The Alpha and his Mate

By B E WAKEFORD

Copyright © 2022 Bryony Wakeford All rights reserved

The characters and events portrayed in this book are fictitious. Any similarity to real persons, living or dead, is coincidental and not intended by the author.

No part of this book may be reproduced, or stored in a retrieval system, or transmitted in any form or by any means, electronic, mechanical, photocopying, recording, or otherwise, without express written permission of the publisher.

ISBN: 9798412921259

Cover design by: The Graphic District, Acacia Heather

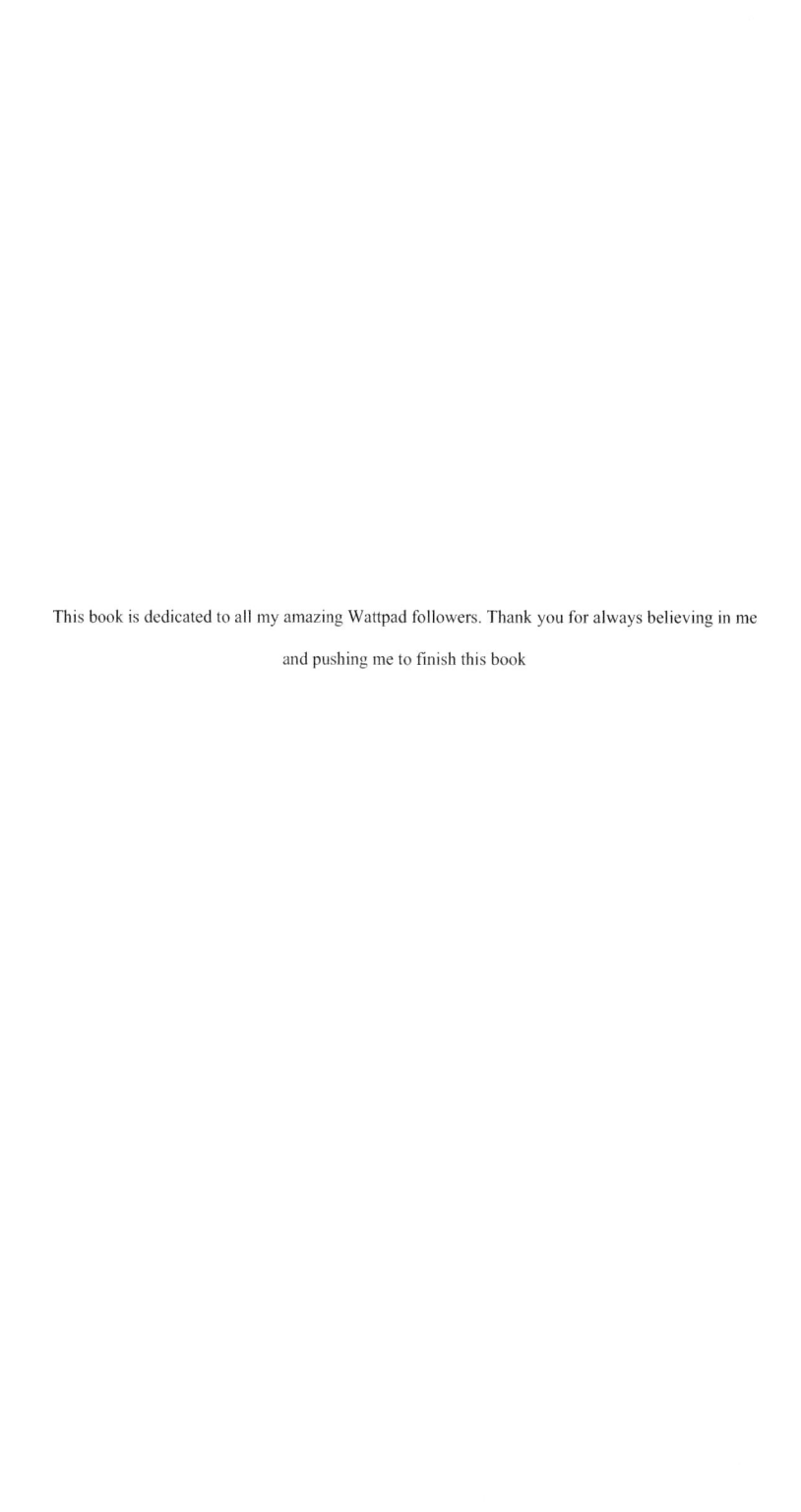

This book is dedicated to all my amazing Wattpad followers. Thank you for always believing in me and pushing me to finish this book

Chapter 1

Annabelle's POV

I wasn't a stranger to pain. In fact, I could barely remember a time when I wasn't in some form of agony, whether it was emotional or physical, I had dealt with it all. At times greeting it with open arms just so I could feel *something* in this house of horrors I called a home.

My first real experience of excruciating anguish was when a stranger, dressed in a police officer's uniform, turned up at my front doorstep with his eyebrows drawn close and a pinched expression on his scared face. He had stated that my Mummy and Daddy weren't ever coming home after they had gone out on one of their date nights. I remember asking person after person what had happened to them, anyone I could find on the street, but no one seemed to have an answer for me, they just walked by as if I were a ghost and they could see straight through me.

Even at the young age of seven I could tell that it wasn't right, that my parents' friends hadn't looked for them and wouldn't talk to me, without so much as an explanation. I had always thought that my parents were well liked in our small community, if the amount of people who always seemed to come around our house to visit was anything to go by. I was so young at the time of their disappearance, and I had been on my own ever since.

I didn't remember much about my parents, my memory of them being washed away throughout the years of grief and misery that plagued my life. I'd managed to clutch onto a few washy memories, things that made me smile when I didn't think I could see the light of happiness again.

I remembered my father being an honest and kind man, both to his family and to the people that seemed to surround us, and his smile was so infectious he could cheer up any room he walked into with just a flash of his pearly white teeth.

My mother was a kind-hearted and free-spirited person, she loved everyone who entered her life and always made time for anyone who needed her, whether it was big or small it didn't matter. Her bright blue eyes were something everyone commented on, looking like they held a secret, one that would one day change the way we all viewed the world and everything in it. They sparkled in the light like rare gemstones, and I always wondered whether I would one day grow up to be just like her and learn the secrets that made them so bright.

The thing that always remained clear in my mind about her was her necklace. I had been fascinated with it. It was a piece that she wore religiously, no matter what she wore or what we ended up doing. I could have sworn the piece had even glowed on occasion, but I knew that was just my child mind seeing something that wasn't there.

It was like it called to me, when even the image of my parents' faces looked more like a watercolour painting than a photograph, that necklace always remained the same. Every twist of the wire and every speck of colour on the gemstone was as crisp in my brain as if I were looking right at it.

It had only been a simple piece of jewellery, a small pearlescent stone which shone blue and gold and white in certain lights as you twisted it in your fingertips. The stone was within a circle of copper wire, an intricate tree made of the same copper wire woven on top of the stone, as if it were the moon at midnight and it was peeking through the branches of the copper, leafless tree. She had always said that it held a small piece of magic in the centre of that stone and that one day the magic would belong to me, when I was ready. I had been so excited at the time, the idea of owning a piece of magic, almost too much for my child-like mind to comprehend.

Flash forward twelve years into the future however and I knew differently. There was no such thing as magic.

My happy family hadn't lasted very long, and now I was living with an abusive, adoptive family. They live on the other side of town, far from my old home, and always loved reminding me that I had meant so little to the town and my friends that everyone had happily forgotten about me within a blink of an eye.

Not long after my parents disappeared, I was removed from my childhood home, the building being quickly torn down, leaving no trace of my parents and the wonderful life we had once lived together. When I had found out about the demolition I had cried for hours, crying for the loss of the household objects that had been destroyed within and the memories that they had held. The feeling of grief was swiftly beaten out of me though, my adoptive father always stressing, *'there was never a time to grieve when there was so much work to be done'*.

"Where the hell is my suit?! It should have been washed, ironed and hung up by now!" My adoptive father, Tony, screamed at me as he stalked forward, quickly getting into my personal space as I dropped the cleaning supplies from my fingers in fright. Before I could explain to him that I had already done the task that he had required of me and that he was, in fact, just looking in the wrong part of his wardrobe, he'd slapped me across the face.

I dropped to the floor due to the sheer force and cradled my burning left cheek with a free hand, feeling the tell-tale signs of heat and tingles that my skin was already omitting, warning me of the inevitable bruise that was to come. "I did Sir," I stuttered, regretting it instantly when I saw the sheer rage in the whites of his eyes from under my lashes.

"Are you calling me a liar?" He hissed as he leant down slightly, intimidating me with the drastic height difference there was between us. He was so close I could smell his morning coffee that was still strong on his breath. I looked up from where I was on the floor, hand still cradling my cheek, to see his face contorted with anger. He had one of his eyebrows raised and arms folded across his chest, with an expression as if to say he couldn't believe that I was even questioning him. To be honest I couldn't believe I was either, I couldn't even remember the last time I had said anything that wasn't *"yes sir, of course sir,"* to him.

I cursed in my head, knowing never to question anything the family ever said, it nearly always landed me in some form of trouble. It never mattered whether I was in the right or not, they never liked to be questioned. "N-no sir...s-sorry sir," I muttered as I got up off the floor to find his missing suit. As I scrambled to my feet however, he kicked my legs out from under me and as one of my hands was still clutching my burning cheek, hoping it would aid with the pain in some way, I didn't have enough time to catch my fall. Before I could blink, my forehead made contact with the wall opposite me, leaving me with a bad headache and an even worse bruise. Thankfully the hit had happened on the other side of my face, so at least my left side wasn't having to deal with a double blow.

"And never question me again you little rat, or you'll get a lot more than just a smack across the face," he sneered down at me before walking off towards the staircase, probably going to watch some form of sports game on the television. I sighed, used to this kind of treatment by now, and made my way over to his and his wife's bedroom which sat at the end of the hallway.

The Leften's house was extremely beautiful, one wall was completely made of glass which covered half of the house, letting in as much of the late morning light as possible as the sun streamed in. A colour scheme of beiges and creams covered the walls and soft furnishings, making the whole house seem open and inviting. To anyone looking in you'd think that this was the show room for the perfect family, open plan with a floating wooden staircase which led up to a mezzanine style hallway before leading off into the four bedrooms and two bathrooms.

I knew differently. This was far from the ideal household when I was the one who had to polish that glass wall every day until it shone and there wasn't a single finger mark on it. When I was the one who hoovered those carpets until they were as pristine and fluffy as the day they'd been installed. I sometimes caught their son vandalising the place on purpose, smearing greasy hands all over the windows and pouring coffee all over the carpets, just so he could watch me and laugh as I went around cleaning up after him. If the place wasn't spotless at all times the Leftens would be extremely angry with me. It usually resulted in me having an empty stomach or a bruised body part of some kind.

I silently made my way across the hallway and over to the master bedroom, slightly worried that my stepmother, Natalie, would be in there getting ready for tonight. After knocking and getting no response I sighed in relief, she wasn't in. She was probably out with her usual girlfriends getting a manicure before their big event tonight.

Natalie was just as bad, maybe even worse than Tony. Her temper rivalled his, and her standards were higher than I could ever hope to meet. The last thing I needed was a run in with her as well.

I swiftly made my way over to their walk-in wardrobe and found the suit he was looking for almost instantly. As expected, it was exactly where I had left it. I rolled my eyes before quickly exiting their room and made my way back down the stairs so that I could hand it over to him. I had learnt the hard way that the longer I took getting something done, the worse my fate would be.

As I made my way down the stairs, clutching the hangers of Tony's suit so as not to drop them and accidently wrinkle it, I was shoved into the banister of the staircase by Damon, Natalie and Tony's son. Damon was a few years older than me and at the age of twenty-three he had achieved almost nothing with his life. He had tried and failed to go to two different universities in the last three years, but both times he had been kicked out within weeks for inappropriate behaviour and lack of respect. I wasn't surprised when he'd turned back up at the front door, the boy didn't have respect for his own parents, let alone faculty members.

He was useful in collecting books though. He had a fickle mind and always believed that he'd be a natural genius in a specific field. Recently it was Palaeontology, but he quickly gave that up when he realised how much work was needed to remember all the different types of dinosaur names. He'd swiftly thrown away all the research papers and encyclopaedias that he'd bought over the short period of time that he was interested in it but seeing as I was the one who emptied the bins, I'd always fish them out and try and teach myself the words. I had always loved reading, even at a young age, so I was always glad to get new material to sink my teeth into, even if it did take me a while to learn how to pronounce certain words.

"Move bitch before I move you," he sneered as he stared down at me. Even with him being on the step below mine his intimidating height still towered over me, which wasn't hard seeing as I only stood at a mere 5'2. I kept my head down as his dark brown eyes swirling with mischief and his brain no doubt thought up a million and one things to torment me with later.

It wasn't uncommon for me to be called things like that; half the time I forget I even had a name due to the fact that it was never used around here. According to them I wasn't worthy of a name so why should they put themselves through remembering it.

"Come on then idiot, come and make me a sandwich before I tell my dad that you said no to me. We all remember what happened last time don't we," he laughed as he gripped my chin harshly between his fingers, forcing my head up.

I painfully nodded as best I could with the restriction of his hold on me before sighing in relief as he finally released me, waiting until he was completely down the stairs and out of sight before following him. A few weeks back I hadn't made Damon's food to his liking and so he'd told his parents that I had refused to make him any food at all. Safe to say the result was not pretty, I ended up with half a swollen face and a few cracked ribs from the beating, not the worst I've ever had from them, but it certainly wasn't something I wanted to repeat.

I entered the open plan living room where I found Tony slouched on the sofa and a beer in his clenched fist as he watched a football game. It didn't matter that it was only eleven in the morning, according to him he deserved it as he had to deal with looking at my face all day. I handed the suit over to him with my head held low, looking at the carpet below my feet, hoping to act as submissive as possible so he wouldn't hurt me further for my mistake.

"Don't let it happen again," he sneered as he snatched the suit from my fingers and got up off the sofa to head back upstairs, probably to get ready for his and Natalie's grand outing tonight. They were vain people and always took the majority of the day to get ready for any event that was in their calendar.

Thankfully he left quickly, leaving me alone with no further injuries. My head was throbbing, and my vision was ever so slightly blurry from where I had hit my head earlier on the wall, but I know that if I complained I would just get a repeat of earlier, so I took a deep breath of air to help clear my foggy head and turned around to start fixing up a sandwich for Damon.

...

Later that night, once Mr and Mrs Leften had left for their gala, I lay in bed, staring at an old photo I had of my parents and myself. It was the only thing I had managed to hide from the cruel family after all these years of living with them. The photo was nothing of value to an outsider, but to me it was everything. It was of the three of us in the back garden of our old house, me in my mum's arms and my dad holding the both of us in his as we all smiled at whoever took the picture. I don't think it was long after this photo was taken that they had disappeared.

The wind had obviously been slightly stronger that day, causing both mine and my mum's golden hair to blow in every direction as we all laughed at our efforts to try and tuck it behind our ears. I looked so young and innocent in this photo I hardly recognised myself, my blue eyes shining bright with the prospect of what tomorrow would bring.

I had managed to keep the small photo hidden from all prying eyes thanks to a loose floorboard I had found in my bedroom. As well as the photo I also hid a few other trinkets and bits and pieces, the odd book for me to read or a dried flower that I had found particularly beautiful. I had so few possessions living at this place, I held the few objects I did have with pride, the photo being the most prized of them all. If it wasn't for this photo, I probably would have forgotten the faces of my parents long ago.

I sighed as I took in our smiling and cheerful faces, even though I don't remember much about them, I still knew that having them as my parents made me the luckiest kid in the world. They were so kind and thoughtful, and happiness just radiated from them.

A lone tear escaped my eyelashes and ran down my cheek after I'd put the photo back where it was safe, my brain reminisced though the amazing memories I held with them. If I was ever sad or feeling particularly low, I'd just look at that photo of the three of us and my spirits would instantly be lifted.

When I heard my bedroom door creak open I startled upright in my bed. I had been so caught up in the memory of my parents that the noise of the door opening shocked me.

"H-hello?" I whispered, asking the question but not really wanting a response. An answer meant someone was in here with me and no good could come from that.

"Be quiet freak," I heard Damon hiss in the darkness of my room and my heart rate suddenly skyrocketed. I was immediately on guard, and I let out an involuntary whimper as soon as I heard the first syllable leave his lips. What was he doing in here? The Leftens almost never come in here, they say that the ugly should remain behind closed doors and should only come out when told to. Whenever I had questioned it as a child, Natalie always told me that they were doing the world a favour by shutting me away. After all, who would willingly want to look at a face like *mine* all day.

"I said be quiet," he whispered as he unexpectedly stumbled in my line of vision, with me lying on my bed and him leaning over me. It was dark inside my room, with no windows to even offer the glow of the moonlight, but I could still see the outline of a sneer on Damon's face telling me he wasn't here to get me to make him a midnight snack.

I flinched at his sudden proximity and my heart started to jump a mile a minute. I tried to sit up and move away to get him out of my personal space, but he just smacked me across the face before gripping onto my wrists, forcing me back down onto the lumpy mattress below me. I whimpered and squeezed my eyes shut at the pain, he just laughed though as his grip tightened further. My head still hadn't completely healed from earlier so that clumsy hit of his sent stars into my vision and my cheekbone to throb painfully.

"Stay still bitch or I'll really give you something to cry over," he growled. "I've been waiting for this moment for so long," he whispered as he breathed in my scent from the crook of my neck. He was so close I could feel his breath on my face and I gagged as I got a strong whiff of whisky. Oh god please no, Damon was a mean drunk, just like his father.

I quickly flung my legs in the air, trying to get enough momentum to get him to release his hold on my arms, but all I ended up managing to achieve was twisting my elbow in the wrong direction, causing me to scream in pain as I heard it pop out of its socket.

"I said stay still," he growled as he quickly elbowed me in the stomach, effectively winding me and making it nearly impossible for me to breathe. Not good, not good at all. The hit rendered me breathless, and I momentarily paused my efforts to escape, my whole focus now on just making sure I got enough oxygen into my lungs and not have a panic attack.

"There, now you be a good little girl and I won't have to tell my father about you not listening to me," he smirked, knowing that the last thing I wanted was to have a drunk Tony angry at me. I looked up at his face with a pained expression and even in the dark I could tell that he was enjoying this, enjoying hurting me and making me cry out in pain. I guess the apple didn't fall too far from the tree.

"Now do as I say and I promise I won't hurt you anymore, okay?" He whispered in my ear, still keeping his full body weight on top of me. His breath caused me to gag, stopping me from answering him, and I received another elbow to my rib cage because of my silence.

I cried out from the pain, feeling my ribs re-breaking from the impact, but he ignored my cry and continued to hold my wrists down, repeating his question.

I nodded my head, tears leaking out from the corners of my eyes. I just wanted the pain to stop.

"Good little girl," he sneered as I felt him move both of my hands into one of his, my elbow screaming in protest at being moved, but I bit back my cry, not wanting to anger him anymore than he already was. With one hand he held both of mine down securely with all his weight whilst the other found its way to the hem of my shirt and started to grip and paw at my skin around my hips and stomach...I needed to stop this, I needed to get away from him and away from this place.

With all my strength and will power I pushed upwards, succeeding in head butting him in the face and I smiled in slight satisfaction as I heard a crunch, ignoring the stars that formed behind my eyes at the impact.

"Ahh what the hell! You freak...you broke my nose!" He screamed as he let go of my arms and sat up to cradle his bloody face in his hands, swaying from side to side slightly due to the high levels of alcohol still intoxicating his system.

I didn't wait another second, worried that if I hesitated even slightly, he would regain his composure and continue what he'd started. As quickly as I could I slipped out from under him and kicked him in the back, shoving his blood covered face into my lumpy old mattress before turning on my heel and making a run for it.

"Crap, get back here you bitch!" Damon screamed at me as I sprinted as fast as my legs could take me, out of my room, down the stairs taking them two at a time and out the front door, thanking whoever was up there that it wasn't locked. I knew where they kept the keys, I just didn't have time to retrieve them and fiddle with the lock as I could hear Damon already stumbling after me not too far behind.

"I'm going to get you bitch," he screamed as he chased after me through the door and down the street. "I'm going to get you and when I do you are going to be so sorry you did that."

Tears streamed down my face as I sprinted as fast as I could down the street and into the surrounding woodland, my bare feet quickly getting bloody and cut up from the gravel and twigs that bit into my sensitive soles. I ignored the pain and forced myself to push on, cradling my injured elbow in my right hand, close to my body. My laboured breathing was causing my ribs to burn and making it difficult for me to suck in enough air, but I pushed on, hoping the adrenaline would keep me going. There was no way I could go back, not after what I'd just done.

"You can't run from me, *little girl,*" he screamed after me, gaining on me with every stride he took, his height causing him to have a clear advantage in his speed.

My eyes looked around frantically, taking everything in as I looked for a solution. I knew I couldn't outrun him, especially in the physical state that I was in. My tears continued to stream down my cheeks, panicked that I couldn't find a spot big enough to hide myself. I wiped my eyes with the back of my hand to help clear my vision and just when I was about to give up hope, I spotted something. I almost cried in relief as my eyes locked onto a small opening in the trunk of a nearby tree. I just had to hide out in here for a while, just until he gave up looking for me, and then I could get away from him, from this place, forever.

I made a dash for the tree and sighed in relief as I managed to scramble into the opening, barely fitting into the small gap, and held my breath to stop him hearing my laboured breathing. My heart felt like it was going to jump out of my chest when I saw his feet run straight past my hiding place. I had to clamp my hand over my mouth, in fear that a whimper would escape and give my hiding space away. I could hear him stumbling around for a bit, the alcohol obviously still affecting his balance and sense of direction as he walked from left to right. I sighed in relief when I heard his footsteps grow quieter and quieter, him obviously giving up in his search for me in this area and moved onto the next.

I always loved playing hide and seek when I was younger, it used to be my go-to game whenever I played with the other kids that would come to my house when their parents came and visited mine. Little did I know a few years later I would be playing the deadliest game of my life, one little noise and I was done.

I sat in the roots of the tree for as long as I dared, feeling the unnerving tickle of multiple insects crawling all over my bare feet and legs, testing my ability to remain still and quiet as I stayed hidden. I sat there in silence for a long while after Damon left, straining my ears for any sort of noise that was considered out of the ordinary. When I came up empty, only hearing the wind in the trees and the animals scurrying around my feet, I cautiously crawled out of the hole. My head constantly turning in all directions with my wild eyes peeled open, looking for any sign that Damon was nearby. I sighed in relief as I came up empty and quickly started running as fast as my body was able to in the opposite direction to where I saw him stumble, hoping to put as much distance between me and the Leftens as I possibly could.

...

I don't know how long I had been walking for, but it felt like hours. The adrenaline had now completely worn off and my injuries that had previously been numbed were now in the forefront of my mind as I pushed my aching legs to keep going. To where I didn't know, I just knew I had to get as far away from that place as I possibly could. Away from that house and away from those people. I was stupid to think that I could have lasted there.

As I walked my brain wandered along with it, taking me back to that place and back to all the times that they had punished me for something. To all the times that I was starved for talking out of turn, for all the times I was hit because I had missed a non-existent speck of dust on the carpet. I had thought about escaping so many times, even attempting it once or twice, but I always ended up being caught. The locals all seemed hell bent on keeping me in that house, if they ever came across me in my attempt to run, they would just pick me up and drop me back at the Leften's house. They wouldn't even look me in the eye and always perform their task with a blank stare, as if I was just a misplaced object that they were just returning to a neighbour. After that I gave up, understanding that no matter where I went I would always be found and brought back to where I belonged. The Leftens, all too eager to remind me of why I should never try to run away again.

I sniffed as a tear fell from my lash line, but I quickly brushed it away and cleared my throat. I am so much better off not being there, I'd prefer to die right now, alone and cold in the woods, then go back to that place.

As I carried on walking, I slowly started to feel the air shift around me, and I frowned at the unfamiliar sensation. I had never felt this feeling before, it was kind of like the air around me was charged in some way, like there was some sort of electrical current in the very air that I breathed. My frown deepened, not understanding what the charged air meant, but as I stumbled on an exposed tree root, I shook my head and cleared my throat. Now was not the time to get distracted.

I pushed on, hoping that I would eventually find a road that would lead me to the next town over where I could get some help. As I walked further and further into the forest though I was getting more and more lightheaded, my feet stumbling in their attempts to walk forward just like Damon had been doing not too long ago.

I stumbled again as my vision went patchy and no matter how many times I blinked; it wouldn't clear. I went to sit down and put my head between my knees, hoping it would help clear the dizzy spell, but before I could I felt my spine start to twist and contort in unnatural directions as I screamed in pain. *What the hell is happening to me?*

I fell to the floor as the pain continued to intensify, the discomfort from my elbow becoming completely overshadowed by the pain that seemed to radiate from within my very core. As time went on the pain spread, going all the way to the tips of my fingers and to the soles of my feet. I'm not sure how long the pain went on for, it felt like hours, but it could have been a mere few minutes, and just when I thought I couldn't take anymore, the pain vanished, and I lay on the ground panting and out of breath.

I lay there for a few minutes, trying to get over the white-hot pain I had just gone through. It was like someone was pouring boiling hot lava throughout my veins whilst simultaneously breaking every bone in my body. I had gone through pain in my life, suffering through more beatings than I cared to remember, but nothing had compared to that.

As I tried to stumble to my feet, trying to stretch out the aches and pains that had started to form in my muscles, I heard a low growl coming from my left in the shadows. I spun around in fright, turning to where the noise had come from, but instantly came up blank as I stared at a small collection of ferns and brambles. *What was that?* Just as I was about to turn, trying to take in more of my surroundings, I heard another growl coming from behind me and my heart rate spiked as I stared at three huge wolves as they came stalking into view, saliva dripping from their teeth and hackles raised.

Well I laughed to myself *you did say you'd prefer to die than go back.*

I stared at the three wolves for a few seconds, taking in the snarl on their muzzles and the way their bodies were coiled up and ready to pounce at any second. I froze in panic, not knowing what to do. I had never even heard of wolves living in this area of the forest before, and I had no clue on how to react around them to try and show that I meant them no harm. I was about to turn and run, thinking that was my best option in this kind of situation, but paused when I saw a man emerge from the shadows of the tree line.

He was obviously the one in charge of the three wolves, once he appeared they stepped back slightly as if they were giving him room to do what he was planning. He had dark brown hair which stuck out in every direction and a slight dusting of day-old stubble across his cheeks and chin, showing that he was older than he appeared. The thing that confused me the most about him though was his choice in attire. Even though it was way into the early hours of the morning and too cold for any person of sound mind to be out he was barely wearing any clothes, just a pair of cut off jean shorts leaving his chest and feet bare and exposed to the elements.

He stood in front of me as he started to make his way over, making slow deliberate steps forward until he stopped just a few feet before me. We stared at each other in silence as I took in his domineering appearance. The guy must have been a giant because even at my 5'2 height I barely came up to his mid chest.

"Who are you," he suddenly demanded in the silence, causing the crickets and other nightlife creatures to pause in their evening song. He folded his arms over his bare chest as he stared down at me, hate clear in his eyes. He looked so much like Tony in that stance I couldn't help but curl in on myself slightly, wanting to make myself look as small and as insignificant as possible.

All I could do was whimper in response as I took a step back with my head held low, wanting to get away from these creatures. As I took a step back the wolf behind me growled and snapped their teeth, reminding me that I was completely surrounded, making escaping from this man virtually impossible. Outrunning a drunk Damon was one thing, but three wolves and a giant angry man? No chance.

"Who are you and what are you doing on our territory," the man growled again as he took another step towards me, shortening the distance between us. I had no idea what this man and his wolves wanted from me, but I remained silent. Natalie had always told me that I should not even be seen, let alone heard. I had their rules ringing in my ears as I assessed the situation, hoping that if I stuck to them, it could save me a beating.

"You are trespassing on our territory, which is punishable by death," he stated before taking another step towards me, putting me within reaching distance of him. If he wanted to, he could reach out and strike me at any moment with nowhere for me to go and no way for me to protect myself.

I tried to stutter out that I didn't mean to cross into his land, that all of this was just one big misunderstanding, but all I was doing was making these weird noises that I had never made before. *Why the hell can I not speak?*

"Shift," he suddenly demanded of me as he stared me down. You could feel the power radiating off him in waves and I curled in on myself further at the sight of him. His blue/grey eyes suddenly spun gold for a split second before returning to their previous colour. I almost didn't believe it, the only thing reassuring me that it wasn't just my eyes playing tricks on me was the fact that the wolves surrounding me had the exact same shade of golden eyes as he'd just had. I frowned in confusion, how was it even possible for a person to have irises that seemed to change colour in the blink of an eye?

"Shift or we will have no choice but to attack," he yelled. "This is your final warning," he growled, his voice too gruff to even be considered human.

I looked down, hoping to find something that could help me in some way, but when I didn't see my feet, I panicked. My feet were gone, and in their place was a pair of sandy, blond-coloured paws, all cut up and bloody, just like my feet had been. I looked around with wide panicked eyes, not knowing what to do and hoping that someone was around to offer me some form of explanation. This was a dream...this had to be a dream. Someone help me, help me please!

My heart was racing faster than it ever had before as I started to panic. My breath became short and fast, feeling like no matter how much I inhaled I still wasn't getting enough oxygen into my lungs. My vision started to go spotty and the last thing I remember was a ferocious growl off in the distance before I lost consciousness and blacked out.

Chapter 2

Jax's POV

I had been feeling agitated all day, both at myself and at the people around me.

I kept finding myself yelling at my pack members throughout the day for no apparent reason. Either someone was working too hard and were going to cause themselves an injury, or they were being lazy and weren't picking up their fair share of the work. They were interrupting me too much; they weren't keeping me informed enough. It was safe to say that the whole pack had been on edge today because of the mood I was in.

I sighed in frustration as I tried to focus on the paperwork in front of me. I had locked myself in my home office for most of the evening and into the early hours of the morning, not wanting to snap at another person for fear my anger would get the better of me.

I had never been like this before, this angry and out of control. I had always taken pride in being a level-headed Alpha, but today something just seemed off and I couldn't figure out what it was. I took a sip of my slightly too strong coffee as I ran my free hand through my black hair, refusing to give into the exhaustion that was trying to take over me, no matter how much caffeine I pumped into my system. I had been putting off doing paperwork for weeks now and it was about time I sat down and got some of it done, my self-imposed isolation being the perfect excuse for me to be left alone.

I had gotten about halfway through the pile of papers that needed my signature and approval when I felt someone trying to push into my mind and gain my attention through the packs mind link. I growled slightly at the interruption, hoping to ignore whoever wanted me, but when whoever it was didn't give up, I released my walls and growled at them, letting my frustration be known through the pack link.

"This better be good," I growled. I had always found the link between pack members fascinating as a child, the ability to talk to people telepathically had almost seemed too magical to be true for my young ears to believe. Who needed a phone when you could talk to anyone you needed at the drop of a hat? Now though it had almost become a hindrance, the fact that I was available to anyone with just a thought was enough to make a man crazy, especially when all he wanted was just a few minutes of peace and quiet to himself.

"I'm sorry to bother you Alpha." Henry, one of my warriors who was on patrol tonight apologised, having felt the irritation coming off me even through our packs mind link. *"We have a lone trespasser on the south side of our border,"* he explained.

I growled in frustration *"then deal with it, you have your training, use it."* Was he seriously interrupting me for a problem as simple as a single rogue trespassing on our territory, surely something as simple as that could easily be handled without me? Especially with Xavier out on patrol tonight.

"Of course Alpha, the only reason I thought it was best you were informed was because she seems rather

frightened and hurt. It also appears to be one of the first times she's shifted and doesn't really understand what is going on or what to do. Xavier is talking to her now but with his history in dealing with rogues and his temperament I thought it would maybe be best if you came out here yourself and assess the situation?"

I frown in confusion; how could you not know what *the shift* was when you grow up your whole life knowing that on your sixteenth birthday your wolf would appear and you would shift. The situation intrigued me and for some reason I found myself walking out of my office and into the cool night air.

I kept telling myself that it was because I just wanted an excuse to get away from my pile of paperwork, but I knew it was because of something else. Sixteen seemed far too young for someone to become a rogue and being out there on her own at this time of night was dangerous.

"I'm on my way Henry, please stall Xavier until I get there," I informed him as I made my way over to the southside of our border.

"Yes Alpha," he replied as he shut the mind link off.

Why did I feel so drawn into this situation? It wasn't like this is the first time we've had to deal with a rogue trespassing on our land. Why is it all of a sudden, I was drawn into the night to see this girl? As I passed through the tree line that lined the outskirts of our small town I stuttered in my steps as an amazing scent hit me, making me stop dead in my tracks. Smelling this scent felt like I had been struggling for breath all my life and I had just experienced my first taste of refreshing air, like I could finally breathe after being submerged under water my whole life.

I broke out into a full sprint as I immediately recognised what this meant. Mate. I felt like I couldn't get there quick enough, couldn't get her in my arms fast enough. I had been waiting for my mate for years and the day has finally arrived when I get to hold her close to me and call her mine.

I was just within hearing range when I heard her whimpering quietly as she was surrounded by some of my warriors and my Beta, Xavier. *Don't worry baby, no one's going to hurt you here* I thought but as I heard Xavier demand her to shift, I let out an almighty howl in anger. If she shifted and if what Henry had told me earlier was correct, she would be shifting into her human form with nothing to change into. She would be naked and vulnerable for four men to see, and my wolf went crazy at the thought, not liking the idea of her being so exposed in front of so many people.

Before I even had a say in it or a chance to think about my options my beast was unleashed, I heard my clothes rip and tear and my bones pop into place as my black wolf materialised and sprinted towards the scene. The first born in the Alpha's bloodline was always a black wolf. Apparently, it was a symbol from our Moon Goddess, to help solidify our role as the rightful future leader of our pack. It also had a hunting advantage, it was easier for me to blend into the dark woods, making it effortless for me to hide and attack.

When I was finally near enough to see the clearing what I saw had anger pumping through my veins, mixing with the adrenaline that was already present. My mate was surrounded by three of my warriors in wolf form, one of them being Henry, and Xavier in his human form whilst she stood in the centre of the circle shaking with fear. Cuts littered her body, and it was clear that she had no clue what was going on. She looked so fragile and lost in that moment that I just wanted to wrap her up in my arms and promise her that everything was going to be okay now that we were together.

"Shift!" Xavier demanded and I let out a ferocious growl at how he was treating his future Luna. No one spoke to my mate like that, not even my Beta.

Xavier turned to me in shock, not believing that I was defending a rogue, but I wasn't paying him any attention. All my focus was on my mate, as I watched her eyes shift to me for a split second before rolling into the back of her head, her legs giving out on her as she passed out.

I growled and started stalking towards Xavier, determined in teaching him a lesson in how to treat his Luna with respect, but before I could take even a step in Xavier's direction, I saw my mate's body start to twitch and contort into odd angles and I know instantly that she was shifting back into her human form.

Xavier was quickly forgotten as I made my way over to her, making it just in time to lay my whole body over hers and hide her nakedness from prying eyes. She was so tiny I could easily hide her slender form with just half of my wolf body. What had happened to my poor mate to make her so thin?

"*Look away,*" I growled at the four of them through the mind link, no one was to ever look in her direction when she was in this state.

"But Jax she's a *rogue*," Xavier stated, bewildered at my odd behaviour. "Why the hell are you protecting her?" He demanded, confused by my actions, but I couldn't respond, the only thing that was repeatedly going through my mind was one word. *Mate.*

I felt a presence just behind me to my right and I growled in warning, not wanting anyone near my injured mate, especially in the state that she was currently in, but when I realised it was Henry I quietened down. He had one of my t-shirts and a pair of jean shorts secured in his mouth that I always had hidden around the territory. I nodded at him in thanks, before growling at everyone to turn around, making sure not one of them could see my mate. Thank goodness Henry had given me some of my own clothing to put on her, I don't think I could deal with having another male's scent on her right now.

Once I was sure no one was looking in our direction I stood up off my mate and quickly shifted, putting my t-shirt on her before pulling the ripped jean shorts on myself. I tried not to look at her too much as I carefully pulled the t-shirt over her body, but I couldn't help but stare when my eyes caught the number of cuts and bruises that plagued her skin. I growled again in rage as I quickly pulled the fabric down and over her knees, trying to cover as much of her skin as I possibly could. Whoever did this to my mate was going to pay… greatly.

I carefully turned around with her secured in my arms bridal style and rounded on Xavier who had, by now, turned back around. "What the hell happened to her?" I demanded. If he had harmed her in any way, he was going to wish he was never born, best friend or not.

He shrugged, a bewildered and confused look across his face, obviously recognising the look of pure rage on my own. "I don't know man; we were all patrolling when we heard a girl screaming on our border line. We came over to see what the situation was, worried that maybe it was one of our pack members in trouble, but instead we found her panting on the floor all cut up and bloody," he explained as he gestured to my mate's form, sleeping in my arms.

"Did you see who did this to her?" I growled, some of the anger leaving me at the realisation that my pack was not to blame for her current state.

He shook his head "no sorry, there was no other scent around either. My guess is that she's just a rogue that got into a bit of trouble and this is where her body finally gave in," he shrugged.

I growled again before looking down at the sleeping angel in my arms. Who could hurt such a perfect and innocent person?

"Why do you care so much anyway man?" Xavier questioned, not understanding why I was so protective of the strange girl who was now secure in my arms.

"Because she's his mate," Henry piped up from beside me and I looked over to see he had already shifted and pulled on his own pair of shorts.

I looked back at Xavier and ignored his shocked expression as I turned and ran back to my house. "Call doctor Tessler and tell her to meet us there," I yelled as I felt everyone run in formation behind me, I don't think I was in any state to mind link someone right now.

Thankfully, I didn't live too far away from where we had found her so it wouldn't be too long before the doctor could look her over. All I could chant in my head as we ran for help was for my mate to be okay, for my mate who I had been waiting years for, to survive.

...

When my house came into view and I saw our pack doctor's car parked in my drive I sighed in relief, thank goodness she got here quick. It did pay to be the Alpha sometimes and this was definitely one of those times. I ran through the front door, being careful not to jar the sleeping angel in my arms, and went straight for my room. I laid her as gently as I could under the duvet on my bed, not caring that the sheets would most likely be stained with mud and blood because of it. I can always buy new ones if I can't get the stains out.

"What seems to be the issue Alpha?" The doctor asked as she walked into the room after me, carrying her medical bag in one hand and a pair of latex gloves in the other, ready to snap them on.

"My mate's injured, I'm not sure what's wrong with her but we found her like this on the edge of the territory,"

I explained, gesturing over to where I'd placed her. If the doctor was at all surprised that I had found my mate she didn't show it, she just quickly walked over to my mate's sleeping form and got to work.

I sat quietly in the corner of my room on the sofa, not wanting to invade my mate's privacy, as the doctor pulled the sheets down and started to lift her shirt up so that she could get a better look at what she was dealing with. I don't think my mate would be too impressed with me if I had watched her whilst the doctor was performing her exam.

It took everything in me not to go over there and hold her in my arms as I watched the doctor poke and prod at her skin. It was practically in a wolf's DNA to want to constantly be physically attached to their mates, especially after first finding them. And if the mate was injured in any way the desire was that much stronger, the wolf needing to be with their mate to help soothe their pain and reassure themselves that they were still alive.

After five minutes of the doctor observing and tending to her wounds, she gently pulled the covers back over her body and walked over to me, peeling her gloves off as she did. My arms had been shaking with the effort not to move and when the doctor had finally turned to face me, I released a breath, I could finally go to her.

"She has quite the list of injuries," the doctor explained. "Not all of them I can treat with the basic kit that I have brought with me. She did have a dislocated elbow though, recently. It was put back into place when she last shifted but as it appears to be one of her first shifts the body may not quite know where to put it. I would recommend bringing her in as soon as you possibly can so that I can scan it and make sure it has been repositioned properly, that way it won't cause her any further issues in future shifts."

I growled at hearing about her dislocation and held my head in my hands, feeling completely useless and out of control. "What else doc?" I whispered, not really wanting the answer but needing to know, needing to know as much as I could so that I could help her.

"From what I can tell she has a few fractured ribs, a concussion and a lot of cuts and bruises, both new and old. She also seems to have an injured ankle so if it is okay with you, I'd like to scan that and the rest of her as well when you get her to the hospital, just to make sure there aren't any other injuries I've missed. If I can get her through at least an X-ray machine, then we would know exactly what we are dealing with regarding the extent of her injuries and trauma her body has endured."

I nodded in a daze, not knowing how to react to the knowledge that my mate had come from such a broken home. "Sure doc no worries, I'll come over as soon as she's awake," I muttered.

"Alpha if I may…" Dr Tessler started to speak but stopped, probably not wanting to go a step too far after the mood I had been in all day.

"Yes doctor?" She needed to speak freely with me, the more information I knew about her the better equipped I would be able to help her.

"Your mate has obviously gone through something very traumatic…" the doctor began to explain as she looked back at my sleeping angel. "I think it's important that you understand that she may not be completely open with you straight away. Yes, you are her mate, but you must take into consideration the state that she is currently in. Someone has *purposefully* done this to her, repeatedly if the scars are anything to go by. I just want you to be aware that she will probably be suffering with some trust issues to begin with, just please don't take it to heart," she explained as she shifted from one foot to the other.

I thought about what she'd said, and I couldn't help but grow both sad and angry at her words. If what the doctor was saying is true, then my mate may be hurting far more than just what I could physically see on the outside.

I nodded as I watched the doctor leave, not bothering to see her out as I went straight for my mate, hoping my presence will calm her in some way. Who could do this to such a sweet looking angel?

I brushed her matted dirty blond hair out of her eyes and tucked it behind her ear, hoping the action wouldn't stir her awake in any way. She was so beautiful I couldn't hold myself back from touching her, even the smallest actions like brushing her hair from her face helped calm me and my wolf. Her face was swollen, one side looking raw and painful as I took in the multiple handprint shaped bruises that marked her skin.

My hands shook at the effort I was putting into not shifting, I couldn't lose control now, not when my mate needed me. I reached out and stroked her less injured cheek, the action causing the telling signs of our mate bond strengthening as my fingers tingle with her warmth.

My wolf and I calmed down at the action, loving the feeling of fire that was licking at our fingertips.

We had waited so long to find her, at twenty-two I was beginning to lose hope that my mate was even alive. Most Alphas found their mates young, not long after they first shifted at the age of sixteen. It was believed that the Moon Goddess, our creator and the one in charge of carefully selecting each and every mated pair, did this to help strengthen the pack and give hope and reassurance to the pack's people. That when the new Alpha took over, he would already have his Luna by his side. The Alpha's mate was usually in a neighbouring pack, making it easier to find each other, but when I had shifted and travelled to each of the packs within a day's run from me and couldn't find her, I got confused. Has the Moon Goddess not selected a mate for me yet? Or worse… had my destined mate died in some horrible accident, resulting in me being forever mateless?

When I hit twenty and my father handed the pack down to me it was a bittersweet moment. On the one hand I was overjoyed at the fact that my father thought I was capable of running the pack, meaning he could retire, but on the other hand I was heartbroken. Heartbroken because the space on my left-hand side, the space that was usually occupied by the Alpha's mate during the coronation ceremony, was empty.

"Where have you been hiding all these years?" I whispered into the warm glow of the room as I continued to stroke her cheek with my fingertips. I sighed as I looked up at the ceiling, praying to the Moon Goddess to give me strength so that I could find the monsters that did this to my mate and give them the punishment they so desperately deserved.

I looked back down at her sleeping form again, intent on looking at her beautiful face all night long. When I looked back at her though the smile slipped from my face as I stared into a pair of bright blue eyes, filled with terror as they looked up at me.

"Little mate… you're awake," I stuttered, not really knowing what else to say to her as I took in her fearful expression as she lay motionless next to me. "Are you thirsty?" I suddenly asked as I remembered the pint glass of water I had on my bedside table. "Here I got you a glass of water in case you were," why was I acting so nervous?

I expected her to take it from my outstretched hand straight away, needing it to quench her dry throat, but she just shrunk away from me as I held the glass out further. I frowned as I took in her fearful reaction, why would she shy away from her mate? Mates were something we were told about and looked forward to finding our whole lives. They were someone who completed us, someone who understood us and we them completely. I held the glass out further to her, hoping she would understand and see in my eyes that I wouldn't hurt her and that she didn't need to fear me. "Please little mate, you need to drink to help get your strength up. You have quite a lot of injuries on you and I'm sure you're thirsty after what you've gone through."

Ever so slowly, like she expected me to pull the glass away from her at the last second, she reached her arm out to take the glass, her eyes cautiously staring just below mine the whole time. I just gave her a nod of encouragement and a small smile in hopes that it would ease her nerves a little more. She was shaking slightly from fright and it killed me to see her like this, but I stayed as still as possible, making sure I didn't startle her or seem threatening in any way. As she took the glass from my hand our fingers brushed together ever so slightly, causing the magical sparks to erupt again throughout my hand. At the shock of the physical contact, she yanked her hand away, spilling the water all over both herself and the bed as the glass fell into the soft folds of the duvet.

I heard her heart rate shoot up and I looked into her eyes to see them on high alert, wide with fear at the realisation of what had just happened.

My mate whimpered slightly as she started to anxiously clean up the mess, using the t-shirt she was wearing to try and absorb some of the water that had been absorbed by the sheets and mattress underneath her.

"Hey...hey it's okay little mate, it was an accident," I soothed, trying to calm her heart rate down before she had a panic attack. "The sheets needed to be changed and cleaned anyway so don't worry about it." I said in the most calming tone of voice I could muster, remembering everything the doctor had told me before she left.

My mate froze in her frantic actions of mopping up the water and looked at me through her lashes with her head down, showing the typical submissive pose everyone showed to their Alpha. Usually it pleased me when people look at me like this, it shows me that they respect me and trusted me to look after them, but that look on her just felt wrong. She was my mate, my equal, and the only person in the world I would hate to feel like they had to submit to me. I reached my hand out and gently tilted her chin up so that she was looking at me, trying desperately to ignore the slight flinch she had when she saw my hand coming towards her.

"No little mate, when you look at me I want to see those pretty blue eyes of yours, please don't shy away from me." I smiled at her, hoping they were the right words to say, but when she didn't react to them I frowned slightly. She was still sitting in front of me in that submissive pose of hers and even with my hand cradling her chin and holding her head up her eyes were still cast down, making it difficult for me to gauge her reaction.

"Would you like to wash up before we go to the hospital?" I asked as I released her, accepting that I wasn't going to be getting much out of her. At my words she frowned slightly before looking down at her appearance. Apparently, she had only just realised that she was covered in blood and mud, twigs accessorising her hair as it sat in odd directions around her face and shoulders. She looked back up at me again, as if waiting for me to answer for her, but when I just carried on staring expectantly, she gave a slight nod.

I smiled, happy that I had finally gotten a response from her that wasn't a flinch. "Come on then, let's get you in the bath, I'm not sure you can stand in a shower at the moment with those cut up feet," I explained as I pointed at the many cuts and grazes that littered the soles of her feet, not to mention her slightly swollen left ankle.

I reached out towards her, intending to pick her up and help her into the bathroom, but as I got closer towards her she froze up and closed her eyes tight, as if she was preparing herself for something unpleasant to happen. My heart broke at her reaction and I retracted my hands slightly as I held them up for her to see, hoping to show her that I meant her no harm.

"It's okay Angel, I'm not going to hurt you, I promise, I was just going to help you get to the bathroom. I could never hurt you my sweet little mate," I muttered, hoping to soothe her a little. She was obviously terrified and the last thing I wanted to do was to cause her more discomfort by scaring her further.

She stared at me apprehensively for a few seconds, deliberating how much truth there was in my words, but when she finally nodded her head ever so slightly I smiled, whether it was in understanding or permission though I couldn't tell. She was still obviously terrified and she could barely stay still due to her shaking, but at least she trusted me enough to touch her.

I slowly inched forward, not wanting to startle her in any way, as I made every move slow and deliberate. When I reached her, I tucked her recently dislocated elbow into her side, making sure it was out of the way before slowly taking her weight into my arms as I carried her bridal style to the bathroom. She flinched slightly as she felt me take her full weight into my arms, but I ignored it, my mind focused on her weight, or more accurately, lack of. I could feel every bone in her body, as if the sharp edges were going to pierce out of her skin if I accidently pressed on them with too much force. I breathed in her scent as I held her close to me in my arms, acting as if I could protect her from even the air around her. This girl was precious and I was going to make sure I did everything in my power to stop bad things from ever happening to her again.

I walked into my en-suite bathroom and quickly sat her down on the vanity counter by the sink. I could tell she was uncomfortable with me touching her and I didn't want to push my luck by holding her more than was necessary.

I turned away from her and proceeded to fill the bath up with some nice warm water for her to soak in, forgoing any products as I knew they would just irritate her cuts and grazes. The doctor had already cleaned them out with some antiseptic when she looked her over earlier, so I knew they didn't require further cleaning from any soap. As the tub began to fill, I turned around to face her. There were so many questions running through my mind, but I didn't know where to begin. What was her name? What pack was she from, if she even was from a pack? How did she end up on the border of my territory and who the hell hurt her so bad? These and many other questions kept rolling around in my mind as I looked into her baby blue eyes, eyes that looked like they had seen way more pain than they deserved.

She suddenly started to fidget uncomfortably, playing with the hem of her wet and dirty t-shirt as she looked at the ground beneath her and I realised that I had been staring at her quite intensely without realising, to lost in my own mind. That was just the effect that she had on me; she was too hypnotising for her own good.

"My name is Jax by the way," I smiled as I introduced myself to the angel that was currently sitting on my bathroom counter. "What's your name?" I asked, needing to know. I bet it was beautiful, a beautiful name for a beautiful girl. I looked at her expectantly but all I got was silence from her as she continued to stare at the tiled floor beneath my feet.

"Please little mate, I need to know your name," I pleaded. I had never pleaded a day in my life, an Alpha never needed to plead, but today I seem to be finding myself doing it a lot.

She frowned for a second as a lone tear ran down her cheek as she shook her head slightly, not wanting to share with me the little bit of information that I had asked from her. I growled in frustration as I turned away from her, not wanting her to see the angry gold swirl in my eyes as my wolf fought to come through. Why would she not tell me her name? I was her mate for crying out loud, surely I deserved to at least know her name!

I heard a whimper from behind me and I quickly turned around to find her silently crying with her arms flying up to cover her face. It was as if she was protecting herself from something, as if she were protecting herself from *me*.

I quickly walked over to where she sat and knelt in front of her, hoping that if I stayed low I wouldn't startle her any more than I already had.

"No-no I'm sorry little mate, please don't cry...I can't stand to see you cry," I whispered as quiet as I could, as if my voice alone would scare her away. I slowly reached out and took one of her hands in mine, loving how the sparks were still there between us. Sparks were a good sign, it meant I hadn't scared her so much that she had rejected me and the mate bond. "I'm so sorry I upset you my angel, I just...I want to know your name so bad and not knowing it is killing me, me and my wolf," I muttered as I held her hand in mine.

She looked at me in confusion before scrunching her nose up slightly and looked off into the distance, as if she were concentrating hard on something. I wonder what was going through that pretty little head of hers. She was gone for a few seconds, but when she came back she looked like she had made her mind up about something because just when I was about to ask her if she was okay she opened her mouth and I heard the most beautiful voice I could have ever imagined.

"A-Annabelle," she stuttered, as if she wasn't used to talking.

"Annabelle," I breathed as my face produced a smile so big it probably looked like it was splitting in two. "I was right, a beautiful name for a beautiful girl."

A slight blush appeared across her pale cheeks as she looked down and slightly to the right of me, trying to hide her reaction, but I gently took her chin in my hand as delicately as I could and turned her face so I could look at her, I could look at her face all day.

Chapter 3

Annabelle's POV

There was something about this Jax guy that made me feel...funny, I contemplated as I lay in the bath that he had run for me to get myself all cleaned up. He was treating me nicer than I had been treated in a long time and I didn't even know the guy.

I sighed as I laid back in the nice warm water, leaving my feet hanging out the edge of the tub so that the cuts didn't sting too much from the soap I had found and used. I had already emptied and refilled the tub once so that the water wasn't so filthy, I hadn't realised how dirty I had gotten until I saw clumps of mud break off my skin and began floating around me.

I also now understood why Natalie would always spend so long in the bath. It was just so relaxing, to be surrounded by nice warm water. I wasn't allowed hot water in the Leften's house, it was too expensive to heat and apparently, to them I wasn't worth the money. I was only ever allowed a ten-minute cold shower once a day and they said that was only for their benefit so that they didn't have to smell me.

As I sank further into the water, I started to drift off to sleep, feeling relaxed for the first time in forever by the calmness that surrounded my aching muscles. I hadn't been this relaxed in I couldn't remember how long. I was just about to drift off to sleep when I heard a soft knocking noise come from the bathroom door that made my heart spike for a split second, reminding me where I was.

"Sorry to bother you little mate but we really should be getting off to the hospital soon. The doctor wanted to make sure she hadn't missed anything when she came to look you over earlier. She also wanted to make sure your elbow was reset correctly after you shifted and that can only be checked with an x-ray," Jax murmured, his voice muffled due to the door that was between us.

I nodded, even though I knew he couldn't see me, before slowly making my way out of the bath and over to the corner of the room where I saw the towels were kept. I grabbed one of the huge, warm, fluffy white towels and wrapped it around myself. It had been resting on the towel warmer, and I sighed at the comforting feeling of warmth and softness as it surrounded me. I was living the life of pure luxury.

I slowly hobbled towards the bathroom door, limping as I put slight pressure on my many open cuts and what felt like a twisted ankle. I rested my hand on the doorknob for balance, proud of myself for making it this far, before I opened it and took in the bedroom to pinpoint where Jax was.

He was sitting on the sofa on the left-hand side of his room and when he heard me coming he looked up from his phone with a huge grin on his face. He quickly stood up and held out a pair of his tracksuit bottoms and another one of his t-shirts to me, but I frowned at him in confusion, not quite understanding what he meant. I still wasn't completely comfortable using my voice around him and so I just stared at him with a confused look on my face, hoping he would understand my confusion. I learnt my lesson pretty quickly not to speak unless spoken to at the Leftens and even then, it didn't always guarantee that my voice wouldn't anger them.

"These are for you," he explained as he continued to hold them out to me. "I'm sorry but they are the smallest things that I have in my wardrobe at the moment," he explained, continuing to hold the clothes out for me.

I inched forward as I made my way towards him, scared it was some form of trick, but when he didn't snatch the clothes away from me I took them from his outstretched hand with a grateful smile and turned around to drop the towel.

"I'm just going to umm...go and stand outside for a second," he muttered, rubbing the back of his neck with one of his hands. Why did he look so nervous? No one had ever been nervous around me before.

I nodded my head in relief as I waited for him to leave the room so that I could change in peace. Once he had closed the door behind him, I quickly dropped the towel to the floor and put on the bottoms and top that he had left me, silently laughing at how big they fell on me. The t-shirt he had given me was more like a dress on my small frame and I had to roll the trouser legs up a fair few times before my feet could finally peek through the bottom, giving me the ability to walk without the fear of constantly tripping up.

Once I was fully clothed, I took a seat on the unmade bed as I waited for Jax to come back from wherever he had disappeared to. As I sat my eyes started to wander around the room as I took everything in. The room had a very masculine feel to it with black and beige being the main colour scheme that ran throughout the room. The king-sized bed with a black leather headboard dominated the room as it sat on the far wall opposite the door to the bathroom. It was flanked by two solid wood bedside tables, both with matching golden lamps on them, and an alarm clock rested on one with red backlighting, telling me that it was five in the morning.

My eyes shifted to the black leather sofa that Jax had previously been sitting on and then further along to the left where I saw an old looking fireplace. It didn't look like it was in use and hadn't been used for many years, it looked more like a decorative piece than a practical addition to the room as I continued to observe it. Before I knew it, I was on my feet again and hobbling over to the fireplace where, on the mantelpiece, sat dozens of pictures all in different sizes, framing faces of happy smiling people.

There was one photo in particular that drew my eye. It was one of Jax with two other people, a boy and a girl, laughing with each other as they had their arms wrapped around each other in a field somewhere. The photo radiated happiness and I felt a pang of jealousy for never having that feeling in my life, one that I could really remember anyway. I'm sure when my parents were alive we did stuff like this all the time, but I was definitely too young to really remember much about it.

A stray tear slipped down my cheek at the realisation that I had left my one and only photo of them back in my old room back at the Leftens. I would never see their faces again, not if I couldn't get that picture back anyway. I just hoped that my memory did them justice.

"Are you okay little mate?"

I silently screamed, not realising that Jax had come back into the room and dropped the photo frame in my shock. I watched in horror as it tumbled towards the floor and broke into several pieces, the glass shattering all over the fireplace's hearth and the soft carpet beneath our feet.

I stared at the mess in horror, not believing that I had done something so careless and stupid, before my brain kicked into gear and I started to panic. Getting hit by anyone of the Leften family hurt, but Jax was bigger and most definitely stronger than all of them and I dread to think about what kind of damage he could do if he ever got angry at me.

I gasped at the realisation that I was just standing there, staring open mouthed at the mess I had made, instead of doing my job and cleaning it up. I must clean it up, the quicker the better, to avoid more punishment than I would already get for breaking something. I immediately fell to my hands and knees, not caring about the fact that the glass was slightly cutting into the skin on the heels of my hands. The only thing going through my mind right now was that I must clean this mess up quickly, before I made things ten times worse for myself.

I hadn't noticed that Jax had also dropped to his knees in front of me until after he had taken my shaking hands gently in his, effectively stopping me from completing my task. I froze as I stared at my tiny hands engulfed in his much larger ones, frowning at the slight calming effect his touch had on me. I had never been comfortable with people touching me, ever since moving in with the Leftens, so why was I okay with his? It was like my body was trying to tell me something but for the life of me I just couldn't figure it out.

"It's okay," he calmly said to me, his voice soft like silk, "it was only a picture frame." He smiled reassuringly at me, but I just stared back at him with wide eyes, not knowing how to react in a situation like this.

He sighed before standing up slowly with my hands still gently cradled in his. I stood up with him, cringing at the weight I unintentionally put on my injured ankle, before limping back over to the bed. I could tell that Jax wanted to carry me, that me walking and cringing at the pain it caused me made him uncomfortable, but I was glad he didn't. I never had any independence at my old house, so I was going to hold onto whatever control I did have for dear life, even if it was just walking on my own.

"You don't have to be scared of me Annabelle," Jax whispered as he kept a hold of my hands in his, gently stroking the top of my left hand with the pad of his thumb. "I will never, *ever* hurt you and I promise to you right now that I will spend the rest of my life making sure that you are never to be hurt by anyone else ever again," he stated with conviction.

I stared at him in shock, not really knowing how to respond to such a statement. My heart was almost jumping out of my rib cage but this time I didn't think it was in fear like it usually was. A blush was slowly creeping its way up my neck and onto my cheeks as Jax continued to stare at me with such faith and determination

I couldn't help but believe him. I think I believed him when he said he would never hurt me...but why? Why did I believe the words of a stranger when I had no reason to?

"Are you ready to go to the hospital?" Jax asked as he brushed a strand of still slightly damp hair that had been hanging in front of my eyes and tucked it behind my ear.

I shrugged before nodding my head, *as ready as I'll ever be*. I went to stand, but as I cringed again at the pain the fresh cuts brought me Jax turned around with a sigh. "Can I *please* pick you up little mate? It is killing me watching you put yourself through this pain when there's something I can do to stop it," he begged as he looked pleadingly into my eyes.

I thought back to all the times he'd already touched me, to all the times that he had already picked me up and gently held me. None of them had been in a threatening or malicious manner and every time he did touch me he always made sure that I was made aware of it and to be as gentle as he possibly could. His touch calmed me and as much as it confused me it had to count for something.

Could I do it though? Could I let this strange man, whom I'd just met only hours ago, pick me up and take away the little bit of control that I had left in my life? I frowned at the thought before taking a tentative step towards the door, testing the pain, but cringed as my ankle gave way. Thankfully Jax was there to catch me before I went crashing to the floor which, knowing me, probably would have resulted in more injuries, and settled me back on my feet.

I sighed as I realised I'd have to let him carry me if we wanted to get to the hospital any time soon. It would be stupid of me to decline his offer of help when I was obviously in desperate need of it. I nodded my head slowly, giving him permission to carry me to wherever we needed to go.

I heard Jax sigh in relief before he slowly bent down and picked me up bridal style, probably not wanting to scare me with any sudden movements. I clenched my fists into the fabric of his top but otherwise didn't make any noise as Jax silently exited the bedroom and walked down the stairs.

I didn't get much of a chance to see much of the downstairs part of his house, but what I did see made my eyes widen in shock. His house was huge, how did one person live in a house this big? I mean presuming he did live alone that is. It was extremely elegant looking and I shuddered at the thought of having to polish the glass that makes up one of the walls in the living room, giving the room a gorgeous view of the forest lining his back garden. I had done that for years and it was a job I wouldn't be missing any time soon.

At my shudder Jax slightly tightened his hold on me, probably thinking that I was chilly seeing as it was dark out and I was only wearing a pair of joggers and a t-shirt.

"I should've gotten you one of my jumpers as well," he muttered near my ear as he slowed down to a stop outside the opened front door, his voice causing slight goose bumps to appear across my arms. "Would you like me to go and get one for you?" He asked as he looked down at me.

I shook my head but otherwise didn't say anything. I wasn't even that cold if I was being completely honest, Jax was like a space heater and with him next to me I was more than warm enough.

After staring at me for a second, probably making sure that I was telling him the truth, he nodded his head as he continued to make his way over to what I'm presuming was his car. It was a glossy black colour with slightly tinted windows and was clearly big enough to comfortably fit five full grown people.

Jax clicked something from inside his shorts pocket and the car lit up with a little *beep.* Once the door was unlocked Jax shifted me easily into just one arm, freeing up his other to open the passenger door and smoothly placed me into the front seat.

"Annabelle, can I just know one more thing about you?" Jax muttered as he started to do up my seatbelt for me.

I could tell by his tone that he didn't really expect me to say yes and the fact that he looked so sad about it nearly broke my heart. I took a breath of courage before nodding my head slowly, nervous about what he was going to ask me.

A grin spread across his face as he took in my small nod but after that we remained quiet. I didn't really know what to say and it wasn't like he had asked me anything specific.

The sound of an owl in the distance broke the silence between us and Jax sighed as he ran his hand over his face before looking back up at me. He was still crouching in front of me as I sat in the front seat of his car and I couldn't help but stare at him expectantly as he looked back at me.

"Please Annabelle, anything at all," he smiled reassuringly but I just remained silent as I stared at him, unable to think of a single interesting thing to tell him. I'm just me, apart from being able to cook and clean there was literally nothing else that I could do. "How old are you?" he asked, when he realised I was struggling for things to say.

I stuttered as I tried to come up with the courage to speak but still no sound came out. Thankfully Jax relented and smiled reassuringly at me before starting to stand back up. Even though I could tell that he wasn't angry at me for not saying anything, I still felt an unwelcome feeling bubble in my chest. It was a feeling I hadn't felt in such a long time that it almost shocked me that I could feel some form of emotion other than sadness and pain. I felt guilty that I had let him down.

I went to grab his hand as he started to close the passenger door and froze as I felt his skin connect with mine. There it was again, that overwhelming feeling of calmness as I looked at my hand in his. We both stood there for a second, marvelling at the feeling of our hand in the others, a connection that for the first time, I had initiated.

I took a calming breath before looking up at Jax's awe struck eyes, still staring at our joined hands. I could do this, after everything he had done for me, the least I could do was give him a little information about myself.

"Nineteen," I whispered, flinching slightly as I watched Jax's eyes snap back to mine. "I-I'm nineteen," I repeated, making sure that he understood what I was telling him.

It was silent for a moment, the only noise coming from the owl as it continued to hoot in the distance. It wasn't long though before Jax released a smile so bright I was afraid it would crack his face. He looked like a kid at Christmas from one of those adverts on the television.

"Thank you my angel," he smiled before leaning down to place a small kiss on my forehead. It was probably the most innocent thing in the world to any onlookers but as his lips connected with my skin a little shiver ran down my spine and I blushed a deep red. What was going on with me? I looked up through my lashes to see that Jax had frozen as he stared down at me with a fearful expression. I'm guessing he was afraid of my reaction, that he had gone a step too far and I was going to have some sort of panic attack.

I waited for the panic within me to bubble to the surface, but when I felt nothing but a slow warmth blossom throughout my chest I blushed. I had no idea what these new feelings meant, but all I knew was that Jax had made physical contact with me without my knowledge or permission and I hadn't freaked out.

I looked in my lap as I fiddled with my clothing, suddenly finding the fabric of the shirt I was wearing remarkably interesting. Did he know what was going on with me? Everything was so new right now I was having a hard time figuring out what I was supposed to be feeling. I risked one sneaky look up at Jax and froze again as I came face to face with his grin that was plastered back on his face. He knew, he knew what my feelings meant and he wasn't telling me.

I frowned as I felt Jax slowly stand up and make his way around the front of the car and towards the driver's side, still not uttering a single word. He silently put the key in the ignition, starting up the engine with a purr and proceeded to backup out of his driveway. There was a soft hum of music that played through the speaker system, but it was too quiet for me to hear, I had never heard anything like it. It was soft and strong all at the same time and I found myself placing my hand on the speaker by my feet as I felt the vibrations tickle my fingertips.

"You like classical music?" He asked, not taking his eyes off the dark road that stretched before us. We were weaving our way through the trees on a country road as the leaves fell around us. The branches acted like a tunnel that blanketed us from the moon's glow and the leaves falling like snowflakes as they drifted silently to the ground. It was very rare for me to experience something as simple as being in a car and even then, I was never allowed in the front seat, always in the back and hidden away from view. Like I was a dirty secret that they refused to air.

I remained silent as I closed my eyes and just immersed myself in the musical notes that had now turned into a soft melody, almost matching the hum of the engine perfectly as they continued their musical duet. I smiled as Jax turned the volume up slightly so that I was able to hear the notes, it was almost magical.

We said nothing else as we continued our short five-minute drive to the hospital, and it wasn't long before we made our way to a clearing with a lone building standing proud in the middle.

I was surprised when we pulled up to the building that was supposedly the local hospital. I had only ever seen a hospital on the television, when Natalie would watch her soap dramas as I cleaned around her, but I thought that the shows were based on some element of the truth. The building in front of me looked nothing like the tall skyscrapers that I had seen on the telly, this building just looked like any other red brick building in the area. The only thing that distinguished this building as a hospital was the sign that was illuminated at the top of the door stating that it was *'Crescent Moon hospital'* in big white letters.

What a weird name for a hospital.

"Are you ready to go, my angel?" Jax asked as he held the car door open for me, his arms outstretched and ready to carry me into the waiting room. I hadn't even realised he'd gotten out of the car and opened my door, too focused on taking in the scene around me to notice.

I nodded my head, indicating that I was ready and let out a little squeal as he lifted me into the air before settling me into his arms bridal style. He smiled down at my reaction before heading over to the entrance of the hospital, the warmth from his chest keeping the chill from the outside wind at bay. "Now the doctor may have to ask you some questions which you will have to answer," he explained as he walked across the carpark and towards the front entrance. "Just be as honest as you can, and she will get the examination over and done with as soon as possible okay?"

I looked up at him, as I felt the worry and anxiety of having to meet new people resurface. My panic was probably clear as day on my face but as I looked up and saw Jax's encouraging expression I suppressed the panic as much as I could, slowly nodding my head in understanding. If I wanted to get better then this was the only way to do it. The sooner I get in there and get this over with, the sooner I could leave. Jax smiled down at me in reassurance as he nodded his head, making sure he didn't jostle me as he went to open the main door.

When he walked through the first thing I noticed was the smell, the smell of cleaning products and antiseptic that was so strong it almost burned my nose. I sneezed from the intensity of it and rubbed my nose. God how was Jax dealing with such a strong smell?

"Don't worry, you'll get used to it," he muttered, as if he could read my thoughts and I smiled shyly at him.

As I looked around and took in my surroundings I started to notice that more and more people, both workers and patients, were starting to stare at us. If I was being honest, I was surprised that this many people were even up and about at this hour. It was way into the early hours of the morning, more towards dawn than dusk, yet there were at least fifteen people here mulling about the place as if it were daytime.

"They're staring," I whispered to Jax as I shrank further into his chest, needing the security of his arms to battle my usual fear and paranoia that always surfaced when people paid too much attention to me.

He grinned down at me and brought me closer to his chest, probably hearing the erratic pounding of my heartbeat as it tried to jump out of my chest. "The sound of your voice is like music to my ears," he muttered as he kissed the top of my head, his action causing a slight warmth to creep along my cheek bones just like earlier.

Jax chuckled but otherwise didn't comment on my reaction as we continued through the reception area and into a long corridor. "They are probably just staring because they're not used to seeing me with anyone like this," he explained as he gestured to me, or more accurately, the situation we were currently in.

I stared at him in confusion, not understanding what he was talking about. Seeing him like what? Was he not usually the kind of person to take someone in and help them in their time of need? I found that highly doubtful, but decided not to comment on it. Jax had a kind and gentle aura about him that I just couldn't explain. It was the main reason why I trusted him so much, he made me feel calm and safe, it was the first time in such a long time that someone had made me feel that way.

He must've seen my slight confusion because he sighed as he sat down in one of the waiting room seats with me firmly held in his lap. I hadn't even noticed that we had exited the corridor and entered another spacious room. This one was smaller than the reception area but kept in with the same theme that ran throughout the building. Lino flooring, bright orange plastic chairs, calming blue wall and the same nearly unbearable smell of antiseptic.

"Most people in my pack don't usually see me this devoted to a particular person," he tried to explain. "Especially after the mood I was in yesterday. I haven't told people yet that you're my mate. I wanted you to be a bit more healed before you officially met any of the pack members as it can be a bit overwhelming sometimes. People are curious to why I'm being so protective of you, that's all," he shrugged.

I frowned, still not understanding what the heck he was talking about. What does he mean when he says words like *pack* and *mate*? I thought when he called me little mate it was just some weird kind of nickname he had given me, like how I've heard Tony call his friends mates when they came round for their monthly poker game.

I shuddered at the memory of the last poker game he had held just over two weeks ago. Let's just say that Tony's friends liked to torment me just as much as the Leftens did.

"Annabelle? Doctor Tessler's ready for you."

I looked up to see where the voice had come from and saw a lady on the other side of the small waiting room as she poked her head out from behind a reception desk. I nodded slightly at her, thankful that she had distracted me enough from my thought trail but then froze when I thought about what she had said.

How did she know my name? I had only told Jax that piece of information and I had been with him the whole time since then, he hadn't told anyone. Unless she knew of me through the Leftens and worked for them? Oh god what if she tells them that I was here and they come and get me? I can't go back to that place again, not now that I know what it's like to have escaped and not constantly live in fear. My heart rate suddenly hit the roof, perspiration covered my forehead and palms as I broke out in a cold sweat.

"Hey...hey little mate it's okay, I'm not going to let anyone hurt you. Not a single person in this building would dare do anything to harm you," he stated as he held my cheek in one of his hands. He had shifted and was now crouched down in front of me, when did he even move?

"Do you trust me?" He whispered, his face close enough to mine that I can feel his breath ever so slightly fan against my cheeks. His touch calmed me, but I didn't allow myself to relax just yet.

Did I trust him? That was the big question I kept asking myself... Did I trust him? Do I trust this stranger whom I've never met before to not lay a hand on me, not only that but to protect me from people who did want to? I looked into Jax's eyes, his soft chocolate brown eyes, and I knew my answer instantly. Yes. I don't know why I trusted him not to hurt me, but I did.

I took a deep breath and offered him a small smile before ever so slightly nodding my head, letting him know that I was okay and that I did, in fact, trust him. My heart started to slow down its pace as I continued to take in slow, calming breaths. I was positive that I had not seen that woman behind the desk before, meaning that she couldn't have worked for the Leftens. *Jax must've told her my name when I wasn't paying attention* I rationalised as I let my fear slip away from me. I trusted him.

Jax let out a breath I hadn't realised he'd been holding and gave me a soft smile which caused a cute dimple to appear on one of his cheeks. My heart stuttered at the sight and I suddenly became very warm, when did it get so hot in here?

"Come on angel, the doctor's waiting for us," Jax smiled as he stood up with me safely tucked back into his arms.

I snuggled into his hold, loving the warmth that always seemed to radiate from him, he was just so comfortable, like a heated blanket that cocooned me in safety. I was so distracted by the feel of Jax's arms around me that I hadn't even noticed that we were already in some form of office. It was a simple room, with a desk and two chairs in one corner, a bed pushed up to the other side of the room and a filing cabinet by the now closed door. An indoor fern tree sat by the open window, making the place feel a little more inviting, but I couldn't help but tense as my eyes landed on a woman in her mid-fifties standing in the middle of the room with her hands clasped behind her back.

Her copper hair was streaked with white and was tied back into a tight bun at the nape of her neck. She had a thin set of glasses balancing on the bridge of her nose and only a very minimal amount of makeup on her face. She wore a white coat over a pair of trousers and a light pink blouse, and she had something weird hanging around her neck. All in all, she looked nothing like Natalie and her friends when they decided to come over.

"Annabelle I'm Doctor Tessler, it's lovely to meet you," she smiled calmly at me. Although she appeared nice when she held her hand out, presumably for me to shake, I shrunk back into Jax's arms slightly and just stared at her.

"Annabelle doesn't speak much," Jax filled in for her, thankfully saved me from anymore awkwardness, and I looked up at him to see his eyes slightly unfocused and looking straight ahead at something. I frowned and looked over at the doctor to notice that she had the same far-off look in her eyes before they both snapped back to reality and went to sit in their respective chairs around the doctor's deck. I frowned but otherwise didn't comment on the weird actions of the two, it was always best to never ask questions.

"Now Annabelle, I gave you a once over when Jax took you back to his house, but I just wanted to do a more thorough examination of you once you'd woken up, that way you could answer some questions for me. Would that be okay?" she asked as she placed her clasped hands in front of her on the desk.

She had a kind smile on her face the whole time she was speaking, making me feel slightly more relaxed, but when she asked me if I was okay with her doing more tests on me I looked at her in confusion. No one had ever *asked* me if I was okay with someone doing something to me before, they just kind of… did it, without concern for me and my opinion. What would happen if I said *'no'*? Would she perform these so-called tests on me anyway, even when I *didn't* agree to them? That sounds like something the Leftens, or more specifically Natalie, would do. She would always do things like that; she'd ask to cut my hair and then after I'd tell her that I liked it the length that it was and to please leave it she'd get a pair of kitchen scissors and just start hacking away at it. She usually left me with some weird lopsided pixie cut which I'd have to wait for it to grow out before I could even it up.

I looked up at Jax for help on how I should answer her question and when he noticed my unease, he smiled a small supportive smile down at me as he nodded his head in encouragement. I turned back to the doctor and copied his actions, trusting in him that he would keep me safe.

"Perfect," Doctor Tessler smiled as she stood up and walked over to the bed on the other side of the room. "Alpha if you could just place her down here, then I'll begin with her physical examination."

...

It was a long process and if I was being honest, I zoned out for most of it. After Jax had placed me on the examination bed the doctor had asked him to leave the room so that she could begin with her tests. He didn't look pleased with her request and made it clear to both me and the doctor that he would be right outside the door if either one of us needed anything. If I was being completely honest, I wasn't particularly a fan of the arrangement either, but between Jax's reassurance that he would be right outside the door and his obvious trust in the doctor, I calmed down enough to get through the examination.

...

"So how'd it go?" Jax asked once Dr Tessler had completed all the tests she had wanted to do.

I was currently sitting in his lap in the same waiting room we were sitting in earlier, before we met the doctor. I shrugged my shoulders and nodded my head, not really knowing how to answer him. Dr Tessler had been very thorough with her tests. I had gone through X-rays scanning my whole body, physical examinations testing joints and reaction times, questionnaires to determine my mental state and even an MRI, these guys spared no expense. The doctor had been very kind whilst she did all this to me, explaining everything that was happening and why she was doing what she was doing. It helped ease my nerves about her enough for me to complete whatever she needed doing.

He sighed slightly and nodded his head, satisfied with my answer.

"Annabelle, the doctor's ready for you now," the receptionist told us, saving us from any more slightly awkward one-sided conversations. This time I didn't freak out at her knowing my name.

As we made our way back into the doctor's office, I weirdly became nervous, this woman probably knew more about me than I did, and the feeling was slightly unsettling and nerve wracking. What if she had found something that meant that I was broken in some way, broken beyond repair? Would Jax toss me aside, thinking that he would be better off without a burden like me dragging him down the whole time?

"So Annabelle, I've correlated everything from today's tests and they've all come back negative, there's nothing a bit of rest and plenty of food and liquid won't fix," she explained as Jax let out a sigh of relief I hadn't realised he had been holding. Was he relieved that I wasn't injured because he wouldn't be lumped with a mess like me to look after?

I nodded my head and leant back into Jax, relieved she wouldn't be doing any more tests on me this morning, I was exhausted. If Jax felt at all burdened by me then I was going to enjoy every single second I had with him until he kicked me out. I had never felt safer than I did with him.

"You're quite malnourished," the doctor continued. "So I'm putting you on a special controlled diet so that you can put some much-needed weight back on," she explained as she wrote something down on her computer. "I'd also like to see you back here next Friday for a catch up and to see how you're getting on. I've emailed the information regarding her diet over to you Alpha and I suggest you stick to it as best you can. Even though you aren't severely emaciated Annabelle we still need to be careful when reintroducing certain foods, I would suggest soups and liquid foods until you feel well enough to stomach something more solid. If you vomit at all or you struggle in any other way, please do give me a ring alright?"

I nodded in understanding as I looked up at Jax, would he allow me to go on such a specific diet? Back at… *that place…* I wasn't allowed to eat any food that wasn't leftovers. Sometimes they would purposely stuff themselves stupid with the food I had put on the table just so I wouldn't have anything to eat. They would tell me I was only allowed to eat when I had earned it.

I would try to sneak food as and when I could, but the fear of being caught always stopped me from taking anything significant. When I was still quite young and hadn't been at the Leftens for very long, I was so hungry I had decided to cook off a few extra sausages along with the ones I had been cooking for their dinner so that I had something to eat. Later that evening Tony found out what I had done and after making me throw up everything I had eaten, including the scraps they had given me after they had finished eating, they didn't allow me to eat anything for two days.

By the time evening rolled around on the second day of my forced starvation I was so weak and hungry I could barely see straight. The family laughed at my clumsiness as my vision blurred from lack of energy. That night they thankfully allowed me to eat some of their left-over food, but not before chewing it up and spitting it back onto their plates. That was Natalie's idea and she laughed as she watched me eat it all, too hungry to care about where it had been or what they had done to it.

It was safe to say I never tried anything like that again, I learnt quickly that you never take anything that would be noticeable. I had later found out that Tony had counted the sausages, that was how they knew I had stolen some from the freezer. After that I only took a spoon full or two of mashed potatoes or a few chunks of cut carrots here and there. Nothing that could be counted or otherwise missed.

I continued to stare up at the beautiful stranger who had rescued me from the woods. No one had looked after me since I was seven years old. I know I said that I trusted him, and I did, but I had been wrong before. I had trusted the police officer who had come to my front door to put me into a good home after my parents had disappeared, that didn't happen. I had trusted the Leftens to look after me after I had found myself alone at such a young age, that also didn't happen. Could I really trust *myself* to know who to trust?

"You okay little mate?" Jax asked, tucking a strand of hair behind my ear and out of my eyes, it was now completely dry and falling in soft waves framing my face. It hadn't been cut in a while, falling just past my shoulders, and I had never been more thankful for that than I was right now.

I smiled up at him slightly and nodded my head, deciding to try my best to trust him until he did something that said otherwise. There was something about him that just made me calmer, more relaxed and I couldn't for the life of me figure out why.

"Thank you very much doctor, we will see you in a week," Jax replied and started to stand with me still in his arms, but the doctor quickly stood with us and stared at Jax as if she was trying to tell him something.

I looked up at Jax to see a slight frown on his face. They stood there in silence for a few minutes, just staring at each other without actually looking. It was as if they had both slipped into a daydream at the exact same moment.

As quickly as they had zoned out they had returned, acting as if nothing had even happened.

"Before you go Annabelle, I have written you a prescription for a variety of vitamin tablets. Alpha, could you please make sure she takes them once a day?" She asked, handing him a small piece of paper.

Why did these people keep calling him Alpha, his name was Jax wasn't it? Unless it was some weird nickname that I didn't know about.

"Of course doctor," Jax replied before taking the piece of paper from her outstretched hand and walking out the room with a final nod from him and a small wave from me.

"Right, let's go home and get you some lunch shall we?" Jax asked as we made our way through the hospital and out to the car park.

I stayed silent, not really knowing how to respond to someone who was offering me food.

"What do you fancy?" He asked as he buckled me up and started to drive back to his house, the tunnel for tree's looking so much different now that the sun was peeking through the leaves. "The doctor suggested only liquid food so how about I heat you up some chicken soup, I'm pretty sure I have some in my fridge that my mum made for me from the other day."

I stayed quiet, last time I had asked for food I couldn't walk for a week. It was ingrained into me at such a young age that food was a luxury I wasn't allowed to ask for. No matter how amazing Jax was or how many times he stated he wasn't going to hurt me, I wasn't going to just break out of that thought process overnight.

I suddenly felt the car jerk to a stop as Jax pulled over to the side of the road and I instantly started to panic, what had I done wrong? I had followed every rule I had been told, stay quiet, head down and don't interact with anybody I wasn't permitted to. My heart rate picked up again and I frantically looked around for an exit, needing to get out of the car as I felt the walls closing in on me. I tried the passenger door, but it had the child lock turned on and the other door was blocked by Jax. There was no sunroof to climb through either and unless I went to the extreme of breaking a window to get out, I was pretty much trapped here.

"Hey, hey calm down little mate...please you're going to start having a panic attack in a minute if you don't slow your breathing down," Jax muttered, but his words fell on deaf ears.

I just stared at him wide eyed, not knowing what to do or how to even begin slowing my breathing down. I had told myself that I was going to trust him, but I don't think my body and mind have the same ideas, I just can't help but flinch and panic every time something looks even remotely threatening. To me, any sudden move was an act of aggression and for him to pull his car over so suddenly made my mind conjure up memory after memory of one of the Leftens hitting me, attacking me.

"I made a promise to you Annabelle," Jax muttered as he leant over the console slightly "and I will reiterate that same promise to you now. There is no way in the Goddess's name that I could ever hurt you. I could never hurt my little mate, not after waiting so long to find you." He was looking deep into my eyes and I found myself getting lost in his chocolate coloured irises which every now and again seemed to swirl with flecks of gold. He hesitantly reached his hand out across the centre console and towards me, so slow it was as if he was helping prepare and warn me that he was going to touch me. He gently rested the palm of his hand against my cheek, an encouraging smile on his face.

His touch was gentle, and warmth radiated over my entire body at the contact. Before I realised it, I began to feel myself ever so slightly leaning into his touch with a small smile on my face, my breathing having now gone completely back to normal. It was like he knew exactly what to do to calm me down. I smiled at him and nodded my head slightly, telling him that I was okay.

He smiled a breath-taking smile back as he kept his hand cradling on my cheek, seemingly not being about to break contact with me. "Please angel, what would you like to eat?"

What *would* I like to eat? I thought about it for a second, never having to think about what I fancied before. The more I thought about it the more my head swirled with possibilities, but I still couldn't seem to pinpoint something that I actually wanted to eat. I was restricted due to the doctor's diet plan so after giving up on thinking about what I fancied eating I just shrugged and looked ahead slightly at the road before looking back at Jax. "Soups good," I nodded as I smiled slightly at him, trying to reassure him that's what I wanted and wasn't saying it just because he'd offered it.

If possible, his smile grew even wider and his cute dimple appeared making him ten times cuter and caused the slight frown that seemed to be ever present in-between his eyebrows to disappear.

He nodded and ran his thumb along my cheek bone "do you know what type of soup you'd like? My kitchen is completely stocked so choose whatever you'd like and I'm sure I could try and make it for you."

"Umm...the chicken sounds good?" I said, it sounded more like a question than a statement though.

"Just chicken? Are you sure?"

I just looked at him confused; did I want anything else? He must have seen the slight confusion on my face as he brushed my cheek with his thumb again before letting go and starting the car up.

"I'll just reheat the chicken soup for you then shall I?" He asked as he pulled back out onto the road.

I smiled and nodded, thankful that I wouldn't have to think and make any more decisions.

...

The drive went by rather quickly and before long we were back at his place. I smiled slightly as he came around the car to pick me up and carry me into the house. I was going to miss this when I finally got a pair of shoes and my ankle was back to normal.

We made our way into the kitchen and I was instantly in awe at the appliances he had. Back at the Leftens place they had a nice kitchen, but I was always forced to do all the cooking and cleaning, so I never got to enjoy it. Here on the other hand, I could imagine myself spending so much time here, because it would be my choice and no one else's.

"Do you like it?" Jax asked with a smile, obviously seeing my expression.

I blushed slightly at being caught marvelling his kitchen and nodded.

He laughed at my slight blush, "well you have unlimited access to it; I hardly ever use it so whenever you feel like cooking something you just go for it."

I smiled happily up at him and nodded again with a lot more enthusiasm.

He laughed again at my reaction and placed me down on one of the countertops before going about making me some food. It was weird, back at the old place I always felt bad about eating, even when Tony had given me permission to, but here I feel no guilt at all as I watched him prepare me some breakfast/lunch.

We sat in silence whilst he worked and once he was sure it was warm enough for me, he placed the biggest bowl of steaming soup I had ever seen next to me on the counter. Did he expect me to eat it or swim in it?

He laughed at my expression and leant beside me on the counter, "you don't have to eat it all if you don't want to, I just wanted to make sure you were full."

I nodded my head and hesitantly picked up the spoon that lay idle next to the bowl. After the first sip of the warm liquid I groaned in pleasure as the flavours exploded on my tongue. The food tasted so damn good and I couldn't help myself as I slurped down scoop after scoop, savouring the taste and the warm feeling as it settled into my stomach.

"Annabelle, can I ask you something?" Jax asked, sounding slightly apprehensive about something.

I nodded my head, my attention only half on him as the other half was still solely focused on the bowl of warm delicious goodness that was in front of me.

"When was the first time you shifted into your wolf?"

I stopped eating, my spoon hanging mid air and looked at him confused.

He sighed and ran his hand down his face. "Annabelle you do know what we are don't you?" He asked, sounding desperate as he looked into my eyes.

I just continued to give him a confused stare before shrugging, not really understanding what he meant by the question. "Umm… people?" I guessed.

He looked at me in shock but otherwise remained silent, had I answered the question wrong?

"Annabelle, how old are you again?" He continued with his questions as I placed the spoon back in the bowl, unsure where the conversation was going but knew it was something important.

"Nineteen?" I don't know why I said it as a question, I knew my age because I remembered always blowing out birthday candles in the summer. I was never sure on the exact date, but it was somewhere in the hotter months of the year, not that I was ever allowed to celebrate it at the Leftens.

For a second a flash of anger washed over his face before it settled into pure hatred. "I'm going to kill them; I'm going to murder them with my own bare hands," he growled as he pushed off from the counter and started pacing in front of me. "I'm going to rip their pack to pieces and feed them to the dogs."

I shrunk back in fright as I could feel the waves of anger rolling off him. Every time Tony had gotten this mad, he had always sought me out to take it out on me. Apparently it was always more satisfying to hit something that would bruise than something that would bruise him.

I couldn't control the whimper that escaped my lips and as the noise made its way to Jax he froze in both his ranting and pacing. At first I panicked, thinking that I had angered him further by making a noise, but when he made his way over, ignoring the fact that the closer he got to me the more I shrunk away, he quickly wrapped me up into his arms and hugged me close to him. Acting as if his arms alone were enough to protect me from the world around me.

"I am so sorry this has happened to you Angel," Jax mumbled into my hair as he continued to hold on tight to me. "I wouldn't wish what they have done to you on my worst enemy," he muttered, cradling my head close to his chest so that I could feel his slightly erratic heartbeat. What was he talking about?

"I...Umm..." I didn't know how to respond; I mean how could I when I had no idea what he was even talking about.

"I know you don't know what I mean, but I promise you we will get everything cleared up. For now, I think we need to have a chat about something you should have known about a long time ago," he muttered as he took my hand in his and kissed it before picking me up and taking me into the living room, leaving my nearly empty bowl of soup on the kitchen counter.

Chapter 4

Jax POV

It took everything in me to leave Annabelle with Dr Tessler as I went to sit in the waiting room. After seeing her worried face when she realised I was getting up and leaving without her my instincts started screaming at me to stay with her at all costs. I knew I couldn't though, she needed privacy if she was going to answer the questions honestly and the last thing she needed was me breathing down her neck and growling at every bit of information she revealed that I didn't like.

"I'll be waiting right outside," I reassured her as I kissed her forehead and went to sit in one of the uncomfortable orange chairs in the waiting room. Did I seriously authorise these? I'll have to look into getting some comfier ones for my pack once I have a spare five minutes. Xavier has been looking after the pack since I first found Annabelle, not wanting to leave her for a second. She was so skittish at the moment I didn't want to leave her with anyone else, just in case she got scared of her new surroundings and made a run for it.

I didn't know what she had been through to make her so on edge, but I can imagine I will not like the answer once she finally trusts me enough to tell me her story.

I clenched my fists in anger at the mere thought of someone hurting my mate, hurting what's mine, and I had to take deep cleansing breaths before my wolf's anger took over and I destroyed this whole room.

...

"Alpha we are finished" Dr Tessler linked me after a few hours of me sitting here and I sighed in relief at the thought of having her in my arms again. She was like a calming balm to me and my wolf and I can't imagine my life without her, even though I've only known her for a total of eight hours.

I walked into the office and found Annabelle sitting in a chair in front of Dr Tessler's desk, her knees curled up to her chest as she wrapped her arms around them. I saw her physically relax as soon as her eyes locked onto mine and I smiled at the thought that she couldn't seem to spend that long away from me either, just like I couldn't spend time away from her.

"Alpha I would like a moment to configure all of my data so if you wouldn't mind taking Annabelle outside for a few minutes I would really appreciate it," the doctor explained as she looked up from typing away on her laptop screen.

I nodded my head in understanding and took Annabelle into my arms, glad I finally had her back with me, and made my way back towards those uncomfortable plastic chairs.

"So how'd it go?" I asked, wanting to find out if the doctor had made her uncomfortable in any way, but she just shrugged and nodded her head, as if that answered all my questions.

I sighed and nodded, I hoped she would trust me enough to talk to me soon. Her voice was music to my ears and I could hear her talk all day.

We sat there in silence for a short while, both just enjoying each other's company, as we waited to be called back into the doctor's office. Even though neither of us spoke it wasn't an awkward kind of silence, just a relaxing one.

"Annabelle, the doctor is ready for you now," the receptionist informed us a while later as she peaked her head up over her desk. I heard her heart flutter ever so slightly when our eyes locked but she quickly cast them down as she realised I was looking at her. I rolled my eyes and stood up, making my way back into the doctor's office.

"So Annabelle, I've correlated everything together from today's tests and they've all come back negative." I sighed in relief at that, happy that my mate wasn't severely affected by what had happened to her. "There's nothing a bit of rest and plenty of food and liquid won't fix," she continued.

"You're quite malnourished so I'm putting you on a special controlled diet so that you can put some much-needed weight back on." I nodded at the thought of my Annabelle putting some more weight on, she was so tiny I could lift her with just one arm.

"I'd also like to see you next Friday for a catch up and to see how you're getting on. I've emailed the information regarding your diet over to you Alpha and I suggest you stick to it as best you can. Even though you aren't severely emaciated, Annabelle, we still need to be careful when reintroducing certain foods, I would suggest soups and liquid foods until you feel well enough to stomach something more solid. If you vomit at all or you struggle in any other way, please do give me a ring alright?"

I nodded my understanding to the doctor but frowned when I saw Annabelle looking up at me with a slight frown set between her eyebrows and a silent question in her eyes. Did wherever she came from withhold food from her? I mean it would explain why she was so underweight, but the thought made me tense slightly. I held back a growl at the thought and looked back into her beautiful blue eyes, instantly calming me.

"You okay little mate?" I asked when I realised she was still staring at me. I tucked a strand of her golden locks behind her ear, marvelling at the softness of its strands.

She smiled up at me and she suddenly looked like a weight had been lifted off her shoulders, I wonder what she was thinking about right now? I can't wait to mark her so that I would no longer have to guess what she was feeling, mates can block thoughts from each other but not emotions.

I smiled back at her before I realised where we were and shook myself out of my trance. "Thank you very much doctor, we will see you in a week," I said as I moved to stand, but Dr Tessler mind linked me before I could take a step out the door.

"Alpha, I don't think Annabelle has any idea about our kind, I asked her multiple questions that most wolves

would know the answer to, like mind linking, but she doesn't seem to know what they are."

I frowned at her statement *"that's impossible, when I found her she was in her wolf form and she's over sixteen, how could she not know?"*

"It's possible that she's blanked that out from her memory due to the sheer amount of trauma and stress she has recently been through. You need to find out whether she has ever shifted before yesterday, that's the only way we'll know for sure."

"There's only one way someone doesn't shift on their sixteenth birthday doctor," I stated, suddenly worried.

The doctor looked at me with slight sympathy in her eyes. *"I know, I just pray to the Goddess that it's not what I think it is."*

"Me too," I replied.

"She has a lot of injuries Alpha," the doctor continued. *"A few new ones, a few a week or two old and a lot of bones that have fracture lines on them where they've been broken in the past. Wherever she came from Alpha, it wasn't a good place, so please watch out for her."*

My wolf growled at the thought of anyone harming Annabelle and the doctor slightly lowered her head in submission.

"I believe it would be helpful for you and I to have a chat alone together, Annabelle has obviously gone through something that we couldn't even dream about and I feel like it would benefit you and help prepare you

for what you can expect with looking after her," the doctor continued and I nodded slightly at her in understanding.

"Thank you doctor," I ended the link before looking down at a confused Annabelle. I hadn't realised how long we had been standing there in silence for and just when I was about to come up with something to say to help ease the awkwardness, Dr Tessler saved me by handing me a prescription stating Annabelle had to take it once a day. I quickly nodded and thanked her and before long we were back in the car park.

"What do you fancy for lunch?" I asked as I buckled her in before sorting myself out and starting the car. I listed off a few things I knew I had in the fridge but when she didn't automatically respond I got frustrated, why wasn't she answering me?

I pulled the car onto the side of the road so that I could get a better look at her, but instantly regretted it as I heard her heart rate drastically increase. I looked over to see Annabelle trying to open the passenger door, tugging at the door handle several times. When she realised it was locked, she started looking round with wild eyes, as if she was looking for an escape route. She looked like a scared deer caught in a set of headlights.

I immediately felt like crap for making her feel trapped and quickly tried to calm her down as best I could. "Hey, hey calm down little mate...please you're going to start having a panic attack in a minute if you don't slow your breathing down." I spoke as softly as I could, but it didn't seem to be working as she just continued to stare at me wide eyed, looking through me rather than at me, caught in whatever memories that were flashing past her eyes.

"I made a promise to you Annabelle," I stated as I changed strategy "and I will reiterate that same promise to you now. There is no way in the goddess's name that I could ever hurt you. I could never hurt my little mate, not after waiting so long to find you," I stated, hopefully in a soothing voice, as I hesitantly reached my hand out to cup her cheek. Physical contact between mates always helped calm the other down.

I breathed a sigh of relief as I heard her breathing and heart rate slow down and before long a small smile graced her beautiful lips. *At least I can help my mate this way, I thought* as I smiled down at her, happy that she had calmed down and wasn't going to hurt herself.

She nodded slightly against my palm, telling me that she was alright, but I couldn't bring myself to let go of her yet. I told myself it was to help her stay calm but really it was just for purely selfish reasons.

"Please angel," I pleaded, hoping this time she would answer me and not have another panic attack, "what would you like to eat?"

She contemplated for a second before slowly whispering that she wanted the chicken soup that I had mentioned earlier. Whether it was because I had offered it or because she actually fancied it I didn't mind, as long as she was eating I was happy.

...

Once we made our way back into my house I went straight for the kitchen and placed her on the counter. I smiled as I looked down at her and caught a glimpse at her expression. She was gazing around my kitchen in awe and I had to wonder whether she enjoyed cooking. I hoped she did because whilst I could cook something edible, I lacked the culinary creativity and the basic patience needed to produce anything of note. After a long day of work, either doing paperwork or training, I would usually just come home and either reheat something my mum had dropped off for me or I would just make something simple like mac and cheese.

"Do you like it?" I asked and I got an immediate blush as her response which I couldn't help but laugh at. "Well you have unlimited access to it; I hardly use it anyway so whenever you feel like cooking something you just go for it." It was like I had just offered her the world with the way she smiled back up at me and my heart couldn't help but stutter slightly at her beauty. She was the most beautiful girl I had ever seen, and I was so lucky that she was my mate.

I silently went about making her food, but I wasn't really paying attention to what I was doing. I was more focused on what Dr Tessler had told me earlier on in her office. What if she didn't know about our kind? How was I going to explain to her what we were, what she is to me, without scaring her off? Could she really handle being Luna of a pack when she didn't even know what a Luna was?

My wolf growled at me at the thought and I quickly agreed to push it from my mind. The Moon Goddess had paired us together for a reason, she believed that Annabelle would make an amazing Luna, the least I could do was trust her and go with her instincts.

I handed the steaming bowl of soup over to her and laughed as I watched her eyes grow wide in shock at the sheer quantity that I had made for her. After quickly explaining to her that she didn't have to eat it all I watched her devour half of it, barely stopping for a breath.

As I watched her eat my brain whirred with questions and it wasn't long before one came tumbling out before I could stop it. "Annabelle, can I ask you something?"

Chapter five

Annabelle's POV

Jax took me into his living room and I couldn't help but stare in awe at this room as well. Was his whole house this amazing?

There was a soft, almost comforting colour scheme that seemed to run throughout this room, with creams and light browns being the dominant colours, from the floors and walls to the soft furnishings. He had three huge sofas, each with a warm fluffy brown blanket that was neatly folded across the backs of the sofas, ready to use whenever they were needed. The sofas sat in a U shape, all facing towards a huge tv that hung on the opposite wall with two shelving units framing the television, filled with more photos as they littered the surfaces.

On one side of the room, on the left-hand side, the whole wall was made of glass, allowing you to look out onto the forest that surrounded the modest back garden. On the opposite wall, on my right, a stone fireplace stood with two dark wooden bookshelves that were built into the walls, covered in books. The fire was on and gently flickering away, giving the whole place a warm and inviting atmosphere. I could definitely picture myself having a relaxing nap here or curling up in front of the fire with a good book.

I snuggled into the fluffy cushions as Jax gently placed me into the corner of one of the massive sofas before turning around and sitting in front of me on the coffee table. He sat with his elbows resting on his knees and his head in his hands, slightly tugging on his hair, looking more anxious than I had ever seen him. I frowned at his actions but otherwise didn't say anything. I didn't even know whether this was normal behaviour for him or not, seeing as I hadn't known him for very long.

I hesitated in reaching my hand out to him, wondering how he would react if I disturbed him from his thoughts. The words he told me in the car, about him never hurting me, rang in my ears and I shook the slight fear away and reached over to take one of his hands out from his hair and held it in mine.

I jumped slightly when his eyes snapped up to mine and quickly went to retract my hand from his, but as I started to, he turned his hand around so that his palm was facing up and interlocked his fingers with mine, effectively trapping my hand in his. I blushed as he brought my hand up to his lips, blushing deeper when I heard him sniff my wrist, before placing a kiss where his nose once was. Well that was… normal.

I frowned as I continued to look him over, he had always been so calm and confident before, but right now he looked so lost, I just wanted to take him in my arms and comfort him. I had never experienced a feeling like this before but for some reason, looking at him, the thought of comforting him didn't scare me in the slightest.

I looked at him in confusion as he stared back at me, what was going through that head of his to make him look so stressed and frustrated? "Are...are you okay?" I whispered, wanting to know what was wrong with him so I could help in some way.

"Oh my beautiful little mate," Jax muttered, still not taking his eyes off of mine. "I don't even know where to begin," he sighed.

"The beginning?" I offered with a shrug. It still felt weird, openly speaking to someone without being punished for it afterwards, I was slowly getting used to it though. The best way to get through a fear is to face it head on... right?

Jax chuckled but it lacked any humour "if only it were that simple," he sighed.

I just shrugged my shoulders again and leant back into the cushions. It seemed like this was going to be a long conversation, whatever it was about, so I may as well get comfortable as I waited for him to sort his thoughts out. He stayed silent for a while, just staring at a spot on the carpet between us. I was about to start drifting off to sleep, exhaustion creeping in on me after being awake for so long, when Jax finally started to speak.

"Are you religious Annabelle?" He suddenly asked out of the blue, waking me up with a start.

I frowned at him before shrugging, I had never really thought about it before.

He sighed before running his hands through his hair, was that the wrong answer?

"Do you know of the Goddess Selene...the Moon Goddess?" He asked, obviously trying a different approach but frowned again when I shook my head. "Well she is the daughter of the Titans, Hyperion and Theia, both Greek gods and Goddesses. Selene controls the Luna cycles; she oversees the driving of the moon across the sky each and every night. One day, as the stories tells us, she got bored of always being out at night when everyone else was fast asleep and so the other gods gave her permission to create a creature of her own, a creature that she could look after so she wouldn't feel so lonely."

I nodded my head, not understanding why he was telling me this story.

"After thinking long and hard about what type of creature she wanted to create she finally decided on merging two existing creatures together, the human and the wolf. Her thought process was that it would cause the line between light and darkness to blur, as the wolf often hunted at night and the human walked around during the day. This would cause other animals to become nocturnal, which in turn would give her more beings to look after and give her existence purpose. She chose to blend the wolf and the human together in the hopes that she could create the strongest species on the planet, the mind and cunningness of a human with the strength, agility and loyalty of a wolf. She had created the first werewolf."

He looked at me expectantly, as if that piece of information would mean something to me, but when I just nodded my head for him to continue, he sighed with a nod before carrying on with his story.

"Werewolves live in packs, with one Alpha male and one Alpha female to lead, called a Luna. They guide and protect their fellow pack members, but the creatures weren't doing so well. They started to turn aggressive towards each other and Selene's parents threatened to destroy her creation if she could not get them under control, and so she decided to give them all a mate. A soulmate. This soulmate would be the perfect match for the other, two halves of a whole and it gave the werewolves something to fight and live for. On a person's sixteenth birthday they would shift for the first time into their wolf form, and they would be paired with someone by the moon goddess herself, someone who can calm their wolf down and give them a purpose in life."

Jax stopped for a breath and I frowned at him confused, "why are you telling me this story?" I asked, desperately trying to understand him but failing to identify the relevance of this story.

"Well...I Umm..." Jax stuttered as he ran his hand through his hair "the thing is...well...the story is...true," he explained, looking up at me expectantly.

I looked at him before laughing silently, is he really telling me that he thinks werewolves are real?

"I promise you that this story is true Annabelle," Jax stated and as I looked into his eyes and I could tell that he genuinely believed that this story was real. He was being deadly serious.

"How?" I questioned, curious about what proof he had.

"That's the thing," he muttered, "I have to show you, but I'm worried that if I do, you're going to get scared and run."

I smiled at how caring he was, I had only known him for under a day, but I already felt so close to him. It was a weird feeling, trusting someone. I couldn't remember the last time I had properly felt safe somewhere but, being here, I felt like I could be happy. I sighed as I suddenly realised that Jax probably won't want me around for much longer, he'd figure out that I was just a burden to him and eventually kick me out and I'd be on my own again. Sooner rather than later now that he knew I had no serious injuries.

A voice in my head whimpered at my trail of thought and I shook my head to hopefully dislodge the image I had of him kicking me out of his house. I don't think my heart could survive with that kind of rejection.

"Show me," I whispered and started to get up even with my aches and pains, but Jax quickly ushered me to sit back down.

"You don't need to move; I promise just stay right there and I'll show you. Just please promise me you won't run away when you see okay?" He pleaded and I couldn't help but stare at him and nod my understanding. Why was he so worried about showing me something?

Without another word Jax pushed up off his knees so he was standing and went around the table so that he was in the large open area in front of the TV.

"Promise?" He asked me one more time and I nodded my head, confirming I wouldn't run from him. At my confirmation he slowly started to remove his shirt and I blushed as his abs and chest were slowly revealed to me and the voice in my head made some weird noise, as if it were purring with happiness.

I looked down to quickly gather myself, but when I looked back up at him, I couldn't help but blush and swiftly looked back down at his sock covered feet. He was starting to undo his belt and jeans.

My body started to panic as I thought of all the reasons why he was taking his belt off but quickly calmed myself down as I reminded myself who was in front of me. *This was Jax and he would never harm me.* I had to chant that mantra in my head over and over again to stop the flood of memories that always seemed to fill my brain when I thought back to that place.

I brought my gaze back up again when I noticed Jax had stopped moving and I found him staring at me intently with just a pair of tight fitted black boxers on. I blushed again and looked back down; I had never seen so much of one person before.

"I'm sorry if I'm making you uncomfortable little mate but just look at me for a second and I can explain everything," he said and as I looked at him, I suddenly noticed that his whole body had started to shake. What the...?

"Just keep looking," Jax pleaded but it came out more like a snarl with a weird lisp. That was when I realised that his teeth had grown and his jaw looked a little disfigured.

I couldn't really tell you what happened in the next few seconds as I stared at Jax's body change from a man into something else, but when he was finished Jax was gone and in his place stood a ginormous black wolf with golden eyes shining back at me. I stared at the creature in shock, not really knowing how to react to the fact that my saviour had just turned into a wolf, but as I opened my mouth to ask a question an ear-splitting scream came out instead.

Suddenly my head felt like it was going to explode, like something was desperately banging on the inside of my skull trying to get out. I clutched the sides of my head in pain and put my head between my knees, what was happening to me?

I felt hands touching my back but if anything, it made the pain worse and I screamed again as the hands took me into their arms and ran me somewhere, but I was in too much pain to see where.

The last thing I remembered was being laid down on something comfy before blackness overtook me.

Chapter 6

Jax POV

After I placed Annabelle down in the centre of my bed, I stared down at her with worry. I knew that watching me shift would have been a shock for her, but I wasn't aware that it was going to cause her *physical* pain. There was very little known about this form of Alpha control, where a person as young as her was forced not to shift. It is a silent, golden rule set amongst all Alphas purely because of the problems it can cause a person and their wolf later in life. Problems she is now obviously struggling with.

I walked back downstairs and into the living room to wait for Dr. Tessler to arrive, when I spotted my discarded clothes that I had haphazardly scattered around the room. Seeing them there brought back the memory of Annabelle's face as it scrunched up in pain, clutching onto the roots of her hair. I sighed, upset with myself that I was the one that caused her pain, before I started picking up the articles of clothing and pulling them back on. I was just putting on my last sock when I heard the doorbell ring. I must've been so deep in thought I hadn't heard them walk up the driveway.

I opened the door and smiled slightly in relief as I spotted Dr. Tessler standing on my porch with her small leather medical bag in hand. This woman was a god sent.

"Hi Dr Tessler, please come in," I muttered as I stepped out of the way so that she could enter my small hallway before walking into the living room.

"So where is she? You sounded pretty worried when you linked me," she stated in a very matter of fact tone. She was straight down to business and for that I couldn't be more grateful, I was not in the current mood to be engaging in small talk.

"She's upstairs in my room," I informed her as I pointed in the general direction to the stairs, not that she needed it seeing as she'd been here just last night when I had found Annabelle.

She nodded as she shifted her bag from her left to her right hand, "if it's alright with you I'd like to check on the Luna alone? I don't want your presence to stir her or her buried wolf any further," she quickly explained once she saw me stand behind her and go to follow her up the stairs.

I sighed before nodding my head. I may not like the idea of leaving her, but I could understand why it was essential. "Of course, please do head up. I will be waiting here when you're done," I informed her as I watched her form disappear through the living room door and up the stairs.

I heard her footsteps as they wandered into my room and I kept a close ear on the two of them upstairs, just in case either of them needed me for anything.

I sighed again as I made my way over to the small bar I kept in the corner of the room and helped myself to a large glass of whisky. The last twenty-four hours has been difficult and it showed no signs of easing up anytime soon.

After a while of sitting alone in my living room I heard light footsteps make their way down the stairs and back to where I was waiting. I quickly downed the rest of the amber liquid that had gone semi warm as it rested in my hand before getting up and helping myself to another. I had a feeling I was going to need it.

"Physically she's fine," the doctor explained as she came and stood in front of me as I nursed my second glass of whisky. "It's more her mental state that I have concerns with," she continued as she gestured to the sofa opposite me. "May I sit?"

I nodded but otherwise didn't say anything as I watched her take a seat on the edge of my sofa, right where Annabelle had been sitting not too long ago. "As I was saying in the hospital, I feel like we should have a conversation about Annabelle's past and how it could affect her in the long term," she explained.

"Her physical injuries and the fact that she was malnourished will heal overtime, her bruises and cuts will eventually fade and she will slowly regain the weight back that she so desperately needs with a proper diet plan and time. Her mental health though is a completely different issue," she paused as she looked over at me to make sure that I was paying attention to her and understanding her words.

"Her mental health is tricky, especially after what she's gone through over the years with that...family. She wasn't very giving with information when I asked her questions, which indicates to me that she has a lot of trust issues that needs to be worked on and looked at. You're also going to have to be very patient with her with regards to some of her characteristics and the way she handles certain issues," she continued to explain.

"What do you mean by her characteristics?" I asked "I'm her mate, mine and her personalities should match perfectly as the Moon Goddess paired us together," I questioned with a frown.

She nodded as she took in my words "yes that is true, but a lot of her personality would have been altered, maybe permanently, because of what she has gone through. The list of symptoms for long term abuse, both physical and mental, are very varied and we can't always speculate how her experiences would have affected her, but be prepared for her to feel tired quite a lot of the time. She may also suffer from anxiety and panic attacks in unfamiliar situations or around new people, which may cause her to regress back to how she would have reacted to a certain action or emotion back in that house. For example, flinching at sudden movements or when someone goes to touch her.

"Low self esteem or even depression can be quite common as well. She has probably been told most of her life that she was worthless and it's very common for people, especially children, to believe others' opinions very quickly seeing as she wouldn't have been told any differently."

My head spun as the doctor continued to list more symptoms that I should be on the lookout for. My poor Annabelle has been through something so horrible and so traumatic it may have ended up affecting her for the rest of her life.

"Should I continue Alpha, or would you like to have a short moment to process?" She asked me in a soft voice, obviously very aware of the turmoil that was currently running through my mind.

"No no please go on, I need to be prepared for anything," I muttered as I took another sip of whisky, feeling the burn as it slid down my throat.

"Very well... she'll also most likely suffer with a tremendous amount of guilt for things that may not necessarily be her fault. Having things blamed on her all her life would make her believe that everything that goes wrong was always her fault. This could lead to over apologising or becoming a social recluse. It is important to remind her, almost constantly, that whatever she is feeling guilty for wasn't her fault.

"It also may help to bring her out of the house every once in a while, without being overly pushy of course. She'd been kept in that house, basically under lock and key, for twelve years, so she may forget that she's allowed free rein of the area and to come and go as she pleases.

"This also brings me to another key point that I wanted to talk to you about," she says as she folds her hands in her lap. "I believe Annabelle's experiences may have caused her to suffer from something called child regression, basically meaning she has the mind of a child. Being only seven when she was placed into this family means she would have had extraordinarily little to no social stimulation throughout her years as a child and early adolescence. She will be extremely naive to certain situations and will not fully understand the full repercussions and consequences of certain acts."

I quickly held my hand up, the one that wasn't holding my now empty glass, as I looked over at her. "Doctor if you're trying to tell me that I shouldn't expect a physical relationship from her anytime soon then there really is no need. I am fully aware that she is in no state to even be thinking about something as serious as marking or completing the Luna ceremony," I reassured her. I wanted to get annoyed at the doctor for even suggesting that I would force or rush anything like that with my little mate, but on the other hand I knew I couldn't. Not only was she just doing her job and informing me on what I should be expecting, she was also protecting her Luna from suffering any more psychological damage than she already had.

"I apologise Alpha," she nodded as she looked down at the floor slightly, showing me that she genuinely was sincere.

"There's no need to apologise," I smiled slightly back at her. "I understand that you just want to protect her. Besides, the more I know about the possible problems I will be facing with her the more prepared I'll be to deal with them," I explained. As much as I hated hearing all the possible side effects my mate may suffer from in the future, it was important for me to know, so as not to affect her negatively in any way. "Please carry on," I insisted as I gestured to her that she had the floor.

"Very well," she nodded. "I also wanted to talk to you about her speech. She is extremely reluctant to talk to or about anything that is new or unfamiliar to her. It is important that you don't push her to talk when she is feeling vulnerable, forcing her to do something she doesn't want to do or what she isn't ready for could actually be counterproductive to our end goal. She has had little to no control over her life, so if you force anything upon her it could cause her to believe that she was back in that place and revert back to how she reacted before she escaped."

I nodded as I took in the last of the information the doctor had to offer. It was invaluable and I found myself trying to absorb it all like a sponge, afraid that I was going to forget some of it and do something that would cause her more pain than she was already in.

I thought about everything that the doctor had told me, about how she may not understand certain social situations or being in a certain type of environment could cause her to have an anxiety attack. My beautiful little mate really had been in the wars, and I was going to do *everything* in my power to make her comfortable and better again.

All I wanted to do was hold my Annabelle in my arms, feel her warmth against my skin, so that I knew she was alive and safe.

I glanced upstairs, as if I could see her through the floorboards of the ceiling. Doctor Tessler must have caught on to how anxious I was feeling because she offered me a small smile before suggesting we follow on our conversation a little closer to Annabelle so that I could relax a little.

This woman really was irreplaceable.

B E WAKEFORD

Chapter 7

Annabelle's POV

What the hell happened?

Why had I passed out?

I frowned and squinted my eyes as a dull headache started to blossom behind my eyebrows. I looked to my right, hoping to find out what time it was, but when my eyes caught the sight of the closed curtains, I realised that it was no longer light out. A bedside lamp had been left on beside me but that was all that lit the room as I looked around for any information that could explain what had happened to me.

I panicked for a second, not understanding where I was, but as I started to take in more of my surroundings, I started to recognise the room as Jax's. Had something happened to him earlier? I had the weirdest feeling that something had happened.

I frowned again and rubbed my forehead as the concentration was causing my headache to throb uncomfortably. I moved the duvet aside so that I could get up and find Jax, but when I heard muffled voices from behind the door I froze.

"But why would her wolf do that to her?" I recognised that as Jax's voice, but why was he yelling? And who was he yelling at?

"I don't know Alpha; my guess is that seeing you in your other form triggered or startled her wolf somehow. I will have to do some research on this type of Alpha control, but my guess is that because she left the pack's territory the command that was originally placed on her is somehow having less of an effect. Adding to that, seeing you in your wolf form for the first time, her wolf must've been trying to escape and shift wanting to meet her mate, but the human side of her is still subconsciously following the command."

"Well how the hell do we break the command?" Jax growled, the sound feeling like it could shake the walls around me. He was so angry, just like Tony or Natalie when they didn't get their way.

I whimpered slightly as memories started to one-by-one flood back into my brain. Memories of them yelling at me for there being no beer in the house, for not organising the jewellery box the way it should be. I whimpered again as I held my head in my hands, praying for the flashbacks to stop and for my brain to go quiet.

All of a sudden it became noticeably quiet outside the bedroom door, as if they could hear the internal turmoil I was currently suffering through.

"Thank you doctor, you are dismissed," Jax suddenly said, in a slightly calmer voice than before.

"Alpha," was all she replied with before I heard her footsteps retreat back down the stairs and out the front door.

The next thing I knew the bedroom door was slowly being pushed open as Jax poked his head through. I smiled for a second, trying to show him that I was okay, but when I looked into those big brown eyes of his everything from earlier came flooding back. The story he had told me about the Moon goddess, him standing by the TV as he started taking his clothes off, him shifting into a giant black wolf before my very eyes.

I whimpered again as the memory consumed my brain, making me watch him shift over and over again on repeat. I froze in my whimpering as I watched the shimmering gold of his wolf slightly swirl into his irises, mixing with his normal chocolate brown colour, the action startling me into silence.

I moved slightly up the bed, planning to put some distance between us and get away from him, but when I saw hurt flash across his features I froze. I didn't understand why but for some reason I felt bad for hurting him. He quickly brushed his feelings aside though and in a blink of an eye he was back to the happy and caring Jax I had grown accustomed to. Even when he was hurting he was trying to make me feel more at ease, and I couldn't help but melt back into a comfortable position at the realisation. He was still the same Jax from earlier, the same person that had assured me over and over again that he wouldn't hurt me.

"It's okay Annabelle," Jax muttered as he took a step towards me with his arms raised, as if he were approaching a wild animal. I smiled slightly at the irony of the situation we were in, if anyone was the wild animal around here, it was him.

"Do you remember what I told you in the car this afternoon Annabelle?" He asked as he took another tentative step towards me and my heart stuttered as he got closer, my irrational fear starting to get the better of me again. I nodded despite my fear though, indicating that I remembered exactly what he had told me. In fact, it was the only thing that had kept me from running for the hills in the first place.

My response brought a slight smile to Jax's lips as he relaxed his shoulders ever so slightly, looking almost relieved that I remembered. "Can you tell me what I told you?" He pressed.

"You...you won't hurt me," I stuttered. My heart desperately wanted to believe him, but my brain still needed convincing.

His smile widened even further as he crouched down by the side of the bed, I hadn't even realised he'd gotten this close to me until he was sitting almost eye level with me. "That's right Annabelle, I could *never* hurt you. I could never hurt the one person who makes my life worth living," he stated, looking into my eyes with an emotion completely foreign to me.

I blushed at his comment and looked down, not knowing how to take it. When you've been told most of your life that you were worthless, and you'd never amount to anything in life, it's hard to accept someone saying anything different. The worst part was that I actually believed them. Those hateful comments that the Leftens would spew my way when they felt like putting me down. I mean I obviously had to have done something horrible in the past to be treated in such a way so maybe… maybe I did deserve everything the Leftens had done to me.

I suddenly felt the bed dip slightly and looked up to see Jax sitting at the foot of the bed, close enough to touch me if he reached out, but not close enough for any contact to be accidental.

"Do you also remember what happened earlier?" He asked hesitantly, obviously wary about approaching the subject of his shifting again after seeing my initial reaction.

I nodded before looking down at my clasped fingers. "I-I remember," I whispered.

"So you remember about the story I told you, about the Moon Goddess and mates and w-werewolves?" He stuttered.

I nodded my head slowly, relieved that my headache was slowly starting to fade now that Jax was sitting close, his presence soothing me.

"D-do you remember anything else Annabelle? Anything about me?" He questioned; hesitation clear in his voice in how to broach the subject.

I nodded again but still remained silent, unable to say the words out loud, that he had changed into a wolf before my very eyes. Instead I decided to go in a different direction, knowing I wouldn't be able to comprehend anything else at the moment. "Why did my head hurt?" I whispered.

Jax sighed and ran his hand through his already ruffled hair, "Well the doctor and I have a theory about that actually. Come downstairs with me and I will make you some hot chocolate whilst we talk, how does that sound?"

I smiled at the mention of hot chocolate and vigorously nodded my head in agreement, making Jax laugh at my ecstatic expression.

"So you like hot chocolate then," he said with a nod, as if he was storing the information away somewhere special in his brain for future reference.

I just shrugged and held my hands out, ready for him to pick me up and walk me into the kitchen. I could definitely walk by now; all the cuts and scrapes had healed over enough so that it didn't cause me too much pain to put weight on them, I just didn't want to waste a chance of being in his arms.

He smiled a toothy grin at me when he realised what I was wanting and quickly came to pick me up in his arms, looking eager to have me close to him.

"I'm so glad you aren't scared of me little mate; I don't know what I would've done if you were," he muttered.

As he sat me down on the kitchen counter, just like earlier, we fell into a comfortable silence as Jax started to get the ingredients together ready to make a hot chocolate.

"Do you like cinnamon in it or not?" He asked.

I shrugged my shoulders, not really knowing how I liked it.

He frowned "you have had hot chocolate before, right?"

I shook my head before shrugging again, the Leftens always said I was never worthy of something as nice as chocolate. Natalie always loved getting me to make it though, another form of torture and making me inferior to her no doubt. She never even drank it because of the high fat and sugar content, she'd just watch me make it, take one sip and then pour it down the drain.

Jax mumbled something under his breath before turning around to gather the squirty cream and marshmallows. "Well you're in for a treat then because my hot chocolates are the best of the best," he declared as he started to heat milk in a saucepan over the hob. "My secret is plenty of sugar and smarties on top," Jax whispered, as if he were telling me a top secret.

I giggled at him and nodded in understanding before pretending to lock my lips with my thumb and finger, letting him know his secret was safe with me.

Jax laughed back with his eyes shining before turning back to the chocolate mixture as he proceeded to pour it into two mugs after he'd deemed it hot enough. One for me and one for him. Once he'd done that he plopped in a few mini marshmallows, squirted loads of cream on top and then finished it off with chocolate shavings, smarties, chocolate sauce and more mini marshmallows with a cinnamon stick and a flake sticking out of it. It was like a sugar overload.

"Voila, my masterpiece," he said in a weird Italian accent which I couldn't help but giggle at.

I clapped at his creation before wrapping my arms around his neck so that he carried me into the living room, settling me back down into my seat on the sofa. When he came back with our drinks, we both got comfortable on the sofa next to each other and I took my first sip. Safe to say it was probably the most incredible thing I had ever tasted.

"Do you like it?" Jax asked as he saw my eyes light up at the taste.

I smiled and nodded my head enthusiastically before dipping my head to take another sip.

"Well don't tell Dr Tessler I gave you that alright? Hot chocolate is definitely not on the list of things you should be having yet," he laughed as he took a sip of his own, causing a small blob of cream to stick to his top lip. My finger twitched, wanting to reach out and wipe it off for him, but before I could he had licked it away.

I nodded again but otherwise stayed silent as I took another sip of the sugary drink, occasionally looking up at him drinking his own. I couldn't even remember the last time I had the privilege of tasting something that was this good. Everything was blended so perfectly together I couldn't help but moan slightly after every sip.

"Annabelle, could I ask you something?" Jax asked, breaking the comfortable silence between us as he looked over at me nervously.

I nodded my head, only half paying attention to him whilst the other half was focused on the hot cup of deliciousness currently clutched in between my palms.

"Okay umm... I don't really know how to go about this so here goes...have you met your wolf yet?"

I froze as I was about to take another sip, confused by his bizarre question. "My...my what?" I stuttered, unsure if I had heard him right.

"Your wolf," he repeated, staring at me expectantly over his own cup.

"I...umm...what?" Was he serious, did he really think I had some wolf stashed somewhere or something?

"Your wolf Annabelle, up here," he elaborated as he pointed to his temple. He had a wolf in his *brain*? I mean I guess that could make sense seeing as he is a werewolf and all but why would he think I had one? I wasn't a werewolf.

I just stared at him in confusion causing him to sigh.

"Annabelle, do you remember the story I told you, about how the Moon Goddess would gift a werewolf with a mate, to help calm their wolf side?"

I nodded, of course I remembered, how could I forget Jax turning into a huge black wolf before my very eyes in the middle of the living room? "Well... to help keep her species alive the Moon Goddess decided that werewolves could only have mates who were also werewolves...do you get where I'm going with this?" He asked, obviously struggling with his words a little. I so desperately wanted to nod and say that I understood, but if I was being honest I didn't have a clue what he was talking about. I shook my head and he sighed, running his hand through his hair.

"Okay let's try this a different way," he muttered more to himself than to me. "What is it that I call you?"

"What?"

"What do I call you when I don't use your name."

I thought for a second before responding in a whisper "your little mate."

He smiled "exactly, you're my little mate Annabelle, my *mate*."

He was looking at me expectantly but all I could do was stare at him in shock, I was his mate? "No...no that's not right," I stuttered. "You said that-that the Moon Goddess d-doesn't pair up a werewolf with a human. You just said that... right now."

He shook his head and leaned towards me so that we were nearly touching. "She doesn't," was all he replied with, a soft smile gracing his lips.

I frowned "but that doesn't make sense...that would mean that I'm a... that I can..." I stuttered, unable to finish the sentence. Was he being serious? Did he really believe that I was a werewolf like him?

I looked into his eyes, and saw nothing but truth and determination in them, nothing to hint that he was lying or pulling my leg.

I stared at him in shock and all of a sudden, I couldn't breathe properly, like I couldn't get enough oxygen into my lungs. I could feel my heart pounding in my chest and my hands started to uncontrollably shake. *This can't be happening... this can't be real* I muttered to myself over and over. I could hear my blood rushing through my ears and my stomach was filled with so many butterflies I felt like I was going to be sick.

Jax was quick to take the hot chocolate out of my fingers before it could spill onto the carpet and placed it on the coffee table in front of us before taking both of my shaking hands in one of his as he placed his other hand on my cheek. "Deep breaths for me little mate, it will soon fade," he reassured me in a calm voice.

The sound of his voice plus the warmth he was generating through his hands into mine helped calm my nerves and before long my breathing had gone back to normal and the butterflies had disappeared.

"Better?" He asked and I nodded my head as I looked up into his calming chocolate eyes.

"How...?" My voice wavered as I tried to formulate a sentence.

Jax sighed as he got comfortable on the sofa, pulling me into his arms so that my head was resting on his chest. I could hear the steady beat of his heart, causing mine to match his as my breathing ease up and calmed down.

"The doctor and I have a theory about the how, we didn't want it to be true but it's beginning to look more and more likely. It's one of the worst things an Alpha could do to someone in their pack," he sighed.

I gazed up at him expectantly, but he was just staring into space with his eyes glazed over, unaware that I was looking up at him as I took in his remorseful expression.

"An Alpha has complete control over his pack," he began, obviously deciding the best way to describe what was going on with me was through another story. "He decides what does and what doesn't happen with everything involving his pack or territory. One of the traits an Alpha has is the ability to bend will, for example if a pack member is being disrespectful to the Alpha then that Alpha can bend the pack members will to submit to him. It's one of the reasons Alphas are so powerful," he explained.

"There are certain unspoken rules regarding this ability to bend will, for example forcing someone to do something they don't want to do, making them commit a crime et cetera..." He pauses for a moment, as if he were gathering his thoughts and I quickly squeezed his hand reassuringly, urging him to continue.

He smiled down at me before taking a breath and ran his hand through his hair. "One of the worst things an Alpha could do is force someone not to shift. Placing that command on someone who has already turned sixteen and has already shifted is bad enough but at least they have already shifted and so have their wolf with them. But placing that type of command on someone who hasn't yet shifted is seen as one of the worst things an Alpha could possibly do. It stops their wolf even coming to the surface and so that person can never shift and never meet their wolf. It's like ripping a part of someone's *soul* away from them. What's worse is that because that person hasn't met their wolf, their wolf is not there to help recognise their mate, without a person's wolf they will never know who their mate is."

I looked up at him again to see him staring down at me in sadness "Annabelle, we believe that's what's happened to you, your Alpha must've placed the command on you at a very young age for you not to remember it."

I frowned and looked at my hands as I picked my nails. Could he be right? Could I really have a wolf trapped inside my head somewhere, unable to get out because of some command put on me by an Alpha as a young child?

"How can you be so sure I'm your mate if you can't feel my wolf?" I whispered, nervous to hear his response.

He kissed the top of my head and my stomach did a little flip. "I can feel her Annabelle, she's hidden away but she's there, tucked away in a corner of your brain. All you need to do is let her out," he encouraged with a soft smile before burying his nose in my hair. "Even if I couldn't feel her I'd still know you were mine, your scent alone would draw me to you, the smell of strawberries and vanilla. It's so intoxicating I could breathe you in all day."

I blushed at what he was saying, did I really smell of strawberries and vanilla? How would someone even smell like that?

"And even without your smell I'd know you were mine, just from a simple brush of my hand on yours. The electricity between our fingertips would light my wolf on fire and instantly let me know that you were mine, just as much as I am yours," he smiled.

He slowly started to trail his fingertips up my arm and I frowned at the lack of this electricity he was talking about, only feeling the smallest amounts of tingles in their wake.

He smiled at me sadly as I looked up at him in confusion. "It's because you haven't met your wolf yet, once you do you'll feel the exact same thing I'm feeling right now," he sighed with gold slightly swirling in his eyes, showing me his wolf was coming through.

"When?" I asked, desperate to meet her so that I could experience these amazing things that Jax was talking about.

He just shrugged at me, "that's completely up to you and how much you want to meet her. You are no longer under your previous Alphas control since you ran away and left his territory, so it's all up to you as to when you shift."

"You're an Alpha, can't you just command me to shift?" I asked, hoping he could somehow help me.

He smiled down at me before shaking his head, "unfortunately I can't, it would probably do more harm to you than good. You'd have two opposing Alpha commands rattling around in that pretty little head of yours and your brain would instinctively try and follow both of them. It would rip you and your wolf in two trying to appease both commands. You need to break through your old Alpha's command on your own before you can even hope to meet her."

I huffed, not liking the answer and crossed my arms.

He laughed at my little tantrum and hugged me tighter. "You've done the hardest part, all that's left to do is just to practice," he said as he continued to chuckle at me.

I frowned "What hard bit?"

"Shifting for the first time, when we found you in the woods you were in your wolf form, I mean I'm guessing that it was your first shift seeing as you don't know anything about being a werewolf," he shrugged.

"I shifted?" I gasped, so confused as to why I didn't remember it.

He nodded and smiled at my shocked face "still believe you aren't a werewolf?" He smirked.

I remained silent, slowly digesting all the information he had just unloaded on me.

"You were the most beautiful golden coloured wolf I had ever seen, similar to your hair but with just a hint more gold in it. You were unconscious by the time I got there but you were absolutely stunning...still are," he whispered as he tucked a lock of hair behind my ear.

I blushed as I looked down, but before I could he caught my chin in his hand and gently lifted my head up so that I was looking deep into his eyes. "You are beautiful Annabelle, don't ever forget that," he whispered, his voice strong with conviction.

I stared into his eyes, feeling speechless. How do you respond to something like that, when you've been told all your life that you were worthless and ugly.

Jax must have noticed that I was starting to feel uncomfortable as he quickly kissed my forehead before changing the subject. "That's why you can heal so fast you know," he smiled, leaning forward so that he could pick up our hot chocolates.

I frowned at him as I took it back in my hands and took a small sip of the luke-warm but just as delicious drink.

"Being a werewolf, that's how you manage to heal so quickly," he explained as he took in my confused expression. "What, you thought it was normal for someone to twist their ankle and then for it to be perfectly fine the next day?" He chuckled.

I just shrugged, I had never really given it much thought, it explains why I managed to survive all the beatings I had received throughout the years at the Leftens. Not many people could break their leg and then walk on it a few days later.

"Anyway, enough of the serious talk for tonight, we can do more of that tomorrow, but now I think that it's time to get some dinner for you," he stated as he placed our half-finished drinks back on the coffee table and got up with me in his arms.

If I was being completely honest, I was still stuffed from the half cup of hot chocolate I had, but didn't want to upset him so I just nodded my head with a slightly forced smile as he walked me into the kitchen.

Chapter 8

Jax's POV

I wasn't going to lie, I was nervous... probably for the first time in my life.

I was carrying my mate up the stairs and down the hallway leading to my room so that I could gently place her on the bed for some much-needed sleep. I hadn't slept in I don't know how long, and my brain was becoming slightly frazzled because of it.

I was nervous because I didn't know how she was going to react to sleeping in the same room as me. I knew she had trust issues with people, and I didn't want to make her uncomfortable by forcing her into a situation she wasn't ready for. Doctor Tessler's words about forcing her into doing something she didn't want to do rang through my head on a constant loop, but I also didn't think I could sleep in a different room to her, my wolf would be climbing the walls at not having her near me.

I stared at her, trying to gauge her reaction to this situation, but when I couldn't pick anything up from her, just her neutral face and wide watchful eyes, I sighed in irritation and turned to get some clean clothes from my wardrobe for the both of us. I'd have to take her shopping tomorrow for some clothes that would actually fit her, I'm not going to lie through, I rather enjoyed seeing her in my clothes.

I cleared my throat and ran my hand along the back of my neck, bringing my mind back to the sleeping arrangements.

"You're going to sleep in here tonight… with me… if that's okay with you?" I tried to say it as if it were a demand, but the more I spoke the more it came out like a question. What was wrong with me, I was the Alpha of a strong pack, but right now I was acting more like a lovesick teenager.

Looking into Annabelle's eyes I could see the uncertainty in them, and my heart sank a little at the realisation and reminder that she didn't fully trust me yet. "I'll sleep on the couch over there so that you're a little more comfortable, but I'm not sleeping in a different room to you. My wolf won't take it Annabelle and neither of us will get a restful sleep," I explained, hoping I sounded a little firmer than last time.

She thankfully nodded her head in understanding before looking down at the clothes that I had just placed in front of her. She then looked back up at me, and I could tell that she was silently asking me to leave the room so that she could change in private.

"Alright, alright I'll leave you to get changed whilst I go and take a shower. I'll be in the bathroom if you need anything," I said before turning around and headed into the en-suit. It took all my self-control not to turn around as I heard the rustle of fabric behind me as she started to change into the fresh set of clothes I had just given her. I managed to get to the bathroom without looking back and quickly shut the door behind me before my wolf won out on what he wanted and I turned around.

I sighed and leant my forehead against the door, she was driving me crazy and she wasn't even doing anything. I shuddered to think what she would be capable of doing to me once she gains enough confidence and has contact with her wolf. She'd have me wrapped around her little finger, not that she doesn't already, or as Xavier would say, whipped.

I quietly growled as I suddenly remembered that someone had forcibly shut her away from her wolf and therefore away from me as I went to turn the water on. Whoever did that to her should be immediately executed in front of everyone, no one hurts my mate.

"Alpha, are you available for a meeting?" Xavier asked me through our mink link, stopping my vengeful thoughts from getting too far.

"Give me ten minutes and then yes I will be, I just want to make sure Annabelle is asleep before you come around." The last thing I needed was for her to see him and get scared. After all, he is the one who forcefully demanded her to shift back when she didn't even know what was going on.

"Sure thing," was his only response before we cut the conversation.

I sighed and quickly finished my shower before dressing into some clean clothes and heading back out into my bedroom. I guess I won't be going to sleep *just* yet.

What I saw when I came out of the bathroom made me angry and my heart break all at the same time. There, curled up on the sofa, was my Annabelle. She had changed into her new clothes and was now cuddled up in the corner of the sofa without even a pillow or a blanket over her to keep her warm. What did she think she was playing at, there was no question that she was getting the bed tonight so why did she go and sleep on the sofa?

I sighed as I walked over to her, taking her petite frame in my arms and brought her over to the left-hand side of the bed. She snuggled in as I brought the duvet up to her chin and I couldn't help but brush her hair back and kiss her forehead as I lovingly stared down at her. She was so beautiful.

I must've been staring at her for longer than I thought because not long after, Xavier mind linked me to tell me that he was waiting outside.

I sighed at the thought of leaving her alone again as I kissed her on the forehead once more before forcing myself to leave my room and head downstairs, quickly making my way over to the front door to let my Beta in.

"Sup man, haven't heard from you all day," Xavier smiled, slapping me on the back as he walked through the threshold.

"Yeah well I've been a little busy," I replied, the lack of sleep making me a little on the defensive side.

"Hey I get it, if she was my mate and I found her in the same condition your mate was in I'd be acting the same way. How is she by the way?" He asked as he took a seat on the sofa in the living room.

My eyes were instantly drawn down to the half-finished and now extremely cold cups of hot chocolate that were still sitting on the coffee table, my mind wandering back to the conversation we'd had earlier. "She's not good man, but she's getting there," I nodded.

I ran my hand through my hair at how useless I felt and rested my head on the back of the sofa. "She doesn't know anything about werewolves Xavier, her so-called *Alpha* ordered her never to shift when she was a child, she has no idea about anything. She can't even feel the full effects of our mate bond because of it."

"I'm sorry Jax, if there's anything you need me to do besides help with the pack just let me know alright?" Xavier reassured me as I looked at him and nodded my head in thanks.

"So what is it you wanted to talk about?" I asked, I just wanted to get this meeting over with so that I could get back to my sleeping mate.

"It's actually about Annabelle," Xavier explained as he ran a hand through his hair. With him just saying Annabelle's name he immediately had my attention as I shuffled slightly more forward on the sofa and I looked at him expectantly.

"I got Henry to follow her scent as far as he could, all the way to the edge of another pack's territory. I don't know whether that's where she came from or whether she was just passing through, but I thought I'd let you know and keep you in the loop. I want to find out who hurt our Luna just as much as you do."

My fists clenched at the recent information, hoping that it was something I could use as a just cause to storm their pack and take my revenge for what they did to my Annabelle. "Which pack was it?"

"That's the thing, it's a pack that doesn't really have the *best* reputation in the world. Just... just don't lose it okay?" He stuttered, obviously a little nervous at my possible reactions.

I rolled my eyes and clenched my jaw "just spit it out Xavier."

"Her scent leads from... the... Rising Dawn pack," he muttered and I instantly felt my blood run cold.

The Rising Dawn pack was known throughout our kind as the lowest of the lows. Their Alpha loved to play dirty and would do anything to get his way. He rules his pack with an iron fist, but no one has managed to get enough proof to get the elders to investigate. The weird thing was this pack used to be an ally of ours, we helped each other out like for like, but out of nowhere the Alpha and Luna resigned their title and gave it to their current Alpha. My dad, the Alpha at the time, had always found it suspicious that his friends would just up and leave their pack, but he could never get close enough to the new Alpha to find out what had happened without starting a pack war.

The idea of Annabelle being in the same presence as anyone from that pack made my blood boil and I quickly stood up and started pacing, I was too jittery to be sitting still. "Are you sure that is where her scent came from?" I asked.

I looked into Xavier's eyes as he nodded his head in a confirming yes.

I growled and punched a hole through the wall closest to me, the idea of my sweet little Annabelle in that pack made my blood boil, goddess knows what she has been through if she came from there.

"There was something else I thought you should know about her too, Jax," Xavier continued, unfazed by my sudden outburst of anger, being so used to it by now after the years of growing up together.

"And what is that," I growled. I could tell my eyes were swirling gold as my wolf tried to make an appearance, but I pushed him back and focused on what Xavier was trying to tell me.

"When I found Annabelle, when she was in her wolf form, there was something about her that was different. I couldn't quite put my finger on it at the time, but it suddenly dawned on me as I was looking through some of my mum's old history books. No matter what status you have in the pack or your eye colour as a human, your wolf always has golden eyes, right? Well Annabelle's eyes were different; they were sort of gold but also kind of transparent as well. It's really hard to describe, but after doing some research I'm sure they were the exact colour of moonstone."

I frowned at him, "Are you sure?" I've never known of a wolf that didn't have golden eyes before.

Xavier nodded "positive."

My frown deepened. "I wonder what it could mean," I muttered, but before Xavier could respond with anything, we were both interrupted by a scream from upstairs and my stomach dropped as I recognised it as my mate's voice.

I bolted upstairs with Xavier hot on my heels and burst into my room to find my mate thrashing in bed and tangling herself up in the duvet as she was in the middle of a nightmare.

I quickly walked over to her and wiped the tears and sweat from her skin as I gently tried to wake her up, hating seeing the look of pain on her face.

"Annabelle...Annabelle wake up little mate...I've got you... it's just a dream, it's just a dream," I kept repeating as I carried on stroking her face, hoping to bring her back to me.

Suddenly she sat bolt upright.

"Annabelle it's me, calm down...calm down before you hurt yourself." I was doing everything I could think of to get her to calm down, but her mind wasn't registering where she was as she just kept screaming and fighting me, thrashing in my arms.

"No Damon no... get off of me... no please... nooooooo," she screamed and lashed out at me.

It took me a second to realise that her fingernails had turned into claws, but it was a second too late as I felt them dig into my chest, causing four deep claw marks to form on my upper body. I grimaced at the pain but otherwise ignored it as I focused on my mate. It would heal quickly as I'm an Alpha but if she got herself with them, she could do some serious damage to herself.

Just then the lights came on and I turned around to find Xavier had flicked them on and was waiting at the door, making sure I was alright and didn't require any assistance.

"Annabelle… Annabelle… come back to me. You're here and you're safe, I've got you. I won't let anyone hurt you I promise," I whispered in her ear over and over again as I held her in a tight hug, ignoring the sting on my chest as the weight of her body pressed into my wounds.

"J-Jax?" She finally stuttered and I sighed in relief as her eyes opened and focused on me.

"Yeah it's me, I've got you," I repeated and held onto her tighter, if that was even possible.

She had stopped struggling as she lay in my arms, and after a few minutes she had calmed down enough for her breathing to somewhat go back to normal.

"Xavier, could you get some water and the medical kit from the kitchen please?" I asked through the link, not moving my arms from around Annabelle so that I could turn to see him.

"Sure, need me to get the doctor or have you got it from here?" He questioned, not moving from his position in the doorway.

I shook my head knowing he could still see me from where he stood, "I *got it thanks."*

"Annabelle, are you okay?" I whispered, afraid that my voice might trigger another panic attack of hers.

She stiffened for a second as my voice broke the silence before eventually relaxing and nodding her head slowly.

"Want to talk about it?" I asked as I brushed her sweat soaked hair from off her face and neck, hoping it would help cool her warm skin.

She stayed still for a second before finally shaking her head and buried herself deeper into my neck.

"Everything you need is outside your room Jax, I didn't want to come in just in case she got scared again".

"Thanks Xavier, I'll see you in the morning."

"Alpha" he replied as I heard him walk down the stairs and close the front door as he left the house.

Chapter 9

Annabelle's POV

It was dark.

The smell of mould and burnt flesh filled my nostrils as I took in a sharp intake of air, the sheer power of the stench making me gag.

Where was I? The last thing I remembered was falling asleep on Jax's comfy sofa after refusing to let him sleep on it. He would have probably dangled off the end with how tall he was and I refused to let him sleep like that after everything he's done for me.

I went to move my arm to brush some hair out of my face which had started to tickle my nose but hissed in pain as they were held back by something. Chains, silver chains. My heart started to pound in my chest as I frantically looked around, trying to see if I could get my bearings at all. All I could see though was the damp stone brickwork that formed the walls of my current prison and a concrete floor with what looked like fresh blood splattered all over it like a Jackson Pollock painting. My blood.

I couldn't help the little whimper that escaped my lips as I continued to stare at the puddle of blood at my feet. What had happened to me?

"Ahh the princess is up," someone sneered from somewhere in the dark.

My head snapped up at the voice and I squinted into the shadows, trying to find the face that the voice belonged to.

"I was wondering when you were going to finally wake up, I have a little someone here that's just been dying *to see you again," the voice continued.*

I frowned as I just about made out the outline of a body leaning against the wall, with his arms crossed over his chest and his legs crossed at the ankles. Apart from that he was just a shadow, a faceless shadow with a sinister voice.

"She's awake," he shouted to someone behind him, making me jump at the sudden volume change. He smirked at my reaction as he kicked himself off the wall and turned around to face the door. I still couldn't make out his face, but I did spot a tattoo on the back of his neck, it was some kind of tribal knot done in a green/black ink.

I frowned at it, following the twists and turns the ink went, before the stranger moved out of my eyesight and instead came face to face with someone I never wished to see again. Someone I thought I had escaped when I ran away from that place.

"Damon." His name slipped from my lips with venom as a shudder ran up my spine and I didn't know whether I wanted to scream in anger or terror.

He smirked at me, obviously happy that I had given him the reception that he wanted, and slowly started to step his way into my cell. I shuffled away from him, ignoring the smell of burnt flesh as the chains rubbed against my wrists. All I could think about was the fact that I had to get away from him.

"Hello little Annabelle," he sneered as he grabbed my chin forcefully and brought my face up to meet his. It was a gesture Jax had done quite a few times since meeting him, but he'd always done it in a gentle, almost loving manner. Damon did it in a way that forced my attention to him in a cruel and spiteful way. "I see you remember me then," he laughed.

I growled at him angrily and ripped my chin from his grasp, not liking the idea of him managing to taint Jax's caring gestures with his hateful ones.

"Oh little Annabelle, when are you going to learn to respect your superiors," he sighed before slapping me hard across the face causing my head to snap back.

I bit my lip so as not to make any noise, Damon always got a secret thrill out of hearing my screams and if I remained quiet the beatings were always less intense.

"Now where shall I begin," he muttered, so quietly I could tell he was talking to himself more than me. "Yes, I think here is a wonderful place to begin, don't you?" He questioned in a sickeningly sweet voice as he got on his knees beside me and produced a knife from his pocket. It wasn't a particularly large blade, measuring roughly a few inches long, but the way it gleamed in the non-existent light I could tell it was sharp, sharp enough to slice skin away from bone if he so wished. "I'm going to enjoy peeling your skin off layer by layer as I watch you scream and beg for mercy," he growled as he flashed the blade in front of my face. "You've had this coming since

the day you ran away from me, little girl. You ruined everything for me and my family the day you left."

And then he started. I couldn't help but scream as he proceeded to hack small chunks of flesh from my legs, feeling strange, invisible hands hold me down as he continued his methodical torture.

It was then that I heard a whisper in my ear, a whisper so low and quiet I had to question whether I'd imagined it. "Annabelle...Annabelle it's me... calm down before you hurt yourself."

Before I hurt myself? It was Damon who was hurting me! I screamed and begged him to stop but he just carried on going, getting a thrill out of my agony as I watched the humorous glint in his eyes grow.

"Annabelle... Annabelle... come back to me. You're here and you're safe, I've got you, I won't let anyone hurt you I promise."

I stopped struggling as I focused on the voice and what it was saying, the volume of it getting louder with every passing second. I knew that voice... that voice belonged to Jax, he had come for me! I ignored Damon and his faceless minions as his torturous actions became less and less effective. All I needed to do was listen to his voice, just his voice and before I knew it, I was out of the mould smelling dungeon and back where I belonged, in his warm familiar arms.

Safe.

"J-Jax?" I whispered, hoping that he really was here with me.

"Yeah it's me, I've got you," he reassured me as his firm grip on me tightened, bringing me closer into his lap. I breathed in his scent, sighing as it instantly calmed me, and before long my breathing had gone back to a semi normal state as I snuggled further into his side.

"Annabelle, are you okay?"

I stiffened, was I okay? That dream seemed so real, I mean I was still half expecting to look down and see blood coating my legs from Damon's torture. I breathed in Jax's scent again, grounding me, before nodding my head. It was just a dream.

"Want to talk about it?"

I shook my head and buried into the crook of his neck, hoping to forget about the whole ordeal. My hand made its way to his chest, hoping the feel of his heartbeat would ground me like before, but when he flinched, I retracted my hand and looked at him with a frown, had I done something wrong?

"It's okay Angel, it's just a few scratches that's all, they'll be healed by the morning," he smiled reassuringly at me.

I frowned again and looked down to see four long, deep wounds across his chest and I gasped in shock. His top was covered in blood as well as my hand as I looked down at it, fighting the slight fear that arose in me at seeing that amount of red on my skin after just waking up from my nightmare. What had he been doing whilst I was asleep? "How..." I let the question hang in the air, hoping he would catch on to what I was referring to.

"You partially shifted during your dream and your claws dug into my skin when I tried to wake you up," he explained with a shrug, a slight grin on his face despite the current pain that he must be in. Why did he look so happy when I had obviously just hurt him? He must've seen my confusion because he kissed my forehead with a slight chuckle, causing his breath to fan across my forehead. "This is a good thing" he explained "it means your wolf is there in your head somewhere. She tried to come out, to try and protect you when she thought you were in trouble, but was held back by the command, hence the partial shift," he explained.

I thought about it for a second before nodding my head to show I understood, I may not like it but I understood why he was looking so happy at being all cut up. I looked back down at the claw marks and frowned again; I better get these cleaned up.

I moved to get off his lap and go to the bathroom, planning to get a damp cloth to clean up the semi dried blood that had been smeared across his chest, but frowned when I was held back by Jax's arms.

"And just where do you think you're going?" He asked, looking slightly amused at my confused expression.

I pointed to his cuts, hoping he would get the hint, but when he just stared down at me blankly, I sighed. "I'm going to clean them," I stated.

He smiled a stunning smile causing his one dimple to appear and my heart stuttered in my chest, god what was going on with my heart lately, it had never been this erratic before.

"I've already got a first aid kit delivered, it's by the door along with a glass of water for you, I'll just go and get it for you."

He started to get up, but before he could I scowled up at him. "Sit," I all but growled at him before I got off his lap and made my way over to the bedroom door. No way should he be moving with cuts like that on his chest, he could rip them open further and make them worse. I felt bad enough already that I was the one who'd caused him the pain, the least I could do was patch him up after.

He smiled as I sat in front of him and got the scissors out of the bag to cut the rest of his shirt off his shoulders, it was ruined anyway so why try and save it now. Once the last of the fabric fell free off his torso I went about sterilising and dressing his wounds, making sure I didn't miss anything as I slowly started to apply a couple of steri strips to the worse affected areas on his chest, using them to help the cuts heal quicker and to prevent scarring.

"How'd you learn to do all this first aid stuff?" He asked as I applied the last bit of dressing to his chest.

I stayed quiet as I finished my task, cleaning up the used packaging and throwing away the scraps of clothing that were now useless. How do you tell someone that you were good at first aid because you were so used to having to do it to yourself on a daily basis?

He must've felt my unease as he took my hands into his and lifted my chin up so that I was looking him in the eyes. My mind momentarily flashed back to Damon in my dream and how he'd done a similar thing to me before he'd started playing his little game, but I squinted my eyes shut to clear my head of the memory. He wasn't here, it wasn't real, it was just a dream.

"Thank you, my little mate," he whispered as he kissed me on the cheek, oblivious to the slight inner turmoil I was going through, before standing up and going into his closet to get out a clean top for him to wear.

When he re-emerged however all he was wearing was a pair of boxer shorts, leaving his chest and legs bare for me to stare at.

"Are you okay?" Jax asked as he took in my slightly bewildered expression.

I smiled up at him and nodded, not wanting him to worry about me anymore than he already does. I could deal with someone sleeping in the same room as me, especially if that person was Jax.

He looked at me sceptically for a minute before slowly nodding his head and walked over to the sofa. "Good night then little mate, sleep well," he sighed as he wiggled around on the sofa to try and get comfy.

My heart rate suddenly picked up at the thought of going back to sleep. What if the nightmare came back? I did not want to experience something like that again.

"What's the matter? Your heart rates going crazy," he whispered from behind the edge of the sofa. The bedside light was still on, but it did little to help me see him, all it did was illuminate his bare feet as they hung off the edge of the sofa.

"I... umm..." I stuttered, not really knowing how to say it. "Can you...I mean...would you mind if-if you umm..." come on Annabelle just spit it out "would you sleep with me?"

Jax grinned at me as his head popped up from behind the sofa and it was only as I took in his amused expression that I realised what that had sounded like. "I mean not sleep *with* me, I just meant that...I mean would you mind...?" I sighed, giving up making it sound better "don't worry."

Jax chuckled from where he was lying before getting up and walking over to his side of the bed to join me. My face was bright red and I could feel the heat radiating from my blush, god that was embarrassing.

"I wouldn't mind at all my Angel," he smiled, kissing my forehead before sliding in next to me and pulling me close to him so that my head was resting on his chest, well the portion of it that wasn't covered in gauze and tape that is. "Sleep well Annabelle, I'll be right here if you need me," he whispered, his voice already sounding dopey as his body began to relax after being awake for so long.

I was tense for a second, never having been in this type of situation before, as I stared down at the bare chest I was currently using as a pillow. I had never slept next to anyone before, let alone a gorgeous half naked werewolf like Jax.

"Just relax Annabelle, your body still needs time to heal so just focus on getting as much sleep as possible," he muttered, bringing his hand to rest on my lower back before starting to gently draw circles on my skin with his fingertips. It felt so nice and relaxing I was out like a light in no time.

…

I woke up the next morning feeling warm, to warm for it to be normal. Had the Leftens suddenly decided that I was now allowed heating in my room? No… that doesn't make sense, if I don't deserve hot water why would I suddenly be allowed heating?

As I came too, I started to take in more of my surroundings and panicked when I realised I wasn't in my usual room. Where was I?

"Go back to sleep Annabelle," a voice grumbled behind me and I froze for a second, fearing that someone had snuck into my room, but when my brain finally caught up with everything and I recognised the voice I relaxed. I was with Jax and I was safe. I sighed in relief and turned over as I came face to face with a still passed out Jax. He looked so tired as I noticed the bags under his eyes, instantly feeling guilty at the fact that I was the reason he hadn't gotten any sleep since I'd arrived.

I sighed and ran my fingertips along his cheek and jaw line, feeling the roughness as his stubble pricked against my skin. I sighed as I thought about the tingles that apparently should come with touching your mate. I wonder when I'm going to feel those tingles of electricity. I hoped soon because I really wanted to feel as close to Jax as he obviously did with me.

Jax shifted in his sleep, muttering something about cotton candy and I couldn't help but giggle at his sleep talk. Who dreams about cotton candy? I smiled down at him, stroking his cheek one more time, before getting up and walking down the stairs and towards the kitchen. The least I could do was make him some breakfast after everything he had done and continues to do for me. After all, he said I could use the kitchen whenever I wanted.

I padded barefoot along the tiled and wooden floors as I made my way into the stainless-steel kitchen where I quickly set about making him the works, opening and closing cupboards to find all the ingredients I needed.

Forty-five minutes later I was just plating the last of the food up and putting it onto the island in front of me when I heard my name being shouted in alarm from upstairs. I frowned as I took in the panicked tone, why was Jax yelling for me? Had I done something wrong?

I walked behind the island in the kitchen, hoping to put some distance between us, as I heard him stumble down the stairs, frantically yelling my name as he did so.

"Annabelle! Annabelle, where are you?" He continued to yell as he ran into the kitchen, looking a little panicked and still half asleep as he ran a hand through his bed hair. He seemed to instantly relax when he caught sight of me standing in the kitchen.

"I thought you'd been taken or something when you weren't in bed..." he sighed as he momentarily closed his eyes in relief. When they opened though they finally noticed the island between us and stared at it in shock. "What's all *this*?" He asked, suddenly changing the subject and gestured to all the food laid out on the counter.

I shrugged as I looked over the food again, making sure it was all there and still looked warm. "A thank you," I muttered, feeling a little embarrassed at his wide-eyed reaction to the food as he continued to stare at all the different options.

"A thank you for what?" He asked, genuinely confused. How could he not know what I was thanking him for?

"For...*everything,*" I smiled as I looked up at him shyly.

A grin was plastered on his face and he ran his hand through his bed hair again, god he looked adorable in the mornings. "I... umm... didn't know w-what you liked so I just made everything I could find the ingredients for," I explained as I looked down at the ridiculous amount of food I had ended up making for him.

Jax looked over to me with a bright smile on his face, showing off his perfectly white teeth. He hesitated for only a second before he walked over to me, slower than he would normally walk, which I'm guessing was because of my obvious rigid posture. He didn't want to move too fast just in case he scared me. When he rounded the kitchen island and stood in front of me he waited all of one second before pulling me into his open arms and towards his chest.

"Thank you my Angel, I really appreciate it," he mumbled into my hair as he kissed my forehead, showering me with his praise and affection.

I blushed at his kind words as I nodded my head, not knowing how else to respond. I was never thanked for doing anything like this at the Leftens, it was always expected of me, so I was still very new to taking compliments and people being genuinely appreciative of what I did for them. It was going to take some getting used to, that was for sure.

After Jax had released me he'd quickly ran back upstairs to put some clothes on and remove the bandaging I'd put on him last night, claiming that it was all healed over and no longer needed the protective gauze on it. Werewolves really did heal fast, even I wouldn't have healed that quickly.

Once he was back, I watched closely as Jax moved around the island, making a plate up for himself as he picked at the breakfast buffet I'd laid out for him. If I wanted to do this in the future, I was going to have to know what his favourites were.

As I continued to watch him my eyes grew wide at the amount of food he was piling onto his plate. He had taken a bit of everything, from the pancakes and waffles to the eggs, bacon and sausages. No wonder this man always made big portions of food for me, next to his mountain of food the stuff he plated up for me looked tiny.

"Oh my god these waffles are *amazing!*" Jax exclaimed through a mouth full of food before he quickly shovelled another fork full into his mouth, his eyes closing every time he tasted something different.

I giggled at him as I went about heating up the last of the chicken soup that I had been eating. I'd have to whip up another batch for myself so that I had something to eat for lunch, that is unless I can convince Jax to let me eat something solid. The soup was amazing, but after staring at the amount of food that was in front of me and not being able to eat any of it yet, I just wanted something solid. It was reminding me of being back in that house, where I was making food for everyone but was forbidden from eating it myself.

"What did you want to do today?" Jax asked around a mouth full of chocolate chip and peanut butter pancakes.

I just shrugged and went back to preparing my food, taking it out of the microwave once the beeper had gone off and stirring it so that the heat could be evenly distributed. I'd never really had much free time in the past, and even when I did, I was never allowed to do anything with it like others could. If and when I did magically have a spare five minutes after I had finished all my chores for the day, I was never allowed to go outside or watch some television. I would usually escape by hiding myself in my room and looking at my small box of treasures that I kept hidden in a loose floorboard, staring at the picture I had or reading the latest book I'd smuggled out of Damon's room.

I had thankfully already been taught the basics of reading before my parents left and so with the help of the stolen books I had managed to teach myself enough words to understand most things. I knew I was still extremely behind in both reading and writing for my age group though. I wonder if Jax wouldn't mind teaching me.

"I could take you to the nearby shopping centre and get you some of your own clothes if you'd like? All before the stores open so you don't panic about being with strangers, it'd only just be us two and a few shop workers who I'll make sure won't come near us. That way you won't have to keep wearing my oversized things anymore," he laughed as he looked at me. I was wearing the clothes he had given me to sleep in last night, another one of his t-shirts and a pair of tracksuit bottoms. The top was so big it reached my knees and the bottoms were rolled up a number of times so that my bare feet were able to poke through the bottom and I wasn't at risk of tripping over.

I stuttered for a second, wondering if I was up for something like that. I had never been to anything remotely like a shopping centre in all my time at the Leftens and I was genuinely curious to see what one looked like. Maybe going shopping could actually be quite fun, as long as what Jax was saying was true and it'd only just be us two. I would like to get a couple of items of clothing to call my own, only ever having hand-me-downs before now.

With one look at Jax's encouraging smile I'd made up my mind. "You'll come with me?" I questioned; I knew I would only be able to deal with such a scenery change with him by my side, calming me down and reassuring me whenever my anxiety rose.

He smiled reassuringly at me, thankfully after he'd finished swallowing his previous mouthful of food. "Of course I will, you can't get rid of me that easily," he joked before cutting up another large mouthful of food to put in his mouth.

I smiled at him and took a sip of soup from off my spoon. I wonder what I'll get from the shops? I hope it's easy shopping, I'd never done it before and I was really intrigued to see what it was like. When I saw the girls on the TV doing it, it looked like they were having a lot of fun, picking out all the different tops and shoes that they liked, I just hope I was good at it.

I got up to clear Jax's plate once I was sure he was finished, but when he took it back out of my hands, along with my own, I frowned at him in confusion.

"It's not your job to cook and clean Annabelle, you don't have to do everything on your own," he explained with a gentle smile as he walked over to the sink and started cleaning up, loading everything into the dishwasher and wiping down the already spotless countertops.

I smiled at his back, slightly overwhelmed by his generosity. I couldn't believe this amazing person who'd saved me from my past and stood by me through everything I'd thrown at him was offering to do even more by helping me with my usual chores.

"JAX!" a voice suddenly shouted as they slammed the front door against the wall and made their way inside. "JAX WHERE ARE YOU!"

I looked over at him in panic, who was this person? Someone who obviously knew Jax well enough to invite themselves into his house without knocking. I quickly edged over to him and slightly hid behind his body as the footsteps got closer.

"In here Hannah," Jax replied with a sigh as he took my hand in his, sensing my nerves and trying to ease them in some way. His hands were still slightly wet and soapy from washing the sides down but I didn't care, the feel of his skin on mine was enough to calm my racing heart.

"Am I interrupting something? There's a strange new scent all around your house-" the voice spoke but suddenly broke off as a girl came skipping into the kitchen. She couldn't have been much older than me, maybe twenty, with shoulder length pin straight brown hair and eyes the same exact shade as Jax's. She was dressed as if she were going to be photographed for a magazine, everything matching perfectly and was wearing more jewellery than I'd ever seen before. Multiple rings littered her thin fingers and bangles ran up her arms, causing them to jingle whenever she swung her arms around.

"You going to introduce me?" She asked, a knowing smirk playing on her lips as her eyes flicked between the two of us and finally down to our joined hands.

Jax sighed and ran a hand through his hair. "Annabelle this is Hannah my sister, Hannah this is Annabelle… my mate."

"Your...I didn't know you had found your mate!" Hannah squealed and I cringed slightly as the high-pitched squeal rang through my ears. "Hi, I'm Hannah, it's so lovely to meet you," she rushed out as she started to quickly make her way around the island and towards me.

I shrunk away from her and hid behind Jax with my head buried in-between his shoulder blades, not understanding what she was doing. Her loud screams told me that she was unhappy or scared about something but her smiling expression and the fact that she couldn't stand still said that she was happy. How could someone be happy and sad?

I felt Jax turn around slightly so that I was now facing his chest instead of his back, my face still hidden in the fabric of his top and my slightly shaky hands covering my eyes. "She's not going to hurt you little mate," Jax whispered in my ear as he brought his arms around me in a comforting hug. "She just wants to say hi to you properly, that's all. Remember what I told you? No one here in this pack is ever going to hurt you," he reassured me.

I nodded my head in understanding and he kissed me on the top of my head with an encouraging smile. Maybe she screamed when she was happy as well as sad?

"Annabelle is a little shy around people at the moment, especially strangers, so why don't I call you tonight and we can catch up another time," Jax said as he turned to talk to his sister, not releasing me from his warm embrace.

"Sure… I guess," Hannah muttered, obviously upset about something I was unaware of. "What are you doing today anyway? Why can't we catch up now?"

Jax sighed, "because we are going shopping today to get Annabelle some clothes, she's probably fed up with wearing my stuff by now."

I peeked out from Jax's chest to look over at Hannah to see her eyes light up at the mention of the word shopping, but I could tell she was holding herself back out of respect for me and her brother. "Can I... can I come with you guys?" She whispered, her voice a lot quieter than it had been earlier.

Jax sighed again as he shook his head, looking uncomfortable at the idea of Hannah tagging along. "Another time okay Han?"

I couldn't help but feel guilty at the sad expression that crossed Hannah's face, she only wanted to hang out with her brother and it was all because of me that she wasn't able to. You could tell they were close, judging by the way they acted around each other, and the last thing I wanted to do was to be a burden and get in the way of Jax hanging out with her family.

I took a deep breath and prepared myself to say the words I may very well regret later. "Y-you can come if you want," I whispered, stepping back from Jax's chest slightly.

Hannah's face immediately lit up like the lights on Christmas Day and she started jumping up and down whilst clapping her hands, causing her bracelets to jingle together with every movement. "Oh this is going to be so much fun," she squealed. "I'll get to show you all of my favourite shops, show you what your colour wheel is and the different types of cuts and styles you'll be needing...I've always wanted a sister and now I've finally got one," Hannah continued to shriek, not stopping in her musical bracelet jingle. This girl sure did squeal a lot, and not in fear or pain like I usually did.

"You have no idea what you have just let yourself in for," Jax mutters with a chuckle as he leant down to kiss my temple, causing the seemingly ever-present blush to bloom across my cheeks.

I instantly got nervous as Jax chuckled in my ear, both of us watching on as Hannah continued to grin over at the two of us. It couldn't be that bad...could it?

Chapter 10

Jax's POV

When we got home both myself and Annabelle crashed straight away on the sofa, exhausted from the day and the fact that we still hadn't fully recovered from our lack of sleep the other night. Who knew shopping could be so tiring?

"So Annabelle, did you want me to help you organise your wardrobe? What would you prefer, having everything organised into seasons, colours or styles?" Hannah jabbered on as she started looking through all the bags we'd brought back with us and I sighed in exhaustion, how did she still have energy after walking about a million steps today already?

I looked down at my mate to see that she was half passed out on my shoulder and I smiled, admiring how cute she looked. She was always ever so slightly tense when she was awake, like she was always preparing herself for something, but when she sleeps, she's so relaxed. "Hannah, I think we're going to call it a day actually," I sighed, saving Annabelle from having to entertain Hannah any longer. Knowing my little mate, she would battle through her exhaustion just to make someone else happy. "I'm shattered and so is Annabelle so we're just going to go for a nap before dinner."

"Fine," Hannah huffed, obviously not impressed with our lack of shopping stamina, as she picked up a few of her own shopping bags and headed towards the door.

"Anna I'm just a mind link away if you need any help with anything or just want someone to talk to," she smiled as she looked over at her semi-conscious state.

She only got a hum in response from Annabelle as she walked out the front door, taking her few purchased items with her.

"Come on then, I think it's time for you to have a quick nap." I chuckled as I watched her head keep slowly falling off my shoulder, shocking herself awake, before placing it back. I carefully picked her up in my arms and carried her up the stairs with ease, she was still so light.

I grumbled at that thought before shaking my head and walking into my room. All of Annabelle's shopping bags were in here, lined up against the wardrobe door and I smiled at the thought that the other side of my wardrobe would finally be filled with my mates' things. There wouldn't be just an empty clothes rail taunting me every time I walked into my closet to get some clothes.

I placed her down on her side of the bed and brought the covers up to her chin once I had taken her shoes and socks off. That's right, she officially had a side of the bed and I couldn't be happier at the fact.

I sat down beside her and stroked the hair from her face. I had gotten so lucky having her as my mate, I could not picture anyone more perfect.

In the end I had ordered takeout for dinner, I didn't think either of us were up for cooking tonight after the morning we'd had.

When the door bell finally rang I ran downstairs to answer the door and collect the pizza and soup I had ordered from the delivery guy. I clutched the food in my hands so as not to drop any of it as I stopped in the kitchen to grab a spoon for her before heading back up to my room. Takeout soup probably wasn't the best thing for her to eat but it was the best I could do on such short notice, seeing as she'd finished the last of the chicken soup she'd been eating this morning.

I walked into the bedroom, making sure the door didn't make any noise behind me, and smiled when I found her hugging my pillow close to her chest, her face buried in the fabric as she breathed evenly. She felt my absence even in her sleep.

I walked over to her, putting the food on the floor by the foot of the bed as I went past, and sat on the edge of the mattress. Goddess I was lucky.

I stroked the hair off her face and marvelled at how soft it felt. I could run my hands through her golden locks all day long and never get bored of it. I moved it slightly off her neck and stroked her skin down towards the area on her neck I would eventually mark. I couldn't wait for the day that I could call her mine, but I knew she wasn't ready for that yet. I would happily wait until the day she was; I'd wait an eternity if I had to.

She stirred in her sleep, causing the duvet to shift down her body and her shirt to ride up slightly and I was just about to look away when I spotted something that made me freeze. Across her stomach and back were small little lines covering her skin, little scars that couldn't be seen unless you were looking closely and in a certain light. I ran my fingers over the few that were visible and growled as I felt the raised skin under my fingertips. Someone had hurt my mate so badly it had scarred.

I lifted her shirt up slightly further and I couldn't help the snarl that escaped my lips as I saw more and more scars the higher her shirt went. Someone had used an all manner of objects to injure her and the more I thought about it the louder my wolf got, causing my eyes to swirl and shift different colours.

I was fighting for control, both on my wolf and myself. We both so desperately wanted to track down the lowlifes that dared to hurt my mate, but instantly froze in our murderous rants with each other as we looked down to find Annabelle frozen on the bed with her eyes wide open, staring at me.

It wasn't the fact that she had woken up that made us freeze, but it was more the fact that the colour of her eyes were nothing like the baby blues I had come to love. I was looking into a pair of almost glowing pearlescent eyes that were staring at me in both curiosity and fear.

My wolf was going crazy in my head, he hadn't acted like this since we had first laid eyes on her in the woods. Who I was staring at right now wasn't my Annabelle at all, it was her wolf.

"Annabelle?" I whispered as I cautiously removed my hand from her skin and held both up for her to see, to show her that I was unarmed and that I had no intention of hurting her. A little growl escaped her lips and before I could blink she was suddenly up in some form of crouch position on the bed, ready to defend herself from me if she needed to.

"Annabelle it's me, Jax, just calm down and I will help explain everything." Her teeth and claws were slightly extended as she slowly started to advance on me, the growl not letting up even an inch as I attempted to calm her as best I could.

I didn't know how to best approach this, if this was a youngster in my pack that was newly shifted I would just use my Alpha control on them to help calm them down, but this wasn't, this was my Annabelle. Not only was she technically not a part of my pack yet, she was also my mate and I didn't want to use that kind of control on her. I couldn't hurt her like that. She had already had some serious mind control put on her once in her life and I didn't want to break her trust in me by using it.

My wolf was going crazy in my head and at first I was trying to block him out, not having enough patience to deal with him as well as Annabelle, but when he continued to shout at me in my head I eased my control on him and started to listen.

Mate, mate! Let me out to calm down Mate.

I thought about it for a second, not knowing what would happen if I let my wolf out with Annabelle being so close to me.

Not to harm mate, never to harm mate.

I looked back at Annabelle again to see her still in her crouched possession on the bed, showing no signs of calming down as her moonstone eyes assessed me.

Fine, but if you hurt her, you're not come out to run for a long time.

He just ignored me and kept repeating the word *mate* in my head and that was enough for me to release some of my control over him. I was never a fan of letting my wolf take the reins when I was still in human form, I felt out of control and for an Alpha, that was a hard thing to feel.

As I let my wolf slowly surface, I continued to stare at Annabelle through my now golden eyes, assessing her reaction. The last thing we needed was for her to react similarly to the last time she'd met my wolf and pass out from the pain. She tensed as she regarded me for a second with her head slightly tilted, unsure on how to process with what was in front of her, but when she slowly inched forward and sniffed the air she grumbled a content purr type noise as her eyes opened wide, fixating them on me.

"Mate," she growled through her canines before springing from the bed and tackling me to the ground, rubbing her cheek into my neck as if she couldn't get close enough. My wolf was extremely happy with her reaction and started nuzzling her back just as fiercely, trying to get just as close to her as she was to him.

"My mate... so perfect," my wolf growled through my lips and I suddenly became very jealous of how much attention he was getting from Annabelle, how come she never showed *me* that much affection.

Mate loves me more my wolf smirked in my head and that little comment was the last straw for me as I forced him back down so that I was back in control, not even caring that it was a petty move.

"Annabelle...Annabelle can you come back to me, little mate?" I whispered.

I stroked her hair back from her face and behind her ear, hoping the familiar action would bring her back. When she finally looked up at me I slowly started to see her eyes shift from her wolf colour back to her normal baby blues and I sighed in relief.

"What...how...?" Was all she stuttered as she sat herself up from me with a sight blush, realising what position we were in.

"Your wolf came out Annabelle, she was completely in control of you," I explained, saddened at the loss of contact from her as she moved away.

"I... umm... I'm sorry, I don't know how she... how that… " she stuttered, confused about what had just happened and how it had even happened. I could understand her confusion, the last thing she probably remembered was sleeping on the sofa downstairs and now here she was lying on the bedroom floor.

"It's really okay Annabelle, great actually, your wolf is getting stronger and stronger every day, hopefully you will be able to fully shift soon," I explained with a grin on my face. As soon as she shifts, she will feel the mate bond and after that I can officially mark her as mine, she can be fully recognised as the Luna of our pack and they will finally have their Alpha female that they rightfully deserve.

Annabelle just nodded, still clearly slightly embarrassed, and sat up crossed legged from me on the floor.

"Did you want some pizza?" I asked, hoping to make her more comfortable again. I knew she wasn't allowed it yet, but one slice couldn't hurt too much. "It might be a little cold now but that doesn't make it any less amazing, cold leftover pizza is sometimes just as good as when you first buy it," I shrugged.

She pulled a face at that, obviously not agreeing with me in the slightest and I couldn't help but laugh at her pinched expression. "It's true!" I exclaimed, defending my opinion.

She shook her head but still reached her hand out towards me as we moved over to sit with our backs against the bed, indicating she still wanted a slice.

"Hmm I don't know... I mean, you did just say you didn't like cold pizza, am I really going to share food with you if you aren't going to enjoy it?" I taunted as I dangled a slice just out of her reach.

She reached out to grab it from me but frowned as I drew it back slightly, bringing it closer to me and away from her. "The price for this slice of pizza is very high, I'm not sure if you're willing to pay for it," I laughed, loving the fact that I'm seeing her more playful side. She had grown so much in both confidence and character since we had first met, and it just made me more excited to see her progress further.

She frowned and stuck her bottom lip out slightly; oh she had the puppy dog eyes down!

"The price for this slice of pizza… is a kiss on the cheek," I smirked. "Are you willing to pay the price my little Annabelle?" I honestly didn't think she was going to do it, but I was pleasantly shocked when she leant forward and briefly grazed her lips against the stubble on my cheeks. The sparks from her touch went flying and suddenly my heart was pumping loudly in my chest. The things this girl did to me.

She must've realised the dazed look on my face because whilst I was distracted, she snatched the slice from my fingers and started to chow down on it.

"Hey, that was *my* piece!" I exclaimed, pretending to be hurt by her actions.

She just shrugged and went back to eating...goddess she was cute.

We sat there for about ten minutes, eating in a comfortable silence, me eating my pizza and her sipping at her soup. I wanted to bring up her scars, but I was unsure on how to approach the subject. The doctor didn't mention how to handle difficult issues like this and I didn't want to make her uncomfortable. Do I just come right out and ask her how she got them, or do I slowly direct the conversation that way? Maybe if I showed her a few of *my* scars she'd feel more inclined to talk about hers?

"Are you okay?" Annabelle whispered, obviously deciding that she's had enough to eat and was now sitting slouched with her back still pressed against the foot of the bed.

I nodded my head and rubbed the back of my neck. It was now or never I guess. "I-I have a question for you...you don't have to answer it if you don't want to, but I was just wondering... well... umm..." I looked up to see

Annabelle staring at me with confusion in her eyes, unsure on where I was going with my questioning.

"Go on," she encouraged me with a small smile and a slight nod.

Well here goes nothing... "How did you get those scars?" I hesitantly muttered. It came out sounding quiet, but I knew she had understood me as I saw her freeze. Had I crossed a line?

Tears slowly brimmed her eyes and she looked down, as if she was ashamed of something, as she fiddled with her fingers.

"I'm sorry, you don't have to tell me if you don't want to," I reassured her. I crawled over to her and brought her into my arms, needing to comfort her in some way as I placed one hand around her waist and the other running soothingly through her hair. She didn't push me away, which gave me hope that I hadn't overstepped her boundaries.

She shook her head before hiding in my chest and all I could do was draw her tighter to me as I kissed the top of her head. I instantly hated myself for making her feel this way, for ruining our seemingly perfect night together by bringing up her past.

We stayed like that in silence for a while, neither of us daring to be the first to speak. Her heart rate dropped back to normal levels and the grip she had on my T-shirt lessened slightly, seemingly drawing comfort from my close proximity. Just when I thought she had fallen asleep, she surprised me by speaking.

"Tony," she whispered, not bringing her head out from her hiding place in my chest.

"Tony?" I asked in confusion, had I heard her right? "Who's Tony?"

"My...my adoptive father," she muttered. "He's the one that gave me the scars, well most of them anyway. Sometimes it was his wife Natalie or his son Damon."

I froze when I heard her say the name Damon, that was the name of the person she was pleading to stop when she was having her nightmare. Was she having a flashback to that place, to what he had done to her? I growled at the thought and struggled to rein in my wolf. If he got out now, I knew there would be nothing stopping him from hunting down those people and killing them in the slowest and most painful way possible.

I took a slow, deep breath to calm myself down before I asked her any more questions. "Why...? How...?"

She sighed, playing with the hem of my shirt. "When I had done something wrong, or if they were in a bad mood, or if...if they were just bored," she shrugged, as if it were no big deal that someone had hurt her through no fault of her own.

I growled again, a bit louder this time and she froze before slowly relaxing, realising the growl wasn't aimed at her but at the sick people who did this. "What did they use on you to cause marks like that?" I didn't really know whether I wanted to know the answer to that particular question or not, but I couldn't stop myself from asking.

She sighed again before slowly moving away from me so that she could lift her top up slightly.

I didn't think I could ever get used to the sight of the scars on my mate's perfect skin. They criss crossed over each other like a spider's web, a web that could only be seen in certain lights, as they created unknown patterns.

"Marks like these are usually from things like belts," she whispered, pointing to lines surrounded by little dots, probably from the holes in a belt made for the buckle. "These ones are from a fire poke, Tony particularly liked to use that one as it caused an instant bruise" she explained pointing to the more raised, thicker ones. "And the rest are from things that have just been thrown at me, like the corner of a blunt object or something," she muttered as she pushed her t-shirt back down before crawling back over to me and snuggling back into my arms. It took a lot of force to scar a werewolf, even one who was malnourished and forced not to shift like her, and I shuddered to think about what could've happened to her if she wasn't a werewolf. She probably wouldn't have survived.

I kissed the top of her head and took in her scent, hoping that it would calm me and my wolf down like it usually did. Thankfully it had the desired effect and my wolf stopped pacing in my head, demanding release, and lay down, calm enough to enjoy the time we were having with our mate.

"I'm sorry you had to go through all that Annabelle, that I wasn't there to save you, but know that you will never be harmed again, never feel pain while I am by your side to protect you," I promised.

I heard her heartbeat skip a beat at my words before she started to relax again and before long, she was fast asleep in my arms. She was such a small, delicate little wolf. I could never imagine anyone wanting to hurt her.

...

The next morning I woke up to the smell of bacon. I rolled over with outstretched arms to find my mate and pull her close, fully intending to fall back asleep with her safely in my arms, but shot up when I found her side of the bed cold and empty.

After a second of panic, my brain caught up with the situation, and I realised the smell of bacon was probably caused by my mate cooking me breakfast again. She sure seemed to be an early riser, the clock on my bed side table hadn't even reached seven o'clock yet.

I quickly pulled on some tracksuit bottoms, forgoing the top, and slowly padded barefoot down the stairs and into the kitchen, where I found my gorgeous mate frying off some eggs while some bacon was sizzling away in a nearby pan. She looked fully at home in front of the hobs, knowing exactly what she was doing, and I couldn't help but smile at the image. She was going to make a fantastic Luna and mother someday. Someone who could take charge and not take any nonsense from anyone.

"Morning baby," I yawned as I leaned against the doorway with my arms crossed, making my presence known. "You know you don't have to make me breakfast every morning, right? You can just sleep in and we can order breakfast delivery or something," I shrugged. "That's what I usually did if I fancied something other than toast or cereal."

She shrugged, still not looking up from her pans and just muttered a quiet "I don't mind." She was getting a lot better at talking to me lately. I think last night brought us a step in the right direction with getting to know each other and I couldn't help but smile at the thought that she was starting to trust me. She was now comfortable turning her back on me to go and do something and she didn't flinch away from me whenever I reached out to touch her, which was a good sign, especially as she hasn't been here that long. I'm sure in a week or two she'd be fully relaxed around me and then we can properly get to work on finding her wolf and getting her fully integrated into pack life.

I padded over to her and took her in my arms, needing to see her pretty face this morning. "So how did you sleep last night?"

She smiled and blushed slightly at our close proximity before nodding her head "good."

I chuckled and lifted her face up so that I could get a good look at her cute little blush. "What's with the blush little mate?" I questioned, finding her reaction completely adorable.

She blushed harder and tried to look down and hide her face from me, but my fingers on her chin were stopping her from hiding. "I... umm... I sleep better when you're next to me. I feel... safe," she muttered and hid in my bare chest as if she were embarrassed with the fact that she liked being around her mate.

I chuckled and kissed the top of her head. "That's normal Annabelle, that's how most wolves feel when they're around their mates," I explained. Sometimes I had to remind myself that she wasn't brought up in our world and even the simplest of feelings for us, like *wanting* to be around our mates, could be extremely confusing and almost foreign for her.

I held her for a minute in my arms, just living in the moment with my mate securely in my arms, until I started to smell burning bacon and reluctantly released her so that she could save the breakfast. I sat on the counter in silence, watching her whilst she finished cooking and plating up the food, thanking her as she placed a full plate of bacon and fried eggs on toast in front of me.

"So what did you want to do today?" I asked around a mouthful of food.

She just shrugged and ate her soup, seemingly not bothered with the plans for today. I smiled as I watched her eat spoonful after spoonful of the liquid, feeling happy that her appetite only seemed to be increasing with each passing day.

"How do you feel about going out again today? Maybe show you some more of the pack lands," I suggested, hoping that she would agree so that I could show her off a little bit. I had found my mate, my perfect mate, and I wanted to scream it from the rooftops and rub it in everyone's face. Not very mature and Alpha like I know but sue me, I was too happy to care.

"We might even get a chance to meet a pack member or two, how does that sound?" Please say yes, please say yes.

"Umm..." was all I got back from her and I smiled lovingly at the nervous look in her eyes.

"It's decided, we can go for a walk around the grounds and if we bump into a few people, I can introduce you to them, but I won't go out of my way to search for them okay? How's that for a compromise?" The doctor had encouraged me to get her out of the house as often as I could, making sure she was constantly reminded that she doesn't have to remain locked away. I just hoped I wasn't pushing the point too hard on her.

She shrugged, not looking up from her nearly finished bowl of soup, "okay I guess."

"Great, well go get ready then and we can make a day of it, I'll even bring a picnic for us." I knew she was nervous, but it was only because she was panicking about the idea of being around new people. Once she meets the pack and gets to know the grounds she'll realise how nice they all are and I'm sure the nerves will be forgotten.

Chapter 11

Annabelle's POV

When Jax had first suggested going outside to see the pack grounds I was nervous to say the least. I had never been allowed outside before I ran away, but I was always envious of those who could come and go as they pleased.

We were currently sitting on a blanket in a field surrounded by wildflowers as Jax offered me more food. Whilst I was getting ready, he had called up the doctor and asked about my diet plan, asking if I was allowed more substantial foods now that they knew I could easily handle liquids and the slice of pizza he gave me last night. She'd said I still wasn't allowed proper solid food and grumbled her annoyance at Jax for ignoring her advice about the pizza last night, but I was now allowed thicker soup and food that had been blitzed up. Basically, baby food, but it was better than the constant chicken soup I'd been eating over the last two days.

I laughed slightly as I watched Jax scoop a spoonful of soup from my container and held it out for me to eat. I genuinely don't think he understood the meaning of the words *I'm full*. After turning down the offered food he shrugged and put it back in the basket. Thankfully not pushing the subject anymore. I think if I took one more mouthful I'd likely burst.

I sighed as I looked over at Jax and took in his relaxed frame. He had denim jean shorts on paired with a bright white t-shirt and red vans on his feet, sunglasses covering his eyes as he lay on his back to take in some of the sun's rays. He looked so relaxed, like he didn't have a care in the world, and I found myself envying him. How he didn't have flashbacks every time he saw or heard something that reminded him of his past, how he didn't constantly live in fear from the very people who were supposed to look after you.

I was currently sitting upright with my knees drawn to my chest and my arms wrapped around them with my eyes darting around at the slightest of noises, making sure it wasn't the noise of someone approaching us. I may trust Jax to keep me safe, but old habits die hard. I was just thankful I'd decided to wear jeans today, so I didn't have to worry about having my knees up with a dress on.

"Just relax Annabelle, I've told everyone not to come into this part of the territory," Jax muttered from his spot on the blanket, not moving his head as it continued to rest on his bent right arm. "No one is going to approach us," he reassured me.

I looked over at him and frowned when I saw that his eyes were still closed and his head was tilted back slightly. He'd known I was feeling tense without even having to look at me.

I sighed and tried to relax by copying him, lying down by his side as I looked up at the cloudless sky, but after a few minutes of trying my body still wouldn't relax. I groaned in frustration and sat back up. "How are you so relaxed?" I questioned him, jealous that he could do it and I couldn't.

He shrugged, still not getting up from his position on the ground. "I don't know, you just have to clear your mind and only focus on the here and now. Focus on the wind in the trees, the sound of the birds, the smell of the grass... everything," he muttered.

I tried again but I just became bored and fidgety very quickly. "Let's play 20 questions," I suggested, giving up on trying to relax as I sat back up into a sitting position. Hannah had introduced the game to me whilst we were shopping, she said it was an 'ice breaker' for when you were meeting new people and wanted to know more about them. My hope was that the conversation would distract my overactive brain just enough for me to enjoy the warm sun without jumping at every twig snapping in the distance.

"Okay sure," Jax smiled, suddenly sitting upright and in front of me "you go first."

"Umm okay... what's your... favourite colour?"

Jax laughed, "That's the best you've got? I thought you'd be a little more imaginative than that," he chuckled and smiled down at me, his white teeth gleaming in the sunlight.

I just shrugged and looked at my knees, hoping he didn't see the blush creeping onto my cheeks at the seemingly common question.

"Orange."

I looked up when he answered my question with a small smile "why orange?"

He shrugged as he looked into the distance. "I don't know, there's just something about the colour. It's so warm and light, you could never feel cold or sad looking at the colour orange," he muttered. "That and it's the colour of a sunset, I love a good sunset," he nodded. "Okay my turn...what's your earliest memory?"

I smiled as a memory flickered through my mind. Unlike most of my other memories that were filled with fear and pain, this one always made me smile. "It was probably when I was around four or five. Me and my parents went to the park one day, I don't remember why or what we really did there, I just remember being really happy as she pushed me on a swing," I smiled. I sometimes felt sad thinking about my parents, about what my life could have been like if they had never disappeared, but I tried not to dwell on thoughts like that. If I allowed myself to feel sad every time I thought about my parents I'd have no good memories left.

I suddenly felt a comforting hand rest on my bent knee and I looked up into Jax's reassuring eyes. "Can I ask what happened to them?"

I shrugged, not really having an answer for him. "No one really knows, they went out for some night out or something, leaving me at home with a babysitter, but they never came home."

"I'm sorry you had to go through that Annabelle," Jax muttered as he pulled me into his chest so that I was sitting in his lap. His touch was so comforting, and I loved the sound of his heartbeat as I rested my head on his chest. There was something so soothing about the repetitiveness of it as my heart calmed to match his beat for beat.

Just as I was about to open my mouth and ask my next question, stating that I was now allowed two because he'd asked two, someone came stumbling into the clearing, sweat visibly dripping from his face, as he panted to catch his breath. "Sorry to bother you Alpha but we didn't know what else to do, you had shut off your mind link and no one could get a hold of you," the poor guy gasped.

I shrunk into Jax, not liking being so close to a stranger as I looked him over. He didn't look threatening, in fact he barely offered me a glance, but that still didn't mean that I could trust him.

"This better be important Jason," Jax growls as he holds onto me slightly tighter, feeling the nerves radiating off me.

"Yes Alpha, we have an issue at the border, Alpha Parker is here and is demanding an audience with you," he gasped.

I frowned as I felt Jax tense slightly, whoever this person was, I could tell he wasn't welcome.

"Do not allow any members of the Rising Dawn pack to enter our territory," Jax growled as he gripped onto me tightly. "Annabelle, I'm going to have to go and deal with this situation quickly, I want you to go with Jason back to our house until I tell you that it's safe." His voice had gotten softer as he spoke to me, but I still couldn't help but frown. I didn't want him to go. I didn't know this man, what if something happened?

"But I want to stay with you," I whispered, not wanting Jason to overhear. I didn't feel safe with anyone else yet, apart from seeing the doctor I hadn't been apart from Jax since I got here, and I didn't feel comfortable leaving him now.

"Please little mate, you don't want to be caught up with this guy... he's not safe," he pleaded.

"W-who is it then?" I stuttered, fearing the answer as I frowned up at him.

Jax sighed and ran a hand through his hair "he's... well he's the Alpha of the pack you used to live in," he whispered and held my chin so that I was looking into his eyes as he said it. So that he could see my reaction.

I thought I would be scared, terrified even, to hear that someone from my past had come back to collect me, but for some reason, looking into Jax's eyes, I couldn't manage it. Knowing that I had Jax by my side and a wolf somewhere in my head to protect me, okay a wolf that I can't get to right now but not the point, it made me feel oddly brave, an emotion I hadn't felt before.

"I want to come with you," I stated, looking into his eyes to show that I really meant it. "I want to meet this Alpha person that blocked my wolf from me."

"No Annabelle," Jax growled and I was momentarily stunned at the fact that he had growled at me and even more surprised that it hadn't scared me. Yes, it made me a little hesitant and uncomfortable, but I trusted him not to hurt me.

"Please Jax, I want to see the man who did this to me," I muttered as I looked down at my clenched fingers.

He contemplated it for a second, but before he could voice his decision Jason piped up again "Alpha sir, please, he is causing quite a commotion and the patrol warriors on scene are worried that if we don't make our way over soon, he will try to breech our parameter by force."

Jax growled at him, not liking being rushed, before sighing in defeat and running a hand down his face. "You promise to stay with either me or one of the guards the entire time?" He questioned as he looked down at me expectantly.

I nodded my head and smiled slightly, trying to show him that I was fine and that I wasn't frightened, which was only partially true, I was terrified, but not enough for me to hide.

"Fine," he sighed. "You can come with us, but as soon as things look like they're heading in the wrong direction I want you escorted out of the area without a single word from you okay?"

I just nodded again and went to stand up as Jax released me.

"Okay let's go and see what this monster wants," Jax muttered as he led me into the surrounding forest, leaving our half eaten picnic on the grass.

As Jax and I made our way towards the border of his land, we started to hear the commotion. The more steps we took into the forest the louder the shouting became and I instantly regretted begging to come with him. Was I even ready to look into the eyes of the man that had basically stolen my life away from me? Could I even bring myself to look at him after everything he had put me through?

I froze as a scent hit me, a scent that for some reason, I recognised. I couldn't quite describe it, almost chlorine like with an undertone of burnt plastic and fake pine wood.

"Are you alright Annabelle?" Jax asked me as he felt me stop behind him.

"Do you smell that?" I whispered, not wanting to draw any unwanted attention to myself as Jason walked on ahead. I didn't know how close we were to this Alpha Parker person, but I didn't want to risk him overhearing our conversation and knowing that I was here.

"Smell what Annabelle? There is nothing out of the ordinary here... well apart from the people at the border but they're a few hundred feet off yet and even then your nose shouldn't be able to pick them up."

I was confused, what was I smelling? "That chemical smell...you don't smell it?" My grip on his hand tightened in nerves and my body started to react in fear at the smell. What was my body reacting to?

"You smell that?" Jax asked and I looked up at his face to see a look of bewilderment in his eyes.

I just nodded as I struggled to keep my body's natural reaction in check. If Jax knew I was frightened he would order someone to take me home in a heartbeat. This smell brought up so much suppressed anxiety I felt my palms begin to sweat and goose bumps to appear on my exposed arms. Where had I smelt that smell before?

"Annabelle that's Alpha Parker, he wears this stupid type of aftershave to mask his natural scent. He says it's to stop his mate finding him as he doesn't want to be weakened and tied down to a single person. Ridiculous if you ask me, but still," he shrugged.

I frowned "how am I able to smell Alpha Parker? My sense of smell has never been that strong before."

He shrugged with a slight smile on his lips, "maybe your body is starting to accept your wolf. Your senses are heightening and getting stronger, with any luck you'll be turning into your wolf soon." I could tell that he was excited, the grin on his face spoke volumes, but if I was being honest, I was more worried than anything. I finally had the chance to fit in somewhere, to be a part of a family, but I didn't want to hope in fear that it didn't happen. Who's to say that once I turned into my wolf Jax's pack didn't accept me, or what if Jax or his wolf didn't like my wolf and rejected me. I whimpered at the thought and shook my head, no point in dwelling on it now, especially when there was nothing I could do to prevent it.

Jax was oblivious to my inner turmoil and leant down to kiss me on the cheek before taking my hand in his and proceeded to lead us closer to Alpha Parker. I smiled as my fingers grazed where Jax had kissed me. My cheeks felt hotter than usual due to the slight blush from the kiss he had given me and my cheeks only reddened further at the reaction my body had to him.

"When we get to him I want you to let me do all the talking okay Annabelle?" The humour and playful Jax had now gone and in his place was what I could only describe as Alpha Jax. His shoulders were back, his head held high and he had an air of authority about him that just couldn't be ignored.

My eyes widened at the sudden change in him. How could he go from cute and playful to serious and poker faced so quickly?

"This is a dangerous man Annabelle and I don't want to give him any more reason to come after you then he already thinks he does. Myself and my pack, *our* pack, will protect their Luna with their last breath, but I don't want there to be any confrontation until you are fully connected to your wolf and healed, understand?"

I nodded my head even though I knew he wasn't waiting for an answer as I looked forward. I didn't want any confrontation either, the last thing I wanted was for people to die because of me.

We remained silent as we continued our walk through the woods, if it was any other morning I'd say this would have been a nice relaxing stroll through the trees.

"Stay behind me at all times Annabelle."

I nodded, having lost my voice again after hearing the violent words that were being thrown back and forth just past the bushes in front of us.

"I will skin you alive if you touch me you worthless mutt, do you really think you could take me on?" The voice snarled as we cleared the last of the bushes that were obscuring us from their vision and entered the clearing.

Once we entered into the mess of people all eyes turned to us, well more like Jax and by default me, as they felt another Alpha's presence. I noticed the people on our side of the territory line relax slightly at the sight of their

Alpha, but the man that was yelling had tensed, obviously not liking the fact that we had interrupted his insults.

"What is the meaning of this Alpha Parker, you know it is against the sacred oath of the wolf coven to turn up unannounced at another pack's border without serious cause," Jax growled. He was definitely *not* happy with the way Alpha Parker was talking to his pack members.

"I apologise for the intrusion Alpha Jax," the intruding Alpha growled, sounding anything but apologetic as he continued to glare at Jax. "I tried to ring ahead but your Beta said that you were not available for the foreseeable future and this issue was far too important to wait."

Alpha Parker was a short stocky man with a bald head and tribal tattoos running up both of his arms. He also had a jagged scar stretching down the side of his face, from the corner of his eye all the way down to the corner of his mouth across his cheek. I frowned; this must have been the guy who had forced me not to shift.

"And what is this so-called emergency?" Jax growled as he squeezed my hand, reminding me to stay quiet and hidden behind him.

"A girl, a human girl, has run away from her family that lives on my pack lands and I fear for her life. She was last seen a few nights ago stumbling through these woods with just a thin nighty on and no shoes." He's a good actor, I'll give him that, the only thing giving him away that I could notice were his eyes. They were cold and emotionless, like the girl he was talking about meant less to him than the gum stuck to the bottom of his shoe. To be honest I probably *did* mean less to him than that.

"And why do you believe that she has crossed into my land? I assure you that if we had found a *human* girl in the woods saying she was lost and needed to get home we would have helped her by now."

"It's not that simple," he continued "you see she is delusional and without her medication she can become quite dangerous to both herself and those around her."

I frowned and looked around at the other wolves in the clearing. None had backed down or relaxed in the slightest, in fact if anything they had tensed further. It was as if they all knew Alpha Parker was lying and was just waiting for the moment when this simple exchange of words would turn into a blood feud.

"Understood, I will keep a lookout for any *human* girls and if we spot anything I will make sure to inform you," Jax growled and nodded his head towards Alpha Parker, obviously a sign that this meeting was over.

I hadn't missed the fact that Jax had emphasised the word *human* when referring to the girl Alpha Parker was looking for. You could tell that the other Alpha had noticed it too as he had lost a split second of control on his wolf, his golden eyes shining though.

As soon as I noticed his eyes changed colour, a memory hit me hard, harder than a ton of bricks, and I had to grip the back of Jax's shirt to stop myself from swaying due to the force of it.

All of a sudden, I was a little girl again, standing at the door as a man in a police officer's uniform towered over me and told me that my parents had gone missing and that I was to go with him.

The next flashback was the policeman walking me to a stranger's house with a tight grip on my shoulders, almost as if he were anticipating me turning around and running away.

The last memory was of the same policeman, this time out of his uniform, sitting in the living room in the Leftens house. He was talking to Natalie and Tony as I hid behind the door, making sure I stayed completely out of sight so as not to be caught eavesdropping.

"She can never know what she really is...do you understand me?" The policeman growled at Tony who shook in fear. "Do this and you will be greatly rewarded."

It was then that I realised why I had recognised Alpha Parker's scent so much, why he looked so familiar to me. Not only was he the Alpha who had taken my shift away from me, he was also the policeman who had taken me from my childhood home and dropped me off at the Leftens all those years ago. Back when I was just a frightened seven-year-old orphan with no family and no home.

I gasped at the realisation and stumbled backwards and away from the man. I had to get away from him, I had to get out of here. Unfortunately, in my panic I had forgotten that he couldn't see me from where I was hidden behind Jax so all I accomplished in doing was bringing everyone's attention to me as I fumbled backwards, everyone's including Alpha Parker's.

"There you are," he snarled as he started to make his way towards me.

Chapter 12

Jax's POV

"There you are," Alpha Parker growled as he advanced towards her with his arms outstretched and an evil grin on his face, his left side slightly dropped due to his distinctive scar. No way was this sorry excuse of a man taking my mate away from me, not after I had just found her.

I growled at him; a growl so loud it even shocked me as my pack mates beside me bowed their heads in respect and submission due to the sheer strength of it. "You touch her and I will take that as an act of war, Alpha Parker." I could tell my eyes were glowing a bright gold as I tried to suppress my wolf as much as I could. He wanted out for threatening our mate.

Parker squared up to me on the territory line, not close enough to physically cross but still close enough to get in my face. "Alpha Jax, she is my property so I will be taking her home with me".

"She is *not* your property Parker, nor will she *ever* be, now leave my land before things get ugly." I could feel my pack members gathering around me, word had gotten out about the possible threat to their Luna and everyone wanted to come and support. I was instantly proud that my pack members, warriors and non-warriors alike, had dropped everything to come and show their support for their Alpha and their new Luna, even if the ceremony hadn't made it official yet.

Parker growled, trying to threaten me back, but with only a handful of wolves behind him I was less than afraid. "What gives you the right to keep that girl from me?"

I growled back and reached behind me, where I knew Annabelle would be. I could feel her terror and wanted to comfort her in any way that I could. This had been a mistake, bringing her here had been a mistake, and I could only hope that seeing this sorry excuse of a man hadn't done damage to my mate in any way. "This *girl* is my mate and no longer your concern, now leave before I get the elders involved, especially after what you have done to her." No way was he getting anywhere near my mate ever again.

"She's not your *mate*, she's just a human little girl with parental issues," Parker laughed as he rolled his eyes. "What meds have you been taking to make you believe that this little girl could ever live up to being a Luna?"

My pack growled behind me, furious with the insult to their Luna and I growled along with them. I'd had enough of this joker. Annabelle was still shaking behind me, her heart rate going a mile a minute and I was worried she would either pass out or regress back into her old self, losing all the valuable progress we'd made together, if he didn't leave now.

"Last warning Parker, leave now peacefully or leave by force...it's your choice."

"What's it like Jax? Having a mate, a Luna, that can't shift?" He sneered, trying to get a reaction out of me as he jabbed insults at Annabelle.

I was just about to pounce on him and end his miserable life forever when a scream was unleashed from my mate's lips. I spun around just in time to catch her before she hit the floor, her eyes rolling into the back of her head as I cradled her in my arms.

"Annabelle? Annabelle, are you okay?" I could feel my pack creating a protective ring around us, making sure Parker and his pack couldn't get to us as I continued to stare down at her.

The only response I got from her was another agonising scream. Her skin was hot to the touch and flushed from the pain she was in and my wolf whimpered at the sight of her in this much pain, not being able to do anything to help.

All of a sudden, I saw fur start to sprout across the backs of her hands and her nails elongate into long claws. Her teeth were also poking through, her lips not being able to contain their size as they slightly pierced the skin on her chin due to the force of her clenched jaw. She was shifting.

I suppressed the slight excitement I felt bubbling inside of me, trying not to get too caught up in the moment and focused on the situation at hand. "Come on Annabelle, you can do it, just ride through the pain and I promise you it will get easier," I reassured her as I placed her down onto the soft grass.

"Have fun with your sorry excuse of a Luna," Alpha Parker sneered from somewhere behind me. "I will take my leave but just know I will be coming for her. I'll come when you least expect it, she belongs to me, to me and no one else, no matter what some stupid Moon Goddess says."

I looked behind me to see Parker smirk at my surrounding pack members before turning and walking into the shadows of the trees, quickly disappearing from sight.

"Jax I think you should move her from the border, we're vulnerable here and I think the pack would feel more comfortable with their Luna deep inside the pack lands where it is safe." I hadn't even realised Xavier had turned up, but in that moment, I was very thankful to have my friend by my side.

I nodded and reached down to take my mate in my arms as she continued to writhe in pain. I remember my first real shift; it was the single most painful experience of my life. This wasn't her first shift, but it was the first time she was shifting whilst being aware of our world. Her wolf was now unlocked from her brain and I am praying that she will remember this shift and finally get to meet her wolf.

When we got to my house I went straight to the back garden, not wanting her to shift in the house. Her wolf would probably panic at the four walls caging her in.

I placed her down onto the grass and a groan escaped her lips at the shift in position.

"Jax w-what's happening to m-me," she whimpered as the pain increased, her canines causing her to speak with a lisp.

"You're shifting little mate, just let it happen and it won't be much longer, I promise." I sat down next to her and started to stroke her hair, trying to comfort and relax her in any way that I could.

"It-it hurts," she gasped as another wave hit her. Her back was arched oddly and I knew from countless times of coaching the pups of my pack through this that her shift was nearly over. I stood up and took a step back, preparing for anything that her wolf might do.

Wolves reacted differently to the shift depending on who they were and who was around them. Some became frightened and tried to run off, whilst others became aggressive and tried to fight off whoever came close. It was a completely natural reaction, an instinct set deep within our bones, I just had to make sure I was prepared for everything so that she didn't end up hurting herself.

After a few more minutes of Annabelle shifting to and from her wolf she finally shifted one last time and with a tear of her clothes, in Annabelle's place, lay a mesmerizingly gorgeous wolf with fur the exact shade of her golden locks.

My wolf was going crazy in my head at the sight of his mate, but I suppressed him as much as I could. Above everything else I had to make sure that she was okay first. "Annabelle... Annabelle, are you okay?" Her ears rotated, signalling that she could hear me, but she made no other move to get up.

I cautiously took a step forward, making sure that she was comfortable with me approaching her and being in her space. When she didn't growl or make a move to attack me, I crouched down and started to stroke her fur, trying to reassure her in some way that everything was going to be okay and that I wasn't a threat. As I stroked her, I could hear a kind of purring sound coming from her and I couldn't help but smile, she was enjoying the attention.

"Did you want to go for a run with me, little mate?" All newly shifted wolves wanted to go for a run. It was as if the wolf that had been trapped inside of us for sixteen years had finally been freed and couldn't wait to explore everything that was around them with their new body. For Annabelle it had been nineteen years, three years longer than most, so I could only imagine what her wolf would be feeling right now.

Her tail wagged slightly and I smiled down at her, happy that she was doing okay, before looking back into her eyes. When I got a look at them, I could see what Xavier had been trying to explain to me when he had seen me last. She had eyes that almost glowed when the sun hit them, looking more translucent than anything I'd seen before.

"You are incredible," I whispered as I slowly bent down and kissed her on her fluffy snout.

She smiled a wolfish grin up at me before slowly starting to stand on her shaky legs. She reminded me of a new-born calf as she unsteadily got to her feet, but once she was comfortable and she had her balance, she smiled as if she was proud of herself and shook out her fur.

My wolf, having been non stop pacing since the first sight of Annabelle's wolf, growled in my head and I knew I couldn't hold him back any longer. He had been waiting so long for the opportunity to run with his mate and to hold him back from that now would have just been cruel. I slowly shifted into my wolf, not wanting to scare her with any sudden movements, and when I had finally shifted into my black wolf I stared over at her, unmoving.

We held each other's gaze for a while, both assessing the other and getting ourselves comfortable being in each other's presence whilst being in wolf form. I knew Annabelle would be feeling a lot right now, not only with shifting for the first time but also with everything that comes with it.

All of her senses would have increased drastically, making everything seem much closer together than before. Things that were previously invisible to her now appeared to be in touching distance. The sound of bugs scuttling across the forest floor now sounded like a heavy-footed hiker as they stomped their way through the undergrowth. The smell of deer off in a distant part of the trees, stopping for a drink of water, now smelt intriguing, almost appetising. I remember feeling so disoriented the first time I shifted, it took me hours to distinguish where things were and how close something was to me.

My sister still likes to laugh at me at the amount of times I ran into trees or ducked when I heard a bird squawk because I had no depth perception, she called it karma for ruining her birthday.

It wasn't just the surroundings she'd be getting used to, it was our mate link as well. The biological reaction our wolves have to our mates can be confusing to some, especially if it hasn't been explained to you from a young age. The pull that we feel, the need to be with and touch our mate, can be confusing and scary to those who don't understand it. The magical tingles we feel could just as much make you flinch away from someone as much as they want to make you grip onto your mate and never let go.

The last thing I wanted to do was to rush her into anything that her or her wolf wasn't ready for.

Finally though Annabelle took a tentative step towards me and I couldn't help but step forwards myself. Every time she took a step, I took a step, matching them like for like, until we were mere centimetres apart. I could feel her warmth as it touched my wet nose, I could smell her scent as it invaded my senses and I could hear her heartbeat as it thudded irregularly in her chest. She was the most beautiful creature I'd ever laid eyes on and I couldn't tear my gaze away from hers, feeling almost hypnotised by her grace and beauty.

Eventually her wolf grew tired of staring at me and before I could react she pounced on me, rubbing her face into the soft fur of my neck as she performed our version of a hug. The sparks that flew between us were like a New Year's Eve firework display and I couldn't help but breathe her scent in as I buried my own face into her neck.

This act was just as much out of love as it was out of instinct. Not only was it so we could solidify the bond between us and commit the others' scent to memory, it was also a display to other wolves out there. Our necks were where our scent was the strongest so rubbing our heads against the others neck transfers their scent onto us, marking us as taken so no one else would dare touch us.

I let my wolf have his time with her as they continued to rub into each other's necks. This was an important moment and I didn't want to interrupt as I continued to stare at her through my wolf's eyes. I would have my time with her when they were good and ready to let me.

After they had finished circling each other and engaging in a bit of play fighting they finally decided it was time for us to make our way into the forest for a long overdue run together.

At this moment, I couldn't be happier.

We ran for hours, just living in the moment as we got to know each other. Annabelle's wolf was seriously mesmerising, I caught myself on more than one occasion staring at her instead of where I was going and ended up either tripping or running into something, usually a tree. Hannah would have had a field day if she'd seen me.

I showed her the whole territory, from the lake that we usually swam in during the warm months of the summer to the dense forest where game such as rabbits and deer usually roamed. Annabelle wasn't very good at hunting yet, it being her first time, but she did have a knack for it. She didn't seem to think so though as she huffed and grumbled at herself every time she missed a kill. I couldn't wait until she learnt how to mind-link so that we could properly communicate with each other. Body language and the occasional bark wasn't really enough for me to express how proud I was of her. Not many people could go through what she went through and come out of it the other side, I was seriously in awe of her, her beauty and her strength.

After a few hours of running, we slowly started to make our way back to the house. We were both exhausted and in need of a good sleep to recharge our batteries after such a physically active day. I could tell Annabelle was starting to get nervous about shifting back into her human form again, her heartbeat had started to stutter and I could taste the fear that was starting to ripple off her in waves. I tried to convince her as best I could that it wouldn't be as bad as her last shift, but that still didn't seem to calm her fears as her heart continued to stutter un-rhythmically.

As we broke through the tree line that separated the edge of the forest from my back garden, I heard a small whimper from behind me and I knew that Annabelle was lagging behind, trying to stay for as long as she could in her wolf form.

I trotted up to her and buried my head into the fur of her neck, trying to reassure her that everything would be okay. This was where the skill of mind linking would really have come in handy.

I whined when the bitter smell of fear tinged the air and I nuzzled her neck again, trying to reassure her as much as I could that she would be okay. I sighed when my actions weren't doing enough to reassure her and so I stepped back from her slightly and prepared to shift back into my human body.

Annabelle's pearlescent eyes grew wide once she realised what I was doing and quickly turned her back before she caught a glimpse of me naked. I laughed and shook my head at her innocence, mostly everyone around here was fairly comfortable being naked for short periods of time around each other. I mean you kind of had to be if you were going to be stripping in and out of clothes to change into your wolf most of your life. It was either that or spend a fortune on clothes that would just get trashed the next day.

I shuddered at the idea of having to do that much shopping as I took a few steps into the woods to find some shorts and a shirt I knew I'd stashed there. There are always emergency clothes hanging around the forest that outlined my pack's territory, just in case an accident happened and the person didn't have any clothes to change into.

I slipped into a pair of shorts and pulled the drawstring tight as I carried the shirt out to Annabelle, knowing that she would need something to change into once she shifted back into her human form.

"Come on my little mate you're going to have to change eventually, I promise you it won't hurt as much as it did last time," I pleaded with her as I crouched down so that I could look into her moonstone eyes. I still couldn't get used to the colour of them. Every wolf I've ever met had golden eyes when they shifted, so why didn't she?

Annabelle just shook her head in response before settling down on the grass, resting her head on her paws and closing her eyes as she breathed in the early evening breeze.

I sighed as I took in her relaxed position. I knew we weren't going anywhere anytime soon so I got comfy next to her and lay back in the grass with my hands behind my head.

"I remember the first time I shifted, it was at Hannah's thirteenth birthday party and she hated me for months after because I had stolen all of the attention away from her," I laughed as I tried to distract her. "She had been planning this party with mum for months, had everything planned down to a T... or so she thought. As soon as it was time for the cake to be bought out and for everyone to start singing happy birthday to her my wolf chose that exact moment to come out. I think we even have it on film somewhere," I laughed, recalling watching it back and seeing Hannah's horrified expression.

Annabelle's ears were facing towards me, telling me that she was listening to my story, but if it wasn't for that telling sign I would have assumed she'd have gone to sleep, she was so still. "Do you want to know the kicker of the whole story? Hannah's birthday is actually a week after mine, but she wanted to plan it before my birthday because she knew as soon as I turned sixteen all the attention would be on me and my wolf and she'd get none," I laughed. "Apparently my wolf didn't like that idea very much and I shifted a week before I was supposed to. She blamed it on my inner Alpha, but I think my wolf just knew how much I loved to mess with her and decided to help me out," I chuckled.

We stayed silent for quite a while after that, just enjoying each other's company, but when the sun started to set behind the trees and the temperature started to dip I sat up and stroked the soft fur on top of Annabelle's head. "Come on little mate, it's time to shift. Every werewolf had been in your shoes, scared of shifting back from fear of the pain, but it won't be as bad as last time and the more you shift the easier it becomes. It's kind of like your body is learning how to shift and the more you do it the more you find little short cuts to make it easier and less painful for you until it's like breathing, like it's the most natural thing in the world to you."

Annabelle grumbled, obviously not happy with the fact that she would have to shift, but slowly got to her feet and stared at the ground in concentration. We stood there for a few minutes, both of us utterly silent and completely still, but after a short while of nothing happening, she growled in frustration.

"Just picture your body Annabelle and all the little quirks that it has. The way it feels to wiggle your toes, to pick something up in your hands, brushing your hair, all the things that make you human and make you, *you,*" I explained.

We stood for a few more seconds, me staring at her and her staring at the grass, before slowly her body started to shake and I knew she was shifting back. I grabbed the discarded shirt that was beside me and held it up so that I couldn't see anything I wasn't supposed to.

My wolf was sad to see her wolf go but was happy that they now had her in our life and she now had the opportunity of feeling the mate bond.

I came back to reality when I heard gasping from behind the shirt and sighed in relief when she was back in her human form again. I swiftly slipped the T-shirt over her head and caught her under her arms before she could fall to the floor in exhaustion. Shifting, especially for the first few times, was extremely tiring. It took a lot out of a person, both physically and mentally and I knew that she was going to sleep for a long time after all this.

I cradled her close to my chest and held her tightly in my arms as I moved into the warmth of the house. Even though she was covered in sweat I knew that if I didn't keep her warm, it could cause her to become sick. It was important to keep her muscles warm after everything they had been through today.

"I feel it," I heard her mutter quietly as I continued to walk through the house and towards the staircase. My heart skipped a beat at the sound of her voice, hoping beyond hope that she was going to say what I thought she was.

"Feel what my little mate?" I whispered as gently as I could, not wanting to startle her with any sudden noises.

She smiled and snuggled into my chest, as if she couldn't get close enough to me. "The sparks."

A grin spread across my face at the thought of my mate finally being able to accept me and me finally being able to claim her as mine, mine and no one else's.

I gently kissed her forehead before making my way upstairs and into my room, to *our* room. "Sleep well my little mate, I'll be right here when you wake up," I reassured her as I lay her under the covers, making sure she was all tucked in and warm before standing up, planning to sit on the sofa and wait for her to wake up.

She shook her head as a cute little 'V' appeared between her eyebrows. "Sleep with me," she mumbled, her eyes remaining closed and her breath almost a whisper as she began to disappear into dream land.

I chuckled before getting under the covers with her and pulled her so that her head was resting on my chest. If possible, the sparkles between us had grown ten times over and I couldn't help but smile at the thought before sleep eventually overtook me and I was out for the count with my beautiful mate safely wrapped in my arms.

Chapter 13

Annabelle's POV

I woke up with a smile on my face as I stretched out across the mattress, my muscles feeling tight and sore from yesterday's run. I don't think I've ever done that much exercise in my life. We had run for hours and I couldn't have been happier throughout the entire experience as Jax showed me the ins and outs of his territory. Our territory.

It was beautiful, the way the sun had danced with the leaves as the wind blew them in different directions. How, even though I couldn't swim, the water felt so refreshing and cool against my paws as we'd paddled through the lake. The whole place was mesmerising, like a scene from a child's fairy-tale and I couldn't wait for my next shift so that we could go back out there and explore further.

I smiled to myself as I relaxed back onto the mattress, thinking about everything that had happened. I honestly couldn't believe that I had actually managed to shift into my wolf yesterday. On the one hand it felt so abnormal, running on all fours around the woods, but at the same time it felt like one of the most natural things in the world, like something I was born to do, which I guess technically I was.

I smiled as I tried to stretch out all the soreness again before slowly sitting up to find the other side of the bed empty and the room dark due to the closed black out blinds. How long had I been asleep for? The sheets on the other side of the bed were cold, meaning Jax had been up for a little while already.

"Jax?" I whispered into the seemingly empty room as I looked around for him.

A few seconds later the bedroom door opened a fraction, causing a slither of daylight to pierce the darkness and create a triangle of light on the soft carpet. A sock covered foot stepped through the open door, creating a shadow, followed by the rest of Jax as he stepped into the darkness of his room with a soft smile. My heart calmed instantly at the sight of him and I immediately felt stupid for feeling anxious in the first place.

"Hey there sleepy head," he smiled as he walked across the room, his feet silent against the plush carpet. "Did you have a good sleep?" He whispered as he took a seat on his side of the bed so that he was facing me.

I smiled and nodded my head, still feeling a little groggy as I rubbed my eyes with the back of my hands. "Yeah I did thanks, what time is it?" I managed to mutter out as my face almost split in two from a yawn.

He smiled as he reached out to tuck a strand of knotted bed hair behind my ear. "It's about one thirty in the afternoon, you slept for a long time. Not surprising though considering you went through the shift and then had quite a long run after," he reassured me. "How are you feeling by the way? You're not feeling nauseous or dizzy or anything like that are you?" He questioned, his eyes raking over my body as if looking for signs that I was anything but perfect.

I mentally assessed myself before shaking my head with a smile, I honestly felt fine. The best I had felt in a long time actually. "I feel good," I nodded over at him, reassuring him that I did, in fact, feel fine.

He let out a little sigh in relief before holding his hand out for me to take. "Come on then, you have an appointment in a few days with Dr Tessler and I want to make sure that you've put on enough weight to satisfy her," he smiled.

I rolled my eyes at him as he pulled me up and out of my sitting position tangled up in sheets, groaning as my sore muscles yelled at me for making them move.

When we got downstairs I sat at my usual spot on the kitchen counter and watched Jax fix me my usual bowl of soup. As I watched him pour a serving into a clean bowl and place it in the microwave I thought about everything that had happened to me over the last twenty four hours. Not only had I shifted into my wolf for the first time, well the first time that I could remember anyway, I had also been reunited with the man that had ripped my childhood away from me and forced me never to shift with the Alpha command Jax had told me about. What didn't make sense to me though was why that man would even want to ruin my life like that in the first place. Why would he put so much effort into taking me away from my parents and making sure that I never shifted just to place me into a fake home? What had I ever done to him to deserve something that cruel?

"Are you okay little mate?" Jax asked with a concerned note to his voice, breaking me from my internal questioning. I looked up from my fingers that were twisted together in my lap to find that he had stopped pouring out the second bowl of potato and leek soup for himself and was now standing in front of me with a concerned look on his face.

I tried to smile and nod my head, not wanting him to panic, but I could tell that he wasn't buying any of it from the stern look that he gave me.

"I just don't...understand," I sighed and looked down, wanting to avoid eye contact with him.

"Understand what beautiful?" He asked as he placed his hand gently on the side of my face, cupping my cheek in his warm palm.

"*Why,*" I whispered, leaning into his hand for a second.

"Why what?" He queried as he moved so that he was leaning with his hip on the counter next to me, his arms folded across his chest and his sock covered feet crossed at his ankles.

"Why would Alpha Parker want to do something like that to me?" I whispered as I wrapped my arms around myself to try and ease the strong sense of loneliness that had suddenly overwhelmed me.

Jax sighed and wrapped his arm around my shoulder and brought me into his chest. "It's not your fault Annabelle. Alpha Parker is the scum of the earth, we knew that long before you came into our lives, this just solidifies it for us. Don't worry, him and anyone else that helped him will get what's coming to them," he mumbled.

I peeked up through my lashes to see that Jax was clenching his jaw so tight I was surprised his teeth hadn't shattered. "Jax are *you* okay?"

"JAX!" A voice suddenly yelled urgently in the distance followed by a massive crash as the front door ricocheted into the wall, "Jax where are you?"

I shrunk back slightly as the voice got louder, causing Jax to jump into gear and stand in the kitchen doorway, ready for what was coming.

"Jax there you are," the voice sighed in relief as he saw Jax appear in the doorway. "I've found something that you are really going to want to see," the voice continued, seeming unfazed by Jax's stiff posture as he refused to move from the kitchen door.

"This couldn't wait until later?" Jax stressed. "I have Annabelle here and I have to watch her just in case she has another uncontrolled shift," he whispered and I couldn't help but shrink back slightly at the thought of the unknown person being in such close proximity to me.

"I know I know, but you *are* going to want to see this... it's about Annabelle." His voice went down in volume as he said the last part, almost as if he was trying to say it without me hearing it. Thanks to my new hearing though it was like the guy had said it standing right beside me.

At the mention of my name I perked up slightly, the fear and panic I was feeling a second ago shifting to the back of my mind as I focused on what the stranger had to say. Has this person found something to explain why Alpha Parker had done what he did to me? I slowly slid off the kitchen counter and tiptoed over to where Jax stood as silently as possible, not wanting the intruder to know that I was here and listening to what he had to say.

I peeked my head around the corner of the doorway to find Jax's shoulders ridged as he pinched the bridge of his nose, looking frustrated as he stood in the corridor. I couldn't get a glimpse of the unknown person, due to the wall he was standing behind, but I could see part of his outstretched arms and the book that he was cradling in them.

I looked back over at Jax as he sighed before nodding his head slightly. "Alright fine, but I don't want Annabelle to be worrying about any of this, she's been through enough already," he whispered, unaware that I could hear him. "Go to my office at the pack house and wait for me there, I'll think of some way to meet you."

The strangers' arms started to disappear behind the wall as he went to leave but before he could take one step, I jumped out from my hiding spot for them both to see.

"I want to know," I whispered as I stood there, feeling slightly awkward at only being in a T-shirt and shorts in front of the stranger.

I looked up at Jax and locked eyes with him as he did the same with me, as if we were in some sort of staring contest, waiting to see who would blink first. "I want to know," I repeated as I held my ground, my hands balled into fists on either side to help ease the slight tremor they had.

Jax sighed and turned to take a few steps towards me. "Annabelle-"

"I have a *right* to know," I muttered, fighting to keep my display of confidence up but failing miserably as my posture visibly started to sag. "Please," I whispered as I looked pleadingly up at him.

Jax ran his hands through his hair, having an internal battle with himself about whether it was a good idea or not for me to find out what this person knew about me.

"Fine," he relented with a sigh. "Just tell me if it gets too much for you okay?" He pleaded as he took a few steps towards me.

I nodded my head with a small smile before reaching out to him and giving him a hug, hoping he could feel the gratitude I felt for him. "Thank you".

I hadn't gotten a good look at the other person yet, if I was being honest I'd kind of forgotten about him, but as we pulled apart and I saw movement out of the corner of my eye I froze, instantly recognising who he was. He was the man that was yelling at me to shift the night I had run away from the Leftens. The one that had told me that he and his wolf friends had the right to *kill* me if I didn't shift.

I shook slightly in fear as our eyes locked together. Jax *knew* this person? Jax was *friends* with this person?

"Annabelle, are you okay?" Jax asked as he took in my rigid frame and fearful expression.

I shook my head and took a few steps back, wanting to get as far away from this man as I possibly could.

Jax looked at me before looking behind him at the stranger and then back at me again, almost as if he were watching a tennis match as he tried to figure out what had made me spooked. He must've figured it out because after a second of looking between us understanding flashed in his eyes.

"Annabelle, this is Xavier, my second in command. You don't need to fear him, he's a friend, my friend" he tried to reassure me as he reached out to try and take my hand in his.

"He-he threatened to *kill* me," I stuttered, not able to take my eyes off Xavier's face as I moved my hand away from Jax.

"He *what*?" Jax suddenly growled as he rounded on his so-called friend, his earlier calming tone shifting to one of anger as he stood protectively in front of me.

"Hey man it was before we knew who she was, when we thought she was just another rogue trying to get onto our land. You know, more than anyone, that I would *never* want to harm our Luna...ever," Xavier defended himself with his hands raised slightly, the book still clutched in one of them. "Come on man, calm down so that we can figure out what this Parker jackass wants with our Luna," he continued as he stared back at Jax.

I looked up at Jax as he looked back at me for a second to see the gold slowly leaving his irises as he became less and less tense.

"Annabelle," Xavier continued as he now directed his attention at me "I am *truly* sorry for what happened the other day in the woods. We thought you were a threat to our pack and our family, but I promise you that it will *never* happen again. I could never hurt you and I would lay my life down for yours in a heartbeat if the situation ever arose."

I stared at him in shock, not really knowing how to respond. I mean how did you respond to a person declaring he would lay his life down for you when he doesn't even know you or you him?

"Do you forgive me?" He asked as he let his hands rest to his sides, seeing that the threat of Jax turning on him was over.

I looked at Jax for help, hoping for some guidance on what I should be doing right now, but when I looked up at him all I got was a questioning look as if he too wanted to know whether I forgave Xavier or not.

I sighed as I weighed everything up before finally giving in. If Jax trusted him then so did I. I turned to look Xavier in the eye before nodding slightly, getting a smile back from both Jax and Xavier in response as they sighed in relief.

"Good, now come on into the living room and you can show us what you found out about Annabelle."

Chapter 14

Jax POV

I was so relieved when Annabelle had said that she would forgive Xavier for what he had said to her when they first met. It has happened in the past, in wolf history, where the Luna didn't trust the Beta due to one reason or another. The distrust in the pack's hierarchy either caused the pack to become unstable or the Beta inevitably having to step down. Both options were dangerous and, more often than not, it spelt the end of the pack.

We made our way into the living room, after I had made sure to grab both mine and Annabelle's soup, and got comfortable on the sofas. I smiled down at her as I watched her sit down beside me and tuck her legs underneath her before reaching her hands out to take her bowl of soup from me. After she was comfy, she slowly started sipping at the food, even though I knew she wasn't feeling particularly hungry, I was glad she was humouring me. Her appetite had slowly been increasing, which was a good sign, but I still needed to make sure she ate a sufficient amount to be sure that she gained the required amount of weight the doctor had asked of her.

"So," I sighed as I turned back to my friend who had sat himself on the opposite sofa. "You said you'd found something out about Annabelle and I'm guessing it has something to do with that huge book you have in your hands," I said as I leant forward with my arms resting on my knees, pointing to the fairly old looking book resting in the palm of his hands.

Xavier nodded as he looked over at Annabelle again before looking back at me. "Well remember when I said Annabelle's eyes were different in her shift than all of ours and that I had read about it somewhere but couldn't remember where?"

I nodded my head as I looked over my shoulder at my mate who had stopped eating and was staring at us in confusion. Of course she was, she had no idea what we were talking about seeing as she'd never seen her own eyes in shift form before. "Annabelle when we change into our wolf forms our eyes shift to a golden colour, no matter what rank in the pack we are or what our eye colour is when we are in our human form," I explained briefly as I looked down at her.

She nodded her head in understanding before placing the half uneaten bowl of soup on the coffee table in front of us and brushed her lip off with her fingers, making sure she didn't have any leftovers around her lips. "So what does that mean for me?" She whispered.

Xavier opened his mouth to answer her question but before he could I turned around and gave her a pointed look. "Xavier will tell us what he found and answer any questions you have but only if you promise to pick up that bowl and continue to eat. I don't want to get it in the neck from Dr Tessler because you're not eating enough and haven't gained enough weight," I chuckled.

She smiled up at me sheepishly before looking back at the food and took another spoonful, quickly followed by another. When I was satisfied that she was going to carry on eating I looked over at Xavier and gestured for him to continue.

"Well this is the book that I originally read it from," he continued. "I had to go through a mountain of books in my mum's old library, but I eventually found it." Xavier dropped the book onto the coffee table that sat between us and started flicking through the pages so fast I was worried he was going to tear them.

"Here, page 267...

The wolf's eyes are remarkable. Whether they are an Alpha or Omega they always remain the same colour. It is believed that the Moon Goddess designed us this way to remind us that we are all special to her and are all of equal value to her and each other. In her eyes we are all golden.

There is however one exception to this rule. It is believed that in every generation there is a messenger who is directly connected to the Moon Goddess herself. This messenger will always be female and will be identifiable solely by the colour of her wolf eyes. Unlike any other wolf, she will have moonstone eyes symbolising the connection she has with our creator and the moon itself."

Xavier went quiet after that and quickly snapped the book shut with a flick of his wrist, obviously finished with the extract he was reading.

"Well what else does it say?" I questioned as I looked down at the book that was resting closed on the coffee table before glancing back up to Xavier again, expecting there to be more about Annabelle and what she was. The more I knew about her and what she was capable of the more I could protect her.

All Xavier did though was shake his head and shrugged his shoulders with an apologetic look in his eye. "That's it, it just goes on about the standard transformation of a wolf after that, but nothing else about the moonstone eyes or what a *messenger* actually is. I may have to do some serious digging to find out but I'm hoping we'll have something in the packs library somewhere," he sighed as he rubbed a hand tiredly over his eyes.

I nodded over at him in understanding as I took a sneak peek over my shoulder to make sure Annabelle was still eating and sighed in relief when I saw that she had almost finished. "Well whatever you need you have, I want to get to the bottom of this," I stated, hoping he knew that he had my undying gratitude for what he had managed to dig up so far.

From a young age Xavier had always been my go-to guy for everything historical related. He suffers from an incomplete blood bond, a mate bond much stronger than the average, causing him to feel extreme amounts of loneliness and pain. He had started reading all his mum's old books to try and find out anything he could about it, hoping he could find something that would help ease the pain whilst he waited for his mate.

No one really knew why the Moon Goddess chose some of us to have a regular bond and others to have a blood bond, but it was believed that the couple would need it later in life to help them get through a difficult time. You couldn't reject a blood bond, no matter what you did or how you felt for the person, you would always be drawn back to them. I didn't know what that meant for Xavier and his future, but I knew that I would help him out with whatever he needed. He was my best friend and Beta and deserved my undying support.

"What if he knew?" Annabelle suddenly whispered from behind me, so quiet I had to rely on my over sensitive ears to hear her. I turned to my left to ask her what she meant, but I was met with a far-off look in her eyes as she focused on the sofa cushions underneath her curled up feet.

"What do you mean?" I asked as I leant back into the sofa cushions to get closer to her, hoping my presence would comfort her in some way and calm her racing heart.

"What if Alpha Parker *knew* about this 'wolf messenger' thing and that's why he did what he did. *That's* why he took me away from my parents and *that's* why he forced me not to shift as a child and made me stay hidden at the Leftens house," she whispered, her voice shaking slightly with fear as she stared at the trees through the glass window.

I held my arms out to her, inviting her in, and sighed in relief when she willingly crawled into my lap with her head resting on my chest. My poor little mate had been through so much in her short life and it didn't look like it would be letting up any time soon.

"She has a point there Jax,'" Xavier sighed as he ran his hand through his hair. "I mean it would explain his weird behaviour at the pack's border yesterday, his desperation to get her back at all costs. No sane Alpha would start a war between two packs over a single runaway, especially if that runaway had found her mate and was a Luna," Xavier mumbled as he scratched his head, trying to work everything out.

"But how would he know? I hadn't even shifted yet when he took me. He couldn't have known about my wolf's eye colour if I hadn't even shifted and met her yet," Annabelle muttered against my neck, her breath fanning across my pulse point. I could feel it tickle the hairs on my neck ever so slightly and I was struggling not to let my goose bumps take hold of me. I was trying to stay in Alpha mode, but with my sweet little mate in my arms and a hair's breadth away from where she'd eventually mark me as her own, it was getting increasingly difficult.

"Good point," Xavier mumbled and sat back in his seat, frustrated in not having all the answers.

"What if it's genetic?" I wondered as I felt Annabelle shift in my arms slightly so that she could see my face better.

"You mean my mum could have been one of these messenger things too?'"

I shrugged as I thought it over. "I mean it makes the most sense, right? If your parents were part of Parker's pack, he would have been able to have complete access to you and your parents. He would have seen the powers she possessed and thought that maybe he could take those powers for himself and use them in some sick twisted way."

"But I would have had to have shifted to be able to access these so-called powers, so why shield them from me if he wanted to use me?"

"I don't know," I groaned as I ran my hand down my face in frustration. "Maybe he's just an idiot that hadn't thought his plan through."

Xavier snorted at the thought before shaking his head and put his hands on his knees to push himself into a standing position. "I feel like these are questions for another night, once I've managed to hit the books and have a few more answers for you guys."

I nodded my head in agreement as I looked down at Annabelle who had made herself comfortable in my arms. "See yourself out will you? I'm guessing she's still pretty exhausted from the shift yesterday," I explained as I made no move to get up and see my friend out as I circled my arms around her in a secure hug.

Xavier smiles before nodding his head and goes to leave out the living room door with his book in hand. "Sure man no worries, I'll give you a message when I know more," he nodded before closing the living room door, giving us some much needed peace and quiet.

"Thanks Xavier," I told him through the pack link, relaxing back into the sofas as he left.

"What if he killed them?" I heard a little voice whisper after five minutes of us being alone. "What if he killed my parents and is planning to kill me all because of this stupid thing that I have no control over."

My arms tightened around her at the mere thought of her being killed by that disgusting waste of space. "I will never let that happen to you Annabelle. You are my mate and it is my job to make sure you're the happiest and safest person alive," I whispered into her ear, burying myself in her hair to try and comfort the both of us.

"You have a pack now Annabelle, a pack that will stand by you until their last breath," I reassured her as I looked down to see her eyelids had closed and her breathing had slowed down and evened out. She was asleep.

Chapter 15

Annabelle's POV

I had been tossing and turning all night, unable to stop myself thinking about everything Xavier had told us.

The fact that I was some kind of magic *messenger* that had a weird connection to an ancient goddess that I'd never even heard of a week ago. I just wish I knew someone who had the answers, who knew what was going on with me and could help me in some way. Someone like my mum.

I genuinely believe that Jax had been right, that she too was a messenger of the Moon Goddess and was taken because of what she could do. Why else would someone want to harm her and rip her away from me?

I looked over to my left to see that Jax was still fast asleep on the other side of the bed, oblivious to my inner turmoil as I lay wide awake next to him. We had kind of just kept the sleeping arrangements since the other night when I asked him to sleep next to me. We're both stubborn and refused to let the other sleep on the sofa so we just thought why bother continuing the fight at all if we both knew the other wouldn't be giving in any time soon. I didn't have a major issue with it, sure it was a bit bizarre that I was allowing someone to sleep next to me when I could barely stand someone touching me not too long ago. But what can I say, he made me feel safe. And safe was a feeling almost foreign to me thanks to all my years at the Leften's house.

I sighed and gave up trying to get back to sleep, I had already slept enough over the last 48 hours anyway so why was I even bothering trying to force my body to have more. I got up and made my way down the stairs and into the kitchen to get myself a cold glass of water. I still found it a bit bizarre sometimes that I was able to just go into the kitchen and help myself to anything that I wanted. I was so used to having to ask permission for years on end at the Leftens that I still caught myself beginning to ask Jax if I was allowed to do anything on a regular basis.

You'd think I would have gotten used to it by now but sadly that little habit was still ingrained into my brain.

I sighed as the cold water soothed my dry throat, quickly draining the whole glass with a gasp, making me realise I hadn't had anything to drink in ages.

I filled the glass back up, intending to down my second pint of water, when a sudden ear-splitting screech rang all around me and invaded my senses. It was a noise so intense that it made my eyes water, my vision to blur and my hands to shake.

I dropped the glass of water, watching it shatter on the floor, as I covered my ears with my hands, hoping to somehow dull the sound down. Nothing happened though, if anything it just made the noise worse. I was aware of nothing, my undivided attention solely focused on the painful ringing noise that seemed to increase with every passing second, and just when I was about to give up hope... it stopped. My vision cleared and I could suddenly hear everything that was going on around me.

What was peculiar though was the fact that I wasn't in Jax's kitchen anymore, in fact I wasn't even in his house. I was in some sort of underground makeshift cell.

I took a few gulps of the mildew air, using it to help calm my nervous heart rate and ease my sweaty palms as I wiped them on the fabric of my shorts. Just when I thought I was calm enough I heard a commotion from up ahead, causing my lungs to hyperventilate all over again.

Curiosity got the better of me as I slowly made my way out of my hidey hole and slowly crept over to the voices. They were muffled at first, but as I got closer, I managed to recognise the sound of a male voice yelling. I couldn't quite work out what he was shouting or who he was shouting at, but whoever it was I felt immensely sorry for them. I had been yelled at like that a lot over my childhood and it never got easier being on the receiving end of someone else's rage. Nine times out of ten you would always end up on the receiving end of someone's fist.

I inched forward, trying to get closer to the angry man until I was satisfied enough with the distance so that I could make out what he was yelling.

"What the hell do you mean you *don't know*!" The man yelled as I inched around the algae covered stone wall so that I could look around the corner, hoping to get a better look at what was going on. As I poked my head out from behind the slimy stone wall I saw a man towering over a cowering figure as they remained crouched on the floor, hoping to make themselves as small and insignificant as possible. I knew that posture anywhere, it was the posture of someone who was expecting a blow at any moment.

The person on the floor must have muttered a response but their voice was so soft and small I could barely make out the quiet whisper of unintelligible mumbles.

"Well then ask again. The only reason we were keeping you around was because of what you knew and what you could do. If your knowledge has now dried up then so has your time on this planet," the man towering over the figure snarled.

I crept closer still, making sure to stick to the shadows, wanting to hear the other side of the story as the crouched figure responded. "I *have* asked again but I'm getting nothing back, our communication bond has been broken," the woman explained, not taking her eyes off the grime covered floor as she did so.

The man grunted in annoyance before delivering a swift kick to the poor woman's abdomen. "You know we now know where she is right? Did your precious little Moon Goddess tell you that? It won't be long before she's dragged back here by the scruff of her neck, back to where she belongs, sharing a cell with you," the man sneered.

"NO!" The woman screamed out, her cry of pain echoing off the stone walls surrounding her. It didn't sound like the kind of cry brought on by physical pain though, it was more the type of broken wail you'd hear from someone who was emotionally shattered.

"Oh would you just shut up and ask again," the man sighed, as if he was already bored with the conversation.

It was silent for a few minutes as the man looked over the women cloaked in shadows expectantly, as if he were waiting for something.

The woman let out a sudden sob and the man sighed again before running his hand down his face in exasperation. "Bring him out!" the man yelled over his shoulder causing the woman to cry out as she got up on her knees and strained in her chains, trying to release herself. I could smell the slight singe of her flesh at what appeared to be silver laced chains digging into her skin at her sudden movements. If the pain she was feeling right now was anything like the pain I felt in the dream I'd had not long ago I was amazed at how little of an effect they had on her.

"It's no use darling, you and I both know you don't have the strength to break out of those chains," the man chuckled, almost taunting her.

"You bastard, don't you dare touch a single hair on his head," she growled, strength returning to her voice.

There was a loud noise coming from the other side of the room, almost like deadbolts, and before long a door I hadn't even noticed opened up to reveal two men walking in, supporting another man by his shoulders with his hands tied behind his back and a ratty old bag slung over his head, shrouding his face.

"You know the drill by now, for every time you don't answer my question your man over here gets a punch. Got it?"

The woman just cried and shook her head. "I don't know, she's not answering any of the calls I put out, I don't know anything," she sobbed.

"Wrong answer," the guy grinned, almost as if he were hoping for that answer, as he nodded at the other two guys as one of them gave a swift punch to the chained man's covered face.

I cringed as I looked away, hearing the crunch as his fists connected with his face. I wish I could help in some way, but what could I do? I didn't even know where we were.

The interrogation went on for several minutes, I honestly didn't know how the guy was still alive after all the hits he'd received. The bag that was covering his face was now soaked in red and he was hunched over from the sheer force of some of the guy's punches as the others struggled to keep him upright.

"Are you really going to let your mate die over some silly secrets the Moon Goddess has asked you to keep?" The man asked the woman as he strode up to her as she continued to sob on the floor. "Is it all really worth making your mate go through this kind of pain?"

The woman stayed silent as she kept her eyes downcast, not wanting to look at the state her mate was in.

"You can't even look at him, can you?" The man sneered as he crouched down to her height and lifted her chin up by grabbing the hair at the nape of her neck, an evil glint in his eyes as he stared down at her. "Take the bag off his head," the guy yelled at the other two men in the room who were barely keeping the poor beaten and bloodied man on his feet.

One of them swiftly nodded before removing the bag to reveal someone who was barely recognisable. Both of his eyes were swollen shut, his nose was broken and his lips were busted open in multiple places.

"Samuel no!" The woman screamed as she leapt forward towards her mate in a panic.

As the woman leapt forward I got the first good look at her since I got here. Her hair was knotted and pulled back into a sloppy updo to keep it out of her face, but even through all the dirt and blood I could tell that it was a light blond colour. She had high cheekbones and a strong jawline as she continued to strain helplessly against the chains.

She looked familiar.

"Samuel please, just stay awake. Stay alive for me," she sobbed as her legs gave out on her and she went crashing to the floor, the chains stopping her from moving more than a foot in her mate's direction.

I looked over at the guy known as Samuel and noticed that his head was slightly raised, as if he was trying to see through the slits that were his eyes.

"Jane?" It was barely a whisper, but thanks to my new wolf hearing I managed to hear him.

Jane? I knew a Jane. Where did I know a Jane from?

Remember... the imaginary voice whispered in my head. *Remember...*

Remember what?!

And suddenly I was slammed with a vision. It was of a man and woman walking side by side in front of me holding hands. They were smiling at each other as they talked, I couldn't make out what they were saying though. The man turned around to look at me and smiled as he reached down to pick me up in his arms.

I felt happy and safe in this moment, like nothing bad could happen.

I looked over to my other side and took in the woman next to me, blond hair, high cheekbones, strong jaw.

Remember...

"M-Mum?" I stuttered as I struggled to get air into my lungs.

I didn't realise I had said it out loud until all five pairs of eyes rounded on me.

"A-A-Annabelle?" the woman stuttered as she looked over at me, disbelief clear in her voice.

"Mummy?" I couldn't believe it; she was actually alive.

"SECURITY BREACH! LOCK THE DOORS DOWN," the man in front of me screamed and started to charge towards me.

"Annabelle run!" My mum screamed but before I had a chance, I was suddenly yanked from the room and back in Jax's living room, lying on the sofa with Dr Tessler looking over me.

Chapter 16

Jax POV

I was shocked awake by the sounds of smashing glass coming from downstairs and before I was even fully awake, I quickly rolled over to cover my Annabelle. If there was an intruder in the house then there was no way I was letting them get to my mate. As I rolled over though I was met with a warm but empty side of the bed.

"Annabelle?" I questioned into the dark and empty room, becoming more and more panicked when it became obvious she wasn't in the room with me.

"Annabelle!" I shouted across the room, hoping that she was holed up in the bathroom somewhere, but there was still no response. I quickly shot out of bed and ran down the stairs, taking them two at a time, to where I could hear her heart racing in the kitchen.

What I found though confused and frightened me all at the same time. I saw Annabelle with her head in her hands, curled up into a foetus position, surrounded by water and broken glass. She must have accidently smashed it and panicked.

I sighed and walked over to her, minding the broken glass that littered the tiled floor so I didn't stand on the shards and cut my bare feet. I crouched down so that I was more on her level and sighed as I looked her over, not seeing any blood on her exposed skin. "Annabelle, it's okay... it's okay. I'm not mad that you broke a glass," I muttered, hoping my voice was soft enough so as not to startle her further. I wanted to reach over and touch her, but with the current state she was in I didn't know whether that would just make her panic attack worse.

When the only response I got was a whimper as she clutched her head tighter I frowned. I reached out to brush a few strands of hair that had fallen in front of her eyes, hoping that the gentle gesture wouldn't increase her panic attack in some way.

When I brushed her face though my frown deepened at what I felt, or more correctly what I *didn't* feel. Our mate's sparks were gone. Not a single trace of tingling could be detected by both myself *or* my wolf. That's when I really started to panic.

Had Parker somehow gotten to her whilst she was still in my pack territory and commanded her to break our mate link?

"XAVIER!" I screamed down the pack link, not even bothering to try and mask my panic and confusion. *"Get over here now! There's something wrong with Annabelle."*

"Why what's wrong? She seemed fine when I left you guys last night," he responded after a few seconds of me prodding into his brain, urging him to wake up.

"I don't know," I replied as I picked Annabelle up off the floor and ran into the living room, not even blinking as I felt the glass pierce my skin as I placed her onto the sofa so that she could be more comfortable. *"Something's wrong."*

My wolf searched through her head as best he could, hoping to find a reason as to why this was happening, but without our bond being finalised there wasn't much he could do.

There was one thing that was startlingly obvious though. Her wolf was gone.

The front door suddenly burst open, revealing Xavier still dressed in his pyjamas, as his eyes flicked across the room frantically trying to find us. When he spotted me knelt on the floor beside a curled-up Annabelle he made his way over and sat on the arm of the sofa next to us, more relaxed now that he realises there isn't an immediate threat of an attack.

"What happened?"

"I don't know," I shrugged. "I found her like this after being woken up, I-I can't feel her wolf Xavier." I hated how my voice cracked as I answered, an Alpha should always be strong and never show weakness, but right now the earth could be crumbling from under my feet and I wouldn't care.

Xavier patted me on the shoulder with a grim look on his face, showing me as much support as he could. Without knowing what was happening though there really wasn't much that he could do.

"Is this something to do with the *messenger* thing or something?" I asked, hoping he had maybe found something that would explain why our mate bond was gone and her wolf had disappeared.

He let out a puff of air and ran one of his hands down his face. "Honestly man I don't know, I mean it's possible, I guess, that the Moon Goddess is somehow involved in this, there aren't many people that can make a mate bond disappear," he shrugged.

"It's not just the bond that's missing Xavier," I muttered as I felt my wolf try to reach out to hers again. "Her wolf is missing too."

It was silent for a moment, the only noise coming from Annabelle and her slightly elevated breathing and heartbeat. She had relaxed out slightly now, looking more relaxed and peaceful as I stared down at her. If I didn't know any better I would have just guessed that she was sleeping.

"I'm getting Dr Tessler over here, maybe she has some logical answer as to what is going on here," Xavier muttered as he stood up and slightly walked away from me with his phone in his hand.

It was common courtesy to not use the pack link at night whilst someone was sleeping unless it was an emergency. It made the person feel groggy and was a real shock to the system if your wolf is woken up by another before your body isn't fully awake yet.

I tuned his voice out as I focused on my little mate in front of me. I didn't know what was going on, but we were going to make it through. We just had to.

"The Doc will be here in five man, honestly you should pay that woman double," Xavier laughed, trying to get a reaction out of me that wasn't stone faced and pathetic.

I just nodded my head, letting him know that I had heard him, without taking my eyes off from Annabelle. *Think Jax. Think!* If we were mated I could know exactly what was going through her head, at least then I'd know if she was scared or not, but we weren't and it just made my wolf even crazier. I'm seriously going to have to bring the topic up soon, just to give my heart a rest and myself a bit of peace of mind.

I suddenly felt a hand touch my shoulder and looked up to find my mother looking down at me, a look of understanding in her eyes as she looked me over.

"Mum? What are you doing here?" I asked as I stood up and pulled her into a quick hug, making sure that I kept one hand on Annabelle just in case the mate link came back and the sparks reappeared.

"Xavier called and said you needed some support; your father and siblings are here too," she explained as she gestured with her thumb to where I'm guessing they were.

I looked behind her to see the rest of my family sitting on the sofa on the other side of the living room, all of them giving me reassuring smiles as their eyes flicked between me and Annabelle. I gave them a brief nod, showing my appreciation for their support, before turning back to my mum. "I don't know what to do mum, she won't wake up and I can't feel the bond. Her wolf has gone. What... what if her wolf never comes back?" I muttered, showing my fears to the one person I knew wouldn't judge me.

"Don't worry Jax, we'll get her back," my mum reassured me as she patted me on my shoulder. There was something about a mother's comfort and confidence that always seemed to ease the mind just a little.

I smiled and nodded down at her before I looked back down at my sleeping mate. *Please come back to me.*

"I came as fast as I could," I heard a voice from behind me and I turned around to see Dr Tessler standing behind me with her medical bag in hand. She was still dressed in her dressing gown and her hair was shoved into a knot on top of her head, but I didn't care, as long as she was here to help my Annabelle she could have turned up in a hula skirt for all I cared.

"Thank you Dr, she seems to have gone into a coma of sorts, when I found her she was in a foetal position on the floor in the kitchen covering her ears. When I first saw her, I thought she was having a panic attack from smashing a glass but when I went to touch her, I couldn't feel the mate bond between us, I still can't even now. Her wolf seems to have disappeared and I can't figure out why," I explained, hoping that I hadn't left out any vital bits of information.

The Dr nodded her head as she took a stethoscope out of her bag and knelt down to listen to Annabelle's heart rate. Yes we could hear it without the aid of a stethoscope, but using one helped with listening to specific sections of the heart as well as her breathing to determine if any fluid had gotten into her lungs. "And when was this?" She asked, getting a device out that she wrapped around Annabelle's arm so that she could measure her blood pressure.

"I don't know, maybe twenty minutes to half an hour?" I shrugged, unsure as to when I had found her. My brain was in such a state the last thing I was focusing on was what the time was.

"An hour," Xavier piped up from the sofa and I nodded a thanks to him before looking back at the doctor.

"Okay and was her wolf missing as soon as you went to her or did it slowly fade away from her?" She questioned, not taking her eyes off of what she was doing.

"Umm... I think her wolf was already gone when I found her." I honestly couldn't remember much from the past hour, all that had been running through my mind was that my Annabelle couldn't die on me, not after I had just found her.

"Okay good, at least her wolf didn't slowly fade away like she was dying, at least like this there is a chance of finding her again and getting her back."

I nodded, trying to take some comfort in that little bit of information, but I couldn't relax entirely until Annabelle was up and about and safe in my arms again. "How long will it take before she wakes up Doctor?"

She looked at me and shrugged. "It's hard to say Alpha, we don't know half of the trauma that this girl has faced over the years, maybe this is just her body's way of dealing with everything that it's gone through," she explained.

"It's quite common for our brains to shut down every now and then so that they can process everything, kind of like slipping into a coma but only less severe. Between the new environment, new people, coming face to face with her previous Alpha and finally managing to shift, I wouldn't be surprised if Annabelle's wolf has just temporarily shut down to try and process everything. Our human brain can cope with such strong emotions, but our wolf side is much more basic, relying more on instinct than emotion and reason. It's possible that her wolf has disappeared purely to protect itself and navigate the difficult situation that it's in," the doctor explained as she removed the blood pressure sleeve from Annabelle's arm.

"We'll get her back son; don't you worry about it," my dad reassured me as he walked up beside me and slapped me on the shoulder.

I suddenly heard a slight whimper coming from the sofa and looked down to find Annabelle's eyebrows drawn into a frown. Was she waking up?

"Annabelle? Annabelle can you hear me?" I knelt down to get closer to her but was pulled out of the way by my dad so that Dr Tessler could get to her.

"Let the doctor do her thing son," my dad explained as I shot him a warning glare, not liking being dragged away from her.

It killed me but I gave a swift nod and let the doctor pass so that she could give Annabelle another quick exam. She pulled the lids back from her eyes and shined a torch into them, checking her pupil reflexes. As soon as she put the small pocket torch away though Annabelle suddenly woke up with a gasp and said one word that made all of us frown in confusion.

"Mummy?"

The Alpha and his Mate

Chapter 17

Annabelle's POV

"You gave us quite a scare there Annabelle, how are you feeling?" Dr Tessler asked as she proceeded to shine a light in my eye.

I didn't know how to respond; how do you explain to someone that you just saw your mum and dad for the first time in twelve years without sounding like you'd completely lost your mind?

"I-I saw her," I whispered as I felt Jax sit next to me and take my hand in his.

"Saw who little mate?" He whispered, speaking softly, probably so as not to scare me.

I looked over at him and my eyes instantly welled up with tears at the thought of what my mum was currently living through. "My mum."

He furrowed his brow in confusion and looked over at the doctor for a second before focusing his attention back on me. "As in you had a dream about her? Or some form of memory maybe?"

I shook my head and licked my lips; I couldn't figure out how to explain it to him, how I *knew* that what I just saw was real and was happening right now and not in my head as a dream. My mum and dad were both alive but kept as prisoners, forced to be apart and beaten when their captures didn't like an answer my mum gave them.

I looked over at Jax and tried to explain to him with my eyes that what I had just witnessed was real. I didn't know how I knew; I just had a gut feeling that someone had brought me there, to see that, for a reason.

"They were prisoners, in some kind of dungeon or cell block. It was definitely underground judging by how cold and dark it was. It smelled horrible… of damp and blood," I shuddered as I thought back to my dream. Jax pulled me into his arms and rubbed my exposed arms where goose bumps had started to appear.

"This guy was yelling questions at my mum, but she didn't know the answers to them, saying that some form of communication bond had been broken or something like that," I whispered, cringing as I remembered the way he had treated her.

I felt Jax tense around me and I looked up to see he had locked eyes with an older man, a stranger, who was sitting on the sofa opposite us. How had I not noticed the amount of people that were in the room before?

I froze and shrunk slightly into Jax's arms, trying to hide from them as much as I possibly could, but as I took another look at them I weirdly felt like I knew them. Hannah was here, Jax's sister, and she gave me a little reassuring smile when we had locked eyes, but I had definitely not met the other three strangers in the room.

"Annabelle, did you see anyone that you recognise at all? Any familiar faces in the dream that you can think of?" Jax asked as he looked down at me with the slight 'V' still between his eyebrows.

I thought back to the dream and tried to refocus on the faces but sighed and shook my head when I came up blank. "No sorry," I mumbled "do you think you know where they could be?"

Jax sighed before running a hand through his hair, making sure to keep his other arm wrapped securely around my waist. "We might have an idea as to who has them, yes, but we need hard evidence before we can do anything further," he sighed.

"Where do you think they are?" I frowned as I looked up at him in confusion. How could he possibly know where they were being kept when I hadn't even truly explained to them what I'd seen.

Jax shook his head before kissing me on the forehead "I don't want to tell you and get your hopes up if it turns out that my hunch is wrong. I'll have some of the pack members do some scouting near the area and see if they pick up anything unusual, if they do you'll be the first to know," he reassured me.

"Be careful son, if it is who you're thinking of then he is not someone we want to get on the wrong side of lightly," the older man of the three strangers spoke up and I looked over to see him give me a soft smile before focusing his attention back on Jax. He had called Jax son, that must make him Jax's father.

"I know dad, I know who we'll be up against, the trackers will just have to be extra careful at hiding their scent," he nodded.

"I'll go with them," the youngest stranger in the group muttered. He couldn't be more than eighteen, but his eyes told me that he knew way more than his age was letting on. A flash of an image ran through my mind and I suddenly remembered where I recognised him from. The first night I was here I looked at a photo of Jax, Hannah and one other person all huddled together and smiling right before I smashed the frame. He must be Jax's brother.

"Thank you Will, I would appreciate your experience in guiding the pack trackers."

He just nodded his head in response but otherwise stayed quiet.

The only stranger left in the room was the woman sitting in between Jax's dad and his brother Will. I'm guessing she was his mum, but I didn't want to jump to any conclusions.

"Jax, are you not going to introduce us to your mate?" The woman suddenly piped up and I realised I must have been staring at her in slight confusion without realising it. I quickly looked down in embarrassment and blushed slightly at being caught.

"Oh yes sorry. Annabelle this is my little brother Will, my father Jackson, my mother Emily and Hannah you already know. Everyone this is my mate Annabelle," Jax introduced everyone whilst pointing to each person on the couch, making sure I wasn't confused about who was who.

"It is so lovely to finally meet you my dear, we have heard so much about you from Xavier and Hannah. It's so nice to finally put a face to the name," she smiled. "If you need anything at all you just let me know okay?" Jax's mum said. She looked like a kind-hearted woman, with mousy brown hair and chocolate brown eyes you could tell that she was a caring woman, someone who did everything they could to help someone out, even if it was someone she didn't know.

None of Jax's family had gotten up to hug me or shake my hand and I had a sneaky suspicion that Hannah had something to do with it, telling them I was still very uncomfortable with strange people I didn't know getting close to me.

I smiled and nodded my greeting at them, but before I could mutter some form of greeting a small yawn escaped my lips. I tried to discreetly lift my hand to cover my mouth and conceal it, but it didn't work, everyone still heard it. I really had to get used to this super sensitive hearing thing they all apparently have, that *we* apparently have.

"I guess that's our cue to leave" Dr Tessler stated as she stood up and gathered all her things into her bag. "My patient needs her rest," she stated as she started to wave everyone out.

I smiled up at them as they whispered quiet farewells to us, one by one getting up off the sofa and headed out the front door. Before long it was just me and Jax sitting on the living room sofa, cuddled up with me in his lap and my head resting on his chest. "I think we should follow the doctors' orders and get you to bed don't you think?" Jax asked as my eyes started to drop. "After all, we have a lot of training to get done tomorrow," he chuckled.

I wanted to ask him what he meant by training, but before I could even form the sentence in my head I was out like a light, with Jax's strong arms around me, keeping me safe.

Chapter 18

Jax's POV

"It's really not that difficult once you get the hang of it Annabelle," I tried to convince her.

We were currently sitting cross legged, opposite each other, in my back garden and I was trying to show her how the mind link works. By law she wasn't allowed to officially become the pack's Luna until she learnt it and becomes connected to the pack.

To say she was shocked when I first told her about it would be an understatement, in fact she outright laughed at the idea of it. I had to prove it to her by calling Xavier over with my mind link and doing a full ten minutes of *'what number was I thinking of'* with him, Annabelle watching closely to make sure we weren't cheating in any way. After not getting a single one wrong during the whole experiment she had no choice but to believe us.

She groaned in frustration and ran her hands over her face "well if it's so easy then why can't I do it yet?"

I smiled at her to try and ease some of her tension and reached over to take her hands into mine. "It's most probably because you and your wolf aren't fully connected yet. Yes, you have now shifted and yes you can now feel the mate link but there is so much more to becoming a werewolf than just turning into a wolf. You have to *feel* her, *know* her, train together and learn what works for the both of you. No two people are the same, so why would that change for a wolf?" I question. "Mind linking works by one wolf talking to another, not human talking to humans telepathically" I explained.

"Well then why are we even bothering if it's impossible for me to do right now? Why don't we work on something else like *strengthening* the connection so I can do stuff like linking in the future." I could tell she was getting frustrated with not being able to link. She was currently frowning down at her feet and pulling the grass out of the ground by its roots and I couldn't help but think that she looked so damn cute right now with her eyebrows drawn down and a pout on her lips.

"This *will* help strengthen your bond with her, everyday your brain is working to try and find new pathways and shortcuts to talk to her and use your link," I tried to explain. I don't think she was aware of just how important it was for her to learn linking. If she couldn't link then she couldn't become the Luna. If she couldn't become the Luna I had one of two choices to make, step down from my Alpha position and be with her or reject her and mate with someone who wasn't my destined mate.

It was an impossible decision to make, if I chose my pack over her then it would surely break both of us, and after waiting so long to find her I knew that I could never break her heart like that. On the other hand, if I chose her over my pack then my sister would have to step up as Alpha. She wasn't the Alpha type; she had never shown any interest in anything to do with the Alpha role and I fear that with me stepping down it would cause the pack to become weak and eventually collapse.

I didn't want Annabelle knowing any of this though, I knew that if she was aware of just how serious it was, she'd panic, causing her to get frustrated and if she got frustrated her brain couldn't function properly.

I could also tell that she was stressed about the 'dream' she'd had last night. I'd known just from looking into her eyes that she'd been telling the truth about seeing her parents, the fear and longing in them had been enough to shatter my heart. I wasn't ready to explain to her what we'd found out though, that she'd most likely Astro-projected herself to where her parents were being kept with the help of the Goddess' messenger touch. I knew it would shatter her if we told her where we thought they were being kept and turned out to be wrong.

I looked into my little mate's eyes and smiled encouragingly at her, "I know you can do it Annabelle."

With my words of encouragement, I could see a new sense of determination in her. She didn't want to fail as much as I didn't want her to.

"Okay so close your eyes... Now focus on your wolf, eye colour, fur colour, height... everything. Focus on trying to connect with her on more than just a physical level," I explained.

She nodded and took a deep breath through her nose and closed her eyes. She was silent for a few minutes, just her even breath filling the afternoon air, and just when I saw her start to give up hope I suddenly felt a slight push in my mind. I smiled a full-on grin at her, not that she could see it, and closed my eyes to try and reach back out to her.

She was just within reach, just one more stretch and we'd brush minds, when we were suddenly interrupted by a pack member forcing their way into my mind.

I growled in anger, not liking the disrespect that the member was showing me, but quickly sobered up when the wolf muttered a few words to me. It was about my brother.

"Annabelle, we have to go. Now," I stated as I shot up to my feet, pulling Annabelle with me, and ran towards my parent's house. All I knew was that my brother was in trouble, no one would tell me anything else, which I found more worrying than anything. If they were waiting to tell me in person then it must be serious.

"Jax what's happening?" I heard Annabelle stutter out behind me between gasps of air, obviously shocked and slightly panicked by my sudden reaction.

"Will's in trouble, he went on a scouting mission with a few other pack members this morning."

Annabelle stayed silent which I was very thankful for, I didn't have the answers to the questions I knew she would be asking me right now.

Thankfully my parents didn't live too far from me and in a few short minutes we were on their property and I was racing up the front porch steps and barged straight through the front door.

What we were greeted with when we walked through the threshold could only be described as an organised chaos.

Pack warriors were running left and right, mobile phones strapped to their ears as they paced the length of the living room. Anyone who wasn't on their phones were huddled around the open plan kitchen dining room, where a large, detailed map of the area was spread out over the table.

"What the hell is going on here?" I yelled and suddenly everyone froze as they felt the power of their Alpha entering the room. Annabelle shrank behind me, not liking the fact that everyone had stopped what they were doing and were now focusing all their attention on us. I tightened my hold on her and wrapped my arm around her waist, hoping I was giving her enough reassurance to get through the next few hours that would undoubtedly be hard for the both of us.

"It's Will son, he hasn't come back from his scout mission," my dad informed me as he came up to us and smiled down at Annabelle softly before placing a hand on my shoulder. "Also, one of the trackers that went with them returned. He was covered in blood and barely made it to the medical bay before passing out. He's there now, Dr Tessler is working on him as best she can, but apparently with all the stress his body has been under it's pretty touch and go."

I closed my eyes for a second and took in a breath, mentally preparing myself for what our pack was about to go though. This was when my Alpha training came into its own, not many people would know how to deal with a situation like this, but thankfully my years of studying and watching my dad deal with similar situations helped me know what to do next.

I walked over to the map on the dining room table without another word and took in what I could see. The map was of the general area, not just our territory but also the territories surrounding us. There were a lot of X's and circled areas covering the black and white piece of paper, but apart from that there wasn't much else. "What do we have?"

"Well we knew they were heading in this direction when they left the pack in the early hours of this morning," one of my warriors explained as he pointed towards the south side of our territory. "The last update we had was ten thirty this morning telling us that they had witnessed suspicious activity and that they were going to investigate further. If they were travelling at their usual speed, then they would have only been able to get as far as this area here at the time of their last check in."

I nodded my understanding before I took a pen and started crossing sections off. "I know my brother and I know that he would not enter any pack territory without permission from their Alpha. As I haven't gotten a call from anyone, we can rule out these areas here," I muttered as I crossed out all of the known pack territories in the area.

"That would mean they could only have gotten as far as this area here." I circled the area where I believed my brother and our trackers could have possibly been, but as I was starting to form a plan in my head my sister suddenly screamed my name from the stairs in alarm.

I dropped the pen and sprinted over to a panicked Hannah to find Annabelle, passed out in her arms.

Chapter 19

Annabelle's POV

I woke up in a cold sweat with beads of perspiration dripping down my hairline and onto my forehead. I looked around in panic and found myself laying on a comfy bed, with my shoes missing and a duvet pulled up over my body and around my shoulders. I quickly kicked the suffocating duvet from my body, hoping it would help cool my adrenaline filled body and stop me from uncontrollably sweating, and sat up to take in my surroundings.

It was difficult as the room was dark due to the blackout blind being drawn, but as far as I could tell I was alone. How did I end up here? I don't remember going for a nap. The last thing I remember was walking through the front door to Jax's family home to find multiple pairs of eyes staring at me.

I slowly sat up and took everything in, I had no idea where I was but for some reason, I didn't feel panicked. Surely a normal person would feel some form of fear when waking up in an unknown room and having no knowledge of even getting there.

It was familiar somehow, well maybe not familiar in the sense that I knew where I was, but more in the sense that it smelled like Jax, it smelt of home.

The voice in my head made this weird purring sound when I mentioned the word *home* and it wasn't till after I thought through my words that I realised what I had just thought. *I had a home.* For the first time in twelve years, I felt like I belonged somewhere.

This was definitely a teenage boy's bedroom at one point. There were posters of cars and bands blue tacked and scattered across the four walls. An old TV sat in the corner of the room on a glass stand with piles of action movies and video games stacked neatly underneath with some form of games console resting next to them.

The walls were a dark blue colour, not unlike the colour on Jax's walls at the moment, with the floor covered in a fluffy cream carpet that had definitely seen better days. I twitched as I felt the urge to go and get the hoover to try and make the fabric fluffy again, but stopped myself when I reminded myself of where I was, or more accurately where I wasn't.

I may not be living in that house anymore and made to do all the housework and cook all the meals, but old habits die hard, especially habits that had been drilled into you since you were seven years old. I had found myself on multiple occasions resorting back to my old ways, getting up early and cleaning the place before Jax had even woken up before getting on with cooking breakfast for him.

He had told me over and over again that I didn't need to do any of that if I didn't want to, that it wasn't my job to do everything in the house. He said that I was now a Luna and if I didn't feel like cooking or cleaning that day he could always do it himself or we could order some food in. If I was being honest though I sometimes kind of liked doing it. It wasn't so much the task itself that I missed, I don't think anyone could miss cooking and cleaning for someone else, but it was more the routine and sense of purpose I'd feel after the job was done. It was a sense of normality in my life as everything else around me seemed to change at the drop of a hat. It soothed my anxiety and helped to ground me when my head wouldn't stop thinking.

Even though the whole room was clean and organised I could tell that it hadn't been lived in for a long time. It was something about the air, it smelled too stuffy and clean to have someone regularly using the space.

I quickly shook my head as I'd realised I had gotten distracted and rubbed my eyes with the heel of my hand, I needed to tell Jax what just happened.

I stuffed my feet into some slippers which were sitting by the side of the bed and gently pulled the door open, cautious of what I was going to find.

As I pulled the door open my view of the corridor was blocked by the back of a guy about the same build as Jax but a few inches shorter. I shrunk back slightly at the close proximity of the stranger and started to shield myself with the door slightly, just in case he wasn't the friendly type.

"Are you okay Luna?" I startled at the sound of his deep voice breaking the silence and looked up at him in confusion. For a second, I didn't know who he was talking to, I even had half a mind to look behind me to see if someone was there, before my brain finally caught up with me and I realised that he was talking to me. I was the Luna of this pack.

I nodded slowly, as I tried to brush back the flyaway that had stuck to my forehead due to the perspiration. The stranger had kind blue eyes as they looked down at me, not in a menacing way but with a look of respect. This small observation gave me the confidence I needed to nod and look up at him. It may not have been in the eye but any form of communication involving me not looking down at my feet was an improvement in my eyes.

"May you please take me to J-Jax please?" I stuttered, internally rolling my eyes at my overuse of the word please.

"Of course Luna," he nodded a swift and business-like nod before turning around and leading me down the hallway. The floors were covered in red floral rugs fringed with beige tassels and the walls were painted a calming off white colour with photo frames littering the surface. Some held drawings done by toddlers, their bright colours standing out against the plain background of the wall, whilst others framed faces of happy smiley people as they stared into the lens of the camera. Some faces I kind of recognised, child versions of Hannah with a bunch of other people surrounding her. I didn't have time to study them in depth though, the stranger in front was walking too fast for me to pause and I didn't want to stop in fear of looking nosey and getting lost.

The hallway ended at a set of spiral stairs which lead down and onto the ground floor of the property. I could hear multiple voices chatting not too far from me and I froze at the prospect of being in a busy room full of people I didn't know. What if, for some reason, they didn't know who I was and thought that I was trespassing? I'd already learnt from Xavier that trespassing on pack land without permission was punishable by death. What if these people killed me thinking that I was some kind of threat?

My brain spun out of control with scenarios on what could happen to me if I walked down there, each one more bizarre than the last. The logical side of me knew that no one here would hurt me, Jax had told me that himself, but the other part of me, the part ruled by fear and anxiety, couldn't help but spit out paranoid thoughts as I stood frozen on the top step.

The stranger looked back at me, confused as to why I had paused, but when he got a look at my fearful expression his eyes softened. "It's alright Luna, no one will harm you here" he reassured me, his voice low and soft so as not to draw attention to us. "I'll personally make sure of it."

I nodded my head slowly, pushing down the bubble of anxiety that was brewing in the pit of my stomach, and slowly made my way down the steps, one hand tightly gripped onto the banister and the other clenched at my side.

As we made our way down the stairs I could hear more and more voices, nearly all of which I didn't recognise. One stood out amongst the rest though, a voice that made my heart rate calm down in a matter of seconds and my rising anxiety to temporarily subside. Jax.

The stranger led me down the last few steps and it was then that I finally recognised where I was. I was still in Jax's parents' house and Jax was exactly where I last saw him, hunched over the dining room table and surrounded by people.

The man that led me down here cleared his throat, trying to gain the attention of the loud people in the room. "Alpha, our Luna is awake and requested to see you."

Jax's head snapped up at the stranger's words and upon seeing me quickly rounded the table and started to jog over to me, the others in the room getting out of his way so he could get to me quicker.

"What are you doing up! You should be back in bed and resting," he sighed as he took me into his arms. "You had me worried sick," he muttered as he kissed the top of my head, before bringing me into his chest.

My cheeks warmed at the audience we had but I quickly forgot about them as I thought about what I had originally come here to tell him. "Jax I had another one of those vision things," I muttered into his chest, "it's about your brother. I know where he is."

Jax's arms tensed around me for a second before he brought me out of his chest and held me at arm's length so that he could get a proper look at me.

"What did you see?" He asked, his eyes burning into mine with the need to know.

I cleared my throat and took a deep breath to steady myself before I looked up at him. "Well I only saw him, none of the others who were taken," I muttered as I played with my fingers in front of me, a nervous habit I couldn't seem to kick. "He was tied to a chair and had obviously been beaten badly. I tried to- to help him in some way but... he was out cold and unresponsive," I stuttered out.

I looked down at my fingers and I continued to fidget, not able to hold Jax's eyes anymore due to the look of pain I saw in them.

"What else did you see?" He asked, trying to keep his voice as level as he could so as not to scare me.

"Jax he…" I stuttered as I took in a shaky breath of air "I had been taken back to the cells where my Mother and Father are being kept. That's where I saw him," I explained. "Whoever kidnapped my parents all those years ago have now taken your brother and your friends," I whispered as the guilt I'd woken up with resurfaced. "I am so sorry Jax," I muttered. "If it wasn't for me being here none of this would have ever happened."

"Annabelle," he whispered as he lifted my chin up with his fingers so that I was looking into his eyes. "None of this is your fault okay? The only ones to blame here are the sick people who did this, do you understand me?" His voice was firm but soft all at once, wanting to make sure his point was made but also not raising his voice enough so that it would startle me.

I slowly nodded my head to show that I understood him and sighed as I let my shoulders drop. Releasing guilt wasn't easy, especially when I was so used to it being forced upon me when something hadn't even been my fault, but Jax was going through a lot at the moment and the last thing he needed was to deal with me feeling sorry for myself.

"He was alive when I found him, I'm sure of it," I said as I tried to ease his worries about his little brother's pain. "I tried to go to him, to check to see if he was breathing, but before I could try and wake him up and get him out of his restraints someone had found me there and h-held me down," I stuttered. Goosebumps rose on my arms at the memory of that man sneaking up behind me and pinning my arms to my sides, his breath fanning across my neck as he breathed my scent in.

"What! Why didn't you lead with that Annabelle? Are you alright?" Jax yelled as he suddenly started checking my arms and face for any form of injury, freezing when he saw the finger shaped bruises that were starting to appear on my upper arms. "I'm going to kill him," Jax roared as he started to pace in front of me. "I'll rip him apart with my bare hands for harming you."

I shivered at the tone of his voice and instinctively took a step back. I had never seen him so angry before and if I was being completely honest it was starting to frighten me.

The way he was yelling and the way he was pacing, it was similar to the way Damon used to react when he didn't get his way with something. He was a spoiled child who had never lifted a finger in his life thanks to me. That sort of upbringing had caused him to become impatient and entitled and when he didn't get something that he wanted, he'd need to find an outlet to release his frustrations. Unfortunately, I was usually the victim.

I looked at Jax as he continued to pace, watching his every move and making sure I was on full alert. He suddenly shifted his head towards me and took a step in my direction and I couldn't help but flinch as I took a step back. It was purely instinctual, I knew that Jax would never mean to hurt me, but it didn't change the fact that my body has certain reflexes I couldn't control. The look in his eyes was so similar to Damon's I couldn't help but be transported back to a time when I was with them.

At the sight of my fear the colour immediately drained from Jax's face, his eyes that were once glowing golden with the presence of his wolf had now faded back to their original brown colour. He was frozen on the spot, not knowing what to do or whether I'd freak out at his next move.

"A-Annabelle I... I'm sorry I didn't mean to-."

"I know," I cut him off, not wanting him to feel like this. He had done so much for me and the last thing I wanted was to make him second guess himself around me. I had to get over my fear and the only way to do that was to suck it up and act brave. Fake it till you make it.

"I just lost it at the thought of someone hurting you, I would never-."

"I know," I interrupted again and focused on slowing my heart rate down, hoping that it would help, both him in feeling better and me in calming my fear down. "You would never hurt me," I finished the sentence I knew he was going to say before taking a few steady steps in his direction.

He just nodded his head in agreement but otherwise remained still, not wanting to scare me again with any sudden movements.

I stood in front of him and smiled slightly, hoping I could get him to relax, but when he didn't I sighed and wrapped my arms around his waist and drew him close, copying what he usually did for me when I was feeling out of balance.

It took a few seconds but thankfully his brain kicked into gear again and responded by wrapping his arms around my shoulders in a bone crushing hug.

We stayed like that for several minutes, both of us calming the other down, before Jax finally felt comfortable enough to let me go and look at me. "I really am sorry Annabelle; I rarely lose my temper like that and you just unfortunately had to witness one of the few times that I do. I promise I will be more careful in the future."

I sighed and shook my head but decided to stay quiet on the matter. He really didn't need to walk on eggshells around me and I honestly didn't want him to. I had overreacted, majorly, but I made a promise to myself that in the future I would try to never react like that again, especially when it was Jax.

"So," I muttered, getting back on track.

"Oh hang on," Jax muttered before his eyes fogged over for a second. Next thing I knew there were people streaming into the dining room, taking up any nook and cranny they could find. When did they even leave? Jax must have mind linked them all I guess. Well at least they didn't have a front row seat to my brief meltdown.

"Sorry I want the others to hear what you have to say, you may continue," he encouraged as he smiled down at me.

I sighed before nodding my head, I definitely wasn't comfortable in a room full of this many people, but I had to get over it. For Will's sake and for the sake of my parents and the rest of Jax's friends.

"So... after I had been found and h-held down," I stuttered. "I was dragged into a room, away from your brother and forced to sit in a chair. They said they wanted to talk," I muttered as I offered them a small shrug. I felt really uncomfortable talking in front of this many people and I think Hannah, who was standing in the far corner of the room, could tell.

"Jax, why don't you get us to broadcast her through the pack mind link? That way Anna doesn't have to feel uncomfortable about talking to this many people she doesn't know but the information is still accessible to everyone?" Hannah suggested as she looked between me and her brother with raised eyebrows.

I smiled over at her, gratefully for her suggestion, before looking up at Jax to see what he thought of the idea.

He thought about it for a moment as he weighed up the pros and cons, before thankfully nodding his head. "Good idea Hannah, dad if you could stay as broadcaster and Hannah and mum for moral support that would be appreciated, everyone else is dismissed for the night, we will reconvene first thing tomorrow morning in the pack hall." There was no mistaking the authority in his tone and before I knew it everyone had quickly emptied out of the house leaving just me, Jax, Hannah, Jackson and Emily.

We all moved over and settled into the sofas, now that they were available, and I wrung my hands together in nervousness.

"It's okay little mate, I've got you," Jax stated as he took my hands in his to stop me fidgeting.

I nodded and took a deep breath before continuing. "It-it wasn't long before whoever we were waiting for turned up. I didn't know who he was, but by the way he spoke to everyone and how they reacted to him he seemed like a person in charge."

"It wasn't Alpha Parker?" Jackson questioned; a deep frown etched onto his face.

I shook my head "no it wasn't him, he did smell like him though," I shuddered as I thought about the smell of burning plastic and fake pine.

"Dad, does Alpha Parker have a possible brother we don't know about?" Jax questioned as he looked over my head at his dad who was misty eyed from relaying everything I'd said through the mind link. "Or maybe that was his Beta?"

"Not that I know of, but no one knows what goes on in that pack," he sighed with a shrug.

Jax's sigh was his only response as he squeezed his hands that were still encaging mine. "Go on little mate."

"Well there was a lot of uncomfortable staring between the two of us before he finally piped up about what he wanted from me and why I was there." I whispered, building up the courage to say the next line. "He umm... he said he was willing to release your brother, my parents and the rest of the pack members that were taken but only on one condition," I muttered. I couldn't look him in the eye, knowing I was about to see a furious Jax all over again at my next words.

"What does he want little mate?" Jax asked, torn between comforting me and pushing me to get the information that could save his pack members.

"He-he wants..." I stuttered as I withdrew my shaking hands from Jax's and held them tightly in my lap.

"It's okay Anna," Hannah tried to reassure me as she got up and sat on the arm of the sofa next to me. I noticed Jackson's eyes were no longer fogged over and I was instantly grateful that he wasn't broadcasting this part to the entire pack. The last thing I needed was for everyone to see me having another emotional breakdown, one of many it seemed today.

I smiled wobbly up at her and took a deep breath, steadying myself before I turned around and took Jax's hands back in mine. "He wants me, Jax. He said he would let everyone else go if I went to him willingly and freely. He said if I didn't, he would just kidnap more and more pack members until we complied with his wishes."

The room was silent for a moment, the only sound coming from the clock slowly ticking away on the opposite wall above the fireplace. It stayed like that for a good thirty seconds, I counted the ticks, before everyone started shouting and screaming all at once. No one knew what to do, on the one hand this was their brother and son that was currently in harm's way, but on the other hand it was their Luna. I mean I know which way I would sway in a heartbeat, but apparently for them it wasn't that easy.

"There is no way in hell I am letting you go anywhere *near* them Annabelle do you hear me? I am *not* letting you get taken by those animals and let them do goddess knows what to you." Jax ran his hands through his hair as he continued to scream profanities and pace across the living room floor. "We'll figure out another way to save the rest of the pack, *without* offering you as a sacrifice," he growled.

I stayed quiet, not wanting to give him any indication as to what was currently running through my mind, that I was strongly considering taking the strange smelling wolf up on his offer. I would do anything for my new pack and if this was the price I'd have to pay, then so be it.

I glanced next to me to find Hannah staring down at me with questioning eyes, looking as if she could read what was running through my head as her parents watched Jax carve a hole into the wooden floor. She knew what I was considering doing. I quickly shook my head and silently pleaded with her to stay quiet, not wanting to give anything away to Jax or the rest of her family.

She squinted her eyes at me in a warning glare, assessing my desperate look, before sagging slightly and nodding her head in understanding. I sighed and smiled gratefully at her before standing up and taking Jax's hands in mine to get his attention and to stop him pulling at his hair.

"Let's go home, we can talk more at the meeting tomorrow," I smiled up at him as I went into his open arms, hoping to ease his nerves and bring him back to a calmer state.

It had thankfully worked and before long we were back home and tucked up in bed with me safely folded up in Jax's strong arms.

"I won't let them get to you Annabelle," I heard Jax whisper into the darkness of our bedroom, his heart rate speeding up slightly as I kissed his bare chest.

"I know you won't," I whispered back as I evened out my breathing and pretended to fall asleep. Little did he know my brain was whirring away a mile a minute, weighing up all my options that were laid out in front of me. On the one hand I could do what Jax says, stay here safe and sound whilst I let other innocent people go and fight my battles for me, or I could face my fear and deal with my issues head on.

The guy in my dream vision thing had given me a time and a place for when I *'inevitably hand myself in'* as he put it. He said I'd have twenty-four hours to decide and if I decided *not* to show then he would take a number of people from our pack and kill them and that the pattern would continue until I gave myself up.

I had seen the place the kidnapped pack members were being held first-hand, seen the filth that my parents had been left in as they sat with their wrists and ankles shackled to a nearby stone wall, bound with silver. I could smell their flesh burning as their skin touched the metal, their bodies not being able to heal quick enough for the burns and welts to completely heal over leaving their skin raw and open to the elements.

How could I possibly allow my pack members, whom I am supposed to protect, endanger their lives in order to give us another measly twenty-four hours to try and figure out what to do? It would just be wrong of me to sit back and allow them to be taken from their homes when the only reason this person was interested in our pack in the first place was because of me. It was always because of me.

Guilt seeped into my soul as I looked up at Jax, who had fallen fast asleep whilst I had been weighing up the pros and cons in my head. To me there was only one clear answer. There was no way I was going to let innocent people die because of me, and with that in mind I formed a plan. If the meeting tomorrow came up completely empty handed and no one could think of a logical plan on what to do next, then I was going to meet this mystery man and hand myself in.

I sighed and looked back at Jax, taking him all in. For all I knew, this could be the last time I get to see him sleep.

Chapter 20

Jax's POV

I was standing on the stage in front of most of my pack as I watched them argue with each other over what they thought would be the best plan of action. Some were saying to go to the elders and let them deal with Will's kidnapping and leave us out of it whilst others were saying to go in guns blazing and grab them.

Everyone was avoiding the elephant in the room, the fact that everything could be solved if we gave up our Luna, but there was no way that I was going to let that happen. She was my mate and the packs Luna, if she were to be taken... I shuddered to think how I'd react.

I signed as I took in my arguing pack members, yelling over each other and not allowing the other to speak, this was getting us nowhere.

"SILENCE!" I bellowed, getting the attention of every individual in the hall. "There is no use in us all arguing. Myself, our Luna and Beta Xavier will take your suggestions under consideration but the main reason I called you all here today was to keep you all in the loop about what was going on and to give you a chance to have any of your questions answered.

"Now, does anyone else have any pressing questions before we terminate this meeting?" I was met with silence, a clear indication that no one had anything further to ask regarding the matter at hand. They all knew what had happened to Annabelle whilst she was in her dream walk. I left it a few more seconds before announcing that the meeting was adjourned and that everyone was free to leave.

I sighed as I watched the last few people leave the room as I turned to find Annabelle watching me with curious eyes. I walked over and took her into my arms, needing the comfort of my mate after such a stressful morning.

"Are you okay?" She whispered, her voice slightly muffled by the fabric of my T-shirt.

I nodded before kissing her on the head and releasing her "yeah I'm okay, just stressed."

"Don't worry, it will all work itself out soon," she reassured me.

I smiled, basking in the confidence she had in me as I tightened my arms around her. "I know it will, I'll inform the elders as soon as we're home to get the ball rolling on the rescue plan. It's just whether we decide to organise an attack of our own before they get here, seeing as they like to drag these things out sometimes."

"I don't think that's what she meant Jax," Xavier stated as he stood up from his seat on the stage. I looked over at him, confused to find him staring at Annabelle with a frown on his face.

I looked down at Annabelle, trying to figure out what he had seen that I had missed, but she had buried herself back into my chest, hiding her face from me. "What does he mean Annabelle?" I asked, but when she didn't answer I extracted her from her hiding place and held her at arm's length. She looked guilty for some reason and wouldn't look me in the eye, what was running through that head of hers?

"You can't do it," Xavier continued, talking directly to Annabelle and ignoring us "Jax wouldn't survive it."

"I wouldn't survive *what*?" I demanded, feeling frustrated at being kept out of the loop.

Xavier stayed quiet as he continued to stare at her. She was now looking right back at Xavier with an almost pleading look in her eye, begging him to keep his mouth shut. "What the *hell* are you two talking about!"

When Xavier saw that Annabelle wasn't going to say anything he sighed and met my eyes. "She's thinking about taking the offer they gave her. Her in exchange for the rest of the pack" he explained, disappointment clear in his voice.

I stayed silent for a moment, not knowing how to respond. She couldn't be that dumb, could she? But one look at her guilty expression told me otherwise.

"YOU WHAT!" I exclaimed, the echo bouncing off the empty pack hall walls. "There is no way in *hell* I am allowing you to willingly give yourself up to those monsters, do you hear me Annabelle? No way." I let go of her shoulders and started pacing around the stage area, needing to move to try and release the anger and adrenaline that was surging through me. How could she do this?

Annabelle sighed and took my hand into hers, halting me in my tracks. "It's for the best Jax, this way no one will get hurt because of me. These... people... will not only let your brother and the rest of the pack members they kidnapped go, but also my parents. It's the least I could do after they have suffered for so long," she explained, a pained note in her voice.

"No. No, no, no I am not letting you serve yourself up to them and that is the end of this conversation. Now if you all will excuse me, I need to go and inform the elders of the developments," I ground out, trying my best to keep my tone in check.

Annabelle reached out to me, presumably in the hopes to calm me down and hear her out, but I just brushed her off and stormed outside. There was no way I was going to let her serve herself up on a golden platter to these… *people.* There had to be some other way to save my brother and the rest of my pack without handing over my lifeline. There just had to be, and I was going to find it.

After all it was my fault they'd gotten caught in the first place, sending them out into the territories of potentially very dangerous wolves without backup or a clear plan of what to do if something went wrong. I was a terrible Alpha, blinded by the needs of my mate over the needs of my pack.

"You okay there son?" My dad asked as he appeared behind me.

I laughed at his question. "Do I look alright to you? I have pack members and a brother missing on one hand and a mate who is so willing to give herself up she's willing to risk *everything* that we have built on the other. I am *far* from okay."

"Well for now let's just focus on one thing at a time. Your mate is perfectly safe, we are all keeping an eye on her, so just take a breath and focus on getting your brother back. We'll call the elders and inform them of the situation we're currently in and then you can talk to some of the pack warriors and get a plan together. We know their rough location thanks to the map so we'll just sweep those areas until we find something," he reassured me. "Also remember what the doctor told you about Annabelle, she feels an extreme amount of guilt for things that aren't even her fault, I can only imagine how something like this is making her feel. It'll all work out, we just need to give her time to sort through her emotions."

I sighed, nodding my head in understanding. I really needed to learn to keep my head in a stressful situation if I ever wanted to become half as good an Alpha as my father had been. "Thank you dad, I really appreciate your experience and level headedness in all this."

Dad smiled and clapped me on the back. "No problem, now let's get back to your mate before she starts to worry about you."

I smiled and nodded as we walked back into the main hall where I found Annabelle sitting on a vacant bench, fiddling with her fingers, and jittering her legs. As soon as she saw me, she released a small sigh before getting up and walking over to me, relieved that I had come back.

I took her in my arms and placed my nose against the side of her head, hoping her scent would aid in calming both myself and my wolf down. If I wanted to come up with a reasonable plan of action, I'd have to learn to remain calm and collected under pressure.

"So what now?" She whispered into my chest as she questioned our next move. "We're going to have to come up with something fast if we want to stop more people from getting taken."

"That's assuming they'll even get that far," I said as I smiled into her hair. "They've now told us what their plan is, all we have to do is make sure everyone stays in lockdown and away from the borders of the territory. If we do this then this mystery guy will have no hope in getting their hands of more leverage." I explained.

Annabelle just nodded into my chest again but otherwise remained silent.

We stood like that for a few more minutes, each using the other to calm ourselves down and try to think of a solution on how to rescue Will and the four trackers that had been taken with him.

"Why don't we all go back to our house," my mum suggested as she smiled at us, "I'll make us all some lunch whilst you lot contact the elders and think of a way to get everyone back safe."

I looked down at Annabelle to make sure that she was up for more socialising and when I was greeted with a small smile and a nod I looked up at my mum and nodded. "Sure mum, that would be great," I replied as I took Annabelle's hand in mine and led her towards the exit.

"I apologise Alpha Jax, but you know we don't assist in these types of scenarios," Elder Bruella explained. We had been on speaker phone with the Elder circle for more than half an hour now and I still couldn't convince them to come down and assist us in our rescue mission.

"But Sir, they have five of my pack members held hostage, one of them being my brother, and are threatening to kidnap many more if we don't comply with their demands," I explained again for the millionth time, getting frustrated at their lack of cooperation.

"Alpha Jax, with all due respect to you and your family, why can't you just figure this one out on your own? Our records show that you are by no means vulnerable and defenceless, in fact as packs go you are one of the most skilled packs out there, so why do you need us to try and sort something out that you can't deal with yourself?"

I scowled at the condescending tone in Elder Bruella's voice but otherwise didn't comment on it. Disrespecting an Elder was a one-way ticket to their dungeons, a place where even the devil would fear.

"Please Sir, as previously stated, I wish not to disclose information as to why they are waging war on my pack or about why I'd prefer not to get my pack involved with these people," I explained. I ran a hand down my face and looked over at Annabelle who was sitting on the sofa in my dad's office, her knees drawn up to her chest and her chin resting on her jean covered knee's. I needed to protect her at all costs and if that meant keeping her a secret from even the Elders I would do so in a heartbeat.

"Then I'm sorry Alpha Jax, without a logical reason as to why you need the Elders involvement, I'm going to have to deny your request and-."

"It's because of me," Annabelle suddenly piped up as she raised her head from her knees. "These people are threatening Jax's pack because of me and what I am."

I looked over at her with wide eyes, silently signalling for her to stop talking. If the Elders found out about her there was no telling what they'd do with her.

"And to whom am I now speaking?" Elder Bruella questioned through the speaker. I could literally picture his wrinkled face pinched with raised eyebrows, unamused at Annabelle having interrupted him.

"My name is Annabelle Sir, I am Jax's mate and the reason the Rising Dawn pack are after us," she explained. She slowly uncurled herself and stood up, making her way over to stand next to me so that her voice was closer to the speaker.

I raised my eyebrows at her and silently asked her what she was doing, but she just ignored me as she focused on the phone. I looked over at my Dad and Hannah, looking for some kind of back up, but I was just met with shrugs as they too stared at her in confusion.

It wasn't that the Elder community was crooked in some way, or that I was worried they were going to come and steal my mate from me because of what she was. I was more concerned with the information potentially being leaked in the future. It only took one person overhearing a conversation they shouldn't be privy to, or someone misplacing a piece of paper and it falling into the wrong hands, that could make Annabelle's identity known and her life in danger.

"And why would they be after you Luna Annabelle?" Bruella asked, slight intrigue clear in his voice.

"It's because of what I am, of what I can do," she sighed as she looked up at me, smiling slightly to show that she was okay with disclosing the information to them, even though she barely knew them.

Well if she was alright with it then so was I, she was just as much in charge of this pack as I was and she had every right to make decisions about what we did and how we would go about it.

"And *what* are you, may I ask, that makes you so valuable to the Alpha of the Rising Dawn pack?" Elder Bruella asked.

"I-I'm a messenger to the Moon Goddess," she whispered as she clasped her hands together in front of her, a habit I've noticed she does when she's feeling awkward or nervous and trying not to fidget.

The line went silent for a moment before we heard yelling in the background, it seems that we had also been on speaker phone and the rest of the Elder's council had heard what Annabelle had just admitted.

"Luna Annabelle, we know for a fact that the messenger lineage had ended more than ten years ago with the tragic death of Jane and Samuel Miller. To impersonate a messenger is grounds for execution which we will not hesitate to enforce no matter what your rank is."

I growled at Elder Bruella's threat, but Annabelle just placed her hand on my chest to try and calm me down as she continued to look at the phone on my father's desk.

"Sir Jane is my mother and Samuel is my father," she explained as she continued to stare down at the phone "and they aren't dead. I have recently learnt that they were kidnapped and have been held hostage by Alpha Parker all this time for the use of my mother's powers and her connection to the Goddess. Her connection has now been severed however and has been passed down to me, they are using my family and pack as a bargaining chip to get to me and regain the power they have now lost with my mother."

Her voice was calm and unwavering as she spoke to Elder Bruella and the rest of the elder's council and I almost burst with pride at the power she held in her voice. She will make an excellent Luna, calm and insightful, but also fierce and protective when needed.

The line was silent for a moment, the only noise being a soft murmur as the council deliberated their options quietly so that we couldn't hear them.

"We will be there in two days' time," Elder Bruella informed us before hanging up the phone, causing the dial tone to ring out through the speaker system.

The four of us sat there in silence for a moment as we digested everything. The Elders now knew about Annabelle's identity, but what was more shocking than that was the fact that they knew about her parents and what her mother was capable of. That information alone gave me a small sense of confidence in the Elders, if they had known about the messenger bloodline and hadn't acted on it in any way then I was fairly confident that the identity of Annabelle and her whereabouts wouldn't be misplaced and that she was safe.

"Well that was fun," Hannah sighed as she pushed herself off from the back of the sofa. "Now all we have to do is make sure we survive the next forty-eight hours until they arrive and we'll be home safe" she muttered sarcastically whilst she crossed her arms and rolled her eyes, her bracelets jingling as she did so. "I mean do the Elders seriously expect us to just sit here, twiddling our thumbs, until they arrive to save the day? I mean I don't know about you, but I don't feel particularly comfortable doing nothing, especially with Will still out there with them doing god knows what to him."

I looked over at Hannah as she tapped her foot on the floor, staring at me expectantly, waiting to hear my plan.

"For now Hannah that's exactly what we're going to do." I sighed as I looked down at my mate who was still standing by my side. "Until we can think of a better plan of action we are going to wait them out and call their bluff."

"You can't be serious!" Hannah exclaimed as she looked at me in bewilderment, her arms flailing wildly around.

"Yes Hannah I am being deadly serious. Will would not want us risking our lives to try and save him because we were too impatient to wait for backup. I hate the plan as much as you do, believe me, but my hands are tied here," I sighed, feeling the weight of the pack on my shoulders.

"But Jax-."

"We have no *choice* Hannah!" I yelled back, "we know nothing about the Rising Dawn pack or what they are capable of, I'd be an irresponsible Alpha to run into their pack lands without knowing what we are up against."

The air deflated out of Hannah as I watched her shoulders drop and the fight leave her body. "Then what are we going to do?"

"I don't know," I shrugged, "but between us we can think of something."

...

We deliberated up until the early hours of the morning, all of us huddled round the coffee table in the living room with a map of the area spread across it. We had come up with a few options on what we could theoretically do, but none of them were particularly great. They all involved potential *what ifs* scenarios that were just too risky for us to take.

Annabelle was all for giving herself up as bait so that we could somehow sneak in, but I just couldn't risk it. We didn't know what these people wanted with her, not really, and I wasn't about to risk her life or anyone else's on a guess that they wouldn't kill her.

The sobering news came just before we were about to break for breakfast and go for a short nap. I had gotten a mind link that our patrol had caught a suspicious scent close to the border and were waiting for their orders to engage.

Without hesitation the five of us dropped what we were doing and ran as fast as we could, making sure the pack warriors were being cautious and alert for any form of suspicious activity whilst they waited for our arrival.

When we arrived I caught the offending scent quickly, the smell of fake pine leaves and burnt plastic was pretty hard to ignore as we all followed the trail to see where it led. All pack members had been warned to stay indoors with their doors bolted and to not answer for anyone unless contacted through the pack link. The last thing we needed right now was for more pack members to be taken from right under our noses and used to further their leverage on us.

"You stay behind me at all times Annabelle, understand?" I warned her as we slowed our run to a brisk walk so as not to miss anything along the trail. Their people could have left anything whilst being on our land, it was important to stay vigilant and to not let our guard down.

"I know Jax," she whispered back as she gripped onto my hand tightly, doing as she promised and staying a step behind me the whole time.

I was just about to respond when I caught a scent that made my stomach drop and my brain to freeze. Blood, dried blood.

"Stay here with the others," I instructed her with a noticeable hard note to my tone of voice as I let go of her hand and walked towards it. Whatever was up ahead, I didn't want her to see it.

"Jax what is it?" She questioned as she took a small step in my direction.

"Please little mate, just stay where you are," I pleaded as I took slow, cautious steps to where the strong smell of blood was coming from.

I could sense a few of my warriors walking behind me, ready to back me up if this was some form of trap. Blood meant bodies and I couldn't help but feel immense guilt as I took the remaining few steps forward until I came face to face with the dead body who had been causing the smell.

He had been a member of our pack, a tracker, who was in the scout hunt with Will when they had been kidnapped by the Rising Dawn pack.

I felt immense sadness as I continued to stare down at the lifeless body, his throat slashed open and covered with blood. If I had worked faster, harder, better, than maybe this wouldn't have happened. I could have potentially saved his life if I had only gotten my head in the game.

"You can't blame yourself son," my dad muttered as he came and stood next to me. "You did everything you could, that's all anyone could ever ask of you," he sighed.

"But I could have prevented this," I ground out; my eyes unwavering as I stared at the poor wolf at my feet.

"You couldn't have prevented this anymore than the next person Jax, deep down you know that" he sighed, trying to make me feel better. "This was no one's fault but the person who dealt the final blow."

"Jax what's going- oh my god!" Annabelle exclaimed as she appeared next to me.

I looked up in shock to find her standing right beside me, her wide eyes glued onto the dead body in front of her with her hands covering her mouth. "What h-happened to him?" She exclaimed as she continued to look him over.

I quickly stepped in her way before she could see anymore and forced her backwards slightly so that she was further away and no longer able to see him. "Annabelle, I need you to look away okay? Just look at me and not behind me," I instructed her as I quickly linked Xavier so he could get down here and help me deal with the situation.

"Is he..?" She muttered, looking up into my eyes as she stuttered out a question I knew she didn't want to ask, her eyes glazing over with tears as she tried to hold herself back from crying.

I sighed before nodding my head and taking her into my arms, "It's going to be alright Annabelle, everything is going to be okay," I muttered. I just wished I believed my own words.

Chapter 21

Annabelle's POV

I hadn't uttered a single word since we'd gotten back. I just couldn't help but replay what I'd just seen over and over again until my head spun. That poor person had died because of me, because I was too stubborn and selfish to give myself up. I mean, I didn't even know the man's name, yet he had died because of the cowardly decisions that I had made.

I wasn't the only one who hadn't said much since finding out about the dead body, we had all been pretty quiet for the rest of the day up until everyone decided to leave and head back to their respective homes. The news had hit everyone hard, especially Jax and his family. That could have easily been Will lying motionless and cold on the forest floor and I shuddered to think about what that would do to them if it had been.

Jax had been on and off the phone all day, trying to rally allies so that we could have the numbers to comfortably form an attack on Alpha Parker, but so far no one was biting. It seemed no one wanted to get involved in an issue that didn't involve them. It's not like we could blame them though, I don't think there were many people out there who would willingly put their lives on the line for someone that wasn't from their family or pack.

I had been thinking about my options all afternoon as I sat quietly on the sofa, cuddled up under a blanket with a glass of water and some potato and leek soup in my lap. I had promised myself that I would wait until it was the last resort before giving myself over to them, that I would only sacrifice myself if I couldn't see any other way of everyone getting out of this alive.

Now someone has *died* because of that promise I'd made.

Yes Jax had the Elders coming and he was currently trying everything he could to rally the surrounding packs for assistance, but for me it just wasn't enough. The Elders weren't coming for at least another thirty-six hours and even when they did finally arrive there was nothing set about what we'd be doing once they got here. For all we knew they'd take even longer to form a plan and for Will and the other three trackers who were still being held hostage, that wasn't good enough.

I only had one clear option, one that would save the rest of the pack and keep those four wolves safe, not to mention my parents. I had to turn myself in. I just had to.

The more I thought about that dead body, lying motionless in the dirt and covered in dried blood, the more my stomach churned and my vision blurred. His blood was on my hands because I had been too much of a coward to give myself up. Well not anymore.

With a deep breath to help calm my racing heart I placed the untouched bowl of steaming soup on the coffee table and flicked the blanket from off my shoulders. I was already wearing something suitable to run in, just a pair of leggings and one of Jax's hoodies, but I still needed to sneak on a pair of trainers and get out of the house without raising suspicions.

Jax was in the kitchen, using the island as a makeshift office desk so that he wouldn't have to go upstairs to his office and stray too far from me. I also knew that Xavier was outside somewhere patrolling the house, making sure that we were protected just in case the Rising Dawn pack decided to try and take me right from under Jax's nose. If I could make it past the two of them then I was safe.

As silent as I could I tip-toed towards the shoe rack by the front door and grabbed the first pair of shoes I could find before hiding them behind my back and walked over towards the kitchen where I could hear Jax mumbling down the phone to someone.

"I'm just going to the toilet," I whispered to him, hoping he wouldn't look up from the numerous papers he had littered across the countertop. I knew if he took one look at my expression, he'd know what I was up to.

Thankfully Jax's only response was a quick head nod in my direction as he continued to mutter down the phone, too quiet for me to hear as he sifted through the seemingly unorganised mess in front of him.

I sighed in relief as I realised he wasn't going to look up at me and backed my way out of the kitchen entrance and down the small corridor until I made it to the bathroom. Once inside I quickly slipped my trainers on my bare feet before locking the door and turning around so that I was facing the bathroom window. It wasn't particularly big, meaning squeezing through the small opening was a slight challenge, even for my small frame.

Thankfully though it wasn't long before I was out on the other side of the glass and hiding in a shrub planted in the surrounding flower beds, keeping my eyes and ears open for Xavier.

When I was sure he wasn't near, I burst through the bush and ran as fast as I could towards the meeting place where the stranger had told me to go.

I panted as I willed my legs to carry me further, further from my mate and further from my new home as I made my way into the forest and towards my potential ending. A tear escaped my lash line as I thought about what I was leaving behind but I quickly swept it away angrily, I had no time to feel sorry for myself, I had a mission I had to focus on.

After a few minutes of sprinting, I leant against a nearby tree as I doubled over from the stitch that was currently stabbing my side. Even though I was a lot stronger than when I had first escaped the Leftens, I still wasn't completely healed. My muscles were screaming at me to take a break, to rest so that they could get the oxygen they desperately needed, but my mind was telling me I didn't have time, Jax would have found out that I was gone by now and sent a search party out to look for me.

I took one last deep breath before I straightened back up and carried on towards the meeting point. I don't know how I knew where I was going, I hadn't gone this far out of Jax's territory since I got here, but somehow I just knew I was heading in the right direction, as if someone or something was leading me there. It was like a golden line had been drawn on the grass, stretching out in front of me and all I had to do was follow it.

All of a sudden, I heard a twig snap behind me and I froze in my tracks, had Jax and the pack found me already? Or was this Alpha Parker's pack following me and making sure I went through with the exchange and that I had come alone?

I got my answer when I saw a faint figure sprinting after me in the distance, quickly recognising it to be Xavier as he ran after me at full speed. He had found me.

I cursed in my head before turning and putting all the reserved energy I had into making my legs go faster, as much as my newfound wolf hated the idea of leaving our mate, she agreed with my decision to save our pack and so helped me as my feet pounded against the ground faster and harder. Her Luna instincts had fully kicked in and she wanted to do everything she possibly could to protect her pack.

"Annabelle!" Xavier yelled behind me, willing me to stop, but I ignored him and carried on going.

"Annabelle please... think about this for a second, this is not a solution!" He sounded closer than he had been earlier and I cursed at his speed. Thankfully though he wasn't fast enough because before I knew it, I had reached my destination. The scent surrounding the scene made it obvious more than anything, the smell of Alpha Parker's aftershave, of fake pine needles and melted plastic, was everywhere.

The meeting point was a little clearing in the trees, wildflowers scattered across the grass offering flecks of colour against the bright green grass. This place was right outside Jax's pack territory, so close to the border that if I'd have taken five steps backwards, I would be re-entering his land. If it wasn't for the current situation I was in, I'd probably admire the beauty of this place, the pureness of it as I watched the blades of grass dance in the wind as they shifted colours in the sunlight.

I turned around to see Xavier skid to a stop in front of me, panting just as much as I was at the physical activity we'd just put ourselves through. "Annabelle you don't need to do this, there's always another way that doesn't involve self-sacrifice" he pleaded.

I shook my head and placed my hand on top of his as he tried to drag me back to the pack lands. "It's too late Xavier, I have made up my mind and I choose to live whatever short life I have left guilt free with Alpha Parker. I'd rather that then live a long life with Jax where the guilt of hurting all those people will eventually crush me. I can't live like that... please... just let me go."

He shook his head "it's not that simple Annabelle, as Jax's best friend and Beta of this pack it is my duty and responsibility to protect both him and you."

I looked into his eyes to see fierce determination in them, swirling around with the gold of his wolf as he fought to keep his control. The slight glazed look in his irises told me he was talking to the rest of the pack and if Alpha Parker didn't turn up soon, I'd fear he'd be too late. This was my one and only shot to buy Jax enough time to save everyone. All I had to do was keep Parker busy long enough for Jax to form an attack.

"Xavier, if I can get Jax just a bit more time, until the Elders get here, then maybe we stand a fighting chance against them," I pleaded with him, trying to get him to understand why I was doing this. "Jax needs time to come up with a plan and save everyone, if I have to give myself up, even just for a little while, then I'm going to do it," I stated.

"But what if he doesn't get you out of there in time? What if Alpha Parker kills you before we can get you out?" Xavier questioned, seeing the obvious flaw in my not so full proof plan.

I shrugged, not having an answer to his question, "then at least I can die knowing I did everything in my power to save everyone."

Before Xavier could protest any further a horrible, artificial smell of fake pine and burnt plastic entered the small clearing, Alpha Parker was close by. We both straightened our backs and turned to see him slowly emerge from the other side of the clearing, an amused smirk plastered on his face as he glanced briefly over at Xavier.

"Ahh Annabelle you finally decided to show up, a very brave and smart decision I must say," he sneered as he looked me up and down. "You seem to have brought an escort though... that wasn't part of the deal little prophet."

I stared at him, not knowing what to say... the mere sight of him freezing me in place. His face brings me back to the day when I first saw him, back to when I was only seven years old, when he was dressed in a police officer's uniform and taking me away from my home. He had destroyed my life all those years ago and now he was about to do the same thing all over again.

"She is not going anywhere," Xavier growled as he took a few steps forward until he was in-front of me, blocking my path to Alpha Parker.

Alpha Parker just laughed at him and crossed his arms, not the least bit concerned with the fact that an angry Beta was currently staring him down, ready to fight.

"Is that so little Beta? Or do you prefer *Rogue Killer*? I've heard a few of my men refer to you as that, although if you ask me, I don't see what all the hype is about," he laughed with a shrug.

I frowned as I looked over at Xavier, hoping to find some form of explanation as to why he would be called that. I got nothing though as Xavier continued to stare down the Alpha in front of us.

Alpha Parker suddenly laughed as he continued his staring contest with Xavier, amusement shining in his eyes. "Enlighten me then, how are you going to achieve getting the both of you out of here when you're so outnumbered?"

I frowned at his words, only seeing him in the clearing, but that soon changed as at least twenty men and women slowly emerged from the shadows, each looking as menacing as the next and all wearing the same stomach churning perfume as Alpha Parker.

My heart rate picked up as I held onto Xavier's arm, the last thing I wanted was for him to get hurt, that was not part of my plan.

"Xavier please just go... I don't want to be the reason for you to get hurt too," I pleaded in his ear. He just shook my arm off him and continued to stare Alpha Parker down, not listening to me and my pleading in the slightest.

Just then we heard a howl in the distance, piercing the silence that had settled around us, and I knew it was Jax and the pack coming for us. They had caught our scent and were making their way over.

Xavier smirked as we saw Alpha Parker's calm demeanour crack slightly, obviously aware of the angry Alpha and his pack that were slowly but surely advancing on us with every second that passed.

"Times up Parker," Xavier growled.

"Nothing's over until I say it is," Alpha Parker growled and before I could bat an eyelid Alpha Parker's pack descended on us. There was little either of us could do being so outnumbered and before I could even think about trying to defend myself, a guy made his way over to me and punched me in the temple, knocking me out cold.

...

The first thing I noticed when I woke up was the smell, the smell of damp and rust. It was the type of stench that I would recognise anywhere and tell me exactly where I was. I knew, without even opening my eyes, that we were in the underground cells where I'd had my dreams and where Will and my family were being held.

I groaned as my body slowly awoke, becoming more aware of itself and how sore it was. I reached my hand up to touch a particular tender spot on my temple but flinched as I felt a burning sensation around my wrist. I looked down at myself and in the little light that the small window offered I saw a pair of silver cuffs attached to my wrists and my ankles, keeping me pretty much motionless in my spot on the cold damp floor as they attached me to the wall I was leaning against.

"Are you alright Annabelle?" I heard a whisper not too far from me. I shot up in alarm at the sudden voice in the quiet room, fearing who could be in here with me, but calmed down when I found it to be Xavier lying next to me, bloodied and bruised.

I sighed and took a mental check of my body before nodding and looking over to him. "I'm fine, nothing I haven't dealt with before," I groaned as I shifted slightly. "Do you know where we are?"

Xavier nodded next to me, but he didn't look happy about it, if anything he looked semi defeated as he lay against the stone wall.

"That bad hu?"

He sighed and looked down into his lap with a shrug "I don't know what to tell you Annabelle, we're slap bang in the middle of Alpha Parker's territory in an underground bunker. Even if Jax and the others could find us, they're going to have a hard time getting through the pack to get here," he sighed before his face contorted in pain as he tried to reposition himself again.

I sighed and rested my head back against the cold stone wall that was currently keeping me upright. "Could you mind link the pack maybe? Tell Jax where we are and see if there's anything he can do?" Why had I not taken those mind-linking lessons more seriously yesterday?

"I can't, we're bound in silver. The pain my wolf is going through right now means he is in no fit state to try and reach out to anybody, let alone someone so far away. I'm sorry Annabelle," he sighed as he closed his eyes in regret.

I nodded my head in understanding but instantly stopped when I felt my temple throb painfully with the movement. "It's alright, it was worth a shot, I mean I asked for this right?" I chuckled as I looked over at him, "don't worry, we just have to hold out long enough for Jax to get here."

Before Xavier could respond the door to our cell opened and bright artificial light streamed into the room causing us both to wince in pain. My head hurt before, but with the added blinding light it was almost unbearable.

"Ahh you're awake, good. I was wondering if maybe my guy had hit you in the head a bit too hard and killed you or something," a voice laughed, the owner silhouetted by the blinding light of the outdoor hallway.

I knew that voice.

As my eyes slowly adjusted to the blue white light, I started to make out a lone figure standing in-front of the doorway. It was too bright for me to catch any key features, just his height and build as he remained a shadow in the light of the hallway.

"Who are you? Where's Alpha Parker?" Xavier growled as he tried but failed to get in front of me, the restraints around his ankles and wrists preventing him from getting anywhere close to me.

"Alpha Parker is currently... indisposed at the moment, so you lucky bunch get me instead," the guy laughed.

I frowned at him, there was definitely something familiar about him. "You smell like Alpha Parker," I whispered cautiously as I continued to observe him. I hadn't realised I had said it aloud until I felt his eyes shift to mine, almost glowing in the darkness.

"Why yes I do," the stranger grinned at me, but it was far from comforting. "You see, we believe that the Moon Goddess didn't create mates to make us whole, she did it to make us *weak*. She saw that we were becoming more powerful than anything, more powerful than her herself, and so created the mate bond to tame us and make us vulnerable. Without our natural scent, we are undetectable and so our mates will never recognise us."

The stranger sounded happy, smug even, as he explained how he had found a way to block the mate bond.

I looked at him in shock, "why wouldn't you want to experience something as amazing as the mate bond? I didn't even know what it was two weeks ago and now I can't imagine my life without it."

"Exactly," the stranger stated as he leaned against the door frame, completely at ease with the situation around him. "Because of your mate bond you are now linked to that stupid Alpha of yours for the rest of your life. If you were mateless you would have had no reason to give yourself over to us, but because of him your Luna instincts kicked in and you just *had* to save your pack. It was inevitable really, no Luna can sit on the side-lines whilst her pack was in danger," he chuckled sarcastically.

I scowled and leaned towards him, ignoring the bite in my wrists as my skin reacted to the silver shackles. "Let me make one thing very clear," I growled, "even if I *wasn't* mated to Jax, or mated to anybody in my pack, I would've still made the same decision. I would still choose saving them over saving myself *any* day."

The stranger smirked "it seems like someone's grown a backbone since leaving the Leftens".

My blood instantly ran cold at the mention of their names and I subconsciously shrunk back in on myself. He knew the Leftens. He knew Damon. He knew Tony. He knew Natalie.

The strangers smirk grew, as if knowing that just the mere mention of their name was enough to have an effect on me.

"They're going to be *so* happy that we found you, they have been worried sick ever since you ran away," he laughed. "Don't worry though, they said they have a *massive* surprise for you when they finally manage to get you back."

My heart began to race and my palms started to sweat. I couldn't go back there, not after knowing what it was like to not wake up every morning in fear of what the day would bring.

The stranger took a step closer to me but before I had any time to react, Xavier let out an almighty roar and launched for the stranger's throat, unconcerned with the burning of his skin as I heard it almost sizzle under the strain of the silver.

"You stay away from her," he growled as his teeth started to extend out from his gum line.

The stranger only smirked, unconcerned with the angry Beta that was only a few feet away from him, tied up, with just a few links of silver keeping them apart.

The reminder that Xavier was here with me gave me a little strength. It reminded me that I was now a werewolf and a Luna, and no one could take that away from me.

"Xavier enough," I yelled, replicating how Jax always sounded when he yelled at someone. I needed to buy Jax enough time to get a plan together and get my people out of here. If that meant playing this guy's mind games, then so be it.

Xavier visibly calmed down at my words and the stranger turned away from him and looked at me. "Not bad for an inexperienced Luna, not bad at all," he chuckled.

I ignored what he said and looked him square in the eye, showing no sign of weakness. I needed to get this done.

"Let him go, let them all go, and then I will do whatever you want."

The stranger suddenly laughed and stared down at me in amusement. "Okay now you're showing your inexperience," he chuckled.

I didn't break eye contact with him, but I could tell my confusion was written clear on my face. I looked over to Xavier, to see if he knew what the guy was laughing at, but when I caught his eye, I could tell he wasn't confused at all. He was angry.

"Oh Annabelle, we had *no* intention of letting any of your captured pack go," he taunted as he turned his back on us and started to make his way out of our cell "They were just bait to get you here," he shrugged "and now that we have you... well let's just say we will no longer be needing their services."

I stared at his retreating form as he exited the cells, but what had me shocked into silence wasn't his traitorous words, it was the tribal knot tattoo he had on the back of his neck. The exact same tattoo as the one I saw in my dream, where Damon had tortured me in a cell just like this one. It seems that the Goddess had known about this guy and his plans for me for a while now and had tried to warn me of what was to come. If only I had paid closer attention back then as to what the dream could have meant, then maybe none of this would have ever happened.

Chapter 22

Jax's POV

It had been just over twenty-four hours since they had taken my mate and Beta from me and I was going out of my mind. I refused to sleep and only ate when my mother practically forced it down my throat, my sole focus was on getting everyone back… safe.

I should have known Annabelle would pull something like this. Ever since she told me about the ultimatum the stranger had given her, I could see it in her eyes that she wanted to hand herself in, I was just too consumed in problem solving to notice.

"Any updates from Xavier, Jax?" My parents asked as they walked into the office. I couldn't imagine what they were going though, not only was their Luna and future daughter in law taken, but also their son and practically adopted son as well.

"No, sorry," I sighed as I ran my fingers through my hair again. "They must have him tied up with silver somewhere, either that or he's unconscious. They're the only logical reasons I can think of as to why he hasn't contacted me… the only reason I can *bring* myself to think about anyway," I sighed.

"I'm sure something will come up," my dad tried to reassure me as he came over and clapped me on the back.

"I'm just so *angry*," I growled. "After Annabelle had her dream walk thing, she said she knew where they were. If I had just shut up long enough to let her finish, we wouldn't even be having this issue. We could be out there, rescuing them right now, instead of pacing the floor and looking like idiots."

"You can't blame yourself honey, you were worried for the sake of your pack and the sake of your mate," my mum tried to soothe me as she came and perched on my desk.

"An Alpha can't cloud his mind with worries mum, otherwise things like this happen," I sighed, sounding more defeated than I thought I ever could. I had only been acting Alpha for two years and look at what I'd achieved in that time.

My mum smiled a sad smile before stroking my cheek. She was a Luna herself after all, it's in her nature to care about everyone. "You can't expect yourself to never have feelings of anger or worry Jax, if you didn't you wouldn't be the amazing boy that I raised you to be."

I stayed silent as I stared blankly at the map in front of me, I had been staring at it for so long I wasn't even sure if it made sense to me anymore.

"Go and take a nap, at least for an hour, to give your brain and body time to recharge. You're no use to anyone if you're so tired you can't even keep your head up," she smiled.

I sighed as I looked up at my mum, knowing she was right but not able to bring myself to leave. What if there was a new development whilst I was away and I missed it?

"How about you take a nap on the sofa over there and me and your father will carry on working, that way if something happens we can easily wake you."

I thought about it for a second before slightly nodding and made my way over to the sofa on the other side of my office. I bought it for this exact reason. I sometimes ended up working so late here that when I finished, I didn't even have enough energy to walk up to my bedroom.

I settled down into the cool leather and as I drifted, I prayed that mum and dad would spot something that I had somehow missed.

I was walking through the woods, way past the boundary of my territory, when I heard a twig snap on my right.

Where was I? How did I get here when I was only just asleep in my office? I couldn't be sleep walking because I knew mum and dad wouldn't have let me get this far out into rogue territory without waking me.

I heard another twig snap and my wolf growled in my head, we were on another person's land and that spelt danger for anyone, even an Alpha.

I turned towards the sound of footsteps that were making their way towards me but frowned at the sound of them. They were noisy, like the person wasn't concerned about being found or trying to conceal their position.

I hid behind a tree, hoping that the element of surprise would be enough for me to get out of here unscathed. As the footsteps got closer, I readied myself to pounce. Three. Two. One. NOW!

"Ahhhh," the person jumped as they screamed, it wasn't until I was on top of them, with their hands pinned on either side of their head, that I realised who it was.

"Annabelle?" I couldn't believe it, she was here.

"Oh my god Jax, you scared the hell out of me!" She gasped.

"Annabelle!" I yelled as I wrapped her up tightly in my arms. "How are you here? How did you get away?"

"I haven't Jax, this is a dream walk, the Goddess linked our minds together whilst we were both sleeping," she explained. "Both Xavier and I are bound in silver so there's no way you could link us."

"You're bound in silver?" I knew how much that could hurt, it was like having hot iron wrapped around your wrists that didn't let up or cool down no matter how much time passed. Not only was it the physical pain you had to deal with, but the psychological torment of smelling your own flesh burning before your very eyes. "Are you okay?"

She shrugged as we got up off the floor "we're both as okay as we can be given the situation."

I nodded in understanding before I brought her into the circle of my arms again. "It's so good to see you, my little mate."

She relaxed in my arms as she breathed in my scent "it's good to see you too Jax."

We stayed like that for a moment, just enjoying each other's company after being forcefully separated for so long.

"Listen Jax, I know where we are-."

"I know, I'm so sorry I didn't let you finish the other day, I was just so concerned about you and wanting to make sure you were okay I completely forgot to-."

"Jax... you're doing it again" Annabelle giggles and I smiled as the sound of her laugh reached my ears. She didn't laugh often, but when she did, it was heavenly.

"Sorry... So where are you?" I asked as I caressed her jaw with my fingertips.

"We're in Alpha Parker's territory, slap bang in the middle and somewhere underground."

"That son of a bitch, I'm going to kill him for what he's doing," I growled.

"Jax, listen... they aren't going to release your brother or the others like they promised. I need you to come and find me so that everyone can come back safe. I'm going to delay him as much as I can, but I don't think I can do it for very long. It seems this pack hates the Goddess as much as we hate them" she sighed. "The strange guy I told you about, the one that smells like Alpha Parker, said that my family and everyone held hostage are no longer needed. I don't like the way he said it so please *find them*

soon" she pleaded, her bright blue eyes showing just how worried she was.

"I will baby, don't you worry" I reassured her as the edges of my vision started to wobble and blur. "I'm going to get all *of you out of there and safe."*

"I'm being woken up so this won't last much longer," she rushed out as she looked at me. "They all wear a certain type of perfume to mask their scent so follow that and use it to help you find us."

I just nodded as I took one last look at her beautiful face as it continued to blur out of sight.

"Be safe," she whispered as she slowly disappeared from my arms.

I woke up with a start, scaring the people in my office that had continued to work quietly around me.

"Are you okay honey?" My mum asked, worry written all over her face as she took in my sweaty forehead and shaking hands.

I nodded as I stood up and made my way over to the map. "I was with Annabelle, she brought me into her dream walk," I stuttered as I reached for a glass of water that had been sitting on my desk, feeling as if I hadn't drank anything in days.

"Is that even possible?" My dad mutters as he looks at me with a frown.

I chuckled as I shrugged my shoulders "is anything she can do possible?"

My dad just shrugged with a small smile as he walked over to my mum and took her hand. "What did she tell you?"

"She said they were in the heart of Alpha Parker's territory, somewhere underground..." I muttered as I started studying the map closer, looking for anything that could help us.

"There!" My dad almost yelled as he pointed to something on the map. "That's an old air raid shelter from back in the forties, I used to play there as a kid with some friends, back before the pack that is now under Alpha Parker's control claimed the land. It doesn't look like much but I'm sure with some modifications they could have easily made it into a dungeon, it's the perfect place to hide someone."

"Big enough to fit a whole cell block down there?" I questioned, sceptical that it could be this easy.

"Most definitely."

"Okay" I sighed, feeling the weight I had been feeling over the last twenty-four hours slowly lift. "We have the where... Now all we need is the how."

Chapter 23

Annabelle's POV

I was startled awake by ice cold water as it was poured over my head. I tried to hold onto the dream with Jax for as long as I could, but the shock of the cold forced me out of my unconscious state and back into the real world.

"Wakey wakey little Annabelle, we have a surprise for you," a voice sang as my muddy brain shifted into consciousness.

I looked up through my semi-sleep hazed eyes and came face to face with the guy with the tribal tattoo.

"What do you want?" I grumbled. The silver around my wrists and ankles was causing me too much pain to care about how I addressed him at the moment. It probably wasn't the best idea to get grumpy with your captor, especially one who didn't mind throwing the odd kick your way.

"Watch who you're talking to bitch," a voice growled at me and I looked up to see a new person standing next to Alpha Parker's scent double. He stood tall, almost 6'6, with broad shoulders and tribal style tattoos running down both of his arms. It seemed to be a running theme in this pack.

"Easy Sebastian, she's alright," the scent double chuckled as he took in my fearful expression. "I just wondered if you wanted to see the show," he continued as he took up his regular stance of leaning against the door frame with his hands and ankles crossed.

I frowned "What show?"

"Well we just thought that as we're going to kill your parents and the members of your pack, you'd like to watch? We're going to put on a little show you see. The guys here have been so bored lately and have worked so hard I think they deserve a bit of fun; don't you think?"

Bile rose in my throat at the thought of having to watch anyone die. "Why are you doing this? You have me, so why not just let them go?" I pleaded, hoping to do as I'd promised to Jax and delay him for as long as possible.

He chuckled "and let them run straight back to that pathetic Alpha of yours and tell them where you are? I don't think so love."

Xavier, who had been quiet throughout the interaction between us, growled at the mention of Jax being weak.

"Oh cool it Beta, I'll get to you in a minute," the scent double shot back as he gestured Sebastian with his head towards Xavier.

I watched in horror as Sebastian stalked over to Xavier and proceeded to punch and kick him wherever he could. Being restrained in silver there wasn't much Xavier could do to deflect the blows, he had no choice but to lay there and take it as Sebastian rained down blow after blow.

Sebastian held Xavier's head up by the hair at his nape and kneed him in the face, causing blood to spew out and a large cut to form on the bridge of his nose before dropping him to the floor and repeatedly kicked him in the ribs.

"No please stop... I'll do anything… please!" I screamed as I saw Xavier's eyes roll into the back of his head.

"Anything hu?" The scent double questioned as he gestured for Sebastian to stop.

I nodded, unable to get any words out through the tears that were currently streaming down my face as my eyes continued to lock onto Xavier's slumped form. *Oh Xavier.*

"Sever your mate bond with your Alpha and mate with *me*," the scent double suddenly growled as a sinister smirk appeared on his face.

"W-What?" I stuttered as my eyes snapped over to his, not able to comprehend what he was asking me to do.

"You heard me, end all your ties with Alpha Jax and willingly mate with me instead. Then and only then, will I let your precious pack go."

He had pushed himself off the door frame and was now crouched in front of me as I lay on the ground in a puddle of Xavier's blood.

"But...why?"

"Why not?" He countered with a shrug as he continued to stare into my eyes.

"But you said you didn't want a mate, that mates were designed to make werewolves weak, why would you want to be mated to me?" I was so confused.

"A destined mate can make you weak, yes, but having the opportunity to be mated to a direct descendant of the Moon Goddess herself? Who would pass up an opportunity like that? What better way to hurt and betray the Goddess more than to forcibly rip her descendants' mate from her and then force her into a mating with someone else against her will? If that happens then the Goddess will have to remove her touch from you and therefore weaken both your family bloodline and her herself. It's the perfect plan," he shrugged with a grin.

I stared at him in shock as everything started to click into place. "This was your plan all along wasn't it? All the scheming, kidnapping my parents, making me live with the Leftens, it was all part of yours and Alpha Parker's plan to get me to be your mate." I felt sick, physically sick, that my whole life has been played out like a checklist for him. I had been a pawn in my very own life.

"Very clever. I have to say when you managed to escape the Leftens it threw a spanner in the works. I had to go and speed things along a little bit when I heard that you had found your mate, but you being so scared and untrusting towards him worked in my favour. I would have never been able to follow through with the plan if you and that Alpha of yours had completed the bond, so I guess I should be thanking *you* for your role in making sure it all went according to plan," he smirked.

This time I did throw up, although seeing as I hadn't eaten anything there was little in my stomach other than bile and stomach acid. "You're a monster," I gasped out after I had finished emptying what little contents of my stomach that I had remaining.

The only thing he did was smirk at my reaction, he was loving every second of my torture.

"And my parents?" I questioned.

"What about them?"

"Why did you take them and torture them this whole time if your whole plan was to get to me? Why not just kill them?"

He smiled and grabbed my chin with his hand whilst his thumb stroked my cheek bone, "They were kept here as a contingency plan more than anything else. We didn't know whether a few kidnapped pack members were going to be enough, so we kept your parents alive, just in case. We then just had to play the waiting game. That and your mother was really handy to have around with getting a Goddess' touch , even if she was useless half the time and tried not to play along," he smirked.

"How do I know you won't go back on your word like last time and keep my family here," I questioned.

"I guess that's just something you're going to have to risk, isn't it?" He laughed at my horrified expression as he got up and made his way back towards the door. "I'll give you till sundown to decide, better make your mind up quick," he taunted as he looked out of the small slit we had acting as our only source of light, before the door was slammed shut behind him by a smirking Sebastian.

What was I going to do now?

After they left, I just sat there in silence, not knowing what to do. Turning myself into these people to save everyone was a no brainer for me, but the idea of having to reject my mate, to reject Jax, sickened me to my very core.

"You can't do it you know," I heard Xavier mumble from his side of the room, I hadn't even realised he was awake. I thought he had passed out from the beating he took from Sebastian.

"Do what?" I asked, acting as if I didn't know what he was talking about.

"I may be hurt but I'm not stupid, I heard what that guy said and I am telling you now that you can't do it," he muttered as he slowly sat himself up to rest against the wall for support. "If you reject Jax then he would spiral out of control, our whole pack would more than likely crumble. If you think what he's feeling now is bad, there is no way to even begin to explain how he would be feeling if he can no longer feel his bond with you."

I frowned as I looked down at my fingers fiddling with the laces of my shoe. "But if I don't reject him, everyone here will die, *including* you. I promised Jax I'd give him as much time as I could so that he could get here and save you all."

Xavier shrugged, cringing at the pain the small movement brought on. "It's a price every pack member would willingly pay if it meant the safety of our Alpha and our Luna, without them the pack would fall into chaos and would easily be taken over by another pack or fall victim to a rogue attack."

My frown deepened, still not understanding. "Why would you lay your life down for me anyway? You didn't even like me and when we first met, if I remember correctly, you even threatened to kill me."

Xavier chuckled "yeah well don't take that personally, I thought you were a rogue looking to make some trouble. I would never have spoken to you like that if I knew who you were."

"Not all rogues are bad though, right? Why do you hold such a grudge against them?"

Xavier stayed silent as he looked down, a look of pain clouding his eyes as he thought back to an unpleasant memory.

"So you're saying that you'd willingly die for me, but not tell me anything about yourself?" I questioned with raised eyebrows.

Xavier sighed before looking up at me with sad eyes. "It's not a very happy story Annabelle."

I shrugged "well neither is mine, but I'm sure you know it."

He sighed again before closing his eyes and rested his head back against the wall. I thought that was the end of the conversation, that he had maybe fallen asleep or passed out or something, but eventually, he started talking.

"It was a few years ago, back when Jax's dad was still the Alpha. I was on patrol with Jax after I'd had an argument with my dad, we'd caught the scent of a few rogues close to the border to our territory. Being the future Alpha and Beta of the pack, we felt we had a lot to prove to both our parents and the pack, so we went to investigate without informing the pack of what we were doing. We wanted to show everyone that when the time came, they could count on us to protect them when our parents inevitably stepped down and we took their place. We ran over to where we could smell the scent, but what we saw when we got there confused us."

"Why, what did you find?" I whispered, not wanting to interrupt him but not being able to stop myself.

"Nothing, that was the confusing part. When we got to the clearing that held the rogue scent, we found nothing but a ratty old T-shirt. That was when we decided to contact the Alpha and let him know what we'd discovered, but when we couldn't get through to him we knew something was wrong.

"We later found out that the scent we followed was just a diversion for what the rogues really had planned for us. They'd gotten rid of the border control, us, so that the rest of them could sneak in undetected and attack the pack.

"The attack didn't last long; they had seriously underestimated our numbers, but it didn't stop us from experiencing some losses. When I found out what was going on I ran straight back to my house, intending to protect my mum and sister who was not old enough to shift yet, but when I got there I came face to face with two rogues who, upon seeing me, ripped their throats out. They showed no mercy for them, they just killed them because they were in the wrong place at the wrong time and I wasn't there to protect them.

"My dad was somewhere else. As he was the Beta it was his job to make sure the pack house and everyone inside was protected, but when he felt the mate bond had been severed with my mum he howled in pain. It was just the distraction the rogue he was fighting needed to go in for the kill.

"In one day I had become an orphan, all because of one stupid mistake I'd made. If I hadn't underestimated the rogues, then my parents and baby sister would still be alive today."

I stayed silent throughout Xavier's story as I felt tears build up in my eyes and spill over. We sat in silence for a while after Xavier had finished his story as I let him grieve the loss of his family, but after a while I cleared my throat and looked up at him.

"You can't blame yourself for what happened Xavier. It wasn't you who rallied the rogues to fight and it wasn't you who killed your family."

Xavier just remained silent and I sighed. I wasn't going to get through to him, but I hoped that he would soon come to forgive himself for something he had no control over.

"That's why Alpha Parker called me the Rogue Killer," he explained as he finally looked up at me. "After they'd been killed I went on a rampage, actively *looking* for rogues to blame and kill, whether they'd been involved in the attack on my family or not," he shrugged. "I didn't care, I just wanted revenge for what had happened to them. It wasn't until Alpha Jackson threatened to take away my Beta position that I stopped.

My dad had passed that title down to me and I couldn't lose that, even if it did mean putting my personal vendetta on hold."

I stayed silent for a second, shocked that someone as amazing and loyal as Xavier had gone through something so horrible. His reaction to me when I first stumbled onto his territory finally made sense and I was so grateful that he had trusted me enough to tell me his story. "Thank you for telling me Xavier," I muttered, wishing I wasn't chained down so that I could console him somehow.

He looked over at me and nodded his head in acknowledgement before hanging his head and closing his eyes, getting swallowed up in his grief and guilt.

"Try and get some sleep, I'll figure out what to do next," I whispered as I watched Xavier's forehead relax and his breathing even out.

I had to find some way to save him and everyone else. But how?

...

I had no idea how much time had passed since the stranger had given me the ultimatum. We were both starving by now and were in desperate need of a glass of water, but we hadn't been offered any, not that I was surprised. At the rate we were deteriorating, I wasn't sure how much longer we would survive in this place. Not only were we suffering from starvation and dehydration, we were also having to deal with our injuries and the silver cuffs. Our wolves were working overtime to try and heal us as much as they could, but to do that they needed sustenance and they'd used what little reserves we'd had long ago.

Xavier has tried to be as supportive and positive as he could, but I could tell he was also struggling, not only with the lack of food and water but also with his injuries. That last beating he took was a pretty harsh one and with the silver going into his system he wasn't healing properly from it.

I couldn't wait for Jax for much longer, if I wanted to save everyone I had to do what the scent double asked of me, but how could I say the words that would forever rip me away from Jax?

"Oh little Annabelle," I heard someone sing from the other side of the door and I immediately tensed up, knowing who it was and what they were here for as the light had dimmed from the window a while ago.

The door swung open after it had been unlocked, hitting the wall with a thud as crumbs of brick fell to the floor at the impact. I shrunk back as the fluorescent light came flooding into our nearly pitch-black cell, burning my retinas.

"It's time to make your decision little Annabelle," the scent double smirked as he came and crouched in front of me. "What's it to be, death for everyone you know and love or sever your ties with your precious little mate and save everyone?"

I stuttered as I looked up into his eyes. They were pure black with a ring of red around the pupil and they terrified me to my very core, I've never seen eyes like them before.

"I-I umm..." was all I could manage to stutter as I sat frozen in my spot on the cold wet ground.

The man before me sighed before dropping his head slightly in exasperation. "Sebastian!" He suddenly shouted, making me jump out of my skin at the invasion of the silence I had grown so accustomed to. "Guard the door," he demanded towards the bulky man that now stood behind him. "Me and little Annie here are going to go on a little *field trip,*" he smirked.

I frowned, confused by his words. Where the hell could we be going?

The scent double pulled a pair of what looked like heavy duty gardening gloves out of his back pocket and slipped them over his hands. He then proceeded to reach above me and over to the wall where my chains were connected to the stone, pulling them until they broke free. Dust and debris rained down on me and I covered my face with my arms as a little squeak escaped my lips.

Without warning he pulled me to my feet by the chains attached to my wrists and started dragging me towards the door and past Sebastian. I took one last look behind me at a still passed-out Xavier before turning back and looking where I was going.

"Where are we going?" I whispered, afraid to make noise in the almost silent stone corridor, my voice echoing as we continued to wherever we were heading.

The scent double chuckled but otherwise didn't respond as he continued to drag me down the hallway. I sighed at his silence and just focused on trying to not trip up on my own feet, still chained together, as I tried to keep up.

"What's your name?" I asked, if I was going to be killed by him I at least wanted to know his name. That way on my head stone it wouldn't have to read *'death by scent double'*.

The scent double chuckled again but this time did answer me with a simple "Matthew."

Hu, so the scent doubles name was Matthew.

Matthew carried on pulling me for a few more seconds before he suddenly stopped at a closed door and turned to face me with an evil glint in his eye. "I think it's time for a grand family reunion, don't you think so?" He chuckled.

I didn't have time to process what he'd said because before I could even blink I was thrown into a room, landing on my hands and knees with a thud, as my skin split open.

"I thought it was time to finally come face to face with the two people who you've been *dying* to see since you were a little girl," Matthew smiled down at me as he walked past me and pulled the hoods off of two figures that were tied up to chairs in front of me.

They were bound and gagged with bruises, cuts and dirt covering them, but even if I hadn't recently seen them in a dream of mine, I still would have recognised them anywhere... my parents.

I sat there, frozen on the floor for a second, as I took them both in. They both looked similar to how I had last seen them in my dream, only this time they were even more beaten and bruised than before. My mum's golden blond hair was almost dark brown with dried blood and grime as it clung to her face and neck in large clumps. Both her eyes were swollen and she had a split lip that looked like it stung every time she licked her lips to try and soothe the dry and cracked skin.

My dad wasn't doing much better, although his hair was naturally much darker than my mum's, his too was ratty and covered in blood as sweat beaded across his forehead, making the roots look that much darker than the rest of it. It was obviously rare for them to allow him to cut his hair or shave his beard off as half of his head was covered in brown matts as they constantly fell into his eyes. I couldn't see much of his face, but I could tell that his nose had been broken and he was sporting a sizable cut that ran from his temple all the way down to where his dimple used to sit.

I sat there as I stared at the state they were both in, I didn't know how to react as tears rolled down my cheeks. I quickly recovered though when I saw them try to turn their heads towards me and I ran over to them, hoping I could help them in some way. I didn't make it far though as Matthew stood on the chains that were still shackling my wrists together as the chain loops trailing behind me, making sure I couldn't reach them. I hissed at the pain of the silver digging into my skin as they yanked me backwards, but I ignored it as I looked over at my mum and dad.

They were facing away from each other and about a foot apart so as not to be touching, but their heads were both turned in my direction, pain and desperation written clear in their facial expressions.

"Mummy?" I whispered as tears continued to leak out of my eyes, "Daddy?"

"Aww...what a heart wrenching moment, all the family back together again," Matthew sighed in a sickly-sweet voice. He took the chains back into his hands before he dragged me to the other side of the room, away from my parents, and secured me to the nearby wall.

Matthew then proceeded to circle around my parents a few times, as if he were the predator taunting his prey, before looking up at me from across the room with an evil glint in his eyes, the red ring more pronounced then I had even seen it before.

"It would be a shame if someone were to... ruin the moment," he chuckled with a shrug and before I could blink, he punched my dad square in the jaw, knocking his head back.

I screamed as I watched him do this over and over again, but my protests only seemed to spur him on. He alternated between my mum and my dad, torturing them in ways I could never unsee. My voice had gone horse from the amount of screaming I had done, and my tears had drenched my cheeks and the neckline of my shirt as the salt water dried and tightened the skin on my cheeks.

"I'll do it... please just stop hurting them," I sobbed as my legs finally gave out on me and I crumbled to the floor, my arm still bound in front of me and unable to catch me as my knees ground into the uneven concrete.

Matthew finally stopped his attack and made his way over to me, blood covering his knuckles as he forced my chin up so I could look him in the eyes. I cringed at the sight of them so close to me but stopped myself, not wanting to anger him further.

"Reject your mate and announce me as your new chosen mate, then and only then, will I let them go," he growled, looking more feral than human in that moment.

It seemed I took a second too long in agreeing to his terms though as he shoved my face away from him and he stood up with a sigh, turning around to face my parents, presumably to continue where he had left off in his torment. I knew I couldn't take another second of it though, so before I could let him get even half way over to them I whispered "O-Okay," as I collapsed onto the ground, all the fight I had left in me now gone. "I'll do it."

Chapter 24

Jax's POV

Since Annabelle's visit in my dreams things here had been moving at lightning speed.

Once we knew where they were being held it was just a matter of how we were going to pull this off.

Alpha Parker's territory was well guarded, with patrols going around the perimeter every half hour, checking for intruders. Even though I was desperate to get my mate and brother back, I didn't want to endanger my pack members' lives in the process of doing so, and with that in mind my dad and I went to find reinforcements.

Ringing the neighbouring packs obviously hadn't worked, none of them were interested in getting involved with the Rising Dawn pack over a few missing pack members. My hope now was that because the Luna and the Beta of my pack had also been taken it would spur them on and help me. After all, a pack without its rightful Luna and Beta was sure to crumble in just weeks, attracting Rogue's and other unwanted wolves to the area.

We first visited a pack a few hours south from us and once we got the agreement from Alpha Troy that he would help us out we went further afield. If we were going to win with as few casualties as possible we would need numbers and numbers meant packs.

Within twelve hours we had managed to gather four separate packs together, not including our own, and were ready to attack. Alpha Troy and Alpha Dixon would go through the south of Alpha Parker's territory with their respective packs, causing as much chaos as possible to draw Parker's pack warriors towards them. Whilst that was going on Alpha Michael and Alpha Caleb would secretly go through the north end, surrounding the warriors and trapping them so they were unable to reach the bunker when the alarm would inevitably trip.

My pack would filter in through the east, a few at a time, so as not to rouse suspicion. Then when the time came, myself and a few other trusted pack warriors would head towards the bunker and rescue Annabelle, Will, Xavier and the others three trackers with hopefully no issue.

I just hoped that it worked. I haven't had a proper night's sleep since Annabelle was taken almost three days ago and all I wanted to do was curl up with her in my arms and sleep for a week.

The one thing that worried me most about all this was how she'd fair mentally to all this stress. It left me with a constant headache, worrying about whether she'd revert back to her old self, the person that was scared to talk, scared to be touched, scared to even breathe. The thought of that happening makes my heart break, she had been through so much throughout her life and the bad just kept on hitting her.

"Alpha Jax, we're all ready to go,'" Alpha Troy informed me as he walked into my office. Alpha Troy was a big guy, standing at 6'5 with the muscle mass to match it. Anyone in their right mind would be wary of him, but put him in the near vicinity of his mate and he turns into a soppy puppy, not that I would say that to his face of course.

I nodded in his direction before closing my laptop and followed him out the door. My wolf was on edge, eager to get on with the rescue and get his mate and pack members back. I had to hold him back though, someone with the powers of an Alpha cannot lose themselves to their emotions, especially at times like this. The consequences could be catastrophic.

I walked out the front door and was met with hundreds of warriors, all saying goodbye to their families as they prepared themselves for a battle. I was instantly overcome with pride, pride for my people and what they are willing to sacrifice for the pack and for each other.

"Everyone!" I yell, gaining the attention of every person in the area. "Today we fight, side by side, not only for the safety of my pack, but for the safety of wolves everywhere. Today we will be sending a clear message to *anyone* who is thinking of crossing us, that we will not lay down and roll over, we will rally together, and we will fight, for our packs and for our friends."

I look around the crowd as I take in the faces of each and every person in front of me. I then look to my left to see the other Alphas standing next to me, their chests puffed out in pride as they too take in the sheer strength and determination of their own packs.

"Today we will show Alpha Parker, and we will show everyone that we are not to be messed with," I yelled, my voice gaining in volume with every word. "Now let's show them what we are capable of, let's bring back our trackers, our Beta and our Luna!" I yelled and was met with hundreds of voices cheering as we started making our way off towards the Crescent Moon pack. He is not going to know what hit him.

Chapter 25

Annabelle's POV

I could hear the weak protests of my parents through their gags as they heard me agree to Matthews terms, but they fell on deaf ears. I couldn't watch one more second of anyone getting hurt because of me, I just couldn't, the guilt would eat me alive and I knew I wouldn't survive it.

I looked into the triumphant eyes of Matthew as he grinned down at me "now was that so hard to say?" He mocked.

I glared at him from my spot on the floor, I had never hated anyone as much as I hated him right now and coming from me and what I've been through, that was saying something.

"Tsk tsk tsk," Matthew tutted at me sarcastically "is that any way to treat your new mate and Alpha?" He questioned with his eyebrows raised.

My glare turned into confusion as my brain registered what he had just said. "Alpha? I thought Parker was the Alpha of your pack?"

Matthew shrugged with a chuckle "that sorry excuse of a wolf was not fit to be an Alpha."

I frowned, my confusion only deepening with his explanation.

"That little *pup* had such small dreams when it came to dealing with you. Do you know what *he* wanted to do?"

He stayed silent for a moment, maybe waiting to see if I would answer his rhetorical question, but when I didn't offer anything, he sighed and carried on.

"His big plan was to kill you, just kill you and that was it. I mean how small minded is that? It's a good job I challenged him and killed him when I did otherwise this thing between you and me wouldn't be happening right now," he laughed.

"But… but why take me and stick me with the Leftens if he was just going to kill me anyway? That doesn't make any sense," I questioned my last attempt at stalling him, keeping him talking to give Jax as much time as I possibly could.

He sighed as he took an old rag from out of his pocket and started to mop the blood off from his knuckles. "He said that he was going to wait until you were twenty-one so that the Goddess was most aware of your presence in this world, or something like that anyway. Then he was going to kill you and your mother in front of her during a blood moon" he sighed as he rolled his eyes.

"Have you ever heard the saying *'attacking a village from the outside in will weaken it but not destroy it, but attacking the village from the inside out will make it implode?'*" He asked as he looked down at me.

I shook my head but remained silent, counting the seconds until Jax got here.

He shrugged, seemingly unfazed with my lack of knowledge. "I heard it in a film once and have never looked back. You see killing you and your mother in front of the Goddess would weaken her for sure, but give her enough time and she'll find some random distant relative of yours to pass the gift onto instead. Now my plan means that she will have to withdraw her touch from your family line all together and that's something that she definitely won't survive," he chuckled.

"So you not only want to destroy my life and kill everyone I love but you also want to kill the Moon Goddess herself? All because you think she sees you as weak?" I questioned, not believing my ears.

"Bingo," he smiled as he pointed down at my kneeling form.

Never did I think that there would be a time that I missed Alpha Parker and his plans. Getting killed sounded so much more appealing than having to reject Jax and live my life mated to this monster.

"Now, we're going to have to start planning the ceremony right away, don't want you getting any ideas and running away from me now do we?" Matthew stated as he started walking towards the door, where my chains were still buried into the stone. I knew I wouldn't be seeing my parents any time soon so I managed to whisper a quick "*I love you both*" to them in their semi-conscious state before I was dragged out of the room by my silver chains in Matthew's hands. Sorry, *Alpha* Matthews hands.

I was dragged back through the tunnel of the underground cell block, to where I presumed I was going back to my cell, but when he walked right past the door Sebastian was guarding I frowned. Where were we going?

My confusion only grew as Alpha Matthew dragged me to a set of stairs that lead upwards. The more steps we took the lighter the stairwell got, and I felt a moment of happiness at the thought of seeing sunlight again. It was short lived though as Alpha Matthew swiftly tugged on my chains, obviously not liking the fact that I was dawdling.

"You'll be getting ready in my house, fully guarded before you get any ideas. If we are to be mated, I can't have you looking like... that," he grimaced as he looked back at me, disgust at my appearance clear on his face.

I stayed silent, not knowing how to respond. Of course I was in a state, that's kind of what happens when you keep someone captive in a room for god knows how long without so much as a shower or even a toilet.

I sighed in relief as we finally made it into the open. Fresh air. I took in as much of it as I could, my lungs feeling as if they were starved of oxygen the whole time I was down there. Up here the air smelt clean and fresh, not like the stuff down in the cellars that smelled like mildew and blood.

Once I was satisfied with my intake of the fresh early morning air I started to take in my surroundings. At first, I thought it looked like any other pack, people were walking around the territory, getting what they needed done and enjoying the warm weather. It wasn't until I looked closer that I realised that everything wasn't as happy as it appeared.

The people who were outside and doing their daily chores were walking around with their heads down cast, with not so much as a morning greeting passed between two friends. There was no sign of affection between the mated couples, walking around town with their hands at their sides. Even the children weren't laughing and playing like normal kids would be, the playground sitting empty in the distant field.

It was like someone had sucked the life out of everyone who lived here.

It was then that it dawned on me, these poor people who were under the command of Alpha Matthew, were just as much of a prisoner as I was. I wonder what happened to them that made them so... lifeless.

"When we arrive you are to get straight into my shower and wash that filth off of your skin," he demanded. "I will then send someone in to help you get ready. You are to be ready by twelve o' clock sharp where someone will bring you out to the front of the house where we will perform the ceremony. Do you understand?" He stated, his tone leaving no room for questions or objections.

I looked up at Alpha Matthew and took in the fire that was blazing in his eyes, he was not messing around. I gave a subtle nob, not wanting to anger him in any way, before walking the last few steps towards his house.

I don't know what I was expecting when I walked in, maybe some form of dungeon with red and black being the main colour scheme, but what I actually saw surprised me. The space was light and open, with the fireplace roaring in the centre of the open plan living room and the counters in the kitchen so clean they shone like a second sun.

"I usually have some of the pack come in and clean my house once a day, but now I have my mate here I don't think they'll be needed anymore," Matthew commented as he quickly dragged me through the house, barely giving me a second to take in my surroundings. "It is your job to make sure this place is cleaned from top to bottom every single day, if you miss something there will be... consequences. Understood?" Matthew finished his little speech as he rounded on me and looked me straight in the eye.

The intensity of his eyes unnerved me and so I looked away before nodding my head in understanding again. It was just like being at the Leftens house all over again.

"Good, now when we have company over you are to remain silent and invisible. Unless I call on you, you're to stay out of sight and out of my way, understood?" It was *really* like being back at the Leftens house, well at least I've had years of practice. I nodded my head again, making sure not to use my voice and potentially angering him.

When Alpha Matthew was satisfied with my compliance, we walked through a door that was on the second floor of the building, me trailing behind him with the chains still wrapped tight around my wrists.

"The bathroom is through there," he informed me as he pointed to a door on the far side of the room "make sure you shower properly; I don't want you embarrassing me by smelling like that during our ceremony," he sneered as he looked me up and down again, his nose turned up at the mere thought of my stench.

I could only nod my head in understanding again, not knowing how else to respond.

We stayed silent for a few moments as Matthew stared at me in an unnerving manner. "In just a few hours Annabelle, you will be *my* mate," he growled as he stalked towards me.

I cowered back in fear for what he would do to me, but sighed in relief as he produced a key from his jeans pocket and unlocked the silver chains that were clasped around my wrists and ankles. The skin was blistered and bruised, blood and fluid oozing from the many welts that had popped, but even through all that pain, it was still sweet relief when they were finally free.

"Get in the shower, you have thirty minutes before I send someone in," were the final words he spoke before stalking out the door, leaving me by myself in this unfamiliar room.

•••

When I stepped out of the bathroom after a much-needed shower I was startled as I saw a woman in her late forties or early fifties standing in the centre of the room, patiently waiting for me. She didn't utter a word as I stepped out of the cloud of steam, she just stood there with her head bowed and her hands clasped in front of her.

"Umm...hi?" I muttered uncomfortably as I waved an awkward hand in her direction. She again ignored me and instead wandered over to the vanity that was sitting on one side of the room and gestured for me to sit down.

I did so gingerly, not really knowing how to react to the woman who refused to speak to me or even look me in the eye. Was this how I acted when I first escaped the Leftens? If it was, I pitied the woman for going through whatever she has to make her act the way she did.

I tried to make her feel a little more comfortable, even though I was pretty terrified of this whole situation myself, by introducing myself. Maybe if she knew who I was she'd feel a bit more at ease around me.

"I'm Annabelle." I waited patiently for a response as I came and sat down in front of her, but I got nothing in response, all the woman did was pick up a hairbrush and gestured for me to turn my head around so that she could brush my hair.

Giving up trying to talk to her I did what she asked, I turned my head so that she could get to work on brushing my hair.

As we sat there in silence my mind started to drift, I pictured Jax and my parents and Xavier and the rest of my new pack, all sitting around and having a picnic with smiles on their faces and the sun bouncing off their sun cream covered skin.

I prayed that Jax would get to me in time, that he would come charging in with the rest of the pack and save the day, but if he didn't, I still wouldn't change the decision I made. Sure I was going to miss them, more than anything in the world, but I was doing this for them, so that they could live a life free of torture and constant fear that Alpha Matthew would be right around the corner at every turn, waiting for me.

I felt a tear gather on my lash line as I continued to think about what I was losing, but mentally scolding myself, I was doing this for them.

I was feeling so much better since before I entered this room, a good shower and being away from the silver chains had done wonders for both myself and my wolf. She was finally free now that the silver was off and she was working overtime to try and fix everything she could.

I frowned as I felt something foreign stir in my brain, something I had never felt before. It was like someone was poking my head from the inside, trying to tell me something. I frowned and closed my eyes, trying to relax my brain so that I could figure out what was going on as the woman continued to brush my hair.

After several minutes of frustration, I finally had a breakthrough as a conscience slipped into my mind. I tentatively reached out to it but jerked back in surprise when I felt the foreign conscience respond by reaching back. What the-

"A-Annabelle?" The voice whispered to me, a voice that sounded oddly like Jax's voice, a little gruff, but still like Jax.

"Jax?" I felt like an idiot basically talking to myself in my own head, but when I felt shock and relief, shock and relief that weren't my own emotions, flooded through my brain I knew I wasn't going crazy.

"Oh my god Annabelle! You're mind linking!" he exclaimed in excitement.

I started to smile at how cute he was being, but I held it in, I didn't want anyone to know that I could now mind link and was communicating with Jax.

"Jax! H-how is this possible?"

"I don't know baby, but I am so happy to hear from you, we aren't too far away. We're coming to get you."

I gasped out loud but froze when I realised I had made a noise. I pretended to cringe as the woman carried on pinning pins into my hair, making it look like she had pulled my hair as I went back to focusing on my mental link with Jax.

"How are you nearly here? How did you even know where I was?"

"It was fairly easy to figure out once you told us you were being kept underground. Alpha Parker hasn't had that land for long, so my dad could guess fairly easily where you were," he explained.

I paused to absorb that information as the woman moved onto making up my face.

"Jax... Alpha Parker's dead. A wolf named Matthew challenged him for his title and won."

319

"Who's Matthew? Did you recognise him at all?"

I shook my head but paused as I took in the woman's face in front of me, pausing what she was doing on my face until I remained still again. "Sorry, just trying to get comfy," I lied. I don't think she believed it, but she carried on anyway.

"No I don't recognise him, he's younger than Parker though, maybe early thirties?"

"Okay well that doesn't change our plan at all, just who we have to stop."

I paused our conversation as I debated telling him about Alpha Matthews plans in mating with me. I probably should, but I didn't want him distracted as he ran into a dangerous situation to save me.

In the end though my conscience won out and I told him. If the roles were reversed I'd want to know every scrap of detail I could before charging in.

"Umm Jax? Matthew killed Alpha Parker because he didn't like his plans for me."

I could feel Jax's confusion through the bond we had *"what do you mean?"*

"Well... apparently Parker's plan was to lure me here and just... well... kill me." Jax growled at that in my head but I ignored it and carried on, knowing I didn't have much time left before the woman was finished making me up. *"Alpha Matthew thought that was too small minded. Jax, he plans to sever our mate bond in the eyes of the Moon Goddess and form a new bond between the two of*

us. He says once he does that the Goddess will abandon me and therefore her people."

Jax was silent for a moment, so silent I thought I had lost my mind link with him, before all of a sudden my mind was filled with unbridled anger. So much anger that even I started to shake from the adrenaline, my eyes beginning to swirl a different colour as I spotted them in the mirror.

"He plans to WHAT!"

"Sever our mate bond and create his own. I didn't even know that was possible."

"It's not," he growled as I still felt the anger rippling through our bond. *"To break a bond and form a new one you need the help of a witch, a powerful witch, and even then, it's not one hundred percent effective. It is a very painful experience and against pack law to perform that ceremony under any circumstance."*

I whimpered as Jax explained the ceremony to me as the woman gestured for me to stand up so that she could fit me into the floor length white maxi dress I was being forced to wear.

"Don't worry baby, I won't let that happen to you. I am going to get you out of this if it's the last thing I do."

…

I was currently standing outside of Alpha Matthews house, wearing a flimsy white maxi dress, in front of hundreds of people. It looks like his whole pack was summoned here to witness this.

After the woman was finished getting me ready, she simply led me out of the front door and then blended into the crowd, leaving me to stand on the porch by the front door with no idea what to do next.

I had the sudden urge to run, but I knew that I wouldn't get far. I was bare footed and Alpha Matthew and his men weren't too far away, they'd stop me before I even made it to the border.

I wrapped my arms around myself as I felt a strong breeze, causing goose bumps to form on my skin and my dress to billow around my bare feet. Could they not have at least given me a jacket? Or a pair of socks?

Just as I was about to give up on standing here, I saw the sea of people part, revealing Alpha Matthew with a woman walking beside him. I didn't recognise her, but I instantly knew she was the witch that was going to be performing the ceremony.

She had jet black hair tied into a scruffy top knot on the top of her head, strands of loose hair hanging down framing her face. A black dress covered her thin frame and a deep red velvet cape hung across her shoulders. I internally rolled my eyes at her look, could she be any more cliché?

They both made their way onto the front porch that was acting as a stage, neither one of them acknowledging my presence as they turned to face their pack.

"Fellow pack members, I have gathered you all here today to witness the joining of your Alpha and Luna. It is a rare and special moment in history when two wolves decide to go against the Moon Goddess' wishes and it should be celebrated for all to see," Alpha Matthew declared, projecting his voice for all to hear.

I frowned at him, confused. I thought Jax said it was against pack law to perform this kind of ceremony? If that was common knowledge, then why wasn't anyone doing anything to stop him?

I looked amongst the sea of faces, hoping to find at least one friendly face in the crowd, but deflated in defeat as I noticed not one set of eyes turned towards me, they were all solely focused on Matthew.

"Isabella will have the honour of performing the ritual." Matthew shouted to the crowd as he turned to his left and took the witch by the hand.

She bowed before Matthew before reaching into her cloak and producing a gleaming silver dagger. I had a moment of relief as I thought she intended to use it on Matthew, but that relief was short lived as I watched her black eyes fall onto mine.

She took confident strides towards me, like a predator whose eyes were locked onto its helpless prey. My entire body was screaming at me to run, to fight this, but I knew that I couldn't. If I did then everyone they held captive would die. I had to remain brave for the sake of my pack and for the sake of my family. Jax was coming for us, I just had to hold out for as long as I could.

The witch extended her hand out to me and hesitantly I copied her, placing my hand in hers as she proceeded to drag me forward until I stood in front of Alpha Matthew. My hands were shaking, both from the cold and the adrenaline as it pumped through my veins, but I refused to let it show as I looked into the eyes of evil.

He smirked down at me, as if he knew what I was thinking, and I couldn't stop the lone tear that escaped my lashes as it descended down my cheek, covered in blush to hide my paleness.

"Hurry Jax!" I screamed in my head as I looked back into the red ringed eyes of Alpha Matthew.

"Aww tears of joy on our special day, how sweet," Matthew sneered as he snatched my hand in his and squeezed until I lost blood flow, my bones crunching together at the grip he had on me. "Remember why you're doing this little Annie, for your beloved little Jax and for your pathetic little family," he mocked.

Another tear escaped but I quickly wiped it from my cheek with my spare hand, this sorry excuse of a man didn't deserve my fear. "Jax is going to find you... he's going to find you and he's going to kill you in the most painful and brutal way he can think of," I growled at him, as I felt my wolf start to come through.

"Ah ah little Annie, careful what you say to me," he chuckled, "wouldn't want your little Beta friend to suffer for your mouth now would you?" Matthew smirked. I frowned at him as he pointed with a nod of his head for me to look to my right. At first, I couldn't see what he was talking about, but quickly spotted it as a gasp escaped my lips.

Xavier was being held up by two men, both of their knuckles covered in his blood, as one held a knife to his throat whilst the other held his head back.

"Don't you dare hurt him," I growled again, feeling anger bubble away inside me at the way he was treating my pack, my friend.

"Go through with the ceremony and I won't," he growled back, red shining bright though his irises.

I ground my teeth together to stop the choice words I desperately wanted to spew at him from leaking out and offered him a small nod, not trusting myself to confirm verbally.

The witch suddenly stepped up to us and moved our palms to where she wanted them to be, palms facing towards the sky and next to each other. As we stood there, the wind blowing my hair around my shoulders and my dress around my ankles, she started to mutter some incantation in another language. I couldn't make out what she was saying, but before I could even blink, she drew the dagger up and slashed both mine and Matthews palms with one flick of her wrist.

I hissed in pain and tried to bring my hand away, but my body wouldn't allow it, like my hand had a mind of its own and wanted to stay rooted in its place next to Alpha Matthews.

"It's no use trying to resist princess, you're in it for the long hall now," Matthew grinned at me from across our blood-stained palms. Our blood pooling and merging into one another's as it trickled across our palms. I glared at him in disgust for what he was making me do, hating him for getting me into this situation and forcing me to leave a life I had barely begun to live.

The witch sprinkled some form of herb across our open palms, causing the opening in our flesh to burn and smoke. We stayed like that for a second as I watched in horror as my blood bubbled away on my palm, before the witch gripped both of our wrists in each of her hands and brought our hands flat against each other in between us, so that the cuts were joined.

She started muttering more sounds in that unknown dialect of hers as she proceeded to tie a blood red silk sash around our wrists, the knots so tight it was impossible to move our hands apart even if we didn't have the spell binding us together. The pain was intensifying by the second, as if someone were pouring acid onto my hand, and no amount of tugging I did would let me release my hand from Alpha Matthews and away from this pain.

I could feel the burning sensation slowly making its way up my arm as the witch continued to mutter to herself, as if the spell was weaving its way through my bloodstream. I tried to slow my heart rate down in the hopes that it would cause the spell to work slower, but it was no use, the burning continued its ascent up and past my elbow. Tears were dripping from my chin as I mourned what I was losing as well as the physical pain that I was currently going through.

To anyone else looking in on this situation, you would think that we were perfectly content, as if standing here and going through this process was the most relaxing experience of my existence. I knew differently though, and one look into Matthew's eyes told me that he was going through just as much pain as I was in this moment. Well at least this situation had a small silver lining, any form of pain Alpha Matthew was in was good news to me.

I suddenly heard an animalistic roar off in the distance and my heart rate immediately spiked as my body reacted to the sound. It was Jax, and he was pissed.

I just had to hold out a little bit longer, just long enough for him and everyone one else to get here and then I could be free from this hell and free from Alpha Matthew.

"JAX HURRY!" I screamed through our mind link as I attempted to contact him, but again I didn't get a response, just static.

I looked back at Alpha Matthew and for the first time ever I saw doubt and fear flash through his eyes, but it was only for a second before the witch proceeded to mutter more words, her voice increasing in volume with every syllable, before stabbing the dagger into our joined hands.

I screamed in agony, this time my body allowing me to move, as I looked at both our hands, joined together by the dagger the witch had recently been holding. It went right through our skin, with the hilt of the handle touching the back of my hand and the tip sticking out of Matthews.

The next thing I knew my brain burst alive as I felt electricity and fire burn through every vain and cell in my body. What was happening to me!

Before I knew it, both myself and Matthew collapsed to the floor, our hands still connected by the dagger and silk scarf, as blackness consumed me.

Chapter 26

Jax's POV

We were all in position. We were just lying in wait on the eastern border of Alpha Matthews territory for the signal from one of our guys so that we could finally put our plan into action.

My skin was itching to shift, to run and find my Annabelle, but I knew that if I did that then I would be putting everyone's life in danger. The plan we had would work, I just had to be patient and hope that I wasn't too late.

Finally, after what felt like hours, we got the signal that we could move in. We had decided to stay in human form until the last possible second. Not only would it save our energy for when it really counted, it would also give us the element of surprise we so desperately needed.

When we shift into our wolf form our scent becomes infinitely stronger. It was used for when we went on hunting trips so that we could find each other easier, it could also be used for defence. As a pack we would be able to smell an attack much quicker if the enemy was in their wolf form. It was a great advantage when we were on the defence, but now that we were on the attack, we needed to make sure we weren't spotted.

We stalked forward through the forest, on high alert for any form of noise that seemed out of the ordinary, but as we made our way forward and we still heard nothing I started to become suspicious. Surely, we would have seen at least one wolf on patrol by now, even with the commotion the other packs were making at the south border.

"Henry, what do you think of the situation? Call me crazy but the lack of border patrol is putting me on edge" I mind linked one of my warriors who was standing not too far from me.

He glanced over at me for only a second, acknowledging my concerns, but that was enough for me to get my answer. He didn't like this either.

Just as I was about to break out of the treeline and take another step closer to the bunker and to the heart of the pack, I felt a splitting pain erupted in my brain, like someone was trying to forcibly rip something from me.

I staggered backwards at the pain as my legs started to give out, what the hell was going on? I forced my lips to remain sealed so as not to give away our position, but if anything, that just made the pain worse.

"Alpha, are you okay?" Henry asked as he ran over to me in concern, thoughts of stealth going out the window as he ran the short distance towards me through the treeline.

"I don't..." I tried to respond but couldn't as I felt the pack link started to shatter.

All of a sudden I had a small moment of clarity as I thought about what Annabelle had told me. Matthew had been planning to perform the breaking and mating ceremony on her.

My wolf was on full alert now, the pain being pushed to the back of my mind, as I jumped into gear. We would not let some little Alpha *pup* steal what was rightfully ours.

I let out a ferocious roar, intending it to reach each and every person who was in this territory. Not only did I want to let the other Alphas know that I was going in for the kill, I wanted Matthew to know that I was coming for him.

I shifted into my wolf form in a flash as I began running towards the bunker where Annabelle had said she was being held. It was as if I had tunnel vision, my mind becoming solely focused on the slightly raised bit of land in front of me, the door to the bunker hidden in the shadows as the grass grew over the archway.

I stumbled in my advance on the bunker though, along with everyone else in my pack, as I heard Annabelle's cry for help though the bond. I was frozen for a second as I marvelled at the sheer strength it would have taken for her and her wolf to project a message through the pack link, especially when she hadn't been fully integrated into the pack yet.

"I'm coming baby, just hold on for me," I tried to tell her as I made it to the bunker, skidding to a stop just outside the door leading down into the cells. I began to descend the concrete staircase but froze when I didn't smell her scent. She was no longer here.

"Henry check the bunker out," I ordered as I turned and started to follow where her scent led.

I paused as I saw out of the corner of my eye Henry and a few of my other warriors fighting with the guards who had obviously heard us coming. I stalled in my departure, waiting to see if they would need my help in handling the situation, but sighed when I saw that they were quickly dealt with. They would be fine without me.

I focused back on the task at hand as I ran with my nose close to the ground, trying to pick up any traces of Annabelle's scent that I could find. It wasn't her normal scent that I was following, more a combination of her natural smell mixed in with different people's blood and urine. It was clear that they hadn't been looking after her whilst she had been here, even refusing to give them all the basic decency of using a toilet when they needed to. I'm not even that cruel when we capture rogues on the rare occasions when we need to get more information out of them.

Her scent of vanilla and strawberries was also mixed with another, something I faintly recognised as fake pine and burnt plastic, and I growled at whoever was so close to her that their scents had merged together on their walk over from the bunker to their new location. I had a feeling that this particular smell belonged to a certain Alpha Matthew, even though half of his pack took it upon themselves to disguise themselves. I know he wouldn't let anyone else deal with Annabelle, just in case she got away. I growled as his stench filled my nostrils and I took comfort in the fact that this was going to be the stench I would be smelling as I watched the life drain from his eyes as I slowly killed him for hurting my mate and pack.

I faltered when I heard a scream coming from a few hundred yards in front of me and I sprinted on to try and determine where exactly it had come from. There wasn't a shadow of a doubt in my mind that that scream belonged to my Annabelle and I was determined to get to her before they could take her away from me for good.

"Annabelle!" I screamed in my head as I continued to sprint forward, gaining momentum with every step that I took towards her, as if the closer she was to me the stronger my wolf became.

"Annabelle's in trouble," I yelled through the link as I pounced on an unsuspecting guard before carrying on. *"Attack now!"* I yelled as I jumped over a small hedge and came face to face with a crowd of people, all staring at the porch of a house where three people stood, one of them being my Annabelle.

My little Annabelle had been stabbed in the hand, forcing her to join with another male, whom I'm guessing was Alpha Matthew, as they lay passed out on the wooden porch. Her body was battered and bruised all over with the appearance of makeup covering her skin to try and hide the trauma it had been through; unsuccessfully might I add. Her feet, fingertips and lips were an alarming shade of blue, indicating that she was ice cold and the white sleeveless dress she had been forced to wear was smeared in red as her hand continued to drip blood, staining the fabric.

I made a move to go and help her off the floor, wanting desperately to feel her warm skin against mine to reassure myself that she was still alive, but tripped in my stride towards her as the blinding pain in my head reappeared. This time it was even stronger, as I watched my Annabelle convulse on the floor slightly as the bond tried to be ripped apart from within our minds.

"No!" I screamed as I tried desperately to grip onto the bond with everything I had. It was like an elastic band being stretched so tight it had snapped and I was stuck in the middle of it, trying to keep the two parts together through sheer will.

My brain snapped back into gear when the bond had momentarily mended itself, like it had slapped a plaster on the issue so that I could refocus on the task at hand and get to my Annabelle before she deteriorated any further. The ceremony that she had been forced to partake in was dangerous, it had never been performed enough in our history to get any specific statistics on it but the survival rate of the wolves who took part in it were slim to none.

The mating bond formed by the Moon Goddess between two werewolves was a complicated one. Not only was it between two individuals in our human form, it was also formed between two wolves. The spell causing the bond to break could sometimes only break one way and not the other, or our wolves could simply not let go of their mate and be ripped from our minds entirely. Both complications were fairly common, and all resulted in death for one or both of the pair. It was as if our brain was split in two with the indecisiveness of what it should be doing.

I shook my head to try and refocus my brain before locking eyes on the male who was, with the help from a blade of a dagger, still attached to my mate. I growled in anger as I ran towards Alpha Matthew at a full sprint, ready for any attack from the crowd surrounding him that would come my way. To my surprise though nothing happened, they just watched me pass with glazed over eyes as they took in the sight of me running up to their Alpha. Some of them didn't even bother to get out of my way as I ran through them, I ended up having to actively try and dodge a few people as I kept my focus on the three figures still there on the porch steps.

The witch was leaning over both of their passed-out forms as she sprinkled something over their still joined hands and muttered some form of spell, her mouth moving too fast for me to make out what she was saying. The wind whipped around her feet as she suddenly lifted her hands up to the heavens, the power of her voice gaining with every syllable she muttered. The bond wobbled again as the witch continued her spell but it held strong causing her to frown down at my mate in confusion, wondering why her spell wasn't working.

I had to think fast as I paused and took in the situation around me. My pack, along with our allies, were easily taking care of Matthews warriors, quickly understanding that the only ones we needed to worry about were the ones that smelled of plastic and pine. The rest were quickly forgotten about as they just continued to stare ahead with an inhuman blankness in their eyes.

The only real threat that remained was the witch herself, who was alternating between continuing the spell and checking her surroundings, her eyes like a snake as she took everything in.

As if she felt my eyes on her she suddenly looked up from what she was doing and stared in my direction, eyes as black as the night staring deep into my soul. I shuddered as a cold chill surrounded me, feeling as if her cold, bony fingers were crawling up my spine. I shook it off, telling myself that it was all in my head, as I started stalking towards her, keeping my body low and wound tight in case of a surprise attack.

As I crept my way closer, I could just about make out Annabelle's heartbeat as I flicked my eyes between focusing on her and my opponent in front of me. The knowledge that she was, in fact, alive, helped me relax enough so I could focus on this witch in front of me. She was alive. I hadn't failed.

"Hello pup," the witch sneered at me as she bent down and placed her hand on the hilt of the dagger currently resting in between the bones of my little mates' hand. "Come to join the celebrations?"

I growled as she slowly started to remove the dagger from Annabelle's hand, blood leaking out of the wound as her skin clung to the metal of the dagger as the witch continued to retract it. Worryingly though Annabelle didn't even bat an eyelid, as the slightly ridged blade was pulled from her skin. Blood continued to drip out of her wound as it pooled around her and onto the wooden floor, her once white dress now turning red with every second that passed.

I wish I could speak and ask her why she was doing this to us, but seeing as she wasn't packed and I was currently in wolf form, I didn't have a hope of communicating with her.

"You're wondering why aren't you?" She asked, amusement lacing in her tone as she stared deep into my eyes, her dagger held at waist height as she pointed it in my direction. "The question shines bright in your golden eyes," she smirked as she read my mind through my eyes.

I just carried on staring at her, waiting for the moment where her attention was distracted enough so that I could strike without fear of the blade digging into my underbelly or throat.

The battle was still raging on around us, cries of pain and sounds of tearing flesh could be heard throughout the clearing as our packs made light work of Matthews loyal followers. Most of them had been rogues, judging by their physical appearance and lack of personal hygiene, so there wasn't much love lost as I heard them one by one being taken down.

"Well it's fairly simple really," she sighed as she smirked over at me, drawing my focus back on her. "I wanted to destroy your little *Moon Goddess* as much as Matthew did," she laughed as she kicked Matthew in the arm with the toe of her boot. "With her out of the picture your species would inevitably crumble, leaving us witches with more land and resources then we would know what to do with. Just like how it was back in the good old days before your filthy little species existed," she sneered, her voice hissing as she delivered her speech.

I squinted my eyes at her as I tried to refrain from portraying the shock that I was currently feeling. If she was telling the truth, that she was alive before werewolves walked the earth, then she must be at least two thousand years old. She didn't look a day over thirty though, her black hair held no grey and her skin showed no signs of the telling lines you'd expect from someone of her age. I pushed that through from my mind and re-focused on the witch. She was more than likely trying to distract me so that she could catch me off guard and make me vulnerable.

I took a step towards her, testing the waters to see what she would do if I did decide to advance on her, but the witch just laughed at my tentative move and took her own step towards me. The gap between us was now only a few short steps, making it extremely easy for one of us to lunge in the other direction and make contact before you could bat an eyelid.

"I wouldn't do that if I were you boy," the witch smirked, amused at the defensive stance that I'd taken. "I've been on this world a lot longer than you could even imagine and I could take you out of it just as easily as I have done with hundreds of your filthy kind."

I growled at the threat as I crouched down, ready for an attack. She had this gleam in her eye which told me that not only was she telling the truth about killing hundreds of my people, she also enjoyed doing it.

I continued to growl as I stared her down. If this was my time, then I was going to go down fighting.

"Oh pup, you have no idea," the witch sighed with an almost condescending tone to her voice, as if she was talking to a child, before she tightened her grip on the dagger's handle and pounced on me, Annabelle's blood still dripping from the blade.

Chapter 27

Annabelle's POV

What happened?

I groggily sat up and rubbed my forehead with the heel of my hand, trying to ease the pounding behind my eyes that was threatening to split my head open. How had I managed to get here?

I was currently sitting cross legged in a field, with more fields attached to this one, stretching out as far as the eye could see, and the sound of a river rushing not too far in the distance. Wildflowers bloomed everywhere, breaking up the sea of rolling green hills with splashes of red, yellow and violet. The place was almost picturesque, peaceful, *tranquil,* and I instantly knew I was no longer in Alpha Matthews territory. Granted I hadn't had the privilege of seeing much of his land during my imprisonment, but the feeling I had, the feeling of utter relaxation, was something I knew I would never feel when in his near vicinity.

"Hello my child," a soft voice spoke, breaking the silence of the scene around me.

I jumped, not realising that I wasn't alone in this serene paradise, before turning around with wide eyes, coming face to face with a woman who was standing a few feet behind me. I couldn't stop myself from staring at her beauty. She didn't have one particular face that she stuck to, instead it was as if she shifted from one body to another, constantly changing her appearance from face to face.

First she was blond, then a red head, then she had black hair, all in different hairstyles ranging from waist length locks to short cropped afros. Her skin also shifted in colour, varying from the palest of whites all the way to the deepest of chocolate browns. She was beautiful and I couldn't help myself as I continued to stare up at her in awe.

The one thing that did remain constant throughout her appearance changes were her eyes, glowing bright with a translucent quality to them as they stared into my own.

She wore a white maxi dress, similar to the one I had been forced to wear for the ceremony, and she had a soft aura about her that just made me instantly relax when in her presence. I knew exactly who she was without her having to tell me. Only a Goddess could look the way she did and make me feel so at ease.

"How am I... where am I... how did you..." I stuttered as I continued to stare at her in shock. I wasn't able to finish the first question before the next one came tumbling out of my mouth.

The Moon Goddess chuckled slightly, obviously amused at my fumbling words, as I continued to stare wide eyed at her.

"Relax," she soothed as she held her hand up. "One question at a time," she softly spoke as she leant down before making herself comfortable on the ground, amongst the wildflowers and the tall grass. She looked completely at home here, as if she were at one with the nature around her, and I frowned at the slight pang of jealousy I felt towards her. She looked so relaxed and at peace with herself, even when everything around her was in the midst of being destroyed with just a simple spell from an old witch.

"Where am I?" I whispered, darting my head from left to right to see if I could find any landmarks to clue me in on where she had taken me.

"We are in your head my child, the link that we share makes it possible for me to appear when necessary," she explained.

I nodded my head, frowning slightly as I started fiddling with the grass beneath my feet, the blades feeling soft like velvet against my fingertips. There was so much I wanted to ask her, so many questions that I wanted to demand an answer for. Like how could she leave me in a house like the Leftens when she knew where I was and what I was being forced to go through? How could she leave my parents to fend for themselves against Alpha Parker when she was the reason why they were taken and held captive in the first place? But most importantly why, out of everyone in the world, did she choose my family and me in particular to be her messenger? I was, after all, damaged goods.

"I chose your family line because I could see the type of characteristics you all held and knew the type of people you'd all become. Your mother, grandmother and even great grandmother were all extremely kind-hearted people who would not take the power bestowed upon them for granted. They were extremely strong willed, just like you, and I knew that you and your family would not crumble under the extreme pressures of becoming my messenger. That kind of combination, being so strong and yet so kind, being so aware of the world around you yet remaining so selfless, is extremely rare in a wolf. It is a combination that should be worshipped and cared for."

I stared at her in bewilderment, at both the words she had uttered and the fact that she had answered a question that I had voiced only in my head.

"We are in your head my dear, of course I can hear what you're thinking. All your thoughts and feelings are broadcasted to me as if you had simply stated them allowed," she explained.

Pink tinged my cheeks as I thought about the other questions that I'd had racing through my mind.

The Goddess' face turned sombre, understanding my embarrassment as to why I had turned shy. "I am deeply sorry for everything you've experienced and everything that you have gone through my dear," she sighed as she placed her hand on top of mine, a warm glow making its way up my arm at the contact. "Interfering with people's will is something that I cannot do, as much as I would sometimes like to," she explained.

"What Alpha Parker and Alpha Matthew did, as awful as it was, was something that I could not stop. It takes a considerable amount of energy, on both my part and my hosts, to interfere in someone's life. It was a type of energy that neither you nor your mother possessed because of the mistreatment you had endured at the hands of others. If I were to interfere back then the likelihood of your survival would have been slim," She explained, a sad look in her translucent eyes.

As much as I would have loved to get angry at her for not helping me, it was neither her job nor her responsibility to rescue me every time I got into trouble. What I had gone through was painful and something I would never wish on another, but it was something that made me who I am today. I was a firm believer in everything happening for a reason, so if me having to live most of my life in an abusive household was what brought me to my family and my mate then I would gladly go through it all again in a heartbeat.

I sighed as a sudden weight lifted from my shoulders. The realisation that I had finally accepted what had happened to me and was no longer feeling anger or hurt from my time at the Leftens helped me breathe easier and put my mind at ease.

"Am I dead?" I suddenly whispered, looking around at the landscape that I could only describe as heavenly.

"No you are not dead my child," she chuckled. "I have placed you into a deep sleep so that we could have a conversation. Do not worry, your mate is protecting your body for now, but we mustn't take much long, the witch is extremely strong."

My heart rate quickened at the thought of Jax being in trouble and I instantly tensed up. There was no way I was allowing Jax to get hurt because of me. "So what did you want to talk to me about?" I asked.

"The ceremony that the witch performed on you," she explained as she continued to stare into my eyes, her gaze unwavering as she stared into my own.

My heart rate increased, if that was even possible, as she brought up my possible broken bond with Jax. Was it gone? Was I now destined to be Matthew's mate for the rest of my life?

"W-What about it?" I stuttered, struggling to get the question out for fear of the answer I would get.

Sensing my nerves, the Moon Goddess smiled at me, a kind smile, before her glow instantly increased making me feel more relaxed.

"Do you wish for me to allow your bond to be broken with Alpha Jax?" She asked.

I was about to scream *no* at her, questioning why she was even asking me that question, when she held her hand up to silence me. "Please be clear with all the options I am offering to you, my child. I am currently still holding your bond together with Alpha Jax and stopping the process of a bond forming between you and Alpha Matthew, but I could just as easily sever both mate bonds for you entirely."

I looked at her in shock, not understanding why I wouldn't want her to keep my bond with Jax intact. He was the most amazing person I had ever met and he deserved to be happy with his mate, the person he's been waiting his whole life for.

"I will happily form a new mate bond for Jax with a different wolf if you wish to remain mate less," the Moon

Goddess explained "but think carefully about your options before you make your decision. Once the decision is made, it can not be undone."

I was about to tell her I wanted to keep my mate bond with Jax, not being able to even stomach the thought of watching him being happy with someone else, when my brain finally clicked. Now I understood what she was asking me. I would never be left alone, if word got out that I had a direct line to the Moon Goddess, that I was her messenger, people would never leave us alone. There would always be a Matthew or a Parker waiting in the wings to ruin everything that we had spent so long trying to build.

I thought about my dad, about how much pain and suffering he had gone through for all these years, all because he had the mate bond with my mother. If the mate bond between them didn't exist, he would have been left alone to live a happy life with someone else, without the fear of being kidnapped and his family put in danger.

Could I put Jax through all of that? The pain of losing your mate and having them kidnapped over and over again? And what about his family and pack? Wouldn't they get tired of rescuing me? I'd already nearly cost them their Beta, could I really ask them to live in constant fear of losing their Luna?

My parent's face's flashed through my mind again. That could very well be us in the future. Could I live with myself if I knew that I was the reason for Jax's pain for all those years?

All these thoughts came flooding through my mind, but all it took was one face as it popped out amongst the chaos, a face that instantly made my choice ten times easier.

"Okay," I whispered as I looked the Moon Goddess in the eye. "I've made my decision".

Chapter 28

Jax's POV

The witch was strong.

Somewhere in the fight I had managed to switch sides with her, having me now standing in front of Annabelle and on the slightly higher ground of the porch. I was standing between her and my mate, who was still lying lifeless on the patio floor, without showing a single sign of waking anytime soon. I could feel the body heat coming from her, confirming that she was still alive, but it did little to calm my nerves.

"Just give up wolf," the witch hissed at me, her black eyes piercing into my soul as she observed my stance. "There is no way you can beat me; you can barely stand as it is," she laughed as she flicked the daggers blade in my direction again, acting almost casual in the action.

Unfortunately, the witch was right, I was starting to struggle. Although we had both caused some damage to the other, I had seriously underestimated her speed and healing capabilities. On two separate occasions now I had managed to clip a claw or a tooth on one of her key arteries, but on both occasions her wounds seemed to ooze this thick, black liquid which seemed to quickly heal the wound back up.

She had gotten one good hit on me with her blade's edge, tearing at my underside, causing blood to flow freely out of the wound and causing my coat to matt in clumps. Thankfully, my black coat was able to camouflage most of the blood, but I think she knew, even without the quantity of blood on show, that she had caused me fatal damage.

But I wasn't going to give up, not for anyone. Annabelle was my mate and under my protection, if anyone was going to defend her, it was going to be me. I drew strength from deep within me, my wolf helping me out, and I coiled for another attack from the witch.

Just as I was about to spring, intending to slash at her throat in the hopes that her body would be unable to heal from a more fatal wound, the witch's facial expression changed. Gone was her fearless and ruthless expression as she zeroed in on me for her kill. She was now looking at something behind me, panic evident in her black eyes.

She dropped the dagger she had been clinging to throughout our whole fight, letting it drop to the floor beside her as it clanged against the paved floor.

I frowned, confused by her sudden change in arrogance, before shifting my head slightly to the right so that I could see what had caught her attention without taking my eyes from her. The last thing I needed was for this to be some kind of trick and for her to suddenly jump back into the fight without me being ready.

I looked out of the corner of my eye, sceptical about there being anything there, but when I saw a blinding light, I couldn't help but turn fully around as I could take in the whole scene.

My mate, who only moments ago was virtually lifeless on the floor, was now floating several inches above the ground. Her eyes shone a translucent moonstone colour, and her skin was radiating a golden glow reminding me of the sun on a warm summer's day. Her hair was being whipped in all directions around her face, like it had a mind of its own, and she was staring at the witch with unadulterated rage.

What the...

"Sorceress Isabella, you have been found guilty of violating multiple of the coven's seven sacred vows and is hereby called upon by the High Courts of Witchcraft for punishment and execution," she stated.

Annabelle didn't sound like herself at all, there was a slight edge to her tone of voice, making me think that the person inside my little mate's body right now, wasn't my little mate at all. She lifted her hand up from where it was resting at her side and raised it high, the earlier knife wound that was there now vanishing with every passing second.

As she spoke, figures made from dust and fog emerged from the ground around us, advancing on Sorceress Isabella who started screaming and begging for mercy as her eyes flicked from one dust cloud form to the other. The figures reacted little to her cries and pleas for mercy as they all grabbed onto a part of her clothing or body as they swarmed her. Within seconds she was surrounded, so much so that I couldn't even make out her figure amongst the debris and mist whirling around and within a blink of an eye, she was gone, vanished along with the dust and wind that had taken her with them.

I stood there for a second, taking in the empty space the witch had previously occupied, before I turned back to face whoever was currently inside my Annabelle.

My hackles raised as I growled at her, how dare they possess my mate.

"Calm yourself Alpha Jax, for I mean your mate no harm," the woman inside Annabelle's body reassured me and a sudden calmness settled around me.

I frowned, confused at my own body's reactions, before everything clicked and I quickly bowed to the floor, showing the Moon Goddess the respect she deserved. I can't believe I just growled at our Goddess.

"Rise Alpha Jax, I do not wish for your submission. I purely came here for an answer to a question that needs answering," she reassured me as I slowly got back on my feet.

I frowned at her as I cocked my head to the side in confusion. I couldn't shift yet because of the wound that was slowly leaking blood on my underside, if I shifted it would split open even further and potentially become worse.

As if she could somehow sense my confusion and frustration, my mate, or more accurately the Moon Goddess, smiled down at me before walking forward and placing her hand on my wolf's forehead.

At first nothing happened, I just felt the comforting touch of a warm palm on my fur, but slowly the cuts and grazes that littered my body began to rise in temperature and become increasingly itchy and painful.

After a second or two the itching became almost unbearable, and I had to force myself not to step away from the Goddess' touch to try to ease the uncomfortable feeling. It wasn't long though before my injuries started to emit their own golden glow, just like the aura Annabelle's body was giving off, as they magically started healing closed. I stared in amazement as she retracted her hand from my skin, taking the warm glow like feeling with her, as I did a mental check of my body.

I shifted from foot to foot, testing my strength, and when I felt no uncomfortable tug, I looked up at her in shock. I was healed. I instantly started to shift back into my human form, needing to be able to speak so that I could get some answers as to what was happening to my mate.

I felt a presence behind me, and I turned around to find Will with a pair of shorts in his hands as he held them out to me. He looked like crap, with more bruises and cuts on his body than I could count. His usual dirty blond hair looked almost brown with the amount of debris he had stuck to its strands and his wrists and ankles were slightly swollen due to the amount of silver poisoning he'd had. Through all that though he still looked like my younger brother, the calm and collected soul who preferred to sit in the corner and read a book whilst everyone else would rather play video games.

I smiled at him in thanks, hoping that he knew it wasn't just the shorts I was thanking him for, but for also lending a hand in finding Annabelle and just generally staying alive. I slipped quickly into the shorts before bringing him into a tight hug. I felt him flinch slightly at the sudden contact, obviously finding my hug a little painful. He didn't pull away from me though, instead wrapping his arms around me and slapping me on the back. "It's good to see you brother," I whispered before releasing him with a smile.

My brother, being a man of very few words, just nodded in response with a smile, his way of saying he was glad to be back.

I looked behind him and suddenly noticed that we had a large audience, everyone that was involved with the rescue had made their way into the clearing and were now staring at us with shock clear in their eyes.

The most shocked people though were the people in Alpha Matthews pack. Gone were the blank stares they'd had moments ago, they were now looking at everything around them, confused as to what was going on and why they were out here with several other packs surrounding them. It was clear that the witch had been influencing them in some way, making them blindly follow first Parker and then Matthew with whatever they needed so that she could execute her plan of destroying us all. But with the witch now gone her spell was lifted, leaving the residence none the wiser that they had basically been controlled by a witch and a few mentally unstable Alpha's for who knows how long.

I looked back at my mate, taking in her appearance as she continued to float about a foot off the ground. Her cuts and bruises had all been healed but the blood that had stained her skin and clothes had remained. Even still, she was the most beautiful thing I had ever laid my eyes on. "What answer are you seeking?" I questioned her, noticing she was still staring at me, her moonstone eyes burning the same colour as Annabelle's wolf's.

She smiled down at me, as a caring mother would smile at her child. "Are you willing to keep your mate bond to Annabelle? Are you willing to stay mated to her after everything that you have learned?"

What kind of idiotic question was that?! Of course I wanted to be mated with Annabelle, she was the most beautiful person I had ever met, both inside and out. Even if she wasn't my mate, I would have still appreciated her beauty. "Yes," I said in a strong voice, trying not to growl at her as the anger of her question ran through my veins.

"Are you sure Alpha Jax?" She pressed, "once you've made your decision it cannot be undone."

"Look, by some miracle you paired me with this amazing person, and I intend to be with her for the rest of my life. I will fight for her, kill for her, *die* for her. I acknowledge that this won't be the last time we experience trouble because of who she is and what she shares with you, but there is no way you are taking away the best thing that has ever happened to me," I growled as my fists clenched beside me.

"Just give me back my Annabelle and I will do anything you ask, just give me back the person that I fell in love with the moment I laid eyes on her." My voice cracked slightly towards the end of my speech, but I cleared my throat, trying to hide the emotion I was feeling.

The Moon Goddess assessed me through Annabelle's translucent eyes, before finally offering me one swift nod as she disappeared from Annabelle's body. As fast as I could, I ran over to Annabelle as she came crashing down to the blood-stained wooden floor beneath her, making sure she didn't hurt herself as she fell.

I caught her and wrapped her securely in my arms, she was finally back where she belonged. Safe

"I love you too," I heard her whisper before she passed out in my arms, feeling the telling tingles of the mate bond running through my veins.

Chapter 29

Annabelle's POV

It had been a week since everything went down with Alpha Parker and Alpha Matthew and things were slowly starting to get back to normal.

The packs that had come to help Jax had all gone their separate ways, minus the odd few people who had found their mates amongst the mass gathering of wolves. It was actually a really good idea, to get loads of packs together into one territory, it helped solidify trust and treaties between each other and also expanded our social circles, helping us find our mates faster and easier. It's something I was going to bring up with Jax, something that we could do each year that everyone was welcome to, no matter what pack you belonged to or your rank.

My parents had decided to come back with us and stay with me in Jax's territory, which I was beyond happy about. It was weird at first, the idea of having that parental figure who would look after you, but I quickly got used to it. It was something I had craved for most of my childhood and I was lucky enough to finally experience it.

Mum was trying to help me get to grips with this Moon Goddess link I had now possessed. Apparently it was the choice of the Moon Goddess when to pass down the responsibility of being a messenger onto the next generation. The only catch was the chosen one had to have found their mate to withstand the amount of strain the link would have on their wolf. Hence why I hadn't become a messenger until after I had met Jax. Once I had met him the Goddess shifted the touch as fast as she could, not wanting my mum to have the burden of the link when she was in such a terrible situation.

It turns out the necklace that I had always admired as a child, the bronze metal ring with a moonstone and intricately woven metal tree holding it all in place, helped channel our powers that we received from the Goddess. No one really knows what the extent of my abilities would be, but from the basic knowledge mum had managed to offer us and the small segments of information we'd found in our pack library, we'd managed to work out a few. The most common was dream walking, a form of Astral projection that the Goddess achieved by taking a part of me and placing me in a different environment. It was risky, as we'd learnt the hard way, as people could see me and touch me as much as if I were really there, but it could really come in handy in the future if anything were to happen.

The Elders had arrived mere hours after we had all gotten home, although I had been asleep the whole time due to the strain my body had been under from hosting the Goddess in my body. They had originally been angered by the fact that Jax had gone against their word and not waited for them to arrive before he formed his attack. They quickly cooled off though when my mum finished explaining to them what would have happened had Jax waited another day for them to arrive.

The one thing I wish I was awake for though was when they took Matthew away. After he had come to from the ceremony, he had found himself in Jax's cells, under the same conditions he had forced upon me and the rest of the pack that he had captured and imprisoned. He wouldn't stop screaming and shouting every time he moved, causing the silver to shift on his skin and burn his flesh. Jax handed him over to the Elders as soon as they arrived, stating that he couldn't stand the sound of his screams any longer.

I had originally asked him why he had handed Matthew over to the Elders in the first place, convinced he would've wanted to conduct his own form of cruel punishment which would have no doubt resulted in his death. His reply though was only a small smile with an evil glint in his eye. I had later learnt from Hannah that being in the Elders prisons was a fate worse than death, something that prisoners feared more than anything else.

They performed torture down there that we could scarcely imagine and I was ashamed to say that I kind of enjoyed the idea of him spending the rest of his life in agony.

Things between Jax and myself were amazing, he's as caring and as devoted to me as when I first stumbled into his life. If I was being honest, I kind of wished he wouldn't treat me so delicately, he acted as if I was a snowflake and the world was a giant ball of flames ready to melt me at any second. As much as I loved him it did get tiring sometimes.

I'm hoping today is going to be the day that things start to progress in our relationship. It was the Luna ceremony today, the day I will officially be welcomed into the pack and given the honour of becoming their Luna.

To say that I was both excited and nervous would be an understatement.

I stared at myself in the mirror as I watched my mum put the last finishing touches to my hair, placing delicate white flowers into my long, curly blond locks in a crown shape on top of my head.

"You look stunning Honey," my mum smiled down at me through the reflection of the mirror, her eyes glazing over with tears as she looked me over. "I never thought I'd get a chance to see you again, let alone be there for the day you took part in your Luna ceremony with your new mate and pack."

I smiled back at her as she kissed the top of my head, my voice too thick with emotion to even try to voice the words I wanted to say. To explain to her just how happy I was that she and my dad were now here, in the Crescent moon pack, and safe from Alpha Parker and Alpha Matthew.

"I love you mum," I whispered as I tried to hold back my own tears, not wanting to ruin the makeup Hannah had spent all morning doing.

"No no no none of that," Hannah ordered as she fluttered around the room, making sure we had everything we needed before going down the stairs. She had taken one look at me and instantly started fretting about my mascara, claiming that it wasn't waterproof and wouldn't be able to withstand even the smallest droplet of water. "We don't have time to redo your makeup Anna, please don't cry otherwise we'll be late," she begged.

I rolled my eyes at her as a smile slipped onto my face. This was my life now, I had people who truly cared for me and I couldn't be happier with how it turned out. I'd go through the hell I went through at the Leftens ten times over if it meant I could have this waiting for me at the end.

"Come on, come on it's time to get going, I've got your shoes, your mum has your garland and you have... well you, so come on!" She yelled, bouncing on her toes in excitement.

I laughed at Hannah's enthusiasm before taking her hand in mine as she led me out of the bedroom and down the stairs, towards the garden where the ceremony was taking place.

My heart was racing as my eyes locked onto the closed back door. I knew that on the other side, hundreds of people were currently sitting and waiting to catch a glimpse of me and bestow their trust and faith onto me as their new Luna.

No pressure or anything.

Just as I started to feel my hands clam up and a cold sweat began to break out across the nape of my neck, I felt a presence behind me that instantly calmed my nerves. Jax.

I could feel his heat radiating through the back of my dress and I quickly turned around in his arms and held onto him for dear life. He was my comfort and my safe place in all this mayhem and right now I needed that comfort.

"You look absolutely beautiful my little mate; I really did get lucky when the Moon Goddess gave me to you," he whispered as he breathed into my hair. His scent was surrounding me as he held me in his arms, and I couldn't help but burrow myself further into his chest.

"I think I'm the lucky one in this pairing Jax, no way would I have been able to survive any of this without you," I muttered as my face hid in his shirt.

I smiled as I felt his deep chuckle vibrate in his chest. "Well then I think on this occasion we may just have to agree to disagree... agreed?"

I laughed quietly with him before nodding my head "agreed."

"Right two minutes love birds!" We heard Hannah shout from outside through the open windows.

"I think she's more excited about this than we are," I laughed, observing through the open window Hannah running back and forth, making sure everything was exactly where it should be for the ceremony to begin.

Jax laughed too before taking my face in his hands and tilting it up so I could look into his chocolate brown eyes.

"Nobody is more excited than I am for this moment my little mate, to finally call you my own. I love you with all my heart and with everything that I have, and I can't wait to tell the whole world that you are mine and that I am yours… forever."

I stood there stunned. It wasn't just his words that made me tear up in that moment, it was the look he was giving me as we stared into each other's eyes. Like I was the air he breathed, the sun in his universe, like I was the one thing in his life that he truly couldn't live without.

I don't know if it was his words, or his expression, or the situation we were in, but before I could overthink it, I reached up onto my tip toes and pressed my lips to his.

He froze for a second, taken completely off guard by my actions and I panicked, thinking I had done something wrong, but I instantly relaxed as I felt him wrap his arms around my waist and drew me in close. Our bodies flush together, fitting perfectly, and I couldn't have imagined a more perfect place or person to share my first kiss with.

…

The time had come for us to finally walk down the aisle together. The Luna ceremony was similar to a human wedding, except instead of two people being joined together in the eyes of their God, it was one person being joined to a whole pack in the eyes of our Goddess.

I had been told that it would be a short ceremony, just a few short words spoken by the previous Alpha and current Beta before the previous Luna would come up on stage and finish the ceremony off.

Jax and I smiled at each other one last time before we turned and proceeded to walk down the aisle. We were both bare footed, helping us to connect with the wildlife, and the grass beneath our feet was covered in handpicked wildflowers which had been picked and scattered by the entire pack as a gift and a blessing to us.

Once we made it to the end of the aisle I sighed a breath of relief as I took the final step onto the wooden makeshift stage where we were met by Jackson. My main fear had been tripping over my dress as I walked, but now that part was over I could sigh in relief and focus on the ceremony.

"It is a joyous occasion when a pack is gifted the presence of their rightful Luna. It is something to be celebrated and shared with the world, under the eyes of the Moon Goddess and the members of her new pack." Jackson's voice was strong and clear, carrying across the winds so that every person witnessing the ceremony could hear. I was entranced by his words, smiling up at him as I basked in the feeling of truly belonging for the first time in my life.

"Before we begin, does anyone present today, pack or otherwise, have any reason why we can not perform the Luna ceremony today?" he asked.

I had been informed of this part of the ceremony, of having to wait in silence to see if anyone rejected the idea of me becoming their Luna. I had been nervous when I first heard of it, thinking that maybe someone would dislike me becoming a part of their pack due to what I was or what I had done, but now that it had arrived I felt nothing but calm. With Jax standing in front of me, holding my hands tightly in his, I knew I had no reason to doubt my pack or their thoughts towards me, just like they shouldn't doubt me and mine.

Once Jackson was happy with the silence that followed his question, he stepped down from the small platform holding the three of us and went to stand on the grass next to us, giving way for Xavier to stand.

I couldn't help the grin that spread across my face as I watched Xavier take his position. Considering everything he had been through, all the beatings he had taken and the silver he had endured, he had come out of it with no permanent damage. He still bore the telling signs of the burns around his wrists and ankles, much like my parents and the rest of the captured pack, but they would soon heal and fade away along with the rest of his injuries.

"In front of all of you today and under the watchful eyes of our Moon Goddess I, Beta Xavier of the Crescent Moon pack, give myself over to you, our Alpha and Luna. I swear to protect you with my life and offer assistance wherever is needed until the day that I draw my last breath," Xavier vowed as he bowed his head at us and held his clenched fist over his heart. "Do you Annabelle, future Luna of the Crescent Moon pack, accept me as your Beta?" he asked as he kept his head bent low and his fist against his chest.

I honestly hadn't seen any reason for Xavier to come up here and pledge himself to me in such a way that he was doing now. He had demonstrated just how far he was willing to go to protect me over the last two weeks and I knew that I owed my life to him. I trusted him without question and it made my answer all the more easier as I smiled over at him. "I do Beta Xavier," I nodded as I watched his head finally rise, a grin on his face as he looked between the two of us before stepping down from the small stage to join Jackson.

Lastly it was Emily's turn. She stepped up onto the stage, holding the garland that her and Hannah had made this morning and placed it over my head. It symbolised a gift from the previous Luna of the pack and from the female members of the Alpha's family, showing that they respect me, believed in me and would protect me until the day I stepped down.

"Annabelle, I stand before you with the offering of this garland to symbolise, both to our pack and to the Moon Goddess, that I accept you as our new Luna with open arms. I offer myself to be by your side for as long as you request, with assistance and guidance throughout your time as Luna. I stand before you as a friend and a confidant, nothing more and nothing less."

I smiled over at her as she looked on at me with glassy eyes, pride swirling in her irises as she looked into my own.

"Luna Annabelle, do you swear to protect this pack with your dying breath, to rule it without prejudice or greed and to help those in need when times get tough? Do you swear to help your mate through thick and thin as you rule, guide and protect this pack?" Like Jackson, Emily's voice was strong and powerful, leaving no doubt in anyone's mind as to what she said or how she felt about it.

"I swear," I nodded, trying to mimic the power in her voice so my promise can be heard by all. I could feel my eyes shine bright with the presence of my wolf as I uttered the two words that would finally connect me with the rest of my pack.

My wolf, who had remained quiet throughout the ceremony, was finally wide awake and prancing in my mind as she worked on connecting us with the rest of the pack. It wouldn't happen all at once, more like my brain would slowly connect itself to each and every person until there was no one left. I was told it could take up to a few days before the pack link was fully connected, but I didn't mind. I had all the time in the world.

"Welcome to your pack, Luna Annabelle," Emily smiled at me before all pretence of formalities went out the window and she pulled me into a bone crushing hug.

I could hear the cheers from the onlookers behind me and I couldn't help but smile as another wave of belonging washed over me. I was home.

Chapter 30

Annabelle's POV

"You don't have to do this if you don't want to," Jax whispered soothingly to me as he stroked my cheekbone with his thumb. "We can just turn around and come back at another time."

I could tell he was worried about me, worried about my mental state, but I needed to do this. I needed to get that photo of me and my parents, needed to face these people who for so long I had been afraid of, and I had to get some closure.

I didn't blame him for worrying about me, far from it. This place had been the setting for all my pain and misery for so many years, even I was anxious about how I would react to seeing the Leftens again.

With one last breath, I turned to face the front door, a door I had scrubbed clean many times in my life, and rang the doorbell.

I was nervous as hell; it had been over two months since I had last been here, but the same feelings of low self-worth suddenly slammed into me as they always had done when I lived here. I started to hyperventilate as I heard shouting come from inside the house, arguing about who was going to answer the front door, before heavy footsteps could be heard moving closer.

As they moved closer a weird sense of calm and determination washed over me and I couldn't help but smile. I was a different person than I was back then, I now had a mate who loved me, a family who supported me and a wolf who would look after me and give me strength whenever I needed it.

I sent a thank you to my wolf for calming me down as I took Jax's hand in mine for some moral support. I could do this. I could face them.

I held my breath as I heard the door unlock and squeezed Jax's hand even tighter as I came face to face with the person who had forced me to run from this house all those months ago. Damon.

At first, we just stared at each other in silence, not really knowing what to say or what to do as we stared at each other. Damon got over his shock with my sudden appearance first, his usual cocky smirk appearing on his face as he looked me up and down.

"Well look who it is… little Annabitch," he smirked.

I froze for a second, having a sudden flash back to all the pain I felt every time he called me that name, but before I could fall too deep into my pit of despair, I instantly relaxed as I heard Jax's quiet growl coming from behind me, reminding me that he was there. *I wasn't alone, I'm not the same person, I can do this.*

Damon paled slightly at the sight of Jax but quickly tried to recover with a fake smirk directed at him. "Who's your friend?"

"This is my husband Jax," I introduced as I looked up at him to make sure he was controlled. He had a slight golden swirl in his eye but other than that, he was okay. When we travelled into the human world mates always referred to each other as husband and wife, it just made explaining our relationship to the curious few humans who asked a lot easier.

"Your *husband?"* Damon exclaimed as he took in all 6'3 feet of Jax. "You sure do work fast don't you."

Jax growled, unable to control his anger at the name I was repeatedly being called by Damon. "I'd be more careful with your words if I were you *boy,*" Jax growled as he took a threatening step towards Damon.

Damon paled further, if that was even possible, as he shrunk back slightly at the size of Jax towering over him, no longer even trying to plaster his usual sneer across his face.

"Who's at the door Damon? If they're trying to sell something, tell them we don't want it!" I heard Tony yell from inside and I froze again.

I wasn't alone, I'm not the same person, I can do this. I repeated the mantra in my head over and over again, until I could feel my heart rate decrease and my breathing return back to normal.

"Come see for yourself," Damon replied as he looked over his shoulder, no doubt looking to his dad for some form of help.

"What could possibly be so important that you had to drag me fro-".

I looked up into the eyes of the man who had caused me so much pain for so long, as he stared right back at me in shock. I was surprised to find that I wasn't afraid anymore, of him or of his family. I *wasn't* alone. I *wasn't* the same person and I *could* do this. That thought brought me more comfort than anything my wolf could do for me and I held my head high as I stared Tony down.

I was a Luna, with a powerful Alpha as a mate. I was a werewolf. I was a messenger of the Moon Goddess and above all else, I had survived. I was strong.

"What do *you* want?" Tony growled at me, probably hoping to inject some form of fear into me like he had done so many times before with that tone of voice, but it wasn't going to work this time. I had grown so much in the short time that I was away from this place, more than either of these two could even *try* to comprehend.

"Tony," I nodded at him, showing my strength through my body language as I held my spine straight and my head high. "I have come for my personal belongings, more specifically a photograph that I had left here."

He laughed "what makes you think we kept any of your crap after you ran?"

I frowned, how was I supposed to move Tony out of the way so that I could go have a look in my old room?

As if Jax knew, he suddenly took a step closer to Tony, dwarfing him as he filled the doorway. "You better move, you sorry excuse of a man, before I move you," he growled, pointing his finger into Tony's chest with every syllable.

Tony grimaced at the pain but refused to crack as he stood his ground with his arms crossed over his front.

Bad move Tony.

Before I could even blink Tony's head snapped backwards, blood pouring from his nose as Jax stood here trembling, trying not to shift from the anger that was currently pulsing through his veins.

"I said *move.*" Jax didn't even try to sound human anymore, there was an inhuman growl to his voice that made the hairs on the back of my neck stand on end and the two men in front of me to tremble. It had the desired effect, as Tony and Damon quickly moved aside so that myself and Jax could enter.

The first thing I noticed about the place was the state it was in. There was rubbish and clothes littering the surfaces of the open plan living room and there was a god-awful rotting smell coming from the kitchen, no doubt from unwashed pots and pans as they sat in the sink unwashed and growing mould.

It looked like no one had even *attempted* to clean this place since I'd left.

I crinkled my nose up at the smell and tried to ignore it as I took in the two people standing in front of me.

"Where's Natalie?" I questioned, more because I didn't want to be unprepared when she popped out from wherever she was hiding.

"That bitch left not long after you did. Apparently having someone to boss about and clean up after her was the only reason she stayed around," Tony grumbled, acting as if it was my fault that his vile wife had left him.

I just shrugged, showing no sympathy, as I took Jax's hand in mine and dragged him through the house, up the stairs and towards the cupboard that was once my bedroom.

It was just as I had left it, even down to the unmade makeshift bed pressed against the corner of the cold dark room, the blankets half hanging off the mattress and in a clump on the floor.

I shivered at the last memory I had in here, of Damon on top of me and forcing himself on me, as I took in the room. So much had changed since I had last been here.

"You okay little mate?" Jax asked cautiously as he took me in his arms, his front pressed against my back in comfort as his arms encircled my waist.

I sighed before nodding; despite everything, I was doing okay. "Come on, let's just get that photo and get out of this hell hole," I said with determination as I made my way over to the bed.

After a little bit of rooting around amongst the thin and splintering floorboards, I finally found the loose one that, not too long ago, held my only belongings. I reached into the small gap that the missing floorboards provided and pulled out the shoe box that held everything safe inside. I discarded the majority of it, the items bringing me more sadness than anything, until I finally came upon the photo.

I carefully pulled it out and smiled down at it as I thought back to all those times I had wished for my parents to come and take me away. I now knew them, had a relationship with them and I couldn't be happier.

I turned around to find Jax standing in the middle of the room, anger clear in his eyes as he took everything in. I frowned and made my way over to him, hoping I could calm him down slightly by taking his hand in mine and smiling at the sparks that always appeared at our contact.

"Are you okay?"

"Am *I* okay? Jesus Annabelle *this* is where they had you living for all those years? With nothing but a bed and blanket for furniture?"

I just shrugged, not knowing what else to say. I knew that if I confirmed it, his anger would only increase, but I also knew I couldn't lie to him and say this hadn't been my room, that just wasn't me.

"I am so glad you managed to escape this place and find me. I am never going to let you go, you will never have to live this type of life again," he vowed. He took me in his arms and held me tight, as if he was scared I was going to disappear with the wind.

"I'm okay Jax, I'm not going anywhere. You saved me," I mumbled into his chest as I breathed in his calming scent.

"Aww well isn't that sweet," we heard a voice comment from the doorway and we looked over to see a smirking Damon standing in the doorway, leaning on the doorframe much like how Alpha Matthew used to.

"What do you want Damon, I've got what we came for and now we're leaving." I went to take a step towards him, expecting him to move aside so that we could exit the room, but when he straightened himself up and blocked the way through, I froze.

"Not so fast little Annabitch... you lost me everything that day you ran away from me, now I intend to get my payback."

Was he delusional? A moment ago he was cowering in fear, terrified of getting punched by Jax like his father had and now he was standing there as if he could take the whole world on and win.

"What are you talking about Damon?" I asked as I pressed myself into Jax, more to comfort him then myself as I felt him begin to shake with rage.

"I'm talking about you running from me so I couldn't hold up my end of the deal. You ruined *everything*."

"*What* deal?" I yelled, frustrated with him and his vague answers as he continued to stare at me with hatred.

"Alpha Parker's deal!" He yelled back as he pointed a finger at me. "Me and my family were supposed to keep you here until you turned twenty-one and then he would come here and get you."

"What?" I whispered, stunned into silence. He knew about that?

He rolled his eyes at me, as if it were the most stupid question he'd ever heard. "Once you turned twenty-one Alpha Parker was to come and collect you and as a reward for keeping you alive and a secret he would share his gift with us."

I frowned "what gift?"

"He said that once he came and collected you, he would thank us by turning us into werewolves by biting us".

"W-What? You know about them?"

"Jax, is that even possible?"

"Not that I've ever heard no, Parker must've just said that so they believed they had something to gain from taking you in".

"Of course I know, my dad and mum told me," he muttered as he rolled his eyes.

"Damon... it's not possible to change someone with a bite, the only way you can be a werewolf is to be born one," I explained. I tried to be as gentle as I could, but Damon was having none of it as he stared at me in disbelief.

"NO!" He yelled as he clenched his fist and punched a hole through the wall, "you're lying!"

"Why would I lie Damon?" I sighed, getting fed up with this conversation as I watched him continue his tantrum in the doorway.

"And even if it was true, Parker isn't coming back to uphold his end of your deal, he's dead. A wolf named Matthew killed him for his Alpha title," Jax explained behind me, him too getting impatient with Damon's childish reaction.

Damon froze for a second before roaring in anger and advanced towards me. "This is all *your* fault! *Everything's* your fault!"

Jax tensed behind me, ready to fight him off, but before he could even take a step in Damon's direction I stepped forward and punched him square in the face.

I stood there, frozen for a second, as I watched blood pour out of his nose. Had I really just done that?

"You little *bitch!"* Damon shrieked as he clutched his nose in pain as tears leaked out of his eyes. I guess I did.

"You'll pay for that," he yelled before standing back up and raised his hand, ready to punch me just like he'd always do when I'd lived here and he didn't get his way.

I moved faster though, thanks to my wolf reflexes, and kicked his knee out from under him before kneeing him in the head and taking his raised hand in mine to lock behind his back, making him fall to the floor with a thump.

"You'll never touch me again, do you hear me? Neither you nor your pitiful family will come anywhere near me or mine ever again, do you understand?"

He stuttered on his answer for a second, making me tighten my grip on his arm as he continued to grunt in pain.

"Do. You. Understand?" I repeated, stressing each word as if he were a child.

"Y-Yes," he finally managed to get out, only letting up when I was sure I'd gotten my point across.

I looked up to find Jax standing there, stunned into silence as he took in my actions, before a massive grin swept across his gorgeous face. "You are so damn sexy when you do that" he chuckled as he looked over at me with pride.

I blushed as I stood up and stepped over Damon who still hadn't managed to get himself together and back up off the floor. "I guess all those self-defence lessons you gave me paid off," I shrugged as I took his hand in mine. "Now come on, let's go home."

Jax replies with a simple nod as he led me down the stairs and back out of the house I had once called my prison. Tony was nowhere in sight as we left the building, probably cowering in fear after the single blow he had received from Jax. Coward.

"When did you get so brave?" He chuckled as we made our way over to the car where a few pack warriors were waiting for us, including Henry and his new mate Sarah.

"Well... I'm going to have to be brave from now on so why not start now?" I shrugged as I rested my hand protectively over my stomach. "I can't expect you to protect the both of us *all* the time now can I?" I smiled.

I smirked as I took in Jax's shocked expression before the widest grin I had ever seen spread across his face.

"I love you so much," he whispered as he took me in his arms and kissed me with so much love it brought tears to my eyes. Oh god these hormones are going to be the death of me.

The End

Epilogue

Jax POV

"Annabelle please, just let me do it for you," I begged as I was forced to watch my heavily pregnant wife try and cook dinner.

"Jax I'm pregnant, not an invalid, so sit down and let me do my thing. Besides, your cooking is rubbish and I actually feel like eating something edible tonight if you don't mind," she stated as she turned her back to me.

I sighed as I watched Annabelle waddle around the house, whilst trying not to comment again on the fact that she shouldn't be on her feet at just under nine months pregnant. Her due date was any day now but my mate, being as stubborn as she was, wanted to cook us dinner and do everything herself. She was just as determined as ever, maybe even more so since we got pregnant and I swear it was doing to be the death of me.

Suddenly I heard a clatter pierce the semi silence and I looked up to find Annabelle staring at the wooden spoon she had accidently dropped on the floor with a scowl.

I held in a laugh as I watched her stare at the spoon in concentration, trying to figure out how she was going to get down there and pick it up.

"Did you want me to pick that up for you?" I chuckled.

"Nope, I've got this," she replied with determination, still staring at the offending object still sitting on the tiled kitchen floor, as if it had fallen on purpose purely to torment her.

"Are you *sure*?" I asked again, already starting to get up from my seat at the island in the kitchen.

"I said I've got it," she snapped as she braced herself against the counter and started to bend down.

I watched her bend into some form of squat, using the kitchen cupboard door handle under the countertop to help keep her balance as she lowered herself closer and closer to the floor.

"Ah ha!" She exclaimed as she got down far enough to reach the spoon, feeling smug in her victory of retrieving the wooden spoon without my help.

I stared at her in amusement, trying to hide my smirk behind my hand. I knew exactly what was coming next.

"You see, I told you I could get it without your help," she smiled as she looked over at me in triumph.

"That's great baby, now you're going to need to get back up if you don't want your sauce to burn," I told her as I pointed towards the pan that was bubbling away on the stove.

"Crap," I heard her mutter under her breath before she placed both hands on the floor and tried to push herself up. Safe to say she didn't get very far in her attempts to be upright again.

"Need a hand there little mate?" I asked, still trying to hide the smirk behind my hand as I watched on in amusement.

"No no... I... got... this..." she strained out as she tried once again to push herself off the floor. "Okay, I don't got this," she finally sighed as she started to wobble and fall back down to the floor. Luckily, I was fast enough to catch her so she didn't fall too hard and injure herself.

"Will you let me help you know?" I laughed as I was no longer able to hide the smirk from appearing across my face.

"*Fine,* if you insist" she sighed as she let me pull her up by her hands, wooden spoon in tow, until she was finally up on her feet again.

"There," I smiled as I set her upright so that she was facing the stove, "that wasn't so hard was it?" I teased.

"Oh shut up," she grumbled with an eye roll, it wasn't long though before she was laughing with me at the entire situation.

"JAX!" Xavier suddenly shouted from the doorway as he ran into the kitchen, letting the front door swing back and hit the wall with a bang. "JAX!"

I was instantly alert as I saw my out of breath best friend and Beta run round the corner and into the kitchen.

"What's the matter?" I asked, on edge due to the wild look in his eyes.

"Rogues on the south border, border patrol are holding them back, but not by much."

I nodded in understanding before taking Annabelle's hand in mine and pulled her towards the hidden door which led to the basement and our safe room. "You know the drill Annabelle, you stay here until either myself, Xavier, yours or my family come and get you. If you get into trouble, mind link Hannah or your mum okay?"

Annabelle tugged me to a stop and I turned to face her in confusion "come on little mate we don't have time for this, get in the safe room," I pleaded, not in the mood for her stubborn antics.

"J-Jax... my waters just broke," she stuttered, looking into my eyes with fear.

I froze, our baby was coming? Now? Crap! We had been planning on what to do for months, we had our overnight bag packed with all the essentials for weeks now and the baby chooses *this* moment to make an appearance?

I was jogged from my internal panic as Annabelle suddenly clamped down on my hand in a vice-like grip and as I looked down at her I noticed the pained look on her face. She was going through a contraction.

Now was no time to panic, my little mate needed me to be there for her.

I picked her up bridal style and walked towards the safe room, there was no way I was taking her out of this building to get to the hospital with rogues threatening our borders. After laying her as comfortably as I could on the bed I sat down with her and did the breathing thing I was told to do with her in the birthing classes we took.

"Hannah get over here, rogues are attacking and Annabelle has just gone into labour. I need to get out there, but I can't leave her on her own."

"Oh my god, timing or what?!" Hannah quickly responded through the mind link. *"Don't worry Jax, mum and I are on the way over now with Jane. Samuel, dad and Will are covering us. You head out, we won't be a minute."*

I sighed before gripping Annabelle's hand and bringing it up to my lips. "I have to go little mate, the rogues... I don't want to but I-"

"You go Jax, the pack needs you," she reassured me with as much of a smile as she could muster. "Besides, I've been through worse right?" She chuckled but quickly sucked in a breath as another contraction hit her.

"I'll be as quick as I can baby, our parents and Hannah are on their way. They know the code so don't worry about getting up to let them in," I reassured her.

She nodded in understanding before reaching up and placing her hand on my cheek. "I love you, be safe. We'll be waiting here when you get back," she smiled.

I smiled a full beam smile at her words. *We.*

I kissed the palm of her hand that was resting on my cheek before getting up and locking her into the safe room. *She would be fine*, I kept reassuring myself as I took the painful steps away from my family.

I shifted as I caught up to Xavier and we both ran off into the woods, towards the south border and the rogues.

Annabelle's POV

What a day for our baby to decide to show up. I had been wanting to get this little cutie out of me for weeks now, but right now I was praying it would stay in me for as long as possible so that Jax could come back in time to help me.

"How are you doing baby?" Jax asked me through our link.

I waited for my contraction to end before I sighed a breath of relief as the pain momentarily subsided. *"I'm- I'm good... you just focus on what you're doing so you can come back here and I'll focus on this."*

"I will baby, I'll be as quick as I can. There is no way I am missing the birth of our first child. Is anyone there yet?"

I shook my head but quickly responded with a *"no,"* when I remembered he couldn't see me.

"Okay well hold on, they should be there any second now."

I nodded my head before shutting the mind link off as another contraction hit me, the last thing I wanted was for my pain to be transferred to him through our link and distract him whilst he was dealing with rogues.

I grunted in pain as I clenched my hands so tight my nails formed crescent moons into my palms. I had definitely been through a lot of pain in my life, but I think this just may trump it all.

I waddled over to the fridge in the room as best I could and took out a bottle of water, no ice chips for me, and slowly started taking sips so that I stayed hydrated.

As time went on the pain started increasing and before long I was screaming in agony, how was it even possible to be in this much pain?

And where the hell was everyone else? I was starting to get worried about Jax and his family, but just as I was about to mind link one of them and ask where they were, I heard a loud thud on the other side of the door.

I know Jax said not to open the door, that everyone that needed access had the code, but what if it was someone I knew? What if they were hurt and couldn't reach the keypad to enter in the code?

I contemplated unlocking the door, but before I could move another wave of contractions hit me. When would this end?

Just when I was finished screaming and wiping the sweat that had started to drip into my eyes, the door to the safe room opened and Hannah, Emily and my mum dragged themselves in.

What the hell happened!

"Are you guys o-okay?" I managed to stutter out through the pain as I took in their dishevelled appearances.

"A few rogues got through the border and snuck up on us, we got away from them, with the help from the guys, but only just," Hannah explained as she sat herself down on the other unoccupied bed. "They're outside guarding the door just in case."

I took a quick glance at them and all I could see was blood, whether it was theirs or their attackers though I couldn't tell.

"The first aid kit is in the cupboard," I managed to get out before I groaned as I felt another contraction hit me.

"You're doing amazing Anna, just breathe through the pain for me," my mum instructed as she came and sat by my head on the bed, stroking my damp hair from off my forehead and taking my clenched hand in hers.

I watched her as I copied her slow breathing, hoping in some way it would help ease the pain I was currently in and as the contraction ended I relaxed back into the bed, I was exhausted.

"How far apart have your contractions been Anna?"

I shrugged "I'm not sure, I wasn't looking at my watch," I explained. "Maybe every few minutes?"

Emily nodded before looking over at Hannah. They shared a look before Hannah's eyes glazed over, obviously using her mind link to talk to someone.

"Honey this is usually the time where we would start to head to the hospital. Now we can't leave this safe room, but you aren't alone, you've got your mum, me and Hannah with you and Hannah has Dr Tessler through the mind link if we have any questions alright?"

I shook my head as my brain started registering her words "but Jax isn't here, and he's my birthing partner. I don't have my bag with me, I packed it over and over again to make sure I had everything. There was this cute little onesie I had that I wanted to put him in when he arrived," I cried.

"I know honey, but we can't get it right now, we have everything we need right here so just breathe. We will get through this, after all, between your mother and me we've had four babies, so we have a bit of experience in the matter," she laughed.

I looked up into Emily's eyes and I knew without a shadow of a doubt that we would all get through this. Together.

After what felt like hours of pain and buckets of sweat, I was finally ready to push. Jax still hadn't turned up yet, but Emily had him through the mind link and Hannah was still talking to the doctor, making sure we were doing everything correctly.

"Right... on three Anna I need you to give me one huge push okay?" Emily said as she held onto my hand whilst Hannah gripped onto my other one, my mum down at my feet making sure everything was progressing as it should.

I nodded, completely exhausted but determined to see my little baby. I pushed with all I had as I forced my brain to think of something else, anything else, so as to forget the pain I was currently in.

I thought of Jax, how he smelled all clean and fresh after he'd just taken a shower. How he'd find my pregnant mood swings more humorous than annoying. How he would cringe at the cravings I was having that day; chocolate ice cream and pickled eggs was a go to favourite of mine for months leading up to now.

I suddenly heard the door burst open as the contraction ended and I looked over to see Jax, dishevelled and slightly bloody and bruised, walk into the safe room and head straight over to my side.

I cried in relief at seeing him and quickly took his hand in mine.

"Where the *hell* have you been?" I growled as I leant into him for support.

"Sorry love," he apologised as he kissed my sweaty forehead and took Hannah's position on the bed, an amused yet worried look in his eyes. "I'm here now, let's get baby JJ into this world," he whispered as my final contraction hit me.

The Alpha and his Mate

Acknowledgments

There are so many people I'd like to thank for this book that if I listed every single one of them this page will be as long as the book itself! With that being said, there are a few key people that I'd like to thank, for without them I'm not sure whether this book would have even happened.

I'd first like to thank my boyfriend Alex, for being the most supportive partner in everything I do and always lending an ear whenever I was stuck or needed a bit of motivation to carry on. He was there the very first time I picked up my iPad whilst we were stuck inside during a snowstorm in the French alps and wrote the very first draft of the very first chapter and was patient with me when I needed talk through my story lines or help me struggle through my writer's block.

Secondly, I'd like to thank my two sisters Tori and Lici, for helping me research into all of my characters to help make them real, especially Annabelle. I'd like to also thank them for helping me edit and edit until I was finally happy enough to leave them alone.

I'd also like to thank my parents, who's undying support helped me keep my head down and never give up on this book, and the ones to come, even when I wanted to.

Lastly, and most importantly, I'd like to thank each and every one of my Wattpad followers and readers. You all mean so much to me, more than I can possibly express into words. You picked me up when I was feeling low and gave me the confidence to continue with my writing and get my stories out there even when I didn't have the confidence in myself. Thank you.

About the Author

Bryony is a trained wig maker working in the hustle and bustle of theatre life.

In her spare time alongside writing, she loves to read one of her many books from her ever expanding 'to be read' list or spend time taking long walks on the beach with her dog, Otis.

Follow Bryony on @authorbryonywakeford on Instagram to keep up with all the latest news.